Henri's Highland

Girl in the Castle

Lizzie Lamb

'I really enjoy Lizzie Lamb's books, she never disappoints, there is always a thrilling storyline with a fine romance, keeping you intrigued and hooked all the way through the book.'

GIRL IN THE CASTLE © lizzie lamb 2017

published worldwide 2017 © Lizzie Lamb

www.lizzielamb.co.uk

All rights reserved in all media. No part of this book may be reproduced or transmitted in any form by any means, electronic or mechanical (including but not limited to: the Internet, photocopying, recording or by any information storage and retrieval system), without prior permission in writing from the author and/or publisher.

The moral right of Lizzie Lamb as the author of the work has been asserted by her in accordance with the Copyright Designs and Patents Act 1988.

Paperback Edition

This book is a work of fiction. All characters and events featured in this book are entirely fictional and any resemblance to any person, organisation, place or thing living or dead, or event or place is purely coincidental and is completely unintentional and not intended by the author.

Cover photograph by kind permission of Nick Fiddes www.scotweb.co.uk

ISBN: 978-0-9573985-7-3

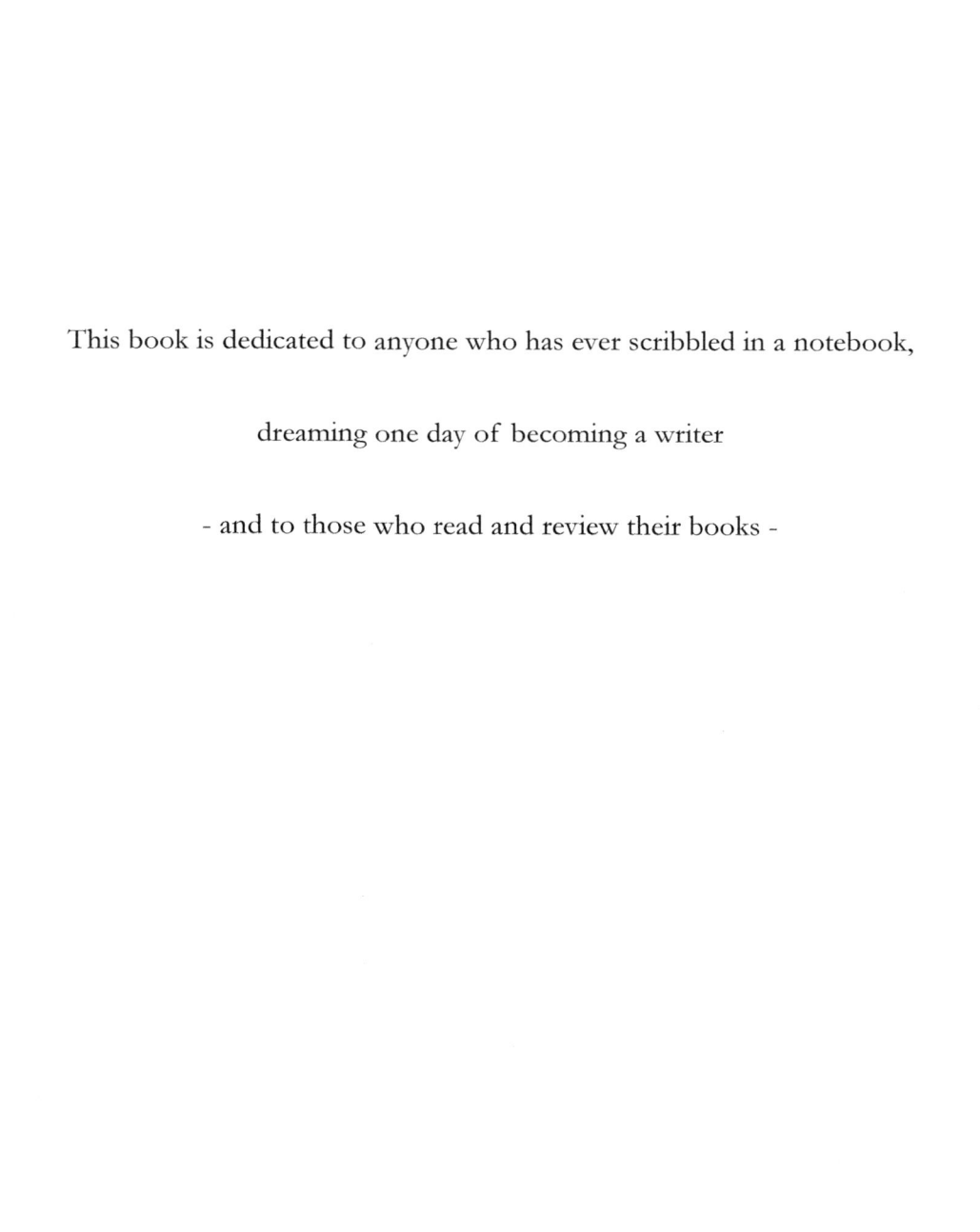

This book is dedicated to anyone who has ever scribbled in a notebook,

dreaming one day of becoming a writer

- and to those who read and review their books -

CONTENTS

Glossary of Terms	7
Chapter One *A Bad Moon Rising*	9
Chapter Two *The Wee Lassie*	12
Chapter Three *Castle Tèarmannair*	20
Chapter Four *Anither Bankrupt Laird*	27
Chapter Five *Breakfast Meeting*	33
Chapter Six *It's What I Do*	37
Chapter Seven *Falling for You*	45
Chapter Eight *A Second Interview*	53
Chapter Nine *The MacKenzie Cousins*	63
Chapter Ten *An Unfriendly Warning*	72
Chapter Eleven *True Confessions*	80
Chapter Twelve *An Unwanted Letter*	90
Chapter Thirteen *The Clash of the Ash*	101
Chapter Fourteen *We play for the Glory . . . and the Clash of the Ash*	110
Chapter Fifteen *Vindolanda!*	119
Chapter Sixteen *All at Sea*	131
Chapter Seventeen *Across the Loch*	138
Chapter Eighteen *The Curse of MacKenzie's Gold*	154
Chapter Nineteen *An Unwise Decision*	169

Chapter Twenty *How Very Dare You?*	*179*
Chapter Twenty-One *Cooking up a Storm*	*190*
Chapter Twenty-Two *Partners in Crime*	*196*
Chapter Twenty-Three *A Conundrum*	*201*
Chapter Twenty-Four *Tam O'Shanter*	*209*
Chapter Twenty-Five *An te a bhreab nead na gasbaid*	*213*
Chapter Twenty-Six *And So to Bed*	*230*
Chapter Twenty-Seven *Next Morning . . .*	*237*
Chapter Twenty-Eight *A Eureka Moment*	*242*
Chapter Twenty-Nine *Romancing the Stone*	*254*
Chapter Thirty *Cas-ual-ity*	*261*
Chapter Thirty-One *Academe*	*271*
Chapter Thirty-Two *Choices*	*279*
Chapter Thirty-Three *Pyrotechnics*	*289*
Chapter Thirty-Four *Romancing the Stone —take #2*	*300*
Chapter Thirty-Five *Is There a Doctor in the House?*	*312*
Chapter Thirty-Six *Playing the Waiting Game*	*320*
Chapter Thirty-Seven *Na Fir Chlis*	*331*
A NOTE FROM THE AUTHOR	*336*
MORE BOOKS BY LIZZIE LAMB	*338*
ACKNOWLEDGMENTS	*342*

Glossary of Terms

Ciorstaidh — **Gaelic form of Kirsty** (or as Alice pronounces it to annoy her, Kursty!)

Mal Choluim — **Gaelic form of Malcolm** — Malchy or Wee Malchy to distinguish him from his father

Slainte mhath — **your good health (a toast)** — slancha vah

Samhain — *Sav-ahn*

each uisge — *a water horse* — ach ooshka

Tulach Ard — **The Mackenzie battle cry.** Tulach Ard is a mountain in the MacKenzie heartland of Kintail — Toolach Aarsd

Sassenach — An English person; a Lowland Scot

An te a bhreab nead na gasbaid — the girl who kicked the hornets' nest

Is tu an solas na mo bheatha — You are the light of my life

Sir Malcolm MacKenzie of that Ilk — 'of the same name or place' — as in, Sir Malcolm MacKenzie of MacKenzie

I have also used words, phrases and sayings from the central belt/west coast of Scotland.

messages — shopping, items you would buy from a supermarket/general store/errands

hen; pet — terms of endearment you would use for a female friend or relative

weans — **children** — pronounced way-ns

dreich — wet and miserable

scunner — a feeling of repulsion, aversion or loathing in (a person),

stapped — stopped up

peely-wally — pale and sickly in appearance

napper — head

lugs — ears

skite — a sharp/glancing blow

clype — (clipe) a snitch or tell-tale

wallies — false teeth

keelie — a tough urban male esp of Glasgow

wee bauchle — a shabby-looking person, especially a small one

bunnet — A head covering for males, including all kinds of caps, but not hats

http://www.dsl.ac.uk (Dictionary of the Scots Language)

Words of Scottish Gaelic origin (Wikipedia)

Chapter One
A Bad Moon Rising

There it was, again—a lament; the kind played from the parapet of a castle high above a loch, the piper hidden by swirling autumn mist and fading light. Unable to ignore it any longer, Henriette Bruar ended the podcast—*Five Historic Hauntings for Hallowe'en*—and, ears straining, glanced half-fearfully over her shoulder in case some madman had got on at the last station, hell bent on making it plain that *here* was no place for Sassenachs.

No place for lone, female travellers either, come to that.

However, the train was empty, as it had been for the past half an hour. For who, in their right mind, would take the last train out of Fort William on a wet autumn afternoon and travel up the line to MacKenzie's Halt?

Only her, of course. Henriette Bruar, lately studying history at St Guthlac University, Hexham, in the north of England, until—well, until she'd screwed things up so badly that she'd been forced to come high-tailing it up to this remote corner of Scotland until the heat died down.

'Stop imagining things!' she admonished herself, her voice unnaturally loud in the empty carriage. That had the desired effect of banishing the piper and restoring her grip on reality. Her iPhone, she reasoned, must have picked up a transmission from a nearby radio station—Highland FM, or similar. That, coupled with the spooky podcast, was enough to make her imagine things.

Yes, that was it.

However, just in case, she cast another look around the carriage. As she did so, the feeling of presentiment which had dogged her since setting foot on Scottish soil returned, accompanied this time by pins and needles and the shivery, shaky feeling which usually heralds a virus. Physical sensations which no amount of foot stamping, arm swinging or cups of lukewarm coffee could banish.

'You need to get your blood pumping, Bruar,' she said in the no-nonsense tone of a games mistress. 'You haven't got time for flights of fancy. You're here for one reason, and one reason only—to undertake a commission on behalf of the university. Keep reminding yourself of that, and how lucky you are to have been given a chance to restore your reputation. Right now, an overactive imagination is an extravagance you simply can't afford.'

Spectral pipers, indeed!

After further foot stamping and curling and uncurling her toes, she sat down, unfolded her itinerary and read it through for the hundredth time. The train would stop at MacKenzie's Halt, where she was to get off. The train terminated further up the line but few, if any passengers, went beyond MacKenzie's Halt. Upon leaving the train, she should cross over the footbridge and make her way to the edge of the loch where she would be taken across to Castle Tèarmannair.

taken across . . .

Forgetting her earlier resolution to stop daydreaming, fancy took flight once more. She saw herself as a Jacobite heroine, plaid wrapped tightly round her to ward off the wind, a white cockade pinned to her hair, being *taken across* the loch by clansmen loyal to the exiled Stuarts. In her imagination, she saw a castle in the middle of the loch where her lover was waiting, piper by his side, to welcome her home.

Then she shook her head and dismissed the image.

Time she remembered that she was no Highland heroine, she was Castle Tèarmannair's newly appointed archivist—hired to catalogue the contents of the laird's library, prior to auction. Most likely it would turn out to be the usual collection of old estate papers, books on the best technique for blasting game birds out of the skies, or catching the salmon with a fly of the laird's own design. There would be no first editions, illuminated manuscripts, or lost family trees proclaiming the laird the Last King of Scotland for her to discover.

'*Castle Tèarmannair.*' She experimented with the unfamiliar Gaelic. '*Meaning Guardian, or Protector,*' she read from her guide book. '*A gift from the Lord of the Isles to MacKenzie of MacKenzie for fighting alongside him at the Battle of Largs in 1263.*' Releasing a pent up breath, she put the itinerary in her bag and, getting to her feet, walked the length of the carriage, holding on to the back of the empty seats for balance, and peered through the windows into the late afternoon gloom.

A thick autumn mist had followed the train out of *An Gearasdan*—Fort William, obscuring the stunning view promised by the guide books and, in a cinematic moment, the train appeared to 'float' above the rails. Nothing was visible on either side—not even the lights from the small settlements flanking the loch. Henri wondered, a little self-pityingly, if the mist was a metaphor for the current state of her life, which was mired in gloom and despondency.

She pulled herself up sharp. 'Positive thinking, Bruar. Remember?'

She was halfway back to her seat when a lilting Highland voice announced: 'We are approaching MacKenzie's Halt. Please remember to take your belongings with you when you alight from the train.' With no more time for introspection, she swung her tote bag over her shoulder, and collected coat, rucksack and suitcase out of the luggage rack as the train came, briefly, to a halt by the short platform.

Chapter Two
The Wee Lassie

Three minutes later, the train pulled out of the station, taking the last of the light with it and leaving behind the smell of hot diesel. Pulling on her coat and setting her beret at a jaunty angle, Henri looked round the deserted platform. Hers was the last train of the day and the station master, no doubt dreaming of his dinner, was already shutting up shop. Anxious that he didn't extinguish the lights before she set out on the last leg of her journey, she coughed and made a great show of reading her itinerary by the light above the entrance to the booking hall.

Now she regretted having listened to the podcast—*Five Historic Hauntings for Hallowe'en*. The mist, the quality of the light and the absence of any other human beings, save the two of them, were the classic ingredients of a ghost story. One where weed-draped creatures rose from the depths of the loch, wrapped sinewy hands round your ankles and dragged you down into its greenish-black depths. Never to be seen again.

Quite a few of her fellow academics at St Guthlac would be more than happy to see that happen, she thought grimly.

'Good evening, Miss.' The station master's voice put her morbid fancies to flight. 'Are ye being met, or would ye like me tae ring for a taxi? Ye'll find mobile phones of little use in these parts. Mah brother-in-law runs a mini-cab business and he'll take ye to wherever you wah-nt. The mist will turn into rain soon and ye widnae wah-nt tae be oot in that, I'm after thinking.'

'I'm being met; only I'm not quite sure where, exactly. My instructions are,' she held out the itinerary so he could read it, '*cross over the footbridge; walk down the gravel track. Ring the bell and wait. You will be collected.'* Collected? Would she have to be signed for, like an Amazon delivery, Henri wondered, looking at the station master.

'Ach, ye'll be going over the watter to the castle, then?' Plainly, he understood the instructions, even if she didn't.

'Yes. Do you know of it?' Stupid question. According to the guide book, Castle Tèarmannair had been a presence in the loch for hundreds of years and its laird, Sir Malcolm MacKenzie of that Ilk, owned thousands of acres hereabouts.

'Aye, I ken it, fine.' He grinned, putting her at her ease. 'C'mohn; I'll help ye over the footbridge and show you the bell. It's not a night for a lassie to be oot on her own.'

The kindly station master made Henri feel about eight years old. She was more than capable of taking care of herself, having travelled the world alone on an extended gap year. She smiled her thanks at him even if he couldn't see her expression in the late afternoon gloom.

The reference to 'the bell', puzzled her and she felt totally out of her comfort zone, as though all the street smarts she'd gained on her travels counted for nothing in this mist-shrouded world on the edge of a loch. Giving herself a mental shakedown, she followed her guide up the stairs and over the iron footbridge. Its white and green paintwork was corroded by the elements and it shook under the trundling wheels of her heavy suitcase. Halfway across, an ornate lamp cast light on the tracks, now barely visible in the mist which had taken on the appearance of theatrical dry ice.

When they dropped down the other side, the station master dragged her case along a wide gravel path sloping towards the loch. Eventually, they stopped at the edge of a shore where water lapped at its margins. Beyond, there was nothing but darkness and the ever-present mist which changed shape as the wind blew in from the west.

'The bell.'

Indicating that she should leave her cases and bags on the gravel path, the station master handed Henri a length of plaited rope attached to the clapper of an iron bell, housed in a mini bell-tower mounted on a granite plinth.

'Ring three times and they'll send a boat over for you. They know what time the trains come in at MacKenzie's Halt—and Mac Mohr will be expecting you, forby?'

It took Henri several seconds to realise that she'd been asked a question.

Fluent in several European languages and a couple of 'dead' ones, too—Latin and Ancient Greek—she was unfamiliar with the word *forby*. What *Mac Mhor* meant, she could only guess at. Her Bruar ancestors had lived in Sutherland until poverty, the Highland clearances and a desire to better themselves had sent them beyond the Sound of Sleet to Cape Breton Island, Nova Scotia. But in their hearts, they'd remained staunchly Scottish, even if they no longer spoke Gaelic, in common with other families on the island.

The station master's lilting accent, swirling mist and the damp seeping through her thin jacket were a timely reminder that she was in another time, another place. She longed to be in the warm, dry castle, sheltered from the elements.

'What if no one comes?' There was a quaver in her voice and she swallowed to hide it. Hadn't she always prided herself on being frightened of nothing and no one? Surely she wasn't going to be defeated by a bit of mist and bone-seeping cold?

'Och, they will. For is Himself not expecting you?'

'Yes. But . . .' Sensing that her companion was anxious to get home to his dinner, Henri released him. 'Thanks for helping me over the bridge. Ring the bell three times, you say?'

'Aye, three times. Someone will come, dinnae fash yersel'.'

Not quite sure what 'fashing' oneself meant, Henri nodded uncertainly. The station master, seemingly taking that as a sign she'd manage on her own, disappeared into the darkness. Henri wasn't timid by nature, but standing on the edge of a loch—make that *menacing loch in a thick Scotch mist*—wasn't top of her things to do on a September evening, less than a month from Hallowe'en.

Or should that be *Samhain* now she was in the Highlands?

Realising that she was wasting the last traces of daylight speculating, Henri took a step towards the ancient bell and tugged timidly on the rope. The sound barely went further than the end of the gravel path before it was swallowed up.

'Don't be such a *girl*, Bruar; ring the bell like you mean it or you'll be sleeping on the platform bench tonight.'

Pushing up the sleeves of her leather biker jacket she gave the bell rope three almighty yanks. This time the sound went straight across the loch to where she imagined Castle Tèarmannair lay. Momentarily, the mist shifted, as if the bell had sent out a sonic wave, pushing it back. Then three echoing tolls came back from across the loch.

Unbidden, Donne's poem came to mind: *'never send to know for whom the bells tolls; it tolls for thee.'* The frisson which ran down her spine was part superstition, part coldness. However, even as the right half of her brain dismissed the superstitious shudder as irrational, the other hemisphere reminded her that many people believed the mystical world co-existed alongside the ordinary. During her gap year, she'd joined in the Day of the Dead festivities in Mexico City dressed as a corpse bride. Compared to how she felt now, alone on the edge of a Highland loch, that seemed like a pantomime, acted out for tourists

This, her instincts told her, was real.

She was about to toll the bell again when the chugging of an outboard motor came from across the water. Letting out a sigh of relief, she pulled herself up to her full five feet eight, threaded her arms through her rucksack, hoisted it on her back and acted as if she wasn't afraid of anything.

She was, after all, Doctor Henriette Bruar, a force to be reckoned with, academically speaking. Keeping that in mind, she watched as a shape emerged from the mist, bringing with it the reassuring smell of engine oil. Eventually, the shape revealed itself as a large orange dinghy complete with aluminium handrails and two rows of seats. It was piloted by an elderly man wearing rolled down wellingtons, a greasy waxed coat and a faded cloth cap. Like his outfit, the ferryman had seen better days.

Tethering the dinghy to a stone jetty, he turned to face her. Instead of the 'welcome to the Highlands' speech Henri had been expecting, she was greeted by a look of incredulity. Then the old man moved closer and shone a torch in her face.

'Why are you after pulling on a bell you have no business to be pulling on?'

'Why am I *what?*' Henri's smiled faltered in the face of such open hostility.

'Ach, way with you now. I'm expecting a verra important visitor to the castle. No a wee lassie, standing on *Himself's* gravel and ringing *Himself's* bell when she has nae right tae it.' Turning, he made his way back to the dinghy, muttering that she should step off the laird's gravel and make room for the aforementioned *verra important visitor.*

Dismissing the feeling that she was a badly-drawn character in a quaint Sunday evening serial, the natural successor to *Monarch of the Glen,* by way of *The Vital Spark,* Henri stood her ground.

'I'll have you know, I am no *wee lassie.* I *am* the very important visitor expected at the castle.' Even to her ears she sounded ridiculous, but she continued. 'By no less than Sir Malcolm MacKenzie. *Himself.*' Clearly, the pronoun carried some weight with the old man. He stopped in his tracks, fumbled in the pocket of his filthy jacket, retrieved the large rubber torch and shone it in her face for a second time, as if she was a species he'd never encountered.

'Ach. You look like a wee lassie to me.' Tutting, he rammed the torch back in his pocket and set about relaunching the dinghy.

'Wait,' Henriette commanded, aware that he was intent on abandoning her on the loch side. 'I demand to be taken over to the castle; or I'll report you to Sir Malcolm.' He spun on the heel of his ancient wellingtons and gave her a hard look, as if reprimanding her for taking *Himself's* name in vain a second time.

'Sir Malcom has sent me over to fetch Doctor Brewer,' he said, shining his torch on a scrap of paper in his hand, and unwilling to concede defeat.

'I *am* Doctor Bruar,' Henri insisted, fumbling in her bag for some means of identification.

'Aye, and I'm George Clooney,' came back the sarcastic reply. It was plain that, despite the brief moment of respect her peremptory tone had gained her, she was back to being the *wee lassie*. 'Can ye no mind seeing me in my last fil-um? Wi' yon Cameron Diaz? ' In spite of her irritation, Henri laughed out loud at the unlikely coupling.

Anyone less like Gorgeous George was hard to imagine.

'And I'm the Queen of the Fairies,' she responded. The old man's head jerked up; he swivelled, crossed himself and then spat on the gravel, seemingly against the evil eye. *Her* evil eye. Henriette cursed her throwaway remark, remembering that many Highlanders believed in the faerie realm, old legends, water horses and shape shifters. Deciding it was time to put a stop to this nonsense, she countered with, 'I insist that you take me across to the castle and we let the laird sort it out.'

'Humph.' This time with less certainty. 'Aye, well, get in the dinghy. Most like you can stay the night, seeing as the last train has gone. But you'll be away in the morning,' he said with an emphatic nod off his head. 'In the morning,' he repeated, in case she hadn't got it.

Henri glared at him, thinking, *dream on*!

She climbed in the dinghy and, to underline her position—Doctor Bruar, not a *wee lassie*, she left him to load her suitcases. This was done with ill grace and much muttering, which Henri took to be Gaelic swearwords. Then he fired up the outboard motor and they were off, scudding across the loch at such a reckless pace that she suspected *George Clooney* wished he could dispose of her in the loch.

'Ah wouldnae lean too close to the watter. Because the *each uisge* will drag you under and that'll be the end of *you*.' He spoke as though he had the power to conjure up the beast from the depths of the loch. 'I'm thinking ye dinnae ken what one of those is?'

'A water horse, a kelpie. I've seen photographs of the ones at Falkirk.'

'For the tourists. Ach.' Another unhygienic spit over the side of the dinghy and a *what-would-the-likes-of you-know* glare. Ignoring him, Henri was grateful that the wind didn't whip the spit into her face. He really was the most revolting old man, faithful retainer to the MacKenzies or not!

Positioned in the front of the dinghy, wearing the lifejacket the curmudgeonly ferryman had tossed at her feet, Henri stared through the mist. Was it her imagination, or were there really lights up ahead? Her heartbeat quickened; Castle Tèarmannair, a bolt hole, somewhere to hide. She forgot all about her woes and thought instead of the castle library she was commissioned to catalogue.

Now she revised her opinion of her task. There *would* be ancient books no one had looked at in years. Maybe even some signed first editions, or some other significant find which would restore her reputation. Why, quite recently, a first folio of Shakespeare's plays had been found in a library on a Scottish Island. Why shouldn't there be a lost manuscript at Castle Tèarmannair waiting for her to discover?

'Here y'are.' The grumpy ferryman slowed the dinghy before mooring up against the moss-draped stones of an ancient jetty. Leaping out with surprising agility, given his age and the heaviness of his wellingtons, he left Henri to struggle up the stone ladder unaided. Standing on terra firma, looking up at the bulk of Castle Tèarmannair towering over her, Henri felt a rush of excitement—as though she was about to embark on some wonderful adventure.

'My cases,' she said in a no-nonsense voice to the grouchy sailor. 'Pass me up my rucksack and bring the rest.' There was a bit of a Mexican—or should that be, Highland standoff—as he weighed up whether to defy her, or do as commanded.

'Here's yer bag.' He climbed back into the dinghy and practically threw it at her. 'As for yer cases, I'll be after leaving those in the boat hoose. No point in lugging them up three flights of stairs. I'll likely be loading them in the dinghy first thing in the morning, when ye catch the train back to Fort William.'

There—that was her told!

'We'll see about *that*,' Henri retorted, although she knew she shouldn't stoop to arguing with him. Once she met Sir Malcolm, all would be well.

Feeling that she'd been rowed across the River Styx by a very surly Charon, she made up her mind not to tip the gruff Highlander. Instead, she'd make it her business to let Sir Malcolm know how unwelcoming he'd been, and leave any reprimand up to him. Slipping on her rucksack, she crossed her fingers for luck and wondered half-seriously if she should follow the ferryman's lead and spit on the ground. Deciding against it, she followed him up a flight of stairs seemingly carved out of the side of the castle, and prepared to meet her new employer.

Chapter Three
Castle Tèarmannair

Moments later Henri came to a halt by a nail-studded door. The crusty Highlander shouldered her out of the way with an ill-mannered *ach*, pushed it open and ushered her into a stone vaulted undercroft. There, all kinds of paraphernalia was stored: tools, boating equipment, fishing rods, nets, outdoor coats, shooting sticks, large umbrellas and pairs of mismatched wellingtons lying on their side. As if the owners had had a good time huntin', shootin' or fishin' and couldn't be bothered to stack them neatly against the wall. Her ferryman switched on a row of fluorescent lights and she blinked in their unforgiving glare. Better illumination did the undercroft no favours. Large cobwebs became visible and Henri speculated that the current inhabitants who were probably the descendants of spiders who'd lived here for aeons.

They might even have known Robert the Bruce personally.

She imagined huge arachnids wearing kilts and bearing targes as they searched out unwary visitors before dropping on their heads and scaring the bejesus out of them.

'This way, *Doctor* Bruar.'

The ferryman, clearly unable to resist one last jibe, snorted and led the way up a short flight of steps to another door. Henri's academic interest, not to mention her romantic nature, was enthralled by the thick walls and narrow arrow slits. A cold draught, emanating from two large cavities dug into the floor of the undercroft, whistled round her ankles. The cavities were covered by padlocked gratings through which the rank odour of decomposing vegetation and something fishy wafted towards her.

Watery oubliettes—was that how they disposed of unwanted guests? Threw 'em in the loch and left the local water horse to finish them off?

Gazing round, Henri reached the conclusion that Castle Tèarmannair had been built to keep people *out*, rather than welcome them *in*! Maybe her guide was simply following tradition in making her feel unwelcome because she wasn't a MacKenzie, born and bred. Maybe the MacKenzies were deadly enemies of the Bruars and no one had seen fit to warn her of it? However, all of that was forgotten as they passed through an archway and climbed a spiral staircase cut into the walls. Grasping the thick rope bannister Henri hauled herself up the stairs. She let out a sigh of relief when she turned the last corner, opened another door and found herself in a well-lit kitchen where dinner was being prepared.

Her stomach gave an unladylike growl and reminded her that she'd eaten nothing apart from a sandwich, bag of crisps and a Kit Kat she'd grabbed at Waverley station, Edinburgh, earlier.

'Well.' Her companion pushed past and headed for a large inglenook which housed an ancient cream Aga. 'Here's our guest. Not a doctor so much as a *wee lassie*.' Again, he emphasised the words. 'Trouble, mark my words. Wait 'till the MacKenzie sees her.' With one last harrumph, he threw himself onto a chair and pressed his hands against the bulk of the Aga to warm them. Two lurchers who'd been asleep on dog beds nearby, raised their heads, gave Henri a cursory look and then went back to sleep.

Clearly, like her newfound friend, they wanted nothing to do with her.

An attractive woman in her mid-sixties, wearing jeans and a striped Breton top, stopped stirring the large saucepan bubbling on top of a modern range cooker on the other side of the kitchen. She blew silvery hair out of her eyes, leaned back against the worktop and sent Henriette a look of consternation.

'Oh my, Lachlan,' she exclaimed, tapping her cheek with her wooden spoon. 'This won't do. This won't do, at ah-ll.' Her accent was pure Lowland Scot and lacked Lachlan's Highland lilt.

'Aye . . .' was Lachlan's response. He shot Henriette another sour look, accompanied by a triumphant sniff to show he'd been vindicated.

'*Aye*, is right; but it disnae fix things.' The cook unfolded her arms and remembered her manners. 'Come away in, hen. There's obviously been a mix up. We were expecting a Doctor Henry Brewer—'

'That's me! Doctor Henriette Bruar.' Henri walked further into the kitchen, determined to put the record straight; it wasn't the first time her name had caused confusion. 'Henri,' she pronounced her name à la française— *Onri*. 'Short for *Onriette*? Most people use the English version—Hen-ree-ette; or, Hen-ree for short.' She was gabbling, but a second less-than-enthusiastic welcome in half an hour, unnerved her. Clearly, there had been a mix up of mammoth proportions. 'Why my parents couldn't have christened me Susan, I'll never know.'

'I bet that Lachlan has been making much of the mistake?'

'He did mention it once or twice.' Henri managed a weak smile.

'Only once or twice? Good God, ye'r slipping, man. It's no like you to miss an opportunity to make a problem seem worse than it is.' Lachlan give a snort but didn't rise to the bait as the cook came forward with her hand extended. 'I'm Alice Dougal, chief cook and bottle washer to Sir Malcolm MacKenzie. Welcome to Castle Tèarmannair. Now, sit ye down, dearie, and I'll pour us a glass of uisge beatha while we work out what to do. Sir Malcolm's away 'til the morrah morning.' She and Lachlan exchanged a look which suggested his absence wasn't unusual. 'So,' she clapped her hands, 'I'll show ye to your room and we'll take it from there?' Removing, three whisky glasses out of a tall cupboard, she poured a shot in each. '*Slainte mhath*,' she pushed one over to Henriette and left Lachlan to fetch his own.

'Sl—slainte,' Henriette stumbled over the unfamiliar phrase. The whisky warmed every cockle she possessed and she began to relax. There was a hiatus as they savoured the laird's best single malt and then Alice Dougal put her glass down, looked around and frowned. 'Lachlan, where are Doctor Brewer's cases?'

'Ah didnae think it was worth hauling them up the stairs. Seeing as she'll no be staying.'

'That's not for you to decide, Lachlan MacKenzie. Now, go and fetch them while I show Doctor Brewer to her room. We sit down to supper at eight o'clock, here in the kitchen; much friendlier than dining in the Great Hall.'

'Please, call me Henri.'

'Very well, Henri.' Alice smiled, but it was a troubled smile. As though she didn't consider it was worth getting on first name terms because Henri'd be leaving once the laird discovered the gender of his newly appointed archivist. 'Follow me.'

Henri put her glass on the large, metal-topped table and followed Alice out of the kitchen and climbed yet another spiral staircase. This one led to the top of the castle where a corridor had been added, with windows along one wall and doors to individual bedrooms along the other. The corridor rendered redundant the practice of going through one room to gain access to another.

Alice paused at the end of the corridor.

'This is you.' She gestured to a large oak door where a brass name holder proclaimed it the bedroom of *Dr Henry Brewer*. 'Wrong on both counts.' Alice laughed, 'The room cards are a bit of a hangover from grander times when guests came and went, all over the summer. And, it has to be said, a certain amount of corridor creeping went on. The names on the doors ensured you didn't get the wrong room at dead of night. It's pitch black once the lights go out.'

They exchanged a look and, much as Henri appreciated the history lesson, she sensed that Alice's forced jollity hid underlying anxiety. She decided to grab the Highland bull by its horns.

'Look, just what is the problem with my being female? I can catalogue the library as well as any man. And, for the record, my name is Bruar; not Brewer; my family originated in Sutherland.' Henriette sensed that establishing her credentials was important and hoped that appealing to the housekeeper's Scottishness would pay dividends. 'Please, Mrs Dougal, level with me.'

'Verr-y well, but it's *Miss* Dougal, not Mrs.' Sighing, Alice pushed open the bedroom door and gestured for Henri to enter.

The room was clean but hadn't been updated in a long time. An oak half-tester, mahogany tall boy and cheval mirror stood on a frayed rug over ancient floorboards. The room had gone past *shabby chic* and was well on its way to becoming down-at-heel. However, a fire burned in the tiled grate, making the room welcoming after the travails of the day. And, to Henri's delight, there was a marble-topped dressing table which could easily double as a writing desk, and ample room on the mantelpiece for her books. It was the perfect spot to write her dissertation on the Highland Clearances. Under other circumstances it would have been the perfect bolt hole until she returned to St Guthlac and cleared her name.

Alice patted the bed and invited Henri to sit. 'The person who recommended you for the post, Maddie Hallam, is a friend of Sir Malcom's— of the family. I'm surprised that she sent you when a *male* academic had been specifically requested.'

'Perhaps she knew that I could catalogue the library,' she paused, remembering what had happened back at her university, 'as well as, if not better than, any man.'

'Aye, I bet you can, at th-aht.' A welcoming smile lit up the cook's face. As though, in the past, she'd come up against her fair share of sexism and misogyny. 'But, your ability to do the job isnae the point, here. It all boils down to—' she stopped herself in time, as though it wasn't her place to interfere or give explanations. 'All I will say, is that decision rests with Himself.' Judging from her tone, she wasn't happy about that, either.

Henri wasn't going to give up without a fight. The job of cataloguing the library was a godsend. 'Look, Miss Dougal, if there's a problem, maybe we could phone Professor Hallam tonight and get it sorted out?'

'Aye, we *could*, except the phone isnae working right now.' Her gaze slid away from Henri and over to the window, instead.

'I could use my mobile—'

'No signal—'

'Send an email?'

'No internet. You'll have to wait 'til until Sir Malcolm returns in the morning. Or, if ye like, Lachlan can take ye over tae the post office where there's a public phone and free internet. You can contact your professor there.'

'I could, except, Professor Hallam leaves first thing tomorrow on a lecture tour of Canada. If I don't get in touch with her tonight, I won't be able to contact her for another week, at least.' Henri's heart sank and she felt close to tears, after coming all this way for nothing. However, she ploughed on, keen to emphasise her suitability for the post. 'I could be really useful, as I believe Sir Malcom plans to sell off the books in the library to pay for repairs to the castle.'

That innocuous statement appeared to anger Miss Dougal. 'Is that what he's been putting aboot? Selling off the family silver to plug holes in the roof? That'll be the day, the auld foo-ul.' Then she pulled herself up, and continued in a more measured tone. 'Of course, it's his to dispose of as he sees fit, but there's Keir to consider.'

'Keir?'

Alice brushed the question away. 'Aye, Keir. Now, if you'll excuse me, I'll away and finish supper. You must be starving, if that hungry rumble I heard earlier is anything to go by.' She didn't quite add that giving Henri a hearty meal was the least she could do, before the laird returned and she was sent back to England. But it was implied.

In what seemed like the middle of the night, there was a tap on Henri's bedroom door and Alice Dougal came in bearing a huge breakfast-cup of tea. Despite her worries, Henri had slept soundly because no noise penetrated the velvety darkness of her bedroom, the only light coming from the dying embers of the fire and the stars above the battlements. Initially, she'd been perplexed to discover there were no curtains at the window and then had laughed at her folly. She was at the top of the castle, only Spider-Man's Scottish cousin would have been able to see into her room.

She pulled a comic face at her own folly and Alice interpreted it as a smile.

'That's better,' she said as she laid the cup of tea on the bedside cabinet. 'Ah dinnae like to see a young lassie looking so worrit. Drink your tea and then come doon tae breakfast. Nae rush; there's plenty of time for a bath aforehand, we dinnae run to showers I'm afraid. Himself will be home and we can discuss what's to be done with you, then.'

We? Done with her?

Henriette gave Alice a more searching look. What exactly was her position in the castle? She appeared to be a member of staff, yet she ordered Lachlan about and referred to Sir Malcolm as though he was her equal, not her employer. This morning she was smartly dressed and wore makeup, and Henri caught the whiff of expensive perfume when she sat on the corner of her bed. With her slim figure, silvery blonde hair and blue eyes, she reminded Henri of Helen Mirren.

Alice Dougal gave the impression she didn't suffer fools gladly—and that included Sir Malcolm MacKenzie.

'I hope that Sir Malcolm will change his mind once he sees my credentials,' Henri ventured as she sipped her tea. Alice gave her an oblique look and muttered something which sounded like: *it's your credentials I'm worrit aboot.* Then she returned to her duties, leaving Henri to wonder what that muttered aside meant!

Chapter Four
Anither Bankrupt Laird

When Henri reached the kitchen door raised voices could be heard. Biting her lip, she paused—anxious not to enter the kitchen in the middle of a heated domestic.

'I'll thank you to remember who exactly is laird, here.'

The speaker's accent seemed to belong to a bygone era. The days when the BBC news was broadcast by a man in a dinner jacket, seated behind a desk with a large microphone.

'Oh, aye? And who might *that* be?' Alice inquired, apparently unmoved by the laird's command. 'I'll remember you're laird—when you start acting like one. I told ye afore, if another wumman comes in tae this castle, I'm away back to Motherwell, for good.'

'And ahm going with her.' Lachlan sounded glum, as though leaving Argyllshire for a town in the Central Belt, near Glasgow, would destroy him.

'*See* what you've done?' Alice asked, as a wife might to a husband who'd upset their child. 'Let's hope it disnae come to that, Lachlan, eh?'

The ancient ferryman, now on a roll, continued in a mutinous voice. 'There are two places unmarried women shouldnae be seen, *Mac Mhor*—ships of the line, and ancient castles. They bring bad luck, and this place has seen more than its fair share o' that over the last years. Most of it, wumman-related, if ye get mah drift.'

The other two, apparently unable to refute what he'd said, remained silent. But not for long.

'She isn't *simply* a wumman, as you so quaintly put it, Lachlan. She's a doctor of letters, well-educated and—' However, the laird was cut off, mid-sentence.

'Oh aye?' Alice repeated. That seemed to be her default expression, and Henri could imagine her pronouncing it, eyebrows raised and hands on hips. 'And what young, *educated,* woman in her right mind would come to Castle Tèarmannair? Ye've got no internet, phone or satellite TV. As for nightclubs,' she snorted in disgust, 'the best we can offer is the Samhain ceilidh in a few weeks' time. And what's she gonnae do when winter sets in? Once she's been through my DVD collection she'll be ready to throw hersel' aff the castle walls.'

'She's right there, *Mac Mhor*,' Lachlan backed Alice to the hilt. "Ah've tae go over the watter if ah wah-nt to watch the racing. It's like living in the dark ages in this castle.'

'I repeat, what young, educated, woman would come to Castle Tèarmannair of her own free will? There's something not right here,' Alice continued. At that, Henri clung more tightly to the door handle as her newly appointed position as castle archivist slipped further from her grasp.

'No,' she mouthed to the impassive stone walls. 'Please. No.'

'She comes highly recommended by Maddie Hallam, who, as you well know, is an old friend and Emeritus Professor at St Guthlac. My alma mater, as it happens,' he added, clearly in a vain attempt to remind them who was the boss round here.

'That'd be the same *alma mater*,' Alice pronounced the phrase in a faux posh accent, 'that sent you down for being caught in innocent lassies' bedrooms, and for the small matter of not writing any essays, or reading a book all the while ye were there? Man, ye threw away a chance many a poor scholar would give their eye teeth for.'

Herself included, Henri guessed from Alice's forlorn tone.

'Believe me, some of those *gurls,* as you describe them were far from innocent. Well, not by the end of the night—if you get my meaning.' His half-snorted guffaw would have done an adolescent proud and Henri could imagine him sending Lachlan a wink-wink, nudge-nudge look, hoping for male solidarity. Plainly, Sir Malcolm MacKenzie of that Ilk was not governed by the same code of conduct as Alice Dougal.

'Och, for guidness' sake, man. Can you no hear yoursel'?' This time Alice sounded resigned, as if she'd fought and lost this battle too many times. 'Ye'll never see seventy again, have lost most of yer wallies, creak when you move and have a red nose and broken veins from drinking too much uisge beatha. Yet ye still see yersel' as God's gift tae wimmen.'

'Noblesse oblige, Alice, darling. Noblesse oblige.'

'A load o' nonsense, wi' knobs on, mair liker it,' came back the swift retort. 'An' dinnae think I havnae seen the wee blue pills ye keep on yer bedside table. If ye're needing chemicals tae work yer hydraulics, it's time ye gave up chasing after wimmen.'

'Niagara?' Lachlan asked, suddenly back in the conversation. 'Can ye get *me* some o' them, Sir Malcolm?'

'They're called Viagra, you great lummox. And, no, he couldnae get you any. Besides, whit would you be needing with them?'

'Yes, we wouldn't want you alarming the sheep, Lachlan, now would we?' the laird added, giving the impression he was trying to win them over with humour. Henri guessed that their friendship went beyond that of master and servant.

'Och, away wi' youse,' Lachlan said, eventually getting the joke.

'Doctor Bruar?' Alice brought the subject back to Henri. 'What *was* Maddie thinking, sending her up here, given your track record?'

'Come on, Ally,' Malcolm resorted to a cajoling voice. 'Doctor Bruar is looking for somewhere to finish her thesis. A new slant on the Highland Clearances, I believe.' He made Henri sound like a blue-stocking, someone with no interest in the usual activities a women in her late twenties might enjoy. 'She'll probably take no longer than a month sorting through the library's contents, papers and so on. Once she's done that, she'll be on her way back to university and the books and estate papers will go to auction. The money raised will go towards replacing the roof.'

'Replacing the roof?' Alice exploded. 'It's gonnae take more than a few worm-eaten books to raise that kind of money. Here,' she could be heard walking over to the dresser on the right hand side of the fire, 'Put your hand on the *Guid Book* and swear that the money from the sale of the library won't end up on the tables at Monte, or being squandered on that mistress of yours in the South of France. The one ye think us and puir Keir, dinnae ken aboot.'

'You go too far, Alice Dougal,' Sir Malcolm protested, slamming the bible down on the kitchen table. 'I'll do what I like in my own bloody castle; it has nothing to do with Keir, or you.'

'And will she be doin' it for love?' Alice interjected, pushing his objection aside. 'Because if she wah-nts paying, she might as well whistle doon the wind. While you've been living the *vida loca* in Cannes, we've been living the *cannae-pay-oor-grocery-bills* in Argyllshire. Lachlan and me have been reduced tae spending oor old age pension on the messages.'

'Aye, that's right,' Lachlan agreed.

'No one will give us any more credit; yer name is *mud* to tradesmen here about. As for the utility bills, don't even get me started.' Alice was on a roll and seemingly unable to stop.

'The name of Sir Malcolm MacKenzie of MacKenzie is held in high esteem, I'll have you know.' Henri pictured the laird pulling himself up to his full height.

'*Was* held in high esteem. Now ye'r just anither bankrupt laird who's blown his inheritance. Any sympathy, or respect, folk aroond here might have felt for you because of the accident, has long since run oot.'

Accident? What accident?

That seemed to put the laird on the back foot. He sighed heavily and then caved.

'Very well, I'll send her back.' He made it sound as if she'd been ordered on line, sale or return. Panicking, Henri pushed the door open.

'No. No. No,' she exclaimed. 'You can't!'

Their heads swivelled in her direction.

Lachlan, sitting at the kitchen table with the dogs at his feet. Alice, standing by the Belfast sink, arms folded across her bosom in a 'they-shall-not-pass' pose. The laird, by the Aga, the back of his kilt raised, warming his arse. No doubt, Henri thought, furious at the turn of events—a skinny, arse at that.

Upon her entry they all adopted new positions.

Lachlan looked to Sir Malcolm, evidently expecting her to be dismissed on the spot. In his mind, he was probably already carrying her cases back down the stairs and firing up the dinghy. Alice, embarrassed because she was aware that Henri had been listening on the other side of the door, and knew the state of their finances. And Sir Malcolm, dropping the pleats of his kilt and brushing down his pilled, cashmere sweater walked towards her—hands stretched in welcome.

'Why, Alice, Lachy, neither of you told me that Doctor Bruar was so—'

'Well qualified?' Henriette finished. She knew that look. The laser beam sweep as men took in her finer points: height, long legs, thick blonde hair and eyes as green as sea glass. Their second sweep often missed the stubborn line of her mouth, the determined set to her shoulders and her death stare that warned—don't come *too* close, if you value your head.

To give Sir Malcolm his due, he read the signs and backed off, after shaking hands politely.

'*Very* well qualified,' he agreed, nodding over his shoulder to the other two. 'I was just explaining to my *staff*, here,' that earned him another derisive snort, but he carried on gamely, 'how you'll welcome the peace and quiet, and the chance to finish your dissertation.'

'Indeed.'

'We all need a bolt hole from time to time,' the laird said. The imperceptible raise of an eyebrow told Henri that he knew chapter and verse of her predicament. It went without saying that Maddie Hallam had invoked every paragraph and subsection of the Old Pals' Act to get him to help Henri, by giving her the job of cataloguing his library.

Convincing Alice and Lachlan to have a nubile young woman in the castle was going to take longer, much longer.

'That's enough for now, leave Dr Bruar alone, both of youse.' Alice's fierce expression warned the laird that Henri was off limits and cautioned Lachlan to mind his manners. Bustling forward, she led Henriette towards a window embrasure where, on a raised dais, a small table had been set for breakfast. The table commanded an unrestricted view of the loch all the way to vanishing point and small islands in the distance. Henriette's breath caught at the beauty of the scene; her stomach flipped over at the magnificence of the vista and she knew, there and then, that she'd do everything in her power to prevent Sir Malcolm from sending her home.

'I'm fair worrit what Miss MacKenzie-Grieves will say when she hears ye've got a young wumman in the castle, Sir Malcolm,' Lachlan added in a loud aside to the laird. 'Especially with Keir being home from Canada.'

'Let me worry about that,' the laird suggested as Alice poured Henri a cup of coffee. Walking over to her table he looked over her head and into the far distance. 'Finest view in Argyll; finest view in the world, bar none.'

All earlier arguments were forgotten as Alice and Lachlan chorused, *Aye. Aye*, drawing out the syllables and demonstrating their love for the place. Was that the reason they put up with the laird's proclivities and worked for no pay? Because they couldn't face living anywhere else?

'So,' the laird said, clapping his hands. 'Breakfast, Doctor Bruar—and then would you please join me in the library? Alice will show you the way.'

Henri looked longingly at the Full Scottish which Alice removed from the warming oven of the Aga and placed in front of her.

'Eat up, hen, you've got a long day ahead of you.'

Whether that meant *a long day getting to know the laird, the library and the lie of the land*, or *the long train journey back to England*, Henri wasn't sure. Shrugging, she momentarily put everything behind her, dipped her potato scone in the egg yolk and set to with a will.

Chapter Five
Breakfast Meeting

Henri found Sir Malcolm seated by an elegant Georgian secretaire bookcase in the library reading *The Scotsman*. It screamed Robert Adam, and was probably worth around eighty thousand pounds, she estimated. Evidently, the MacKenzies had once been wealthy, but what they had done with that wealth over the years was anybody's guess. It was typical of the rundown state of the castle, that the bureau's pigeon holes were haphazardly crammed with bills, (doubtless unpaid), personal papers and sun-bleached writing materials.

A complete romantic, Henri saw herself as a cross between Indiana Jones and the Relic Hunter. Someone who could tell the difference between a clever forgery and the genuine article—be it a manuscript, painting or artefact. Knowing she was in danger of losing focus, Henri squared her shoulders. She had to persuade Sir Malcolm to keep her on, even if only for a trial period. The fact that she was prepared to work for no wages might be a clinching factor in him doing so. She had her back against the wall and nowhere left to hide. She couldn't run to her parents in Switzerland, they simply wouldn't understand how she'd got herself in this predicament in the first place.

Their loving, disappointed faces and the inevitable, 'Oh, Henriette—why can't you think before you act?' was more than she could face, right now.

'Darling girl!' Sir Malcolm got to his feet and with olde-worlde charm guided her over to an ancient leather chesterfield by a roaring fire. 'Come. Sit. Make yourself comfortable.' He held onto her hand a little longer than good manners dictated and Henri prised her fingers free, as subtly as she could without causing offence.

Once her position was secure she'd make it plain that touchy-feely was out of the question. He wasn't the first man to cross the boundary between friendliness and loutish behaviour, but she knew how to deal with them.

Unaware of the thoughts running through her mind, Sir Malcolm sat on a matching leather chesterfield, crossed his legs and arranged the pleats of his kilt to best advantage. A low coffee table covered in dog-eared copies of *Tatler*, *Country Life*, *Horse and Hound* and, incongruously, *Classic Car* magazine, separated them. Glancing round the library, Henri took in the boudoir grand covered in dust, piles of books stacked on every surface and a vintage wooden globe on its own stand, its once vivid colours faded to sepia. She'd lay even money on the MacKenzies having had better taste than to have turned it into a drinks cabinet.

Finishing her hasty sweep of the library, she turned her attention back to Sir Malcolm. 'Maybe I shouldn't call you that?'

'What? *Darling girl?* I suspect not,' she agreed, not wanting to encourage him.

'I'm afraid I'm not very PC. I belong to an era when one opened doors for ladies, put oneself between them and the traffic and paid them effusive compliments whenever possible. It made us all feel special. Now?' He shrugged. 'You're likely to be hauled before the beak if you so much as tell a lady she looks pretty, or that her hair is nice.' He looked like a small boy who'd had his toys taken away by Nanny. There was a pause as he waited for her to contradict him, and when she didn't, he continued, forlornly. 'As for doors ... today's sporty Amazons look as though they want to kill me if I stand to one side and let them pass through.'

Oh, he had charm alright, by the bucketful; but Henri wasn't about to fall for it. She sent him another chastening look and kept her expression neutral. Now wasn't the time to share her views on post-feminism with him; time enough for that, once her position was secure.

'How well do you know Professor Hallam?' she asked, pretending she hadn't overheard his conversation with Alice, earlier.

'Maddie? Oh, we go way back. We were at Grotty Guthlac together,' he said, using the unflattering nickname for the august institution. 'She was a real blue stocking while I was a bit of a wastrel.' Again, a pause to allow her to contradict him. When no platitudes were forthcoming, he adopted a sad but slightly impish expression. 'She knows,' he gave a discreet little cough which encompassed all his money problems, 'the lie of the land. And when I told her I wanted to sell off the contents of the library, she suggested you, straightaway. Said you might appreciate the remoteness of the castle and the chance to get your dissertation finished?' Again, the faint raising of his eyebrow, as if inviting her to reveal her reasons for leaving St Guthlac in a hurry. 'Maddie told me you were a bit of a *divvy*; had an instinct for how much things were worth, understood the value of provenance, and had the ability to separate wheat from the chaff.' He took in the room with an expansive gesture. 'As you can see, there's lots of chaff.'

As with her bedroom, everything had once been of the best quality but was now tired and faded. The walls were lined with bookcases whose leather-bound volumes were held in place by copper wire strung across the front of each shelf. The mahogany shelves ran from floor to ceiling and a serviceable rolling library ladder on brass runners stood halfway along one of the nearest shelves. That would prove invaluable in getting the books down.

Whoa, she curbed her enthusiasm. Apart from calling her his *darling girl*, nothing had been settled. 'Okay, Sir Malcolm.' She turned her back on the books which were calling to her, begging to be catalogued and sold to a good home. 'Level with me—am I sacked before I take up my position?'

She tried to look hard-faced, to gather together phrases like *breach of contract, mediation, arbitration and compensation* to let him know she was no pushover. Instead, her chin wobbled as she realised how much she wanted this post—unpaid or not.

'Darling g—' He checked himself and then continued in a gentle but business-like manner, as though he sensed her distress and wanted to help.

'The job's yours if you want it. The roof needs repairing, and I have *expenses*,' a little pause, 'which must be met and—well, without going into too much detail, matters are a little pressing.'

'I see.' If his cook and odd job man had to contribute towards the bills and hadn't been paid in months, things must be pretty bad. 'And what about this *Keir* person? Do I need to be interviewed by him, too?'

The good humour slipped from Sir Malcolm's face. 'Oh, yes, he'd love that,' he said, bitterly. 'However, here at least my word is law. So, my dear, if you're willing to take on the task, I'm happy for you to stay.'

'I'd love to stay.' Henri held out her hand and then paused, feeling she should be completely honest with him. 'About that business back at university . . . I'm sure Maddie will have told you something of—'

Sir Malcolm brushed her explanation away. 'We're all running away from something, Dr Bruar. Me, Keir, all of us—including Lachlan and Alice. Best not to dig too deep, eh?' Reaching across the table, they shook on the deal.

'Do I start straightaway?'

'Certainly. I'll go and square things with Alice and Lachlan and leave you to become better acquainted with these precious tomes.' The last was said with dry humour as though he thought them better suited to a bonfire than an auction house in Edinburgh.

Square things with Alice and Lachlan? Henri didn't know how things worked between a Highland laird and his staff, even an impoverished one. However, it seemed unlikely that he would have to run everything past them. She was still pondering the question when she realised she was alone, perched on the edge of the sofa, hands balled into fists, nails digging crescents into her palms.

And, breathe . . .

Letting out a shaky breath, she unclenched her fists and relaxed into the leathery embrace of the chesterfield, allowing herself a moment to relish the warmth of the fire, the feeling of fullness after the excellent breakfast and the little skip of excitement which made her heart beat faster.

The job was hers and that was all that mattered.

For now.

Chapter Six
It's What I Do

'I gather that you're hired?'

Plainly, Alice wasn't happy with the situation. If the way she slammed a tray of coffee and homemade biscuits onto the top of the piano was anything to judge by. Henri wanted to ask what exactly the problem was with her staying on. If it was the laird's wandering hands and eye for a bonnie lassie, she'd soon sort him out; hadn't she she'd spent most of her adult life fending off unwanted male attention?

Or was it something to do with Miss MacKenzie-Grieves who Lachlan was 'worrit about'?

'Oh, has he left the castle?' she asked, more as an icebreaker than a desire to know the laird's whereabouts.

'Aye, he's gone over to the garage on the mainland to fetch his E-Type, to take it for a spin along the shore. When there's better things he could be doing, like . . .'

'Here, let me do that. I'm sure you have enough to do without waiting on me. I'm quite capable of fetching my own coffee from the kitchen, too, if that helps.' Henri tried to sound friendly and accommodating but Alice was having none of it.

'Aye, and nae doot getting under my feet into the bargain,' she snapped.

Shrugging, Henri picked up the coffee cup. If Cook didn't want to play nicely, there was nothing she could do. Cataloguing the library shouldn't take more than a month, six weeks at the outside. She'd be out of here, before they realised it. Until then, Himself had better watch his step and keep his hands to—well, himself! And as for his staff -

Without being aware of it, she adopted a fierce expression.

Apparently realising that she'd been rude, Alice continued in a more conciliatory tone. 'Och, it isnae you that's the problem, lassie, it's that auld foo-ul, Malcolm MacKenzie, acting like he's still thurty-five. And,' she encompassed the library in a sweeping gesture, 'the fact that he's dismantling the estate, piece by piece, with ne'er a thought for Keir.'

Him again.

Much as she wanted to know more about the mysterious *Keir*, Henri held her peace. She didn't want to start Alice off on another rant. Instead, she bit into one of the biscuits as Alice tended the fire.

'These are delicious,' she said, with a mouthful of crumbs. The biscuit, consisting of two layers of shortbread, filled with jam and topped with sweet icing and a cherry, was like nothing she'd ever tasted.

Mollified, Alice turned round and smiled. 'We called them *German Biscuits* when I was a wean, growing up in Motherwell. Our mammy owned the local bakery and oor daddy worked at the Ravenscraig steel mill.' She broke off, as if that was a story she wasn't quite ready to share with Henri. 'They were renamed *Empire* biscuits after the war, but they'll always be *German Biscuits* to me.' She sighed, as though there were memories in this castle which were too much to bear. 'Well, I must get on. Lunch will be served at one o'clock, in the kitchen. With or without Lewis Hamilton.'

'Lewis Hamilton?' Henri frowned, bewildered—and then the penny dropped. 'The Laird?'

'Aye, he'll be tear-arsing round the loch in that bluddy ridiculous sports car, like it's 1965, he's twenty years old and The Beatles are playing on the eight-track. He'd be better off helping you in the library. You'd get the job done in half the time.' She slanted a look at Henri which suggested the sooner she was out of there, the better.

'No.' Henri's answer was most emphatic. 'I work alone. It's quicker, and besides, I've had enough of . . .' She stopped herself in time. 'I'm going to clear some space on these tables and make a start. Is there any chance of a couple of trestle tables, or even an old pasting table to lay the books on?'

'I'll get Lachlan to bring a couple up to the library. He's over on the shore side idling his time in the café drinking *lattes*—if ye please, gossiping while he waits to bring Himself back to the castle. He should be chopping wood for the fires, clearing leaves out of the battlement guttering and such. Och, whit I wouldnae give to have a bridge linking us to the shore, then I could come and go as I pleased.' Her expression implied that castles were all very well and good, romantic even, but deeply impractical. Wiping her hands down the side of her apron, she paused and turned to face Henri. 'Did he mention wages?'

'Not as such . . .' Henri answered vaguely. She wondered why Alice had mentioned the café on the far shore in such disparaging terms. Perhaps Calvinism ran through her veins and she disapproved of such pursuits as driving E-Types, Beatles' music, and lattes laced with gossip, when there was work to be done.

'Fancy that,' Alice said dryly. Henri was about add that wages weren't important so long as bed and board was included in the deal. But she held her peace; if she offered to work for nothing, Sir Malcolm might expect Lachlan and Alice to do the same. That wouldn't go down well; worker solidarity, and all that.

'One more thing,' Alice paused in the doorway.

'Yes?'

'Dinnae go loaning the auld bugger any money. No matter how hard he presses ye. Ye'll never see it again.'

With that she was gone, leaving Henri to drink her coffee and finish her biscuit.

Making the most of the quiet moment, Henri rested her head on the wide back of the chesterfield and looked up at the vaulted ceiling. Everything was so *old*—a complete contrast to her family home in Basel, Switzerland, where her parents worked in the biotech industry. Her mother, a great fan of modernity, constantly changed the furniture, having no time for anything over ten years old, or which didn't scream *design classic*. Her father was the exact opposite, spending most of his time hunched over a microscope in a stained lab coat, searching for new drugs to cure pandemics like Ebola or Zika virus. Henriette wondered why her mother hadn't traded him in for someone, or something more up to date. Perhaps in his way he was a *design classic* and her mother was happy to keep him.

Thinking about them, Henri smiled. She knew she was loved, but was aware that she'd always been a distraction, getting in the way of their important research. It had been a relief all round when they'd sent her to an international school in Switzerland; near, but just far enough away from the family home to make weekend visits impractical. Consequently, they got the peace and quiet they craved and she gained a ready-made 'family' of school friends, and the chance to excel in a range of outdoor activities her parents didn't have the time or inclination for. As a result, she was independent, self-reliant and happy in her own company.

Henri was a romantic at heart and she put that down to her father's Scottish genes. Her mother came from a long line of Franco-German mathematicians, engineers and scientists—practical, rational and with not one fey bone in her body. If they were disappointed that she'd shunned a lab coat in favour of a magnifying glass, CSI gloves, and an interest in dead languages and precious manuscripts, they hid it well.

Now, *they* would have explained the phantom piper in scientific terms: acoustics, atmospherics, subsonic sound waves. And not, as she saw it, as the reawakening of her ancestry which had been dormant until she'd set foot on Scottish soil. Pulling a wry face at the fanciful thought, Henri walked over to warm her hands by the fire.

The marble mantelpiece was supported by two naked caryatids carrying its weight on their heads, flanked by two huge baskets—one filled with logs and the other with squares of peat turves. She guessed that both came courtesy of the estate and helped to supplement the heat from ancient radiators between the bookcases. They looked like coiled, iron-forged dragons, but gave out hardly any warmth.

—*coiled, iron-forged dragons?*

She smiled, imagining her parents shaking their heads at having produced a dreamer, when they viewed the world as something which could be quantified, based on practical, scientific evidence. Turning her back on the flames, Henri warmed her derriere, much as the laird had done earlier. Then she made her way round the room, touching the leather-bound books and tutting. Many of them had peeling spines and she guessed that when she came to examine them, she'd find the pages foxed, mouldy and riddled with bookworm.

But, surely, there had to be some treasures amongst them?

If there were, she—Dr Henriette Bruar—would find them.

Climbing up and down the ladder and removing books from the shelves was a filthy job. After lunch, Alice pressed an unflattering wrap-round floral pinny and silk headscarf on Henri. Now, hours later, she was grey with dust and festooned in cobwebs—complete with a full complement of dead insects and scuttling spiders. She'd suspected that cataloguing the library wouldn't be an easy task, but *this* was worse than anything she'd imagined.

Books lay piled on top of each other, with scant regard for the Dewey System. Some of them, due to damp, insect infestation, discolouration, mould and distortion, were fit only for a bonfire. Others had missing spines, detached boards, broken sewing, rusting staples and pages stuck together with damp. She had no idea of the age or subject matter contained within their worm-eaten pages, as prising the pages apart would result in further damage.

Using crumpled up sheets of writing paper she'd found in the wastepaper bin and a cracked biro which leaked ink all over her fingers, she'd written makeshift labels and placed them on top of the tables which two estate workers had carried up to the library. The labels were her first attempt to classify the books; a rough guide to the physical condition of each volume, irrespective of its worth. Depressingly, she was beginning to suspect that the whole collection would fetch pennies at auction, barely enough to replace the roof, or to treat the laird's ladies to a few spins of the roulette wheel in Monte.

At three o'clock, announced by the delicate chimes of an ormolu clock on the mantelpiece, Alice brought in a tray of tea and a packet of wet wipes.

'Here.' She tossed the wet wipes to Henri. 'Clean yersel' up, lassie and take a break.' Henri tore open the packet, wiped her hands and face and threw the filthy tissues onto the fire. Alice placed the tea tray on the table between the two sofas (no banging, or huffing and puffing this time) and wandered over to see what Henri had accomplished. 'You work fast, I'll gei ye that. Och, look at you—forced to reuse old sheets of paper and covered in ink. Make a list of what you need and I'll send Lachlan to the post office for supplies.'

'That's be great. If you're sure he won't mind.'

'He'll mind, aw'right, but he'll do as I say.' Fleetingly, fierce Alice was back in the room, then her expression softened. 'I'll make sure he goes afore the post office shuts. It's his job, anyhow, to collect the post every morning and bring it over to the castle. The postman disnae wah-nt to cross the loch after all the tales Lachlan's been spinning, aboot—'

'Water horses, and such like?'

'You, too, eh? But, you have the look of a lassie who disnae scare easily. Dinnae fash yersel', you'll have the things for the morrah.'

The morrah—ah, tomorrow, Henri was becoming more accustomed to Alice's accent. She took the cup of tea proffered and sat on the large padded fender in front of the fire.

'No chance of the internet, I suppose?' she asked, without much hope.

'Aye, ye'll be wah-nting to go on Facebook; surf the web, that sort of thing?'

'More to look up some of the authors I've unearthed and to send an email to Professor Hallam.' She tried to sound scholarly and professional, when what she really wanted to do was make contact with the outside world. She'd spent less than twenty-four hours in the castle but was already feeling removed from her other life, which was a godsend in one way.

'Professor Hallam? What I cannae understand is why Maddie sent you up here, knowing the trouble we've had in the past with—' she stopped short.

'Wee lassies?' Henri ventured.

'Exactly. But you're here now,' and then she changed tack. 'I'll get Lachlan to take ye over to the café attached to the post office when you're ready; they've got free Wi-Fi.'

'Thank you.'

'We have a telephone line in the castle, but it's out of commission. Ach, it's time this auld pile was knocked down and rebuilt, or dragged into the twenty-first century.' Alice showed scant respect for the history of the place or its family, yet it was plain that she'd been Sir Malcom's cook for many years. So—what kept her tied to this *auld pile*? Hands on knees, she pushed herself to her feet and her bones creaked in protest. Maybe she was older than first appearances suggested?

'Has Sir Malcolm returned? There are one or two things I need to ask him.'

'Yes, he's back aw'right. Ah'll tell him ye were asking after him and he'll come doon to the library. Now,' she said as she made for the door. 'It'll be dark soon and the lights in here are next tae useless. Work for anither hour and then go and get cleaned up. Thanks tae the estate, there's always plenty of wood for fires, so have a long, hot bath if ye wah-nt wan. Dinner will be at seven o'clock, in the kitchen. Ah've told Himself that ah'm getting' too auld to go carrying dishes through to the dining room. This isnae Downton Abbey; once maybe, when it was overrun with staff. But nae mair.'

Her expression was thoughtful as though remembering better times. Behind her fierce demeanour, Henri detected an air of sadness and regret and wanted to know more. But she knew she would have to tread softly around Alice, win her confidence and hope that, in time, they would become friends.

'The kitchen's fine,' she affirmed.

'Aye.' Alice stood in the doorway, hand on hip and gave the library one last despairing look and then was gone.

For several moments Henri sat staring into the fire, and a poem by Robert Louis Stephenson came to mind:

Armies march by tower and spire
Of cities blazing, in the fire;
Till as I gaze with staring eyes,
The armies fall, the lustre dies.

Watching the armies marching, she zoned out and went over the events which had brought her here. However, she was unable to arrange them in any kind of logical order because her brain refused to accept how badly she'd been treated, how appallingly she'd been let down by people she'd trusted. What did find its way into her brain was a series of flashing images: a scrap of illuminated manuscript, a smashed television, a circle of shocked faces . . . and, for an encore, the realisation that she'd flushed her promising academic career down the toilet.

'Enough!'

Smiling humourlessly, she paraphrased the tag line from an old movie— *in a castle, no one can hear you scream.* Chasing away her demons, she finished her tea in one thirsty gulp and got on with cataloguing the library. At the rate Alice was feeding her sticky buns and three-course dinners, she'd be the size of a house in no time.

'All the more for the water horse to eat—eh, Lachlan?' she said, climbing the ladder to the top of the bookcase.

Chapter Seven
Falling for You

Walking over to the window, Henri looked down over the loch as her 'shift' for the day finished.

The light was fading and there was no wind. Trees on the margin of the loch were reflected as a perfect mirror image of themselves, in ochre, vermillion and acid yellow. Pushing her reading glasses on top of her head, she focused on the middle distance where two small islands, topped by scrubby vegetation and gnarled trees bent over by the prevailing wind, gave perspective to the view.

Did the MacKenzies really own everything she could see? Small wonder the laird had such an inflated opinion of himself!

Nearer home, she picked out the jetty on the far side, where Lachlan had picked her up last night. Behind the railway station, round, green hills rose towards the sky, and behind them the mountains towered over them, like their big brothers and sisters. Was that snow on the peaks, or a corrie, catching the last rays of the setting sun?

Loch—castle—endless sky—mountains—ancient legends.

It was all too romantic for words. She suspected that if she prised open the window, the air would smell sharp and clean—not full of diesel fumes and the odour of the takeaways found on every street corner. Resting her head against the window embrasure, she closed her eyes. In her daydream, she fancied that she heard the lament which had made her doubt her sanity on the train. This time, there was no chance of it being feedback on her iPhone or a radio signal. She knew—felt it in her bones—that setting foot in Scotland, in this ancient castle, had awoken something buried deep within her.

She was beginning to understand that the piper was simply a physical manifestation of her DNA, Bruar genes and Celtic heritage. Accepting that made her feel better and she opened her eyes; she was back in the library and her flight of fancy ended. A long, hot bath was called for, without a phantom piper on hand waiting to pass her the bath towel. Last night, she'd noticed scented candles in the bathroom, probably left behind by one of Sir Malcolm's *ladie*s. She felt sure no one would mind if she used them, but she'd check with Alice first.

Rolling up her sleeves, she prepared to bring the last pile of books down from the top shelf. When that was done, one half of one monumental bookcase would be empty. At this rate, it would take her a week to fetch the books down off all of the shelves; cataloguing them would take much longer. It would have helped enormously to have someone to pass the books down to. Instead, she was forced to climb down the ladder with an armful of books, hanging on for dear life with her spare hand.

Or grim death, depending on your point of view.

It was quite a climb to the top of the ladder, even for someone fit and foot-sure. One false step would result in her, and her armful of books, crashing down onto the floor. Perhaps, in days of old, the laird had employed a wee boy to fetch books down for him. The equivalent of sending small children up chimneys, perhaps? Dismissing the thought as pure whimsy, she wheeled the ladders into position, straightened her shoulders and started the last ascent of the day.

Moments later, just as her foot was stretching down towards the last rung of the ladder, someone grabbed her round the waist. Startled, and with a split second to choose between losing her balance and falling backwards, or letting the books slip out of her grasp, she chose the latter. The books cascaded onto to the floor, she lost her footing and bounced off someone's chest.

Make that, *someone's scrawny chest.*

'Steady the buffs,' Sir Malcolm breathed against her cheek, grasping her firmly round the waist.

'What—what are you *doing?*' Henri demanded as her feet touched the library floor. 'You *bloody idiot*. I could have fallen off the ladder and broken my neck.' She pushed his hands off her waist and spun round, ready to give him a piece of her mind. If he considered manhandling female staff the last remaining perk of the landed gentry, she was about to disabuse him of the notion. As far as she was concerned, *droit de seigneur* had died out with the Normans, and she was not about to encourage its revival.

She'd had her fill of men who considered her fair game. Men who thought they could call the shots and take advantage of her. Time to lay down some ground rules.

With the rungs of the ladder pressing painfully against her bottom, Henri gathered all her strength and gave Sir Malcolm an almighty push backwards. This time, it was he who lost his balance, clutching at the air and reaching out for her. Instinctively, Henri did just that. After all, he was an elderly gentleman in his seventies, and she'd been a tad too rough with him, even if he deserved it. Seconds later they landed on the floor in an ungainly heap. He, kilt askew and showing his thin, sinewy legs to their worst advantage. She, half-blinded by the silk scarf, which had been holding back her hair but was now draped over her eyes, as if this was some kind of bondage game.

'Oof.' Her breath was knocked out of her when her breasts came into contact with Sir Malcolm's aforementioned scrawny chest.

'Tally ho,' he exclaimed, seemingly enjoying every moment of the encounter. Henri suspected that he regarded it as some kind of game; foreplay, even.

Then he cried out *'tulach aarst'*, which Henri assumed was a reference to her arse, which was within reach of his wandering hands.

'Sir Malcolm. Get off me!' Horrified, Henri levered herself upwards, taking her weight on her outstretched arms and putting space between them. The laird, surprisingly strong for his years, knocked her hands away and she fell on top of him again. 'I swear to God,' Henri began, drawing back her arm ready to poke him in the eyes with her first two fingers, as she'd learned in self-defence class.

But it never came to that.

The stone floor rang out with the sound of iron-studded boots, she was lifted off the laird as though she weighed no more than a feather and thrown over someone's shoulder in a fireman's lift. Next thing, she was lying face down on the leather chesterfield gasping for breath. Righting herself, she pushed the headscarf over the crown of her head and straightened the floral overall which had ridden up over her midriff, like a badly-made festoon blind.

'What the bloody hell—' Henri exclaimed at her rough treatment.

'What's all this?' Alice demanded from the threshold where she and Lachlan were standing—arms folded, lips pressed together and wearing identical *'did we no say that having a wee lassie in the castle would bring nothing but trouble?'* expressions. Sir Malcolm, on the other hand, looked pleased with himself and not in the least bit embarrassed at being found under said *wee lassie*.

'Who is this—person?'

A new participant in the game; someone with black hair pulled back and knotted on top of his head in a man bun and sporting the bushy beard of an Old Testament prophet, regarded Henri and the laird with eyes, bright with anger.

'Aye, whit's going on?' Lachlan parroted, seemingly anxious not to miss an opportunity to land Henri in further trouble.

Unfazed, Sir Malcolm replied, 'Calm down, all of you. I was simply helping Doctor Bruar to carry some books over to the table when we lost our balance and landed in a heap on the floor. Gallantly, I threw myself under her—to break her fall.' He acted as if he couldn't understand why they were all so put out. He extended his hand, and the man with the beard hoisted him to his feet in a manner which showed little consideration for his age, or respect for his title. Sir Malcolm took a few unsteady steps, dusted himself down and adjusted his leather sporran. 'All innocent and *perfectly* above board. Chivalrous, you might even say.'

Girl in the Castle

'We heard ye call out *Tally Ho*, you eejit,' Alice said.

'And *Tullach Ard*. The MacKenzie battle cry,' Lachlan snarled, openly affronted at it being wasted on a Sassenach, and a female Sassenach at that.

'Et tu, Brute?' Sir Malcolm demanded, with a sad shake of his head.

Lachlan looked between Sir Malcolm and the man with the beard, openly weighing up where his loyalties lay. He came down on the side of the stranger in the thick tartan work shirt, combat trousers and safety boots.

'Ah dinnae ken who this *Brute* is, or what clan he belongs to, but—aye, since ye ask, I think ye were *both* up to nae good.' Lachlan took a step away from Henri and the laird, and sided with the dark-haired man.

'Now, look here.' Henri scrambled to her feet. However, the man with the beard ignored her and rounded on the laird.

'Sexually harassing the new cleaner? That's a bit low, even for you.'

Cleaner? *Cleaner!*

Now, while Henri in no way considered cleaning houses beneath her, she hadn't spent years studying to gain a PhD only to be dismissed as some over amorous Mrs Mop—by, by *him*. Whoever he was.

'I'll have you know,' she began, pulling on the sleeve of his tartan shirt, 'that I am Doctor Henriette Bruar, late of St Guthlac University; engaged by Sir Malcolm to catalogue his library, with a view to its contents being auctioned.'

At that, Sir Malcolm groaned and covered his eyes with his hand.

Too much information?

'You're *who*? And you're doing *what?*' the bearded man demanded. 'Father, is this correct?'

Father!

Feeling like an extra from *The Empire Strikes Back*—the scene where Luke Skywalker discovers that Darth Vader is his father—Henri could only stand mouth agape. THIS—this man with the piercing blue eyes, thick black hair and disapproving countenance was the *Keir* they'd all been referring to? Sir Malcolm's son; heir to a diminished kingdom she was commissioned to reduce even further?

Now it was her turn to groan and to look between father and son.

Of *course* he was Sir Malcolm's son, she saw it now, even if in colour and stature they were nothing alike. Sir Malcolm, tall and rangy; fine blond hair arranged in a skilful comb-over to hide his balding pate. Keir MacKenzie, tall and well-built, without an ounce of excess flesh on him, looking as if he ran ten miles a day with a rucksack full of stones—just for the hell of it. They held themselves with the kind of easy confidence which comes from knowing your place in the hierarchy. Even if these days good breeding and social standing was all that was left of a once prosperous Highland estate.

Where Sir Malcolm's fair complexion was raddled from high living and time spent in the south of France, his son had the dark hair, olive-pale skin and cobalt blue eyes typical of a Highlander. The other thing they had in common, apart from their haughty demeanour, was that they spoke the Queen's English without a trace of Scottish accent. Evidently, some elite boarding school—Gordonstoun most likely—had ironed all Scottishness out of them.

'*Doctor* Bruar, is it?' Judging by the stress he put on her title, he was unimpressed. In fact, his scathing tone made it plain that he thought her academic title as phony as she was. 'Doctor of what, exactly? I'm guessing you're one of those lifestyle gurus whose qualifications come via the internet. I bet you've got a vlog and thousands of followers on Instagram.'

This was her chance to put the record straight, and she had the feeling the opportunity wouldn't present itself again.

'I am Doctor Henriette Bruar. At the start of the next academic term, I will be appointed junior lecturer at—' She wasn't allowed to finish her sentence.

'Really?' A dark eyebrow shot up in disbelief, followed by a swift onceover of her unflattering wrap-round pinny and headscarf. '*Really?*'

'Yes; really,' she asserted. 'I didn't bring my diplomas with me, but I can have them couriered over.' There was no mistaking her snarky tone or her false, bright smile.

'That won't be necessary. I think I know what we all believe of you, Doctor Bruar.' He included Alice and Lachlan in his gang of three.

'This is getting us nowhere,' the laird broke in. 'What you witnessed was a genuine accident, I surprised Doctor Bruar—' Henri's gracious nod acknowledged his use of her title.

'I'll bet ye did,' Alice hissed under her breath.

'She lost her balance and I, nobly, broke her fall. End of.' Snorts of derision greeted this. 'Let's hear no more about it. To be honest, Keir, I think you owe Doctor Bruar an apology.'

Keir MacKenzie's expression suggested there wasn't a snowball's chance in hell of that happening. The laird plainly thought so, too, because he tried to defuse the charged atmosphere and save face in front of Henri and the other two.

'We weren't expecting you home for another couple of weeks. I thought I'd miss you.'

'Don't you mean you *hoped* you'd miss me?' Keir MacKenzie's sweep of the library took in the trestle tables, Henri's makeshift, ink-stained labels and the first, empty bookcase. 'And I have no say in this, I suppose? The fact that you're selling my inheritance from under me?'

'It will be yours when I'm dead,' Sir Malcolm said, 'Until then, it's mine to do with as I please.'

Henri was puzzled. Before the appearance of his son, she would have said that Sir Malcolm was affable and easy-going, even if a little *too* hands-on for her liking. Now his jaw was set in the same implacable line as the younger MacKenzie's and his eyes glittered with suppressed rage. It was like witnessing a young buck locking antlers with an aging stag.

What lay behind their antagonism, she wondered? Surely it wasn't *all* about money?

'Please tell me that funds raised from selling off the library will be put to good use on the estate and not spend on those avaricious harpies you consort with in the South of France.'

Sir Malcom countered with, 'I suppose you'd deny me some fun in my declining years. God knows there's nothing here to keep me,' he added, bitterly.

'If it means safeguarding what's left of the estate—yes. And, don't worry, I won't be under your feet for long and the castle's large enough for us to avoid each other. Once the Beach House is aired, I'll move in there. That way, you and Doctor Bruar can get on with destroying this ancient library—and whatever else you have planned, without my help or interference.'

There was anger in his voice, but sadness, too. However, Henri didn't have the time to become involved in the MacKenzie soap opera, she had enough on her plate.

'Och now, Keir,' Alice came forward and put her arm through his. 'This is no homecoming for you, laddie. Come away intae the kitchen and leave Doctor Bruar alone. She's only doing what she'd being paid to do, after all.'

'Quite,' was his cutting rejoinder.

That put Henri on a par with Sir Malcom's *avaricious harpies* on the Cote d'Azur, if not worse. However, she held her peace. She was more interested in the way Keir MacKenzie behaved towards Alice Dougal, how he didn't automatically cast her off, but allowed her to rhythmically stroke his arm, and smooth his ruffled feathers.

'Very well,' he said, walking towards the door with Alice's arm threaded through his. 'Father? We can talk later. In private.' Henri felt the last was aimed at her, but she kept her feelings to herself and wondered instead what lay behind over the dysfunctional relationship between father and son.

Chapter Eight
A Second Interview

The following morning in the library Henri was glad she was wearing woollen wristlets.

She'd learned soon after arriving at Saint Guthlac that sitting in university libraries, even centrally heated ones, was chilly work. And, while cold hands were a boon to a pastry chef, they were the bane of an academic's life, along with icy feet. But today, none of that mattered because she was wearing Uggs and thick socks, a pashmina, and an Aran sweater under an old pair of denim dungarees, and Lachlan, at Alice's insistence, had built up the fire.

It cast a warm glow over everything and the scent of the peat turves as they burned was comforting. Beyond the library, the sun shone in a cloudless sky, melting the overnight frost riming the battlements. Henri gave a contented sigh and relaxed. *This* was her work; *this* was what she was good at, what she loved. Castle Tèarmannair was the most romantic of settings, even if there was a large fly in the otherwise paraben-free, hypoallergenic ointment.

Keir MacKenzie.

At Alice's suggestion, Henri had eaten supper in her room yesterday evening, keeping out of his way. Alice had hinted, this was probably *'for the best'* until *'things settled down'*. And, to be honest, Henri was in no hurry to renew their acquaintance—although, she was keen to put him straight on a few things. The chief one being that she had no designs on his father. She had a job to do and would make a bloody good stab at it, and raise money for their bankrupt estate. Professional pride and self-respect demanded no less.

What she didn't need was the son and heir getting in the way and cramping her style.

Luckily, by the time she'd come down to breakfast, he'd left to check out the Beach House, and the well-rehearsed speech which she'd spent all night composing with the intention of putting him in his place, was left unsaid.

Somehow she doubted it would go to waste!

With luck and a following wind she might never meet MacKenzie Junior again. That thought cheered her as she walked over to the secretaire bookcase where the tools of her trade were laid out on the pull-down, desk top: two reams of paper, an assortment of pens and other items of stationery. All purchased in the local post office by Lachlan, on Alice's instructions. Now, she could rewrite the labels for each table, make notes and get on with the cataloguing. Her initial plan—to spend most of the day indexing the books and her free time working on her dissertation at the marble-topped dressing table in her room—had been blown out of the water by Keir MacKenzie's arrival.

The sooner she was out of there, the better.

She frowned, lost in thought. She couldn't imagine addressing either of her parents in the tone he'd used with his father yesterday. And in front of other members of staff, too. Obviously his grasp of the tenet regarding honouring thy father and thy mother was shaky. She frowned more deeply, consternation puckering her normally smooth brow. *Mother*. There has been no mention of the laird's wife since she'd arrived. There were no photographs of her on top of the rosewood piano, or any other recent family photos, come to that. Was she dead? Divorced? Or, missing in action as a result of the laird's womanising? She wouldn't blame any woman for bolting from this castle, lovely though the surrounding hills and mountains might be.

Wrapping her pashmina round her neck, muffler-style, she pushed MacKenzies, plural, out of her mind and got down to the intellectually satisfying task of cataloguing the library.

Later, hunkered down in front of the window seat, carefully prising apart the pages of an old Bible, she became aware that she was no longer alone.

'You're different from the others, I'll give you that,' a voice broke into her thoughts.

'Wh—what?' Startled, she lost her balance, rocked back on her heels and landed painfully on her bottom. Spinning round, she clocked the now-familiar safety boots, khaki combat trousers and tartan work-shirt.

Him! Like the proverbial bad penny, Keir MacKenzie apparently had the knack of turning up when he was least expected—or wanted.

Quickly, she scrambled to her knees. It wouldn't do for him to believe that she threw herself at the feet of every passing MacKenzie in an attempt to . . . to do what, exactly? Seduce them, win their trust, become mistress of this crumbling pile of stone; help them spend their last bawbee?

'I said, you're different from the others,' he repeated, waiting for her response. He held out his hand to help her to her feet.

'Am I now?'

Ignoring his hand, Henri stood up, dusted herself down and glanced up at him, keeping her expression neutral. She'd made up her mind to take a deep breath before she spoke, giving herself time to counter whatever ridiculous claim he laid at her door. However, tall as she was, she had to raise her head to look him in the eye, otherwise he'd think she was kow-towing to him. When she did, the sight that greeted her, nearly made her lose her balance a second time. The black, bushy beard had been shaved off and his long hair, which had been pulled back in an unbecoming man bun, was cut in a style which showed off a well-shaped skull, and cheekbones capable of slicing cucumbers.

Henri swallowed, hard; the Old Testament Prophet had morphed into Rock God! Or, at the very least, given his work clothes, Man of the Woods; Bear Grylls's sexier, Scottish cousin.

One thing hadn't changed, however; his eyes were the same remarkable dark-denim blue, even if, today, the antipathy in them was banked down, hidden. His white-toothed smile which superficially appeared charming and welcoming, didn't fool her for a second. It was the smile on the face of the wolf before it pounced on an unsuspecting lamb. It was apparent that MacKenzie had embarked on a charm offensive and, judging by his calculating regard, believed there was more than one way to skin a rat.

That she was the rat in question, wasn't up for debate.

'Did you want something? Something other than preventing me from getting on with my work, that is.' Her cool looked made it plain that she was no ingénue who turned into a blushing schoolgirl, simply because the son of the house smiled at her from his lofty height.

'Merely,' he paused a split second for effect, 'checking things out.'

By *things*, Henri assumed he meant her. That smile again—apparently he was keeping his powder dry until he'd determined what her game was. The fact that he assumed she had a 'game', spoke volumes. Henri turned away and returned to sorting through a pile of books as though he wasn't there.

It was a pile she'd already sorted through several times, but he didn't need to know that.

'Yes; different,' he repeated when she didn't respond. Plainly not used to being ignored, he walked round to the far side of the table and stood there for several moments; watching, waiting—getting in her way. Henri recognised the steel in the man, and knew that it would take more than a few cold looks and brusque answers to deflect his interest and put him in his place.

'Different in what way? Excuse me—' She paused with a pile of books under her arm and waited for him to move out of her way. She hoped that by carrying on regardless, he would realise she wasn't easily intimidated by the male of the species.

'Younger for a start. How old are you? Twenty-five, twenty-six?'

'What's my age have to do with anything?'

'I was merely observing that you are younger than—'

'Younger than what?'

'Father's usual *women*.' He put enough stress on the word to make it sound like a slight.

Commendably, Henri maintained her composure and came back with, 'It's none of your business how old I am. I'm employed by your father. So, if you think you're about to conduct a second interview, forget it. I'm answerable to Sir Malcolm. If you have any issues, take them up with him. All *you* need to know, is that I am old enough, and qualified enough, for the task in hand.'

'Which is?'

'Cataloguing this library.'

'Nothing more?'

'Such as?'

'Seeing yourself as the new mistress of Castle Tèarmannair.'

It was such a ludicrous suggestion that she laughed out loud. 'What— become your stepmother? As you've been keen to point out, your father is old enough to be my grandfather. '

'Then why are you here?'

'I've told you, cataloguing the library so that Sir Malcolm can raise enough money to prevent the castle from falling into further disrepair.'

'All very commendable and I would be inclined to believe you but for two things.'

He moved towards the table bearing the label, '*BEYOND REPAIR*' and started rearranging books on there.

He was, Henri reckoned, taller than her by a good head and a half. She wasn't above exploiting her height advantage and caustic wit when the covert sexism in the history department became too much for her. This was no different. If she showed any sign of weakness—physical or emotional, he would exploit both. She had to become *Hard Hearted Hannah of the Highlands;* stand her ground, or he'd have Lachlan take her across the loch to the station in double-quick time, once the laird left for France.

The ormolu clock on the table chimed the hour, a gentle reminder that time was passing. Henri sighed theatrically to signify she didn't have time for this third degree.

'You were saying,' she prompted. 'Two things?'

'One. It's no secret that Father would happily see the castle sink into the loch before he spent another penny on it. And, two, you were recommended for the post by one of his old friends. I'm guessing that they have an equal opportunities policy in place at your university? So, I'm wondering—why did Professor Hallam choose to bypass it?'

'Two reasons,' she mocked. 'Your father wanted an expert. My name came up and I was free.'

'Isn't that *three* reasons?'

'Okay, three,' she conceded. 'Now, if you don't mind . . .'

'You had to leave St Gulthac, and Hexham, in a hurry, I gather?' He made Hexham sound like Dodge City, as if there was a mob of vigilante academics on her tail. In place of six guns and Stetsons, they were wearing academic gowns and mortar boards, and brandished iPads. 'I'm guessing that a castle in the middle of a loch, hundreds of miles away is as good a place as any to hole up.' Again, the raised eyebrow as he waited for her to fill in the gaps.

'Hole up? I'm sure I don't know what you are alluding to.' Walking round to his side of the table she took the books out of his hands and rearranged them on the table with exaggerated care. 'Professor Hallam may have a shared history with Sir Malcolm, but I was chosen to catalogue the library because I am the best person for the job. And, in any case, why would your father bother to employ me if he would rather see the castle sink into the loch?'

'My point exactly, why would he?' Obviously, he had no intention of enlightening her on *that* point. 'Makes you think, doesn't it?' Whether he was referring to his father's predilection for spending his fast dwindling inheritance on the tables at Monte, or was harking back to what little he knew about her, wasn't clear.

'I have to get on, so, if you don't mind—'

'That's my point, I do mind. Take pride in destroying ancient libraries, do you?'

That was so far from the truth and insulting to her academic prowess that Henri slammed the books on the table and then rounded on him.

'Look—if the library is so precious, how come it's been allowed to get into this state?' She picked a book at random. '*Regardez*—Adam Smith—*The Wealth of Nations*. When this book was published, America was a British colony. It's a seminal text and it's been treated so disrespectfully that it makes me want to weep.' At that point, her voice did catch and she banged the book down on the table and picked up another. 'And this? *Culpeper's Complete Herbal*, printed in the late seventeenth century when there was a *Scottish* Stuart king on the throne. You know? The pages are stuck together, some have been ripped out and,' her voice rose an octave, 'some *idiot* has coloured the original drawings with felt-tipped pen. An early nineteenth century copy sold recently for over one thousand pounds. And *this*,' she took a step closer, 'James Audubon's *Birds of America*, published in 1840. Some philistine has ripped out the prints and . . . done, I know not *what* with them.'

He had the grace to look sheepish. 'I think great-great-great granny had them framed for her sitting room, next to her parrot's cage. The prints are in a storeroom, somewhere.' She threw her hands up in the air in a gesture of exasperation and disbelief. Then she pointed an angry, accusatory finger at him.

'So *don't* you lecture *me*. Mate.'

He didn't look as though he was used to being addressed as anyone's *mate*, let alone by a woman over whom he considered he held the high moral ground. Seemingly affected by her passionate outburst, he took the book out of her hands and put it on the table, as if suspecting she might use it to brain him. His hands, Henri noticed, were used to hard, physical work; however, his fingers, were long and slender—like a poet's.

'I see what you mean. But you must understand, these books have been neglected for years. No one has read them or—or taken care of them.' There was a note in his voice which she couldn't identify. One which made it plain that someone had once loved this library but now there was no one left who cared for first editions.

'I noticed that these precious paperbacks have been looked after.' Walking over to a Georgian revolving bookcase crammed full of John le

Carré, Barbara Taylor Bradford and a selection of Eighties *sex and shopping bonk-busters*, she stood with her hands on her hips. 'Well, shame on you. And shame on your family,' she added before she could stop herself. 'When did Jackie Collins take precedence over a King James version of the Bible?' She pointed at the large tome she'd been working on when he crept up on her.

'I don't know much about King James versions of the Bible but I do know that those other books are Alice's guilty secret.' His eyes softened and his expression became forgiving. Henri was blown away by the change in him. 'As are the Mills & Boons,' he said, pointing to a shelf devoted entirely to the slender volumes. 'She's the only one who has entered this library for years, mostly to dust it and check for leaks.'

Again the faraway look, as if remembering someone who had once loved this library. The softening of his fierce demeanour, the way his eyes had turned a deeper, softer blue affected Henri. In spite of the antipathy she felt towards him, she wanted him to be on her side, to acknowledge that she had no ulterior motive for staying in the castle, didn't fancy the pants off his father, and had no intention of applying for the position of stepmother.

Instead she said, 'Alice?' hoping he would drop his guard and give an insight into their relationship. Perhaps even explain why the cook's word was law in Castle Tèarmannair.

'*She who must be obeyed*,' he quoted H Rider Haggard, and grinned. Something nascent, and unlooked for, turned a little cartwheel in Henri's solar plexus. She laid her hand over the chakra, midway between her navel and her breast bone, as one might do when supressing a hunger pang. Taking in a breath, she returned to the subject of the library, but he beat her to it. 'To be honest, I rarely come up to the castle, let alone into the library. I didn't realise it was in such a state.'

'In which case,' she crossed her fingers behind her back, 'leave me to do my job and I'll be on my way. I'm in enough tr—' She stopped herself in time, but the word, *trouble,* hung in the air.

Luckily, he didn't pick up on her chopped-off sentence. Nor did he appear in any rush to go about his business; instead he parked himself on the edge of the trestle table and swung his free leg backwards and forwards. She didn't need to be the seventh daughter of a seventh daughter, or whatever constituted a Highlander with 'the sight', to know that Keir MacKenzie was trouble with a capital 'T'.

So,' he asked, pleasantly enough. 'Is *this* you? The real Doctor Henriette Bruar?' His sweeping gesture took in her ancient dungarees, Arran sweater, and the silk scarf she'd tied, bandana style, over her blonde hair. Henri shifted restlessly under his gaze and pulled the wristlets further down over her knuckles, as if to ward off his scorching regard. 'Bit of change from yesterday.' There. He was back to his old self; suspicious, guarded, wary of her.

'The same could be said of you.' She mirrored his all-encompassing gesture and raised eyebrow.

'Oh the hair, you mean?'

'Precisely.'

'Alice insisted.' Then he pushed himself off the table and headed for the library door. 'Oh, by the way—you didn't answer my original question.'

'Remind me,' she said, as though she was too busy to give his questions too much thought.

'How old you are?'

I'm twenty-eight and *three quarters*, and have all my own teeth, if you must know. Well past my teenage years but not quite ready to be grouped with those—what was the phrase you used—*avaricious harpies*, your father consorts with? FYI—my birthday's in January, which makes me a Capricorn: responsible, disciplined, self-controlled, and a good manager. How about you?'

She fired the question at him and, off-guard, he came back with, 'May; like my father.'

'Which makes you Gemini. Rest easy,' she said, walking over to the ladder to begin the ascent of the north-west wall of library. 'An astrological no-no as far as Capricorns are concerned. So you see, you and your father have nothing to fear from me. We're incompatible.'

Turning her back on him she climbed to the very top of the ladder and pretended to sort through the books. Leaving him, as they say, to stew in his own juices as he made his way back to the kitchen.

Chapter Nine
The MacKenzie Cousins

Some days later, when Henri walked into the kitchen, Alice was banging saucepans over at the cooker. Judging by her expression she was far from happy and Henri was anxious to find out if she was responsible for Alice's bad mood. They seemed to be making friends, if somewhat guardedly, and she didn't want anything to spoil that.

'Are you alright, Alice?'

'The MacKenzie-Grieveses are coming for lunch today.' She made it sound as if the Clancy Gang was about to ride into town and shoot up the sheriff. Having delivered the message, she turned back to the stove and stirred a large pot of soup in an agitated manner, giving the impression that she neither liked, nor approved of the MacKenzie-Grieveses.

Unsure of what to say, Henri hesitated and then asked, 'Does that mean you want me to have my lunch in the library?'

'No; it disnae. But,' she turned to face Henri again. 'Tidy yersel' up, lassie, before you join us.' She gave Henri a straight look, as though they were co-conspirators. 'No dungarees, get rid o' that old scarf and put on a wee bit of makeup. Ken?'

Henri didn't 'ken', but she knew enough of Alice Dougal to recognise that if she said 'tidy yersel' up,' she'd better do just that. Having survived a second interview with the son of the house, she didn't like to think she was about to be interrogated a third time, and by people who had no business nosing into her affairs.

The smell of cock-a-leekie soup and freshly baked bread greeted Henri when she re-entered the kitchen. Alice was no longer alone and the kitchen seemed crammed with people—three familiar figures and two complete strangers. Keir stood apart from the group, leaning against the small table in the window embrasure where Henri took breakfast every morning. He didn't seem too pleased to be there and Henri suspected that he had a thousand and one jobs he should be getting on with—just as she did. Evidently, Alice had dragooned him into putting his work clothes aside and tidying himself up; clean jeans and a smart shirt worn under a microfibre gilet. Henri hoped that he hadn't been told to put on a 'wee bit of makeup', too.

Smiling at the thought, she walked over to the Aga where the strangers were drinking whisky, and waited to be introduced. Sir Malcolm, full of olde-worlde charm as ever, did the honours.

'Alexander, Ciorstaidh, this is Doctor Henriette Bruar who is cataloguing the library.' He pronounced her name 'Onriette, à la française—much to her embarrassment.

A young man roughly about Henri's age, sporting well cut moleskin jeans and a cashmere sweater under a tweed jacket, walked over to her.

''Onriette? Enchanté, Mademoiselle.' Much to Henri's surprise he didn't shake her hand, but raised it to his lips and kissed the air above it. 'Do I detect French blood running through your veins?'

'On my mother's side, yes; Scottish on my father's.'

'Ah.' He appeared in no hurry to release her hand. 'The Auld Alliance—France and Scotland, united against the English. I'm a great believer in keeping that association alive. Aren't you, Keir?'

Keir, it appeared, had no opinion on the subject, and continued to scowl at them all from his vantage point. Henri removed her hand as politely as she could without giving offence. What was it with the men round here? They were either curmudgeons like Lachlan and Keir MacKenzie or considered flirting an Olympic sport.

'Well, for the sake of international relations, I'll reserve judgement on that one,' Henri said, diplomatically.

Like his Uncle, Alexander MacKenzie-Grieves looked uncrushable as he shrugged off the put down. 'Ciorstaidh, come and meet Henriette.'

'Henri, please.' Smiling politely, Henri turned to shake hands with his sister.

'How do you do?' Like Venus rising from the waves, Ciorstaidh MacKenzie rose from the armchair. Wearing a mini-kilt in MacKenzie tartan, black suede over-the-knee boots, ruffle-edged green cardigan and burnt orange silk shirt, she touched fingers with Henri and then glided over to Keir. The mid-morning sun picked out the russet highlights in her hair, contrasting it with Keir's, which had the dark bloom of a chough's wing.

They made a fine couple, Henri reflected, and Ciorstaidh seemed keen to emphasis the point.

'When youse have all finished bowing and scraping and—for the love of God, kissing hands, Sandy? Mah soup's getting cold.' Alice banged a large enamel ladle on the table. 'Sit. If you please. Sandy, Ku-rsty,' she indicated their places at the table, using the ladle as a pointer. Henri gained the impression that pronouncing the cousins' names in broad Scots was Alice's way of countering the high esteem in which they held themselves.

'I'll sit by Keir. We have lost time to make up, haven't we?' Ignoring Alice, Ciorstaidh MacKenzie laced her arm through Keir's and practically dragged him off the raised dais. 'Alexander, you can sit on one side of Dr Bruar and Sir Malcolm on the other. Lachlan and Alice can sit at the far end of the table.' She didn't quite say *below the salt*, but it was implied.

There was an unseemly scramble as Alexander and Malcolm jockeyed for position on Henri's right hand. When she took her place between them, their knees pressed against her thighs in a wholly inappropriate manner and she squirmed uncomfortably. She didn't want to make a fuss, otherwise Keir MacKenzie would accuse her of—somehow—bringing their unwelcome attention on herself. However, she felt like elbowing them in the ribs and telling them to back off.

In contrast, Ciorstaidh stood by her chair and waited for Keir to pull it away from the table. Then she sat down and shook out her napkin. Malcolm and Alexander fought for possession over Henri's napkin and an unseemly tug-of-war ensued, finishing with the linen napkin being rent asunder. In the end, Sir Malcolm won possession of the two halves and spread them over her right knee with a great show of gentility. Not to mention a light trailing of his fingers along her thigh.

Wanting to slap them both and feeling things were getting out of hand, Henri spoke plainly. 'I take it that I'll be allowed to feed myself?' To make her point, she picked up the soup spoon before either MacKenzie could claim it.

'Quite so.' Malcolm frowned at his nephew and issued a warning, as though he was innocent of all crimes. 'Sandy, behave.' Alexander's eyes widened in protest but he said nothing.

'Is this bread gluten free?' Ciorstaidh asked, pointing to Alice's freshly made loaf in the middle of the table. 'I take it the soup has been made with organic vegetables and the chicken is free range?'

Lachlan regarded her with a baleful eye.

'It is that. I wrang its neck and plucked it mysel', just yesterday. Eat up lassie, yer too thin. In my opinion a man likes a bit more lying beside him in his bed of a winter's night.' With that, he plonked his elbows on the table and starting sucking soup off his spoon, like Dyno-Rod clearing a blocked drain. Ciorstaidh shot him a look of distaste, giving Henri the strong suspicion that she would prefer Lachlan to take his lunch with the dogs in their kennels.

'What are you up to these days, Sandy?' Keir asked his cousin. 'Still working in your uncle's bank in Edinburgh?' The stress on *bank*, underlined Keir's obvious belief that being a pen pusher wasn't a fit job for a man, let alone a MacKenzie. Knowing the MacKenzies' parlous financial circumstances, Henri guessed that bank managers, financial advisers and accountants were on their black list.

'We aren't all cut out for the great outdoors,' Alexander drawled, looking pointedly at Keir's jeans, shirt and gilet. Henri gave Alexander an oblique look; she couldn't imagine him getting his hands dirty or doing anything more physically demanding than opening a bottle of champagne. He had the air of being used to money and the privileges it bought, and considered Keir uncouth. Henri glanced between Keir—who was breaking bread with strong brown hands and getting stuck into his lunch, and Alexander—who was crumbling bits of bread before popping them into his mouth, as delicate as a girl.

'What about you, Doctor Bruar? Do you spend all your time cooped up in a library researching . . . or whatever one does at university these days?' Ciorstaidh pushed her half-eaten soup away from her and left the bread on her side plate untouched, as though she found Alice's food unpalatable.

'I'm writing a paper entitled: *The Highland Clearances—ethnic cleansing or economic pragmatism?* which I hope to publish next summer. The main thrust of my argument being that defeat at Culloden led directly to the destruction of the clan system and a form of feudalism over a thousand years old.' Henri was on a roll and warmed to the subject. 'After the Forty-Five, lairds no longer needed rent in the form of military service from their tenants. They wanted rent paid in coin of the realm which, obviously, their tenants did not have. Putting self-interest first, the lairds cleared the land for sheep rearing, with little regard for their tenants' welfare—where they went, or what became of them.' Pausing, Henri dipped her napkin in her water glass and dabbed at the dribble of soup which had dripped off her spoon and landed on the front of her blouse. 'If the research is well received,' she went on, still dabbing away, 'I will explore the topic in greater detail, contrasting the Scottish Diaspora with the mass emigration which followed the Irish Potato Famine.'

When she raised her head, she became aware that they were regarding her, soup spoons paused halfway to their mouths, as if she was an alien species. Considering that there were two lairds and the son and daughter of a wealthy landowner present at the table, Henri realised that she'd dropped a clanger.

'I see Doctor Bruar is a historian born and bred in the Marxist tradition,' Alexander quipped. 'Better watch out, Malc, or she'll have us all lined up against the wall.' He took aim at each of them in turn and mimed a shotgun going off. 'Bang. Bang. Bang. Getting rid of the ruling classes is much more fun than shooting pheasants, isn't it, Doctor Bruar?' Ciorstaidh frowned at him and then turned her attention to Henri. Her flint-hard grey eyes missed nothing—Henri's empty soup bowl, butter-smeared side plate, or the soup stain spreading across the front of her blouse.

Henri supressed a groan. They must think her a closet revolutionary *and* a slattern.

'What you need to understand is that, in order to gain attention outside of one's university, an academic must raise a controversial topic, back it up with rigorous research, publish it and hope it will be well received. It's nothing personal . . .' she added, tailing off.

'I'll remember that when the tumbrils roll up the drive,' Alexander said.

It was Keir and then Alice who came to her rescue.

'Not our finest hour, I think we all agree on that point.' Keir put down his spoon and regarded Henri as if seeing her for the first time.

'I understand what Henri's trying to say. Keir's mother, despite being the laird's wife, was a member of the Labour Party all her life. She named Keir after Keir Hardie, the first Labour member of Parliament—a miner's son, born not a stone's throw from Motherwell where we grew up.'

We? Henri waited for Alice to qualify the statement but Alexander MacKenzie-Grieves interrupted and the moment was lost.

'Two revolutionaries at the table. Bravo. Or should that be three, if we're to include Keir?' He laughed, touching Henri's hand, lightly, to show *he* was impressed by her academic prowess. When his foot pressed against her instep suggestively, it took all of her self-control not to leap out of her chair like a scalded cat.

'That's enough, Sandy,' Alice warned as she started to clear away the first course. However, Alexander MacKenzie-Grieves was clearly having too much fun to let the subject drop.

'God, Keir, don't you find a woman with long legs and brains an incredible turn on?' Keir's countenance darkened, evidently he was not amused by Alexander's flippant remarks. Moving her foot away from the amorous Alexander, Henri steered the conversation onto safer ground.

'I'm not just another academic, beavering away in an ivory tower, in case that's what you're all thinking. I'm also an excellent skier and captain the dons' mixed-hockey side. I like to keep fit—an academic faculty is a snake pit of ambition, the struggle to win tenure and an academic chair. I have to be at the top of my game. Each faculty member is only as good as their last piece of published research.'

Her expression became pensive as the memory she kept pushing to the back of her mind elbowed its way forward. Zoning out from the group, she recalled the events surrounding the last hockey match of the season. She'd arrived at the Dean of Faculty's rooms where colleagues from the history department had gathered, just in time to catch the opening titles of a BBC4 history programme. The documentary spotlighted the rare manuscript she'd discovered, pressed between the pages of a medieval psalter in the university library. Trustingly, she'd handed the manuscript over to the Dean who, elated by her discovery, promised to fast track her application for the junior lectureship she sought, once her doctorate was awarded—naturally.

'Naturally,' she'd agreed, echoing his words. Idiot! She should have known better.

During the time she'd been at university, she'd spent most of it as the Dean's unpaid research assistant, practically writing his latest academic paper for him. Sure, she'd been awarded her doctorate; however, the Dean, unwilling to lose a valuable research assistant had blocked her every attempt to gain a teaching post. Feeling overlooked and undervalued as she watched less able colleagues promoted above her, Henri's had felt her resentment grow, until . . .

She frowned, what had brought this up? Ah, yes; captaining the dons' hockey team.

She remembered every detail of that evening—sitting cross-legged on the floor, hockey stick across her knees, watching the programme, waiting patiently for it to finish. Waiting—and expecting to have *the find of the decade* attributed to her, to hear her name read out; to appear in the credits at the end. As the programme drew to a close, it became clear that the Dean had claimed the find as his own. Although, according to the voice-over, he'd been assisted by a junior researcher in his department.

Junior! That was the moment when she finally snapped.

'Henri, are you aw'right? Ye've gone awful peely-wally . . . '

'Which is Alice's quaint way of seeing you look rather pale.' Alexander spoke slowly, annunciating each word as if Alice was a simpleton. She threw a bread roll at his head and he dodged it, allowing it to land on the floor where the dogs set about devouring it. Their snarling and barking brought Henri back from her waking nightmare. Brushing away Alice's concern, she tuned back into the conversation, but it had moved on. So, she never found out if Keir MacKenzie preferred women whose IQ outstripped their bra size.

Probably just as well.

'Hockey? A Sassenach's game,' Alice interjected. 'You should see oor Keir when he plays for the local shinty team. It's a sight for sore eyes, Henri, because they play the last game of the season in kilts. Awful braw,' she added, finishing her soup.

Oor Keir? Was that just a figure of speech? Or was Keir MacKenzie somehow related to Alice Dougal?

Evidently displeased that the spotlight had moved off her, Ciorstaidh MacKenzie leaned into Keir's side, slid her arm round his waist and looked up at him. 'I could have gone to university. *Should* have gone to university, but I wanted to learn how a Highland estate is run. I'll make the *perfect* wife for a Scottish landowner.'

No prizes for guessing who that landowner might be!

When all heads swivelled in Keir's direction, Henri decided it was time for her to exit, stage left. As if choreographed, she and Keir stood up from the table at the same time, pushed their chairs back and muttered something about 'getting on'. When she glanced over at him, she saw the humour in his eyes as he acknowledged the shared moment.

'Quite,' Ciorstaidh agreed, clearly wanting to appear busy, too—and evidently none too happy that Keir and Henri were on the same wavelength. 'We'll take coffee in the sitting room, Alice,' she said, as if mistress of the castle. Muttering something which sounded suspiciously like, *feck off and get it yersel'*, Alice cleared the table, crashing dishes together with scant regard for their age or value.

Making the most of the diversion, Henri slipped out of the kitchen and headed for the library. Suddenly, the physical act of climbing up and down a ladder with an armful of books seemed *very* appealing.

Chapter Ten
An Unfriendly Warning

Fifteen minutes later, the heavy library door opened and Ciorstaidh MacKenzie crossed the threshold, huffing and puffing as though she'd performed one of the twelve labours of Hercules. Ciorstaidh's mime was evidently designed to underline the fact that she was petite and fragile, whereas Henri was tall and athletically built. Standing at the top of the ladder with an armful of books, Henri stifled the urge to drop them on the fragrant Ms MacKenzie-Grieves's head, and dumped them back on the shelf instead.

'Was there something you wanted, Miss MacKenzie-Grieves?' she asked, frowning to make plain that Ciorstaidh's intrusion was unwelcome.

'Oh, sorry. Am I interrupting you?' Ciorstaidh asked, all wide-eyed innocence.

Biting back the obvious—*what do you think?* Henri ran with, 'Of course not. Come in.'

Ciorstaidh walked further into the library, wrinkling her nose at the smell of damp and dust, as if the thought of touching one of the grimy, mouldering volumes was repellent. So dirty, so ancient, carrying who knew *what* diseases. In the end, good manners overcame irritation and Henri joined Ciorstaidh by the piano.

Ciorstaidh cut to the chase. 'How long is this going to take, Dr Bruar?'

'By *this*, I take it you mean cataloguing the library?'

'Obviously.'

'Well, *obviously*, it will take some time. A month, minimum, to get the books down and into some sort of order—and then they'll have to be valued by an expert and sent to auction.' She looked at Ms MacKenzie-Grieves, not quite sure what her point was. 'Is that a problem?'

'Not if we can reach an understanding.'

'An understanding?'

The helpless maiden act and simpering tone vanished, replaced by a look of pure steel. 'In case you aren't aware, Keir and I are promised to each other.'

'Promised?' Henri laughed at the quaintness of the expression. 'What is this, the Middle Ages? You mean, you and Keir are *engaged?*'

Ciorstaidh confidence wavered, briefly in the face of Henri's amusement and apparent disbelief. Then she rallied and continued. 'Not officially, you understand. But—look, you're a smart cookie, Dr Bruar, I'm sure I don't need to spell it out . . .'

'I'm rather afraid you do,' Henri replied, refusing to play ball.

Ciorstaidh sat on the leather chesterfield and swept her legs to one side in a pose straight out of a finishing school manual. She sighed, as though resigned to explaining all to Henri, as one might to a none-too-bright child.

'I'm sure you're up to speed on your Scottish history?' She inclined her head and indicated that Henri should take her place on the other chesterfield, across the coffee table from her. Henri complied, curious to find out what all this had to do with Keir—and, she supposed, her. 'The Jacobite Rebellions, and so forth.' Ciorstaidh's gesture encompassed the library's ancient walls hung with threadbare tapestries of battle scenes.

'Of course. Although, it is more accurate to refer to some of them as risings, rather than rebellions.' Henri couldn't resist the chance to establish her scholarly credentials. 'Any rebellion in particular?' She felt like holding out a pack of cards and saying: *pick a rebellion, any rebellion . . . now, don't show it to me; let me guess.*

As if sensing Henri's amusement, Ciorstaidh frowned. 'The seventeen nineteen; the battle . . .'

'Battle of Glen Shiel? Which, I believe, is just up the road?' She pointed towards the window and then continued. 'The rout of the Spanish troops sent over by Cardinal Alberoni to join the local clansmen; Eilean Donan castle being blown up by the English.' She rattled off a potted history, but had clearly missed the point, because Ciorstaidh gave an irritable tut.

'A bad day for the MacKenzies.' She made it sound as if it had happened only yesterday. 'They lost the battle and, as a punishment for supporting the Jacobite cause, Sir Malcolm's ancestors were heavily fined and their estate sequestered. They narrowly escaped death because *my* ancestors intervened, bribing officials and asking for mercy to be shown.'

'Wait; aren't his ancestors and yours one and the same?' Henri frowned, her scholarly curiosity piqued.

'Back then, we were the *Grieves* and they were the *MacKenzies*. We'd long had our eye on Castle Tèarmannair and it was our money and influence which saved the MacKenzies' skin, the laird's head, and the castle from suffering the same fate as Eilean Donan. The laird married one of my female ancestors, and basically,' she looked down at her bright red shellac nails, 'we've been doing the same, ever since.'

'All a bit *Gone with the Wind*, isn't it? Cousins marrying cousins, simply to keep the money in the family. Are you telling me that Sir Malcolm married into your family, too? Wouldn't that make a connection between you and Keir genetically . . . ill advised?' Henri struggled to get her head round the concept of cousins, half-cousins, and cousins twice removed marrying over the last three hundred years.

Seemingly, that touched a nerve. Ciorstaidh's head snapped up and she gave Henri a hard stare. 'We're far enough apart, genetically, for it not to be a problem. I've checked.'

'I'm sure you're right. Only . . .' Henri was about to say something but then changed her mind.

'Don't hold back, Dr Bruar.' Her smile held little warmth or humour.

'I'm thinking of the old stories, about so-called monsters, bricked up behind walls in Scottish castles, their remains shown to the laird on his coming of age. I'm wondering if they are the offspring of first cousins who married.' She left Ciorstaidh to join up the dots.

'As I said, not a problem. No MacKenzies have married for at least two generations. Sir Malcolm *should* have married into my family—instead he married Keir's mother.' She paused and then turned up her nose as if a dirty smell had entered the room. 'Not a Highlander, of course, and not of our class.'

'A love match?' Henri asked, silently applauding Keir's mother and Sir Malcolm. But—if it'd been a love match, how had things turned out so badly; father and son estranged, no sign of Lady MacKenzie, Sir Malcolm living in the South of France, spending his son's inheritance?

There was so much she needed to know, wanted to know. But who could she ask without seeming too nosy? Not Ciorstaidh Mackenzie-Grieves, that's for sure. She wasn't certain how it worked with the landed gentry; her parents had met at university, fallen in love when they'd joined the debating team, cemented their relationship over a Bunsen burner, as her father jokingly put it, and remained sweethearts ever since. That's what she wanted, a great love which never faltered. One which grew stronger over the years. Was such a thing possible nowadays, when everyone shacked up together after a couple of dates, reluctant to commit, to give up their freedom?

'Not *quite* a love match. But that's another story,' Ciorstaidh said at last. 'What you need to understand is that Keir is mine and always has been. He needs me; needs the money my mother will gift us when we marry—money which will restore his estate and his fortune. The last thing he needs—*we need*—is for him to become distracted, to lose sight of his . . . obligations. His destiny if you like. To put it bluntly, Dr Bruar—to become involved with someone who, for all the letters she has after her name, doesn't understand how it works here in the Highlands.'

'I get all that,' Henri said, hiding the fact that she wanted to make Keir a widower before he was a husband. 'What do you want from me?'

As if she didn't know!

'I want your assurance that you aren't interested in him and, once you've finished your work here, you'll go back to university and we'll never hear from you again.'

'That sounds very . . . final.' She couldn't resist stringing the haughty heiress along a bit longer.

'It has to be.'

Ciorstaidh's arrogance in assuming she could be brushed aside reminded Henri of how the Dean and the hierarchy at St Guthlac had treated her and she responded more vehemently than intended.

'Dowries, arranged marriages, family expectations—give me a break! Unlike you MacKenzies, I live in the twenty-first century and have to establish my academic reputation, build a career and, hopefully, earn a living from it.' Standing, she sent Ciorstaidh a get-over-yourself coruscating look. 'Rest assured, Miss MacKenzie-Grieves, I have no designs on your darling Keir; he's not my type. And, for the record, shouldn't he have given you the family ring to wear, the one doubtless left to him by his heilan' granny? Thus rendering this conversation unnecessary?'

Ciorstaidh, patently not amused by Henri's flippant reference to darling Keir/heilan' grannies, snapped back. 'He will, at the Samhain Celebrations. As for not being your type,' Ciorstaidh gave a snort of disbelief and followed Henri as she walked over to the ladder to resume her work. 'Have you *seen* him? He's every woman's type, you just need to get to know him.' Then she smiled, a secretive little smile, intimating that she and Keir MacKenzie were more than kissing cousins.

For reasons Henri could not explain, that statement made the lunch curdle in her stomach and left a bitter taste in her mouth.

'Thanks, but I haven't got the time—or the inclination, to study his finer points. I've seen enough to know he's not for me. So, rest easy, *sistah*,' she said the last in an American accent, clicked her fingers and traced an 'S' in the air. 'Ah don't want your mah-n.' She sounded as though she was a guest on the *Oprah Winfrey Show*, but she didn't care. 'Now, if you'll excuse me, I have work to do. And, as I'm sure even you can work out—the quicker I do it, the sooner I'll be out of your hair and you can have your precious Keir all to yourself.'

At that moment, Ciorstaidh's 'precious Keir' entered the library.

'Everything okay, ladies? I heard raised voices.' He looked from one to the other before his gaze finally rested on Henri. 'Dr Bruar, is there a problem?' Was it her imagination, or was he accusing her of upsetting his future fiancée? Despite what she'd just said to Ciorstaidh, his words cut her to the quick. Eyes pricking with angry tears and more affected by the encounter with Ms MacKenzie-Grieves than she cared to admit, Henri gripped the rail and started to climb the ladder.

Why did everyone assume she was the villain of the piece?

'Everything's tickety-boo, Mr MacKenzie,' she replied in a false, bright tone. Scooping up an armful of books, she descended the ladder, holding onto the rail with her free hand. When her feet touched the stone floor she spun round and gave an impatient sigh. 'Still here are we?'

Ignoring her snarky tone, Keir relieved her of the books.

'Well, it is my home, which probably means I can go anywhere I like; without seeking anyone's permission,' he said with dry humour. 'However, now I've seen you teetering on that ancient ladder, I'm not happy with the situation.'

'Worried I'll fall and sue your arse off?' she snapped, still rattled by Ciorstaidh's inquisition.

'Sue all you like, but it'll be a hollow victory,' he said, referring to the dire straits the estate was in. Ciorstaidh sent Henri a *see, I told you so,* look. Then, with a glimmer of the humour, he added, 'We can't always rely on Sir Malcolm to be on hand to break your fall. I think you need an assistant.'

'Break her fall?' Ciorstaidh inquired, but no one paid her the slightest attention.

'Speed up the process, you mean? Good idea.' Henri implied that she couldn't wait to get out of here.

'That isn't what I meant,' Keir said, a tad wearily. 'Look. I didn't come here to argue with you, again . . .'

'*Again?*' Ciorstaidh was ignored a second time.

'Let's save this discussion for later. Ciorstaidh.' He turned to his cousin. 'Lachlan's ready to take you and Sandy over the loch back to your Land Rover.'

'Oh but, Keir, I wanted *you* to take us across. Maybe come back with us to the house to see Mother and the aunts? We all want to hear how you've got on at our cousin's lumber business in Canada.' The slight emphasis she placed on *our cousin* was another shot across Henri's bows. This was Mackenzie business—*you* back off, sistah! Walking over to Keir, she laced an arm through his and looked up into his face, her eyes soft and limpid. 'Please? Lachlan's such an old grump.'

'That I cannot deny. Unfortunately, I must decline your invitation. I'm leaving the castle in my own boat and going over to the Beach House, which, as you know, lies in the opposite direction. Earlier, I lit the wood burner and the old kitchen range in an attempt to air the place. I intend to sleep there tonight, damp and mildew notwithstanding. I can't breathe in this place.' He took in the room, the loch and the hills beyond in one despairing sweep. 'Old memories; too many ghosts.'

Ghosts? The phantom piper!

Catching Henri's interested look, Keir muttered, '*A la recherche du temps perdu.*' Was it Henri's imagination, or did he seem bereft as he pulled up the zip of his gilet?

'*In search of lost time.*' Henri translated the title automatically. Then putting the books she was carrying on to the table, she picked up a copy of Proust she'd found earlier. 'It this yours?'

'It is. I haven't seen it in years. Thanks.'

'You're welcome.'

They stood rooted to the spot, each holding an edge of the slim volume, Ciorstaidh all but forgotten. But she was not so easily side-lined, and soon drew the conversation back to herself.

'Ghosts—of course there are ghosts. This castle is over a thousand years old, what else would you expect. I *do* hope you have time to enjoy the Samhain celebrations before you leave, Dr Bruar. That's *Hallowe'en* to you;

but you'll find it has nothing in common with all that trick or treat nonsense imported from America. To Highlanders, Samhain is a time for remembering the departed, those lost spirits who haven't found their final resting place.' She slanted a glance at Henri and then drew Keir towards the door. 'I'd better not say anymore, or you'll be too scared to leave your bed in the middle of the night to use the bathroom.'

In one fell swoop she implied that Henri was timid *and* incontinent.

'Oh, I suspect that Dr Bruar is tougher than she looks,' was Keir's deadpan response.

'It's not the dead you need to fear in this life.' Henri gave them both a hard stare. 'In my experience, only the living have the power to hurt and betray.'

There. Let them make what they will of *that*. Climbing the ladder, she stood balanced at the top, back towards them, and waited until a loud click told her that they'd left the library.

Chapter Eleven
True Confessions

At the sound of Lachlan's boat revving up, Henri rushed to the window. Sure enough, Keir, Alice, the MacKenzie-Grieveses and Sir Malcolm were on the jetty exchanging farewells and promising to meet up soon. Beset by a sudden yearning to breathe in the crisp, autumn air and get the dust out of her lungs, Henri fetched coat and scarf from her bedroom, rushed down two sets of spiral stairs, and through the undercroft—just in time to see Lachlan's boat head for the farther shore.

'A nippy wee sweetie, that one,' Alice observed when Henri reached her. Her smile held until the boat's occupants were too far away to read her expression, then her shoulders sagged and she exhaled.

'A what?' Henri was beginning to understand some of Alice's quainter expressions, but this one beat her.

'A nippy wee sweetie—hides a sharp tongue behind a sugar coating. I'm guessing she warned you off Keir?' They stood shoulder to shoulder watching him untie his boat and prepare to head up the loch in the opposite direction to the Beach House. Fortunately he was out of earshot so Henri could speak freely.

'You guess right. However, we also discussed the 1719 rebellion and how the MacKenzies were saved by the Grieveses' money.'

'Is that what she told you? She didnae mention that the laird of Castle Tèarmannair had no choice but to marry the Grieves heiress and hand the castle over to them? Or that the Grieves were all that stood between him and a beheading? It wouldnae surprise me to discover that the Grieves had denounced them to the English in the first place.'

'Blackmail; eighteenth-century style? Nice.'

'A determined lot, the Grieves,' Alice observed as Keir walked along the short jetty towards them. The wind off the loch whipped colour into his cheeks, giving his hair a just-got-out-of-bed look. He looked in rude health and much suited to an outdoors life, Henri reflected, harbouring her first non-murderous thought about him since her arrival. It wouldn't last, she knew that! But one thing she did know, if he married Ciorstaidh, neither of them would be happy. She watched him lean forward, kiss Alice on the cheek and give her a bear hug.

'You'll be back the morrah to discuss the Samhain celebrations, Keir? I have enough to do without taking that on single-handed. And Himself's about as much use as a chocolate fireguard.' Holding him at arm's length, Alice regarded him with a steady eye, making plain it was a command, not a request. 'But, if you're too busy, I'm sure Ciorstaidh will only be too pleased to come over and help.'

They exchanged a conspiratorial look and then laughed.

'I'll never be *that* busy,' Keir quipped and Alice slapped the top of his arm in playful reprimand. Poor Ciorstaidh, if only she knew what they thought of her! Poor Alice, should Ciorstaidh become mistress of this castle, she'd be on the first train back to Motherwell, no returns—for life! Feeling excluded, and wanting to be part of a gang that exchanged quips and easy laughter, she spoke up.

'*I* could help, although I have no idea what the Samhain celebrations entail. But I'm good at following instructions.' Keir MacKenzie's swift look showed he very much doubted that.

'At least she knows to pronounce it *Sav-ahn*,' Alice replied, straight-faced. 'Whatd'ya say, Keir?'

'I'd say that you've never had a *doctor* help you make clootie dumpling before. And Doctor Bruar strikes me as very capable.' Henri wasn't sure that his statement was entirely free of irony but she took it at face value.

'Is that a *yes*?' she inquired, hands on hips in an unconsciously challenging pose.

'Och, Keir, stop teasing the puir gir-ul,' Alice reprimanded, before addressing Henri. 'I was hoping ye'd say that, lassie. But I widnae want to get in the way of the library business, or your—what was it, Highland Clearances thingummy-jig.'

'I'm sure I can fit in both. As for my thingummy-jig, well . . . I'm not sure I'll be finishing it, the way things stand.' Her voice trailed off—and when she raised her head, the other two were looking at her quizzically and waiting for her to qualify the statement. Rubbing her hands together, she blew on them and gazed out across the loch, thus bringing the conversation to a close.

The mood broken, Keir climbed into his boat and made his way up the loch and out of sight.

'I know what you're wondering,' Alice said a while later as they sat by the Aga, the work for the day completed. 'You're wondering, how come Tèarmannair's head cook and bottle washer orders the laird's son around and kisses him on the cheek.'

'I'm not. I didn't. Oh hell, okay, I *am* wondering that.' Henri laughed and settled herself more comfortably in the old armchair. One of the lurchers at her feet raised its head and laid its long muzzle on her knee. Its piteous expression implied that it was never fed and could she please give it some of her biscuit?

Beyond the window, the dusk settled round castle and loch like a cashmere shawl; purple, and shot through with rose. 'I'll let you in on the secret—I'm his auntie.'

'His . . . his *aunt*?' Henri failed to keep the incredulity out of her voice. 'But, how—'

'How does a woman raised above a bakery in Motherwell come to be aunt tae a Highland laird?'

'Well, yes.'

'Simple. His mother, Lady MacKenzie, was my sister.'

'You mean, you were separated at birth? She was raised in the Highlands and married Sir Malcolm, while you were brought up in Motherwell?' Henri tried to make sense of what Alice was telling her.

'Och, not at all. I'll tell ye all about it, if *you* tell me what trouble brought you here. Ok?'

'Deal,' Henri sighed. It'd be a relief to unburden herself to gruff, kind-hearted Alice Dougal; aunt to the future laird and sister-in-law to Sir Malcolm MacKenzie. 'Me first?'

'If ye like.'

'Long story short?' Alice nodded, encouragingly. 'I spent the last three years gaining a PhD in history—writing my thesis under the supervision of two dons—Maddie Hallam, Emeritus Professor History, who you know—'

'Aye.'

'The other was the Dean of the History Faculty who, in theory, was there to oversee my thesis and help me gain my doctorate. However, in reality I was nothing more than his dogsbody. *Do this, Miss Bruar, fetch that, Miss Bruar,*' she mimicked his supercilious tone. 'He even sent me to buy cards and birthday presents for members of his family when I should have been studying. On top of which, I spent more time undertaking research for *his* post-doctorate work than I did for my own thesis. He was a bully and had wandering hands.' Shuddering, she recalled the number of times he'd 'accidently' brushed against her, or trailed his hand along her arm as he'd reached for a pen. His favourite ploy was to creep up on her in the library when she was burning the midnight oil doing *his* research, put his hands over her eyes and whisper: *guess who?*

'Why did ye no report him to Maddie?'

'Professor Hallam spends most of her time abroad on lecture tours trying to attract benefactors who'll give large donations to the university. I wasn't the only female he tried his 'tricks' with, but he pestered me more than others.'

'Why did ye put up with it, hen? You dinnae look as though ye'd take that sort a' thing lying down.'

Henri pulled a face.

'I'm ashamed to admit that I put up with it because I wanted to finish my doctorate. After which, I would work for a year as a research assistant, with a view to becoming a junior lecturer when a post became vacant. All of which he could make very difficult, if not impossible for me, if I didn't play ball. I should have stood up to him, I know that. However, it's all academic, now—if you pardon the pun, because I've screwed up big time.'

'Go on.'

Henri stroked the lurcher's long muzzle and played with its silky ears as she explained.

'I found a scrap of illuminated manuscript tucked between the pages of a medieval psalter in the university library. The psalter was hidden at the back of one of the bookcases, possibly by a student who intended returning later to retrieve it, with a view to selling it to a collector. But that's not the point—'

'Go on,' Alice urged.

'I guessed, from the colour, penmanship, and subject matter that the manuscript was original—and extremely old. Dating, in all likelihood, from the time when The Venerable Bede was writing *On the Reckoning of Time* at his monastery in Jarrow. About, oh, thirteen hundred years ago. Bede wrote the book to aid his students' understanding of computation and the calendar.'

Although she was recounting the tale of the worst day of her life, her eyes shone as she remembered finding the precious scrap of paper. Her enthusiasm was contagious because Alice was hooked and hanging on her every word.

'And? Go on—ye cannae stop there, Henri.'

'Sorry for the info dump, but I want you to understand how important this find was—is.' And so she continued. 'The university had a copy of *On the Reckoning of Time*, courtesy of a rich benefactor in the late 1800s, whose son was a theology student at the college. I'd seen the original and recognised the piece of manuscript straightaway.'

Seeing Alice's frown of concentration, Henri stalled. How dull and dry this must seem to a non-academic. Alice clearly needed a short intermission, because she walked over to the corner cupboard, brought out a bottle of uisge beatha and poured out two glasses.

'A wee dram, to wet your whistle.' Henri accepted the drink and then went on with the story.

'Can you imagine my excitement? It was the best day of my life. Our university would hit the headlines, we had the missing piece from an important manuscript which the British Library had on permanent loan from St Guthlac. But, do you want to know the best bit?'

'I do.'

'The rough notes, scribbles and practice letters on the reverse side of the vellum were clearly the work of the great man himself. It was the discovery of the decade and I thought my academic career was assured.'

'And it wisnae?'

'Sorry, long story short, I said—' She started pacing round the kitchen in an agitated manner. 'I was on my way to take the manuscript to show Maddie, when I remembered she was on a lecture tour. I bumped into the Dean of Faculty in the corridor and, unable to contain my excitement, I showed him my find.'

'Let me guess, hen. From that moment onwards it became *his* find; *his* discovery?'

'Correct. As luck—bad luck, would have it, he had contacts in the media and got straight on to them. It was but a short step from there to a BBC film crew turning up on our doorstep and St Guthlac making the end of the six o'clock news.' She tossed back the contents of her glass and slammed it down on the table before taking her place by the fire.

'There's more, I'm thinking . . .'

'I was promised credit for the find. Not simply *young research assistant finds rare manuscript*. More than that. He promised that I would be interviewed for the programme, after which, I would be a shoe-in when a junior lectureship became vacant.'

'So, what happened?' Alice cradled her whisky glass, too interested in Henri's story to raise it to her lips.

'A few weeks ago, before the start of this academic year, the programme was scheduled to be aired. I was invited to his rooms to watch, along with colleagues from the history department.' As she recounted the last act in this story of betrayal she had difficulty forming words.

'Straight from your hockey match,' Alice encouraged her to continue.

'The credits rolled, everyone applauded, clapping the Dean on the back. Congratulating him on the find. *My find.* I stood up, thinking—hoping—as the seconds ticked by, that he would put the record straight. But—'

'He never did?'

'No. So—and this is the part I'm *not* proud of—I went in for the kill.'

'Oh my God. I'm guessing that you brained him with your hockey stick and he had to be lifted to the nearest hospital.'

'Next best thing. I smashed his television to smithereens and was just about to do the same to him when the hockey stick was prised from my fingers and I was bundled out by Maddie Hallam.'

'I would'ah done the same.' Alice sent Henri an admiring look. 'What happened next?'

'I'm in deep dung and the university doesn't know what to do with me. I found the manuscript, I made that plain, but I'd also smashed up an eminent prof's property. I was trouble with a capital 'T' and had to be dealt with.'

'I'd love tae get mah hands on him,' Alice declared and Henri managed a weak smile.

'So—Maddie sent me up here to catalogue the library; got me out of the way until the heat dies down. But it's not over.' Henri's voice caught in her throat as she relived the terrible day when she was summoned to the chancellor's office. 'I'll have to face a disciplinary hearing for '*Gross Misconduct*—fighting or causing a disturbance/ malicious damage or destruction to property'.' Henri quoted from the letter she'd received from Human Resources, prior to setting out for MacKenzie's Halt.

She covered her face with her hands and Alice made comforting noises. 'Och, ye puir wee thing—'

'As a result of my hot-headedness,' she said in a muffled voice through her fingers, 'I've wrecked everything; my chances, my future. I expect I'll be asked to leave the university and told to forget all about the promised junior lectureship. Oh, Alice, how can I tell my parents? They are so proud of m— my achievements?'

'Och, c'mere.' Getting to her feet, Alice held out her arms. Henri was only too willing to be enfolded in them. 'Things always appear darkest before the dawn. I've lived long enough to know *that*. Is there no one who can speak up on yer behalf? Maddie perhaps?'

Henri shook her head. 'Getting me out of the way is as much as she can do, for now. As the Dean's superior she'll probably be asked to chair the disciplinary hearing, so she can't be seen to be siding with me, or granting me any favours. The general consensus,' Henri sniffed and dabbed at her eyes with the piece of kitchen towel Alice handed to her, 'is that I'm lucky the university hasn't pressed criminal charges, and has decided to handle the affair, internally.'

'Maybe you'll find a rare book or something else in the castle library. Claim it as yer own; rebuild your reputation.' Shaking her head, Henri adopted a sorrowful expression. 'Nae chance of that, then?'

'Sadly, no. Most of the books have been ruined by damp and age. Those which are salvageable will hardly raise anything, once VAT and the auction house's commission are deducted from the sale. The most precious thing I've found are the household accounts, which stretch back to the late seventeenth century.'

'Those auld books?'

'Yes; you see, historians aren't only interested in scraps of illuminated manuscripts stretching back a thousand years, or more. They love evidence of how people used to live; diaries, private letters, estate papers. Primary sources which can validate hours of research; improve the chance of their post-doctorate work being accepted and making a name for themselves in a crowded field.'

Alice looked sceptical. 'So, how many bushels of wheat or cattle were slaughtered for a Samhain feast back in 1716 wid be fascinating, then?'

'Correct—so, unless I find Castle Tèarmannair's hoard of buried treasure, those household accounts are our best hope of raising money. The volumes covering the Jacobite rebellions are rare and I'm hoping that museums and academic libraries will start a bidding war for them, once word gets out.' Alice's head jerked up at the mention of 'treasure,' and a look of pain crossed her face. Henri wondered what she'd said to upset her, but when she next looked, Alice had herself under control and the moment passed. 'Please don't mention any of this to Sir Malcolm or—or, Keir. It's nothing to do with them and it won't affect my work in the library. Although I suspect that Sir Malcolm may have an inkling of it, via Maddie. I'll be finished and out of your hair before you know it. No one needs to know the trouble I'm in, apart from us.'

'Alice Dougal knows how to take a secret to the grave,' she declared, referring to herself in the third person. 'Aye, she does that.'

Henri didn't doubt it. For a few moments neither of them spoke. Then the door of the kitchen burst open and a very disgruntled Lachlan entered, muttering uncomplimentary things about Miss Mackenzie-Grieves, and it was business as usual.

'That bloody wumman fair gives me the scunners,' he asserted and plonked himself by the fire, not in the least concerned that he might have interrupted something important. 'Ah'm parched, Alice. Give me a wee drap of the laird's finest, will ye?'

'Indeed I will not, tea's all that's on offer. And, take yer bunnet aff indoors, man. How many times dae I have tae tell ye?'

'Ah take mah bunnet aff for no man. Not even the Queen,' he declared over his shoulder as he slid the kettle onto the hotplate.

'You'll do as I say, Lachlan MacKenzie, or ye'll be getting yer own dinner tonight,' Alice asserted and a full blown row ensued. Henri made the most of the diversion to slip out of the kitchen unnoticed.

Girl in the Castle

It was only later, as she tidied up in the library, that she realised Alice had told her nothing of how a girl, born above a bakery in Motherwell, had come to be sister-in-law to a Highland laird whose lineage was older than Braveheart's.

Chapter Twelve
An Unwanted Letter

True to his word, Keir MacKenzie found Henri an assistant in the shape of Lachlan's sixteen-year-old great-nephew. As Henri passed another armful of books down to Young Lachy MacKenzie, she supressed a smile. He was completely smitten and blushed to the roots of his red hair when she addressed him. He refused, point blank, to call her Henri—instead stammering out D-Doctor Br-Bruar every time he spoke to her.

'Last lot for today Lachy.' Descending the ladder, Henri directed him to place the books on the 'sorting table'. Smiling, she remembered how he'd declared on the first day they'd worked together that *it was just like Hogwarts and the Sorting Hat,* and then had almost imploded with embarrassment at his gauche remark. 'A wee cup of tea?' she asked, walking over to the tray which Alice had provided, accompanied by a warning of what would happen to Lachy, if he *messed Dr Bruar aboot.*

Henri supressed another smile. It was almost two weeks since she'd arrived at Castle Tèarmannair and she was beginning to think and speak like a Scotswoman. By rights, she should have been suffering from claustrophobia because she hadn't set foot outside the castle and had no means of communicating with the outside world. However, with each passing day, the debacle of the television programme and its aftermath receded and she hunkered down in her Highland hideaway. In fact, she'd started to feel quite light-hearted, humming *Don't You Worry 'Bout a Thing,* as she went about her work.

Some days, she actually convinced herself that everything *was* going to be alright.

'No thanks, Hen—Doctor Bruar, I've got shinty practice.'

'Shinty?'

'*MacCoinneach Camanachd*—MacKenzie's Shinty Team. We're really glad Keir's home, it's the last match of the season on Saturday and we might stand a chance of winning if he plays. Will—will ye come and watch us?'

'I might at that,' she mused. 'I read, somewhere, that Quidditch in the Harry Potter books, was inspired by shinty. Or, is that too great a leap of imagination?' she teased him.

'Och, well, I—I dinnae ken,' he stammered and turned a deeper shade of red.

'Is this the match when the team play in their kilts?' she asked, hoping to put him at his ease. However, having to answer a direct question rendered him speechless.

'Yes, it is,' Keir answered, entering the library. The look he threw her suggested that she was teasing the poor boy for her own amusement. Then, as if realising that he'd been unfairly harsh, he continued in a conciliatory, if slightly ironic, tone. 'Coincidently, it's the match most ladies choose to attend.'

'Funny, that,' Henri said, matching his inflection.

Then she turned away, tutted, and riffled through the pages of yet another damaged book. With Lachy's help, she'd spent most of the day emptying those bookcases which butted up against the outward facing west wall, only to discover that rain water had seeped in and ruined most of them. Seemingly, little structural work had been carried out on the castle in years, and the mouldering book in her hands was a casualty.

'That's because the l-ladies like to see the men in their k-kilts,' Lachy stammered, in case Henri didn't get it. 'Only . . .' He looked at Keir, seemingly for permission to say more, but then his courage ran out and he clammed up.

'I think what Young Lachy is trying to impart, is that—contrary to common belief—the men will be wearing shorts, or at least compression leggings, under their kilts.'

"Elf and Safety?' Henri raised an eyebrow and then sighed, elaborately. 'Such a shame when old customs aren't strictly adhered to.' There! Let him make of that what he would.

'You'd know all about that—being an historian, I mean.' Leaning against the back of the chesterfield, Keir folded his arms across his chest and crossed his feet at the ankles, perfectly at ease.

'My interest is purely academic, I assure you,' Henri said, mirroring his sardonic expression as she moved books from the 'sorting table' to a different location.

'I called in the post office,' Keir said after a pause, 'to collect the mail destined for the castle. It's Lachlan's job, but he's very laid back about it. There's a letter for you. I thought I'd deliver it personally because it looked important—' He handed Henri a thick, manila envelope bearing St Guthlac's frank mark.

Practically snatching it out of his hands, Henri ripped the envelope open and read the contents. The letter confirmed her worst fears. Crashing onto the chesterfield, she let out an almost inaudible, 'Oh.' Then she re-read the letter more thoroughly.

An investigation had been carried out by Human Resources at the behest of the governing body regarding the incident in the Dean's study, and it had been decided there was a case to answer. As a result, Dr Bruar was required to attend a disciplinary hearing, the date of which would be communicated to her after all relevant parties had been consulted. HR would forward all necessary documentation to her: the investigating officer's report, witness statements, and any other papers deemed appropriate to help her to answer the complaint brought against her.

Tucking the letter into the bib of her dungarees, Henri tried to marshal her thoughts into some kind of order. *Come on, come on—this is what you're good at,* she reminded herself. However, her brain had frozen and refused to cooperate. Forgetting she had an audience, she groaned and buried her face in her hands.

'Bad news?' Keir moved round to sit on the chesterfield opposite. 'Or, is that none of my business?'

'Bad, but not unexpected.' She raised her head and, with a false smile intimated that the letter was of no consequence. She was used to fighting her own battles, this was no different.

'You sure?'

'Thanks for bringing it over; really—and don't worry, I won't shoot the messenger.'

'Glad to hear it,' he said, in a valiant attempt to lighten the atmosphere. Then he sent her a steady look. 'If there's anything I can do . . .'

'Thanks, I've got it covered.' She tapped the letter inside her dungaree's bib with her pencil and forced her brain to kick up a gear.

First, she'd write to HR informing them that all communications would have to be conducted via snail mail, and explain that she had no access to the internet, landline, or mobile signal. Once she had all the documentation in her possession she could start organising the case for the defence. She shouldn't have smashed up the Dean's television; but equally, he shouldn't have taken the kudos for finding the scrap of manuscript.

'I'd expect nothing less of you.'

'Hm? Yes; of course.'

Dispirited, and only half-listening, Henri gave a 'whatever' shrug to demonstrate that she was cool about the contents of the letter. In reality she felt sick, her fingers were numb with cold, and she was desperate for the sugar rush which a cup of tea and slice of cake would bring.

Perhaps, if she didn't engage him in conversation, he'd take the hint and leave.

'See you after the weekend, D—Doctor Bruar. K—Keir.' Lachlan said from the doorway, slinging his messenger bag across his body and scuttling out of the library.

'Thanks, for all your help, Lachy,' Keir called back.

'Yes—yes. 'Bye.' Momentarily distracted by Lachy's departure, she lost her grip on a heavy tome she'd picked up from the coffee table and it crashed on to the floor close by MacKenzie's foot. She was glad of the distraction and used it to avoid MacKenzie's too perceptive gaze. He wasn't an idiot, he sensed something wasn't right; it wouldn't take long for him to work out that it was somehow connected to her being in Castle Tèarmannair.

'Allow me.' Bending, he picked up the book and handed it to her. Their fingers touched; his warm, hers cold as the grave. 'Cold hands, warm heart—isn't that what they say, Doctor Bruar?'

He spoke casually, as though commenting on the weather, and as she took the book from him, the unthinkable occurred to Henri—and she froze. Was Keir MacKenzie *flirting* with her? No—it was unconceivable. Just because they weren't at each other's throats, didn't mean that he sanctioned her presence in the castle, or condoned what she was doing there.

This new, empathetic Keir was hard to resist. The longer he stayed in the library, the more chance there was of her dropping her guard, and revealing all. Time she moved the conversation along.

'Not sure I can remember being *that* young, or that embarrassed. Can you?' Henri jerked her head in the direction of the door.

'Not sure I can.' Keir grinned, revealing white, evenly spaced teeth. Evidently the laird hadn't stinted on the orthodontist while his son had been growing up. The smile reached his eyes and they crinkled at the corner; clearly he was making an effort to be welcoming and friendly. Then, his lips quirked in a warm smile—making her feel . . . well, simply making her *feel*. And she didn't want to feel anything. She wanted to remain separate from the world, anesthetised from feelings—not think about the world beyond the castle walls.

At least, not today.

'I've done nothing to encourage the boy, in case you're wondering.' Anxiety sharpened Henri's tone. She found it easier to think of MacKenzie as her enemy, than to imagine they could, in some way, become friends. Time to raise the drawbridge; time to get him out of *her* library.

Keir's straight black eyebrows drew together and his smile vanished.

'Even you wouldn't stoop so low as to make a teenager fall in love with you for fun . . .'

'Even me?'

'Sorry, it came out wrong. What I meant to say was, someone like you . . . oh, dammit. Now you've got me tongue-tied. Is that the effect you have on hapless males, Dr Bruar?' Pushing himself away from the leather sofa, he walked over to the sorting table. Henri was glad to have a barrier between them, it gave her time to gain command of herself. 'Sandy MacKenzie-Grieves is obviously smitten with you.'

'Sandy MacKenzie-Grieves,' she declared heavily, 'is a mischief maker. I haven't the time or the energy to think about him, or any other man come to that. I've got this library and—and other things—to sort out. Besides which, I suspect that the moment he left the castle he stopped thinking about me.'

'I don't think that either of us believes that.'

Was that a compliment, Henri wondered? Lord, that drawbridge was proving more difficult to raise than she imagined.

'For your information, my taste in men runs to something rarer than a boy who's just started shaving, a man of Sir Malcolm's age or an out-and-out flirt like your cousin.' Her words landed like well-lobbed hand grenades and Keir held his hands up in mock surrender.

'I suppose that rules out Auld Lachlan, too? He'll be verra disappointed, ken?' he mimicked, peering at her through his fingers. Then he dropped his hands and adopted one of Lachlan's disapproving faces. That made Henri laugh and she relaxed—maybe she was overthinking MacKenzie and his actions. '*Pax*, Doctor Bruar?' He held out his hand.

'Pax.'

Grasping his hand firmly, she pumped it several times in manly fashion. She wouldn't want him to think she was weakening, or coming over all girly and compliant just because a ceasefire had been declared. Although she wished he'd go away and leave her in peace to read the letter through again, some part of her wanted him to stay. And, okay—actually *liked* him being in the library. He was a thorn in her side, *sans doute*—but intuition told her that if she won his trust, convinced him she had no hidden agenda, things would improve between them. Which, in turn, would make it easier for her to finish the job and get back to university.

Something of her inner turmoil must have shown on her face because he countered the friendly handshake with one of his long, straight looks.

'Somehow, I don't quite believe you mean to keep to our pact.'

'You don't?'

'No. Your lips say one thing but your eyes say something entirely different.' He smiled, taking the sting out of his words, evidently making a conscious effort to preserve their newly formed accord. Then he waited, as if expecting her to contradict him. When she didn't, he called her bluff. 'Prove you're serious about our truce, come to the shinty match on Saturday afternoon and cheer on the home side. It's the last match of the season and everyone will be there.'

'By *everyone,* you mean—'

'The whole village, crofters, folk from miles around; our tenants—the MacKenzie-Grieveses, of course.'

'Of course.' Henri pulled a face at the idea of seeing Ciorstaidh again. Choosing to ignore her less than enthusiastic response, Keir waited for her answer. Then a thought struck her, perhaps he didn't really want her there; maybe he just wanted an extra pair of female hands to help prepare the shinty 'tea' after the game. Her father played for an ex-pats cricket team and her mother, along with the other wives, spent many a fine summer afternoon preparing tea for the players. She'd vowed never to put herself in that position.

He'd turned away from her and she coughed to gain his attention.

'Yes?'

'One thing—I don't, that is to say—you won't, find me in the pavilion with the other woman, missing the match and making tea for you conquering heroes to consume once the game's over.'

He turned to face her. 'Let go of your misconceptions, Doctor Bruar, shinty is unlike cricket in almost every respect. For starters, we don't have a pavilion, we have a rickety shed which stores the equipment and doubles up as changing rooms. Afterwards, there will be no delicate cucumber sandwiches with the crusts cut off—or fairy cakes.' The last was said with disdain, as though it would be an affront to his MacKenzie ancestors to eat such effete, *English* fare. 'It's the last match of the season and after it we'll all repair to the MacKenzie-Grieveses' house for whisky, Dundee cake and a hot buffet, prepared by their staff. There will be no need to compromise your feminist principles or get your hands dirty, if you don't want to.'

Put like that, it made her sound as if she was a spoiled princess who didn't know how to 'muck in' with the people.

'I simply meant,' she said, using a steady, quiet tone, 'that I don't believe in women standing on the touchline while men have all the fun.'

'So, you'll come?' he asked her, his eyes lighting up—as if he really wanted her there. Just to show, Henri surmised, that he was good at games. Unaware of the seditious track her mind was taking, Keir continued. 'You can stand with Alice and Sandy.'

'Not Miss MacKenzie-Grieves?' She was in no hurry to renew their acquaintance, however, in view of their last close encounter, forewarned was forearmed.

Keir gave a bark of laughter.

'What? Get her suede boots wet and muddy? God, no.' He raised his eyes to the ceiling in an *as if* expression, before continuing in a more diplomatic vein. 'Ciorstaidh will grace us with her presence towards the end of the match and present the cup which her family has generously donated.'

She couldn't help but hear the stress he put on *generously*, and knew she was opening a can of worms, but needed to know more. 'Her family?'

'Yes.' A flash of pain crossed his face and his smile faded. 'Father sold the original cup to pay off gambling debts and finance a summer cruising the Greek islands on a chartered yacht.'

'But, surely it's the laird's place to host such a gathering in the castle?'

'Well, yes. And it would be—should be—but we can't afford it. So it's down to the M-G's to do the honours.' His voice was upbeat, but it was clear from his expression that he was aware how far his family had fallen. No money, nothing but an empty title and a grey slab of castle perched on an island in the middle of a loch. Not knowing what to say, Henri said nothing. Then Keir rubbed his hand across his eyes, as if banishing dark thoughts. 'So—yes, or no?'

'What? Oh, the shinty match. Yes, I'll come. As I think I mentioned a few days ago, I was captain of the university hockey team before . . .' Now it was Henri's turn to clam up. Her cut-off sentence apparently piqued Keir's interest because he sent her a questioning look.

'Good,' was all he said, when it became clear she had no intention of qualifying her statement.

It was on the tip of Henri's tongue to say: *I can't wait to see you in your kilt.* But she stopped herself in time. Their relationship didn't allow for flirting or jokes and she guessed that poking fun at his culture would earn her no brownie points.

'Oh, nothing. I've lost the thread of what I was going to say.'

'That, I seriously doubt. One last thing—stand at the west side of the field, you'll be sheltered from the cold wind there.' For a brief moment, Henri was touched that he was thinking about her welfare, then reality kicked in. Of course. He thought her nothing more than a Sassenach, a wimp who would drop to the floor in a dead faint if the wind threw icy October rain into her face.

'Thanks for the tip,' she said, smiling pleasantly. Again, they exchanged a look, one which acknowledged neither of them was saying what was really on their mind.

'Laters,' she said, waving her hand at him, as she might one of her contemporaries at university.

'Laters,' he repeated, his mouth quirking at her turn of phrase, as though he was more used to sayings like: *haste ye back and bide a while.* Archaic expressions—no doubt used by The Young Pretender, back in the day.

Two days later, on the morning before the match, Alice dispensed advice over coffee and shortbread in the kitchen as they waited for Lachlan to take them over to the far side. Henri hadn't seen Keir since their discussion in the library and Sir Malcolm had been absent, too—preferring to spend his time with the Mackenzie-Grieveses because, as he put it, *their house was warm, the uisge beatha never ran out and there was no nagging old woman to remind him of his shortcomings every hour of the day.*

Not that Alice seemed in the least bit bothered by the unflattering description.

'If it gets warm,' Alice broke into Henri's thoughts as she sat warming her stockinged feet against the Aga, 'ye can take aff a few layers. But if the wind comes whistling doon the loch towards the shinty field, ye'll be grateful for every stitch of clothing on yer back.'

'So Keir informed me. Don't worry, Alice, I'll be fine. I'm looking forward to a day off and seeing my first shinty match.'

'Aye, ye've earned a day aff, hen, working flat oot so that auld foo-ul can find money to spend on his lady friends. And he disnae even have the manners to thank ye, let alone pay ye, I'm guessing? But let's forget about him. It's a fine autumn day and the crowd will make it all the better with their good-natured insults and name calling. The final is always a rare sight, as is Keir in MacKenzie tartan. Wait till ye see him. Och, it's just a shame he hardly ever wears the kilt these days. I'm guessing that it reminds him of how low the family has sunk.' Now it was Alice's turn to look pensive, as though remembering happier times. Then she gave herself a shake. 'I hope it disnae spoil yer enjoyment of the day, if we give the earlier matches a miss? It'll mostly be the wee ones in the playoffs. The proper matches don't start until after well after lunch.'

'Matches? Plural?'

'Aye, there's a six-a-side game played by the women's team just before the main event. It warms the crowd up, ye ken? There'll be a big crowd there today because the final's a local derby between our side, *MacCoinneach Camanachd* and the *Linnhe Camanachd.*'

'Camanachd?'

'After *caman*—Gaelic for shinty stick? It can get a bit rough at times, what wi' body tackling allowed. But that all adds to the excitement—and, of course, hacking's oota the question.' Registering Henri's puzzled look, she went on to explain. 'Coming down on your opponent's stick with your caman. It's a great day oot and a grand finale to the season.'

'It makes the inter-varsity hockey matches sound like a game of tiddlywinks,' Henri laughed, amused at the light of battle in Alice's eyes. No prizes for guessing which side she supported.

'They say that the game was brought over from Ireland by St Columba. But who knows the truth of it? It was all so long ago.' Alice looked at Henri, as if her PhD made her an authority on all historical periods.

'Agreed. Does Alexander MacKenzie-Grieves take part, too?'

'Sandy? Ach, no. He'll be shouting his support from the side-lines, making sure he doesn't get mud on his fine, handmade tweed coat.' Her derisive snort made clear what she thought of *that*.

'Do you think we'll win?' Henri was surprised to find that she considered herself a supporter of the *MacCoinneach Camanachd*. She'd been in Castle Tèarmannair just over a fortnight and already felt part of the clan.

'Aye, we've got a fighting chance—if the lure of the trophy proves stronger than the lure of the *MacKenzie Arms*. It widnae be the first time the team let us all doon by drinking too much the night before a match and being hungover next day. Mind you,' she collected Henri's cup and saucer and put it in the dishwasher, 'with Keir as their captain they widnae *dare*!'

Not that you're in any way partisan. Henri smiled, finding Alice's faith in her nephew's ability to manage the team touching. It balanced out her voluble and scathing opinion of Himself and his henchman, Lachlan.

'Come on, hen, go and fetch your things and let's be on oor way.'

Obeying, Henri got to her feet and headed for her bedroom to collect hat, coat, gloves and scarf. She felt ridiculously excited at the thought of watching some amateur shinty team getting muddied up before her very eyes, but excited she was!

Chapter Thirteen
The Clash of the Ash

'Today just got better,' said a smooth voice at Henri's elbow.

Turning, she found herself face to face with Alexander MacKenzie-Grieves. As predicted, he was immaculately turned out in green herringbone shooting coat, brown tweed trousers and matching waistcoat. The whole was topped off by an expensive-looking felt trilby and his wellingtons were an upmarket brand costing over three hundred pounds. He looked as though he'd dressed for a day at Perth, or Musselburgh, races and had somehow stumbled on to this muddy, windswept shinty field by accident.

'Dressed for the occasion, I see,' Henri remarked.

'I'm afraid I don't own a fleece, cagoule or a woolly hat. This is how a gentleman looks when in the country, it distinguishes him from the tenant farmers, and so on.' He not only submitted himself to Henri's amused inspection, but obligingly turned round slowly in front of her so that she didn't miss any details. 'Damn, now look what you've made me do.' He regarded the mud on the leather uppers of his *Le Chameau* wellingtons and looked annoyed.

'Sorreee,' Henri laughed at his plight.

'Bloody Scotland,' he murmured. 'Mud, snow and rain from October to June and then midges the months in between.'

'Don't apply for a job with the Scottish Tourist Board, will you?' Henri giggled at his woebegone expression. 'But you're exaggerating; there've been some lovely days since I arrived—sunshine, a warm wind, crisp mornings with blue skies. Typical autumn weather. Besides, wearing expensive wellingtons is only asking for trouble. Didn't you expect to get them muddy on a shinty field? They don't look as if they were designed for jumping in puddles.'

'The bad weather will start to close in, you'll see,' he remarked with a weary but knowledgeable air, taking her teasing in good part. 'After Hallowe'en it'll be downhill, weather wise, all the way 'til Christmas. That's why I live and work in Edinburgh and spend a month in the Bahamas in February, if funds allow.'

'An admirable work ethic,' Henri observed. She knew men like Alexander MacKenzie-Grieves; spoiled rich boys who played at being bankers, hedge funders or entrepreneurs (generally in the family firm), subsidised by the bank of mum and dad until their trust fund kicked in. Men whose working week ran from Tuesday to Thursday, after which they spent a long weekend in the country with friends or relatives.

'I normally only attend smart race meetings, the Royal Highland Show, Chelsea, Henley—that sort of thing,' Alexander said, confirming all of the above. 'All this,' he gestured at the shinty field surrounded by mountains on one side and the white-capped freezing waters of the loch on the other, and sighed. 'Not quite my milieu. But, noblesse oblige and all that. The MacKenzies must be seen by the people.'

'Bit elitist, isn't it?'

'Believe me, if I wasn't terrified of my sister I wouldn't be here at all.' Removing his felt trilby, he ran his fingers through his well-cut auburn hair and then replaced it.

'Terrified?' Henri send him a quizzical look.

'I don't usually turn out to watch cousin Keir get down and muddy with the locals, but,' he pulled a comical face, 'I have been charged with keeping an eye on *you*, Doctor Bruar.'

'Me? Why on earth should you need to do that?' Henri's green eyes widened in astonishment.

'My dear girl.' He slipped his hand through her crooked arm, pulled her closer and whispered in her ear. 'Because of cousin, Keir. Oor Wee Ciorstaidh,' he pulled a droll face and adopted a broad, Lowland accent, 'has earmarked him for hersel' ye ken, and has been in a right state ever since we had lunch at the castle and saw *you*—the opposition. She's convinced hersel' that you are after her ma-ahn. And has charged *me* to keep *you* away from *him*.' At every pronoun, he gave her arm a shake for emphasis.

'How ridiculous,' Henri spluttered, red in the face.

'Agreed. However, should I fail in this task, she'll have my balls for earrings. And, it turns out, I am quite attached to my wedding tackle. Pun intended.'

Dramatically and for effect, he surreptitiously moved his left hand protectively over the lower half of his body. Henri knew she should be annoyed with him and his bloody control freak of a sister, but she burst out laughing. Heads swivelled in their direction, including Keir and Alice's; the former making it clear that he disapproved of them larking around in front of everyone. Thinking it wise, Henri withdrew her arm from Alexander's and turned her back on Keir and his disapproving face. Leaning back against the rail which separated the spectators from the players, she addressed Alexander.

'Whatever gave your sister the impression that I have *designs* on Keir MacKenzie?' She put a comic stress on the word.

'You mean you don't?' Henri shook her head and Alexander looked at her in disbelief. 'Well, good for you, Doctor Bruar. You're the only female within a twenty-five-mile radius of MacKenzie's Halt who doesn't go weak at the knees every time the Master of Mountgarrie —to give Keir his full title —walks by.' He sighed heavily and then glanced down at his feet. 'Shame I don't have the same effect. Could it be the wellingtons, do you think? Not butch enough?'

Henri laughed at his woebegone face, not taking him seriously for a moment. 'Don't be ridiculous. Since I arrived at the castle I've seen Keir less than half a dozen times. Not long enough to form an impression of him,' she lied.

She knew *exactly* what she thought of him and none of it was for his cousin's ears.

'Once would be enough for Ciorstaidh, she's determined to marry the poor sod and will allow nothing and no one, to get in the way of her becoming Lady MacKenzie.' Henri opened her mouth to protest but Alexander continued. 'I'd give good odds that she'd already warned you off. A nice girly chat where no one could overhear? In the damp ol' library, for example . . . last time we paid a visit to Malcom's crumbling pile? I can tell from your expression that I'm bang on the money.'

'She did. But on that occasion I made it plain that I'm here for one purpose and for one purpose only—to dismantle the library, have the books valued and then I'll be on my way south. Back to university where—where I will take up a position as junior lecturer at the start of Hilary Term. In January,' she added in case he didn't believe her. Like the fox whose colouring he resembled, Alexander's sharp ears picked up her stumble over the words.

Cocking a russet eyebrow, he put a hand on her shoulders and looked at her with shrewd, blue-grey eyes which saw right into her soul.

'Are you telling porky pies, bonnie lass? About your reasons for being here *and* your feigned disinterest in the future laird of Castle Tèarmannair? No matter; we all have secrets. But do me a favour, will you?' He glanced over his shoulder. 'Ciorstaidh usually only turns up at the end of the match to present the cup, however, she's making an exception today. She's got some silly notion in her head that you and Keir are *already* romantically involved. That he finds his way to your bedroom in the wee, small hours of the night, candle in hand, wearing his Wee Willy Winkie nightshirt—and then . . . ' Again the raised eyebrow as he paused, giving her a chance to confirm or deny his sister's suspicions. 'So when she drives up —with Mother and a troupe of aged aunts with whiskery chins, look enamoured of *me* and not my penniless cousin. There's a good girl. As you say, you'll be gone before we even know it and Ciorstaidh will get off my case.'

Henri shook his hands off her shoulders and gave a huff of annoyance. So, they all thought she was just passing through, did they? Like a bird of passage. Time she squeezed Alexander MacKenzie-Grieves's pips and made him squeak.

'Don't you MacKenzies think of anything *but* money?' she demanded.

'Ah, there speaks the daughter of two eminent scientists who has never, I'll wager, had to wonder where the next euro is coming from.' He leaned over the fence and examined the grass at their feet, his hands stuck deep in his pockets to keep them warm. Henri didn't like the idea that he knew so much about her and was quick to tell him so.

'How do you know about my parents?' She was surprised at the strength of her anger; annoyance mixed with fear. If he knew about her parents, what else might he know? She sensed that his Hooray Henry act was a front for a sharp brain. He might look like an advert for his Jermyn Street tailor, but it wouldn't do to underestimate him. Like his cousin, Keir, he had a thousand years of breeding and warrior genes to draw upon. Whereas she, as Lachlan was keen to remind her, was just a *wee lassie*.

'I Googled them, of course, Doctor Bruar. I have to do something when I'm at work—and, to be honest, snooping on people's lives is about as exciting as it gets in my office, waiting for stock exchanges round the world to open. Unless, that is, I can sneak a bet on a long-legged thoroughbred via my bookie, without my uncle finding out and dobbing me in to Mother.' At that point, he turned round, leaned back against the fence on his elbows and gave *her* long legs a professional examination. 'I'm a great judge of form; an expert, you might say, on flighty fillies.'

'Really?' She sent him a scathing look.

'Yes; really. I think you're the sort to stay the course—and dear Ciorstaidh might have her work cut out to clear Becher's Brook.' The racing analogy, combined with the thought that Henri might foil his sister's matrimonial plans, seemed to cheer him up. He let out a low guffaw, and nearby spectators glanced in their direction.

'If you don't behave, I'm going back to the car to sit the match out.'

'What? And miss the sight of himself in his kilt, looking all heroic and manly. That'd be a shame.' He gave her a petulant look which didn't sit well with him. 'You know the trouble with my cousin, don't you?'

'No, but I suspect you're *dying* to tell me.' If Alexander registered the irony in her voice, it didn't prevent him from letting her know just how much he envied Keir.

'In Scots Gaelic our surname is *MacCoinneach*—meaning 'comely' or 'handsome'; thing is, Keir has bought into the legend, believing himself quite the dude. Unfortunately, so does everyone else around here—including my bloody sister. *I* don't get a look in.'

'Aren't you a MacKenzie, too?'

'MacKenzie-*Grieves,* sweetie, with emphasis on *Grieves.*'

'So?'

'So—explain to me why the fair lassies round here would prefer an impoverished laird's son to a well-heeled hedge funder like . . . well, like *me.*'

Henri glanced between the two men and raised an eyebrow which said: *do you really want me to answer that?* Although Keir wasn't 'quite the dude' in her eyes, it was plain to see that next to him, Alexander MacKenzie-Grieves was but half a man—too manicured, too smooth, too mannered. She longed to remove his hat, throw it onto the muddy grass and jump up and down on it. Obviously detecting a cooling in the temperature, Alexander gave Henri's arm another *we're pals, right?* shake.

'Och, c'mon, hen; don't let's fall out.' He looked at her with pathetic puppy dog eyes, raised one hand in the air, bending it over at the wrist to make a paw. Then he started to whimper like a whipped pup and pawed her sleeve.

'Stop it,' she hissed as the whining grew ever louder. 'You're mad.'

'Not mad, just terrified of mah wee sister.' Now both 'paws' were held up in front of her and he tilted his head on the side. Despite being annoyed with him for pushing her into a corner, an involuntary giggle escaped Henri.

   'And why is that?'

He exhaled and dropped the dog act. 'I have a weakness for the gee-gees which far outstrips my income from uncle's bank. Ciorstaidh helps keep my gambling debts from Mother; as simple as that. In a couple of years I'll come into the fund set up for me on Father's death, until then . . .'

'God, you're as bad as your uncle Malcolm,' she reprimanded him.

He threw his hands out wide and bowed. 'Guilty as charged. It's in the blood, alas. Mother is tight as a tick with cash, so Ciorstaidh has had to bail me out on several occasions—which gives her a degree of leverage over me. So?' He cast her a pleading look.

'Okay, I'll play along,' she said, knowing what it felt like to be in trouble, to be held to ransom. He stretched his hand out and touched her, just as Keir jogged over to them, not in his kilt as promised but in a muddy tracksuit, and treated them to one of his glowering looks.

'Sandy,' he nodded at his cousin, and then immediately dismissed him. 'Doctor Bruar—Henri. I have a favour to ask.'

'Yes?' There was astonishment in her voice at the thought of having it in her power to grant him a favour. She gave him her full attention as he moved closer. Next to his smart cousin, Keir MacKenzie looked rugged, part of the elements. A man used to giving commands and having them obeyed.

'Can we talk hockey for a moment?' It was the last thing Henri expected and all colour drained from her face. Had he found out about her moment of madness in the Dean's study and was about to demand that she left Tèarmannair ASAP?

Sir Malcolm had asked for a librarian and academic and had been sent a mad bunny boiler.

'H—hockey? W-why?' Damn her stammer, it made her sound nervous and defensive when she needed to act cool, calm and collected. She glanced between the two cousins and her stomach plummeted, as though she'd descended in a very fast lift. This was immediately followed by an adrenaline rush which left sparks of fire trailing along her skin.

'You told me you were captain of the varsity hockey team?' Showing puzzlement at her reaction to a simple question, his face clouded over, as though he suspected her of lying. 'Was that the truth? If it was, then *great*, because we have a bit of a crisis. One of the players in the women's side,' now it was his turn to look uncomfortable, 'took a pregnancy test this morning and it came back positive.'

'Pregnancy test?' Henri assumed that the whole *peeing on a stick and waiting for the result to appear in the window,* routine would be beyond his remit as laird-in-waiting. Then realisation dawned. 'And you're the father?' For reasons she couldn't quite explain, her stomach met her boots for a second time. Irrationally, she felt let down. Pulling herself together, she swung round to face Alexander, wondering how he was going to square *this* with Ciorstaidh.

'I'm *what?*' Keir regarded her as if she was raving lunatic. 'Good God, woman, I most certainly am not.'

Relief swept over her. She registered the feeling and sent it to the back of her mind to be examined later. 'Then, why are you so concerned?'

'She's the wife of one of our tenants and has had problems conceiving. She's miscarried several times, and . . .' Alexander took several steps back from the rail, as if all this gynaecological stuff was not to his liking. Keir didn't look particularly comfortable having this conversation with her either, but soldiered on. 'The point is.' Keir frowned at Henri and then looked over his shoulder to the women's team which was warming up, passing the ball between their *camans.* 'The point is, she doesn't want to take any unnecessary risks. We're a woman down and I wondered if you'd . . .'

Henri saw where this was going and was keen to cover up her earlier gaffe.

'Make up the numbers? Certainly. Why didn't you say so in the first place?' Keir let out a long, exasperated breath, as if pushed to the edge of reason by emotional, illogical women. He gestured for her to climb over the fence and join him on the other side. 'But I know nothing about shinty and haven't got any kit . . .'

'You are about to receive a crash course and we'll find something to fit you. Come on.' He rested his hand lightly in the small of her back and guided her towards the changing hut, just as Ciorstaidh MacKenzie-Grieves's Range Rover Evoque drew up in the carpark. Sandy glanced between his cousin, the car, and Henri and then sent her a despairing look. He mimed throat-cutting (and worse!), but Henri was too preoccupied with the thought of playing an unfamiliar game, with people she didn't know, in front of an expectant crowd—and Keir MacKenzie— to feel much sympathy for him.

'Ready?' Keir asked as they climbed the rickety steps to the wooden hut/changing room.

'Ready,' she said, squaring her shoulders and preparing to do her best. This was her chance to redeem herself in his eyes and she wasn't about to blow it by spending time thinking about some spoiled madam. Or an amusing wastrel like Sandy MacKenzie-Grieves.

Chapter Fourteen
We play for the Glory . . . and the Clash of the Ash

'So let me get this right,' Henri addressed the captain of the women's shinty team as she fastened on her shin pads. 'I can play the ball in the air, use both sides of the hockey stick, and—'

'*Caman*,' the captain corrected. 'Go on.'

'I can use the *caman* to block and tackle a shot, but I can't come down on an opponent's stick?'

'Correct. And . . ?'

'And . . . I can tackle an opponent using my body, as long as it's shoulder-to-shoulder?'

'Right, again,' Shona the captain said approvingly. 'Not so different from hockey, after all. Is that why Keir asked if you'd help? Has he seen you play?'

'Not exactly,' Henri mumbled. So far, she'd escaped the third degree but she could tell they were curious to learn more about her relationship with Keir, and life 'up at the castle'.

'Don't forget, Henri,' one of the other players reminded her, in a lilting Highland voice, 'a goal can only be scored with the caman. It will be deemed a 'no goal' if the ball has been kicked, carried or propelled by your hand or arm into the net. So be careful; it's easy to get carried away in the heat of the moment.'

Heat of the moment? She knew all about that. Didn't she?

'Got it,' Henri assured them, holding the caman between her legs and plaiting her long blonde hair into a braid before securing the end with a shoelace. Then she grasped the caman in both hands, pulled down her too-small team jersey and made sure her borrowed boots were tied securely.

'We might only be the 'B', six-a-side, team, but we like to make Himself and the community proud of us,' added a woman in full goalkeeper's kit.

'Especially Himself,' Shona laughed. 'Eh, ladies?' This was followed by a chorus of *aye, aye* and much head nodding. 'It's the highlight of the year when Keir returns to Castle Tèarmannair for the last match of the season. He plays for a local shinty team in British Columbia, to keep his hand in and remain match fit, so returning to play in the men's side isn't a struggle for him, at all.'

'Every year,' a younger player went on to explain, her eyes shining, 'we wait to see if he'll return with the future Lady MacKenzie on his arm. But each year he returns alone.'

Henri held her peace, keen to get their slant on Keir MacKenzie.

'Thank the lord for *that*,' another player opined. 'There's plenty of braw Scottish lassies here for him to choose from. No need to import someone from Canada or—' They eyed the Sassenach in their midst and left the rest unsaid. Henri felt it was incumbent upon her to define her relationship with Keir.

'What? *Me?* Oh, no. I'm just here to do a job of work and then it's back to university.' She had the distinct feeling that, pleasant and welcoming as they had been, they would rip her limb from limb if they thought she'd set her cap at *their* Keir; *their* laird-in-waiting. Honestly, what was it with the women round here? First Ciorstaidh, and now six members of a shinty team, all on her case.

Cheeks flaming, Henri clattered over to the door in her studded boots, using the pretence of breathing in the cool October air to deflect their attention. She looked beyond the shinty field to the mountains that framed two sides of the loch, focusing on a wispy cloud which grazed the summit of the highest peak. Taking in another deep breath to calm her nerves, she admitted that no inter-varsity hockey match had got her so worked up and nervous. Or had been played in such a beautiful setting.

The highlight of the day, Shona had grumped as they changed into their kit, would be the Men's Championship Match. In deference to that—another far-from-resigned tut—her team would only play for thirty minutes. In the past, it turned out, the women had fielded a full twelve-a-side team and played for ninety minutes. However the natives had grown restless, regarding the women's match as a mere filler; something to pass the time until the *real* match—the *men's* match—played out before them.

Wee Lassie Syndrome, yet again, Henri reflected, remembering the less than enthusiastic reception she'd received when she'd arrived at the castle.

'Och, leave the lassie alone,' the goalkeeper barged her way through the group of women surrounding Henri, and returned to the topic of Keir MacKenzie. 'What good would a laird be to a clever girl like Doctor Bruar? Eh?'

Another chorus of *aye, right enough.* Then Henri was handed a protective helmet with a chin guard and a left-handed glove to enhance her grip on the caman, and followed them out onto the field. The crowd roared and shouted encouragement as they took up their places ready for the start of the match. A heady mix of excitement and adrenaline coursed through her veins as the two captains raised their sticks high above their heads and the referee tossed the ball even higher, signalling the start of the game. Shona was quick off the mark and flicked the small ball through the air and towards the opposing team's goal, with Henri in hot pursuit.

If the past fifteen days had been the longest in Henri's life then, by the same measure, the next half hour was the shortest. Game over, her ears ringing with the noise from the crowd, she made her way back to the changing room where she was stopped by Keir MacKenzie who laid a detaining hand on her arm.

'Well done, Doctor Bruar. Two goals scored, at this rate you'll never be allowed to return to university.' Although his tone was light and congratulatory, Henri detected something different in his demeanour towards her. Respect for her prowess as a player, certainly; gratitude that she'd stepped into the breach and helped the team win the match, undeniably; but something else.

Grudging admiration and—please God, the dawning realisation that he'd got her all wrong.

Henri remembered a television programme about ocean liners, how long it took them to turn round. In many respects, Keir was like an ocean liner. However, she had neither the time nor the inclination to wait until *he* turned full circle and admitted his mistake; or that his initial impression of her didn't stand up to scrutiny.

'Thanks,' was all she said, as the other players rushed to congratulate her.

'Well done, Henri!'

'Way to go!'

'You did a great job,' they called, high-fiving Henri and slanting Keir and her an *ah, that's how things stand, is it?* look as they clocked his hand on her arm. She wanted to shrug him off, stand at the top of the steps and shout: *no, that's **not** how things stand!* However, that would have appeared churlish, childish even, and she didn't want to spoil the mood.

Instead she said, 'Thanks, ladies, I enjoyed it.' Then she turned back on Keir, hiding her feelings beneath a genuine smile.' I'd forgotten how much I love hockey—shinty; the fresh air and exercise has worked wonders, blown away the cobwebs.'

'I—' Keir started to say something but the team's mass exodus from the changing hut, arms full of their belongings, prevented him.

'Henri, get your things before the men enter the changing room,' Shona called to her. 'See you later at Glen Shiel House—the MacKenzie-Grieveses' place?'

'Er-m, sure,' Henri replied, not fully comprehending what she was agreeing to. She turned to Keir for enlightenment.

'After the match, the players are invited to Glen Shiel House where tea is laid on. On behalf of his late father, Alexander presents the winning team with a cask of uisge beatha and Ciorstaidh draws the winning lottery ticket. To be honest, she does all the organising while Sandy gets in the way and Aunt Grizel and her sisters stand around looking pained and disapproving.'

'Ah yes, Alexander mentioned something about whiskery aunts when we were talking earlier.'

'Yes; it looked like you two were getting along.'

Henri sent him a sharp look. 'Meaning?'

'Nothing, except—Sandy is an amusing companion, but it wouldn't do to get involved with him.'

'*Involved?*' she asked in a quiet voice. 'Involved in what way, exactly?'

At last, Keir had the good sense to realise that he'd dropped a clanger. 'Never mind. I spoke out of turn . . .'

'You most certainly did. Do you think I have designs on every man between Glen Shiel and Inverness? Thanks for the character reference. Or should that be, character assassination?' On the periphery of her vision she saw the men's team advancing towards the changing hut. Time she was out of there.

'My God, you're touchy,' he exclaimed, his tone implying that women were charming, but their mood swings defeated him. 'Our truce didn't last long, did it?' If that was a vain attempt on his part to win her back, it failed dismally.

'Seemingly not,' she replied, climbing the steps to the changing hut door. Pausing, she turned. 'And for your information, *bonnie laddie,* there's one man in the glen who need have no worries about my setting my cap at him.' Slamming the door behind her, she stood in the middle of the empty changing hut, hands shaking and stomach squirming after yet another exchange of words. Gathering her clothes together, she stood rooted to the spot, unsure of what to do next. She could hardly walk down the stairs and past him after that dramatic exit; could she?

In the end, Shona who came to the rescue.

'Henri, I'm so sorry. What was I thinking! Come back to my house, get showered and changed, then we'll return to watch the last half hour of the men's game.'

'I'll just shove my old clothes back on, no worries . . .'

'Indeed you will *not*. If it hadn't have been for your two goals we would have finished the season at the bottom of the league. For the third year in a row. Besides which, ye cannae go the Big Hoose looking like Tattie Bogle.'

'Who?'

'Tattie Bogle. The female scarecrow in an old Scottish poem, she was too nice to the birds until she learned to sing and they were driven away. Ye dinnae ken it? And you a Doctor of History?' She took the sting out of her words by helping Henri gather her belongings together. Straightening, she turned and grinned. '*Her gowden hair wis made o' oo,*' she quoted and then translated. 'Her golden hair was made of wool. Not that I'm implying your hair is in need of conditioner,' she laughed, 'but golden it is. Come on, Tattie!'

Giving her own thick dark hair a vigorous shake, she led the way out of the changing hut and down the stairs where, to Henri's relief, Keir MacKenzie was nowhere to be seen.

Shona was as good as her word, returning with Henri and the rest of the shinty team to watch the last half an hour of the men's game. Although by then, it was the middle of the afternoon and the light was fading. Autumn mist rose from the loch, banishing the golden afternoon and inching its way towards them, carrying a hint of decay and the harsh winter ahead in its dank breath. The shinty action seemed confined to the far side of the hundred-and-seventy-yard long field, and the players were lost in the mist. Then, as they emerged from the gloom and headed up the field in pursuit of the ball, the spectators saw them and roared their support.

And, just as Young Lachlan had promised, the men wore kilts over their dark compression leggings.

When Keir came into view, Henri sucked in an involuntary breath and blinked several times. It *was* Keir yet—somehow—it *wasn't* Keir. At least, not one she recognised. He seemed different, as if being lost in the swirling mist had wrought some kind of metamorphosis over him, and everything connecting him and his team to the twenty-first century. The changing hut, car park, even the burger van parked at the entrance to the field seemed wrong, out of place. And, for the first time, Henri understood *who* Keir Mackenzie was; saw him as a warrior, a man out of his time, tied to the land and its people by tradition and right of inheritance.

And in that transforming moment, he was no longer the son of a bankrupt laird. In dark green Hunting MacKenzie tartan he looked valiant, heroic even. Not that she'd tell him that. Or let on that *MacCoinneach Camanachd's* advance through the mist towards the Linnhe goal brought to mind a scene from *Braveheart*, or the shinty match in *Outlander*. Dismissing the thought as absurdly romantic and putting it down to the atmosphere and the surroundings, Henri concentrated on the finer points of the match. Watching, as Keir stopped the ball with his chest, let it drop onto the turf and then gave it an almighty whack which sent it airborne. Another team member stopped it in mid-air, knocked it down and sent it towards the Linnhe goal. Catching up with the ball, Keir administered the coup de grâce which sent the ball into the back of the net before the goalkeeper had time to react. The referee blew his whistle and the players rearranged on the pitch, ready for the final assault.

Standing shoulder to shoulder, the women's six-a-side team put up the battle cry:

MacKenzie! MacKenzie!
Tulach Ard! Tulach Ard!
Clash the ash! Clash the ash!

The spectators took up the chant as Keir and the Linnhe captain crossed their camans in the air, their breaths coalescing as they waited for the referee to toss the ball above their waving camans. To Henri's heightened senses, the camans resembled the heads of two sparring water horses. Seizing his chance, Keir whipped the ball towards another team member who picked it up and dribbled it towards the goal. The Linnhe captain, seeing that Keir was lining up for another goal, shoulder-barged him out of the way. Henri winced at the force of the tackle which bowled Keir over, making her glad—for his sake —that he was wearing leggings beneath his kilt!

Gritting his teeth, Keir stood up, flexed his shoulders and to cries of: *MacKenzie! Clash the ash. Take the glory*! headed after the ball.

The anger Henri had earlier felt towards Keir was forgotten. Standing close to Alexander MacKenzie-Grieves and watching the men compete against each other, she conceded that shinty knocked inter-varsity hockey into a cocked hat for sheer excitement, possession of the ball and the physicality of the game. Blinking, she almost missed the moment when Keir shouldered the other captain out of way and fired one straight into the back of the net, just as the final whistle went. The women's team jumped up and down and embraced each other. Henri was so carried away by the moment that she threw her arms round Alexander's neck, hugged him and kissed his cheek.

'Good girl,' he whispered into her ear, holding on to her longer than strictly necessary. 'That'll get Ciorstaidh off my back!'

Henri, realising he'd misread her motives, drew back from him. 'I wasn't doing it for that reason, I was—oh, never mind.' Moving away, she caught Keir looking towards her with an expression she couldn't quite fathom: a mixture of irritation, displeasure and . . . something darker.

Here we go again, she thought, *now I'll have to explain exactly why I was hugging his cousin. Damn it.*

Then Keir was hoisted on the shoulders of his team mates, declared Man of the Match and became lost in the melee.

Deciding she had no stomach for the MacKenzie-Grieveses' revels, Henri slipped away and sought Alice out in the crowd.

'Any chance of Lachlan taking me back to the castle? I've developed a headache—'

'No need to explain, lassie. Ah dinnae want to watch Ciorstaidh acting like she's mistress of Castle Tèarmannair already, and lording it over us. I'll come home with ye. As for Lachlan, he'll do as he's told, or I want to know the reason why.'

Henri laughed. It felt good to have Alice on her team.

Arms linked, the two women went in search of Tèarmannair's resident curmudgeon, hoping they'd find him while he was sober enough to take them across the loch to the castle.

Chapter Fifteen
Vindolanda!

Henri gazed out across the loch, shrouded in a shifting veil of low-lying mist. The castle appeared to float above it and the world beyond it seemed unreal, until she spotted Lachlan piloting his boat towards Tèarmannair. His head and shoulders were just visible above the swirling fog and Henri smiled, remembering Alice saying he could find his way home dead drunk or half asleep. A heron skimmed over the shifting mist, its spindly limbs trailing behind it as it hunted for breakfast. No doubt Lachlan would be looking for his, too, once the large dinghy was moored alongside the jetty.

She'd been at Castle Tèarmannair over a month now, long enough for the spirit of the place to work its magic on her. As an only child of busy, career-focused parents, she'd often been left to her own devices and had learned how to make friends, seeking out the company of others to make up for her lack of siblings. She worked hard at maintaining those friendships—remembering birthdays and anniversaries, marking them with cards and little gifts; keeping in touch with the girls who'd attended her boarding school. Latterly, she'd built up a network of university friends and colleagues, spending her time with an inner circle of like-minded young academics.

However, since arriving at the castle, she'd become happy in her own company. Most of the time it was just her and Alice and the days had settled into a steady routine: breakfast, fetching books down from the shelves, cataloguing them, lunch; repeat, as above, until afternoon tea. Then a welcome bath before an early supper after which she'd put in some time on her dissertation.

She saw little of Sir Malcolm as, with Lachlan in tow, he spent most of his time away from the castle. Not that she minded—she relished the peace and tranquillity exuded by centuries-old stones and liked to imagine the whispering stories they could tell, if they had a mind to. Now she was feeling less stressed, she'd managed to rationalise the lament she'd heard on the train, dismissing it as nothing more than an ear-worm; an echo of the medley played by a busker outside Fort William station.

After the excitement of the shinty match and the attentions of Alexander MacKenzie-Grieves, the quietude of the castle was a blessed release. She'd made a promise when she'd first arrived to maintain a low profile until things settled down back at her university. Now, thanks to the shinty match, she'd done the complete opposite.

Thinking about the match brought to mind Keir MacKenzie's reaction to her throwing her arms round Alexander's neck. MacKenzie had seemed angry and, now she came to think of it, *disappointed*? Not that he had the right to make judgement calls about her, flattering or otherwise. The moment they'd shared when he'd brought her the letter from the post office and had seemed genuinely concerned for her welfare, now felt in the distant past.

Really, the man was impossible and had too high an opinion of himself. He knew nothing about her, *nothing*; and she was happy for it to remain so. Perhaps, as Alexander MacKenzie-Grieves had hinted, impoverished laird's son really did trump wealthy hedge funder? The shinty girls had spoken about MacKenzie as if he was God's gift to the female race. Maybe in their eyes he was.

But not hers.

And if she rushed to the window every time a boat chugged towards the castle it was because she wanted to check if it was Lachlan with a letter for her. It had nothing to do with her wondering when she might see MacKenzie again.

Releasing another pent-up breath, she touched a stack of books on the table and admitted that she was dragging out the task of dismantling the library. She didn't want to leave Castle Tèarmannair, and take the train to Inverness. She didn't want to travel back to her university where a disciplinary panel was waiting to crush her hopes and dreams.

Talking of which—the HR department was taking its time getting back to her about the date of the hearing, and forwarding the necessary documentation to her. She'd give it a few more days and then ask to be taken over to the post office where she could phone the university. With a bit of luck, Maddie would be back from her fundraising tour and offer good counsel.

'Gah,' she exclaimed, her head a muddle of jumbled thoughts—not wanting to return to England, phantom pipers, disapproving laird's sons and a thesis on the Highland Clearances which had ground to a halt. So unlike her former, uber hardworking, self. She frowned; what had started her on this train of thought—ah, yes, the Master of Mountgarrie. There was no point in trying to second guess him or his motives. He was a law unto himself and was as complex as his father was straightforward.

Sometime later, as if conjured up by her thoughts, Keir MacKenzie slipped into the library. Was it simply the case that he didn't want to disturb her? Or was he hoping to find her up to no good; secreting away a couple of precious volumes in her tote bag, to sell at a later date? Maybe he'd like to frisk her, just to be sure. The idea of Keir MacKenzie running his hands over her body while she stood, arms outstretched, waiting to be patted down, made her lose her grip on the handrail.

He was at her side in an instant.

'I thought we'd agreed that you wouldn't climb the ladder unless there was someone else in the library?' He walked over and held the ladder to steady it as she climbed down. He half-raised his hand and then dropped it to his side, obviously wary of repeating the scene where she'd landed on top of his father.

'Just doing mah job,' she said cheerfully, squeezing past him but leaving a good bit of space between them. He cut straight to the chase.

'Everyone was disappointed when you didn't come to the after-match shindig at Glen Shiel House.'

'Everyone?' The event had taken place over two weeks ago and she wondered why he was mentioning it now.

'Everyone,' he repeated, adding, 'especially Sandy Mac-G.'

'You don't say.' Her tone implied that if he had a problem with her so-called relationship with his cousin, now would be a good time to spit it out.

Keir looked as if he wanted to qualify his original statement but then changed tack. 'Pax. Remember?'

'How could I forget?'

'I bet you have an eidetic memory.'

If he meant to trip her up with the unusual word, she put him straight. 'You're right. I can remember and recall most things I've seen and heard. A must for an academic, wouldn't you say?' She slanted him an oblique look which implied—*and in my dealings with you*—and then continued, 'So what brings you here on this fine autumn morning?'

'Well, it *is* my home.' His lips quirked in response at the way she'd—unintentionally—made it appear as if she was the mistress of the castle and he an unwelcome visitor. 'For good or ill. But, on this fine autumn morning, I have something for you.'

The long-awaited letter from St Guthlac! Henri shivered as if someone had poured a jug of cold water over her head. 'You do?'

'Indeed.' He reached down into the side pocket of his cargo pants and withdrew a small, ribbon-tied package and handed it to her. Henri viewed the package with suspicion. Why was he giving her a present? Was it a parting gift, his way of telling her it was time to leave Castle Tèarmannair? Apparently sensing her uncertainty, he put her fears at rest. 'Don't worry, it isn't from me, per se; I'm merely delivering it. Go on, open it.'

'If you insist.'

'I do.'

First she untied the ribbon, wrapping it round her knuckles to form a tidy loop before tucking it into her pocket. Next, she tore off the gift wrap to reveal a blue rectangular box inscribed with the name of a jeweller in Inverness. Hands trembling, she removed the lid of the box.

'Oh—' Inside, nestling on a bed of kapok, was a caman fashioned in silver attached to a small silver chain. 'Oh,' she repeated, words failing her a second time when she saw her name was inscribed on it.

'All the ladies in the six-a-side team received one. Even the mother-to-be. Ciorstaidh ordered them from the jeweller before the match and presented them at the post match party.' He frowned, as if to remind himself that it was his father's place to host the after-match celebrations, to commission and present the prizes. 'I didn't want you to feel left out, especially after your two goals; so, I had one made for you, and here it is.'

Ah—so he'd commissioned it, not the lovely Ciorstaidh. No surprises there. Ciorstaidh would happily see her hung in chains of a different sort and dropped into the deepest part of the loch, if she had her way.

'I would have brought it over sooner, but—' He removed it from her shaking hands and then, coughing theatrically, re-enacted the prize giving ceremony for her benefit. 'Doctor Bruar, it gives me great pleasure to present you with this token of our esteem and to thank you for stepping so gallantly into the breach at the shinty match—and clinching victory for *MacCoinneach Camanachd*.' Then, suddenly serious, he added, 'We may never let you go back to England—'

Henri didn't know how to take that, so she focused her attention on the silver caman instead. Keir removed the necklace and placed the box on the arm of the chesterfield. 'It was nothing,' she murmured, her throat suddenly dry, 'my pleasure.' Mesmerised, she watched as he unfastened the clasp and held the necklace out in front of her.

'Am I permitted?' Keir walked round and stood behind her.

It was Henri's custom to cover her head with a scarf fashioned into a turban in the style of workers in a WWII munitions factory. It kept her hair free of dust and insects which had a habit of dropping on her from above.

The turban left her neck exposed and the touch of the cold silver chain on the nape of her neck and the trail of Keir's warm fingers across her skin as he fastened the necklace, made her tremble.

Yin and yang. Ice and fire.

She hunched her shoulders defensively, and resisted the urge to lean back against him, to feel the solidity of his chest and ribcage against her body's softer contours.

No, no, no. What was she thinking? This would never do.

Covering the silver caman with her right hand, she took several dancing steps away from him, rubbing the back of her neck to exorcise his touch. Her gesture intimated that the trail of his fingers against her neck was unasked for, and unwelcome. It denied the fact that his touch made the delicate hair on the nape of her neck curl of its own volition.

When she faced him, he shrugged in manner which suggested her reaction was no more than expected. Then he picked up the box off the arm of the chesterfield and handed it to her. After that, he took up his favourite position, resting back against the broad back of the leather sofa—arms folded, feet crossed at the ankles.

'So pleased you like it,' he said, boot faced.

Henri knew she must seem rude and ungracious and, quite frankly, bonkers. Time to undertake damage limitation. 'Thank you, it's lovely. I'll treasure it as a reminder of the time I spent in Castle Tèarmannair and . . .'

Keir was quick to change the subject, as though tired of it—and her posturing.

'Let's forget unwanted and unasked for presents, shall we?'

'Oh. But, I —you, see . . .'

She was about to explain that she *loved* the necklace but the moment had passed. She doubted that they would ever be able to hold a reasonable conversation without one leaving the other with the wrong impression. Keir, clearly being of the same opinion, moved the conversation on.

'So, the books? The library?'

'What about them?' The books were hardly a neutral topic.

'In your considered opinion, are they worth anything?'

Looking round the almost empty library, she shook her head. The books on the table labelled WORTH SAVING barely covered its surface. Other books, those deemed better suited to a bonfire or recycling, spilled across three tables and onto the floor. Their combined sale would hardly raise enough to buy pay off some of the MacKenzies' more pressing debts.

It wasn't her fault, but she felt responsible, as though she should have found something, *anything*, which would have gone at least part-way to restoring the MacKenzies' fortunes. This castle had provided her with a temporary bolt hole, a hideaway—and she'd given nothing back in exchange. Perhaps Keir would have to step up to the plate, marry Ciorstaidh and use her fortune to restore the castle to its former glory.

'Just a couple of shelves to empty and sort through and then I'm tackling the secretaire bookcase. The bookcases on the east wall appear much drier than the rest and I have high hopes of finding something . . . a first edition, maybe. However, *these* are the real treasure.' Anxious to re-establish her credentials, she only half-registered the look of pain which crossed his face at the word *treasure*. With a flourish, she pulled a cloth off four large books stacked on top of the boudoir grand and a collection of small, wooden chests. 'Someone, possibly in the nineteenth century, gathered together all the MacKenzie Papers: marriage deeds, land transactions and so on. Over three hundred years of MacKenzie life, all catalogued, bound and safeguarded for future generations. The documents stretch as far back as 1689—the time of the first Jacobite rebellion.'

'And these are precious, *how*?' he asked.

'Okay. Forget the things on the piano for a moment and let me ask you a question. What would you say is the most precious treasure in the British Museum?' Her green eyes were bright as sea glass, her expression animated— as though she'd asked this question many times, but no one had come up with the right answer.

'The Sutton Hoo Ship Burial? The Mildenhall Treasure?'

'Wrong. Try again.'

'The Rosetta Stone, the Parthenon Sculptures . . . Anything Egyptian and wrapped in bandages, the blessed left fingernail of some saint, preserved in a gold reliquary.' He was openly amused by her enthusiasm and the earlier frisson between them was forgotten. 'Okay, I give up—enlighten me, Doctor Bruar.'

'The Vindolanda Tablets,' she revealed, like a magician pulling a rabbit out of a hat.

'The *what-o-landa?*'

'Let me explain. The Vindolanda Tablets are over four hundred postcard-sized slivers of wood on which notes and letters were written in ink. The tablets, found near Hadrian's Wall in 1975, have been dated to 121 AD, making them one of the earliest written records ever found in Britain. Although I believe that earlier tablets have recently been unearthed in London as part of the Cross Rail excavations.' Knowing she was getting off-topic, she reined herself in.

'Go on.'

'The tablets, written between 90–120 AD, are postcards from the past, giving historians a rare insight into the lives of people living and working at Vindolanda nearly two thousand years ago; *two—thousand—years—ago.*' Her voice rose and she spoke slowly to emphasis her point. 'Other things were found, too: shoes, bags, leather buckets, purses; why there's even an archer's thumb guard. Everything from wagon axles to parts of furniture, tent pegs, combs, a child's sock; a smattering of animal bones. Not to mention what most laymen,' she looked straight at him, 'would regard as treasure: jewellery, bronzes, weapons.'

'I still don't see the connection,' he said.

Walking over to the piano, Henri picked up the smaller of the wooden chests; she flipped back the barrel-shaped lid and held it out to him. 'Look inside.' As commanded, he bent his dark head over the box, then raised it and regarded her in a puzzled fashion.

'Just a load of papers. Only things a lawyer would be interested in.'

'Wrong. These are things an academic library would be *very* interested in purchasing, should you care to sell them. Like the Vindolanda tablets, all of life is here: marriages, baptisms, deaths; every legal and contractual document concerning the MacKenzies and their estates over the last three hundred and twenty seven years. They cover key events—The Acts of Union and Settlement, the first Jacobite Rising of 1689, the ill-fated Darien Scheme, harvest failures, the rocketing price of corn . . . all the way through to the Highland Clearances.'

'Throwing tenants off their small holdings so we could raise sheep and create deer forests. 'Not something a twenty-first century laird can be proud of,' he interjected, his expression grim.

'It's a sad subject, agreed, however these documents would help our understanding of it. It's all documented in these ledgers—the tenants' names, their crofts. I would find them immeasurably useful when writing my paper. I know your cousin suggested that I was a Marxist historian, but many academics *are* likening the clearances—especially what happened in Sutherland—to ethnic cleansing. They'd give their eye teeth for a chance to study the primary sources you have here. Why, one of your ancestresses kept a diary covering the years from the '15 Jacobite Rebellion and the rout at the Battle of Glen Shiel. I'm longing to read it, but I don't want to touch it without wearing CSI gloves.'

'CSI gloves? Oh, yes, I see.' She was in danger of being swept away by her enthusiasm for the subject and was glad when Keir's next question brought her back to earth. 'You say university libraries would be interested in these papers?'

'Lord, yes; we'd have to seek expert advice, naturally. But we—that is, you, should insist that the papers are sold as one lot, otherwise they would lose their value.'

Holding his chin in right hand, Keir pressed down on his lower lip with the inside of his thumb and considered what she'd told him. Then he raised his head, stuck his hands in the pocket of his gilet and then paused, as if giving thought to what he was about to ask her. 'A small favour—'

'Yes?'

'Can we keep this from my father? He'd sell to the highest bidder, even if that meant splitting up the collection.' Henri nodded. That idea had also occurred to her and that's why she hadn't mentioned discovering the papers a few days earlier. She couldn't bear the thought of them being dispersed across the four corners of the globe. They belonged to Scotland and deserved to stay where they could be studied and evaluated properly.

'Of course. That—that's why I've kept them safe until you now. I hope that doesn't seem underhand, after all, Sir Malcolm is the one employing me.' He said nothing for a few moments as he took time to evaluate everything she'd told him. Then, she saw hope in his eyes, where usually there was only a haunted look, full of darkness and despair. Her heart picked up a new rhythm and beat faster because she was responsible for giving him hope.

Her and the *MacKenzie Papers*.

'You've done good, Dr Bruar,' he joked. 'Thank you.' Unused to basking in the warmth of his approval, Henri blushed.

'But there's more,' she added, 'look.'

She handed him a ball of screwed up newspaper. Keir pulled the sheets of newspaper apart to reveal a miniature of a young man in eighteenth-century Highland clothes. The small frame was oval, made of old gold and nestled in Keir's hand as if it belonged there, by right.

'I thought Father had sold off all the miniatures of my MacKenzie ancestors,' he breathed, walking over to the window to examine it in greater detail. Henri followed after him, taking a letter from the collection with her. 'I wonder who he is. Perhaps he's the MacKenzie who fought at the Battle of Glen Shiel.'

'Not him.' She handed the letter over to Keir who read it through several times before handing it back to her.

'What does it mean? Who is this young man?'

'I don't want to build up your hopes until I'm one hundred percent sure—but this letter would suggest that you are holding in your hands a miniature of Prince Charles Edward Stuart, the Young Pretender—'

'Bonnie Prince Charlie?' Keir asked in a whisper.

Henri nodded. 'In the letter, dated 1744, he asks your ancestor for his support, should he lead an uprising to regain his throne from the Hanoverian usurper. A letter from the prince to his cousin, King Louis XV of France, written after Culloden and asking for money and troops sold at auction recently for twenty-five thousand pounds.'

'Twenty-five thou –' Keir's eyes lit up.

'Let me stop you there. This letter wouldn't be worth anything like that, I'm afraid. The Bonnie Prince famously sent letters such as this one, accompanied by a royal selfie, to Highland chiefs in an attempt to win them over to his cause.'

'I see.' Keir made himself comfortable on the window seat, and examined the artefacts in better light. 'Sorry to be crass, but—'

'How much would it be worth? Between five and eight thousand pounds. However, you might do better to keep the letter and the miniature with the *MacKenzie Papers* and auction them as a whole. But that's up to you—and the laird, of course.'

'I wish we could afford to keep them, but we can't. But what we *can* do is keep Father from finding out about them until you, we, carry out more research. Agreed?'

'Agreed.' Henri smiled, she liked the sound of 'we'.

'Here's what we do. I'll take the papers over to the Beach House while my father's visiting the MacKenzie-Grieveses. They'll be safe there and he'll be none the wiser.' He walked over to the piano and replaced everything in the chest and covered it with the cloth. Henri's concern for the welfare of the papers was written large on her face. 'Won't that suit?'

'I—I'd feel happier if I came over with you and saw that they were stored somewhere warm and dry.'

He nodded, seeing sense in her words. 'Very well, this is your area of expertise—you call the shots; I'll consult with you every step of the way.' Henri believed him, knowing that above all else, the Master of Mountgarrie was an honourable man, so different from the Dean who made Machiavelli look like a Sunday School teacher.

'Thanks.'

'Can you be ready to travel across to the Beach House at a moment's notice? I want them out of here before the Samhain celebrations. The castle will be overrun with MacKenzies that day and I—we, don't want people poking around in here and seeing them. Although,' he smiled and Henri's heart did a curious little flippy thing, like a penny spun on its edge coming to rest, 'they've been here all this time and no one has realised their value.'

'Up until now.' She was pleased to discover that the suspicion which had clouded his eyes ever since their inauspicious first meeting had completely vanished. 'Do we tell Alice?'

'I tell Alice everything,' he said simply. 'She can cover our tracks this end, otherwise Lachlan will be wondering why I'm taking you over to the Beach House. We wouldn't want him getting the wrong idea and spreading it up and down the loch, as is his way.'

'The wrong idea?' Henri frowned and then she realised what he meant. 'Oh, I—I see. *That* wrong idea . . . No; quite.'

'Quite,' he agreed, laughing at her confusion. 'So, until the next time.' He held out his hand and she took it. 'Partner.'

'Partner,' she echoed, feeling ridiculous light and happy. Keir stood there, not moving. Looking down, Henri realised that she was still holding his hand. She gave an embarrassed cough and released it, rubbing her hands down the sides of her dungarees. 'If that's everything, I'd better get on,' she stated in a brisk, business-like voice.

'I'd better bring Alice up to speed.' He walked over to the door, turned back to face her, as if he wanted to say more, but appeared to change his mind. Then he was gone, leaving Henri to touch the silver caman around her neck as though it was a talisman.

Chapter Sixteen
All at Sea

Alice's sitting room commanded a fine view of the loch and was the warmest room in the castle, thanks to the fire kept burning twenty-four-seven, at her command. Alice was a movie buff and had bought a flat screen television to view her impressive stock of DVDs. They lined a modern bookcase covering one wall and were a standby for when the television didn't receive a signal from the ancient roof aerial—which was more often than not.

It was one of Lachlan's jokes, (his only joke, in fact) that the astronauts in the International Space Station rang up every night to ask which movie Alice was showing.

The room was a modern day equivalent of a housekeeper's room and entry was by invitation only. That way, Alice could get away from Lachlan's whinging and Himself's demands as he, evidently, regarded the castle as an open-all-hours café where food and drink was produced to order. Most nights Alice invited Henri to join her for a movie after dinner. Tonight, Henri chose *The Holiday*, from Alice's collection. It was one of her favourites, her version of a comfort read, and she was happy to kick back in front of the fire with a hot chocolate, feet up on a large footstool, knees covered in a tartan throw.

The room had two large windows set at right angles to each other, and on the remaining walls tapestry hung to keep out the draughts. At night, it was easy to imagine the castle was a ship sailing untroubled across a wide ocean, the only light visible the beacon on the jetty at the far side of the loch. This evening, the castle—for all its leaks, creaks and lack of modern day facilities—

felt solid and dependable and Henri relaxed, secure in the knowledge that no one could cross the loch unless Lachlan fetched them.

Tucking the tartan rug more tightly round her legs. Henri wondered how the Beach House felt on a night, such as this. Her only experience of beach houses, this side of Malibu, were the brightly painted beach huts found on some British beaches. She couldn't imagine Keir MacKenzie living in such cramped quarters and wondered why he preferred the Beach House to the castle, where he had his own bedroom, bathroom and sitting room. She glanced over at Alice, and frowned. Despite her promise to explain how she came to be sister-in-law to a Highland laird and chief chatelaine of this ancient castle, so far she hadn't made good on it.

Perhaps tonight was the night for such confidences?

'Where's Himself tonight?' Henri asked, getting the conversational ball rolling. Alice gave one of her disapproving harrumphs, as she always did when discussing Sir Malcolm MacKenzie of that Ilk.

'Over on the far side, shooting some harmless animal along with the *cousins*,' she said with another telling harrumph. 'Last time he shot a goat by mistake.'

'A *goat?*'

'Have ye no seen the signs on the side of the road? Beware of feral goats? The place is overrun with them.'

'I came by train, remember?'

'Aye, so ye did. Mind you, the signs should read: BEWARE OF FERAL LAIRDS, if ye ask me. He's taken Lachlan as his gillie, and if they don't end up blasting each other's head off, or falling in the loch, I'll be most surprised.' Henri couldn't imagine the grumpy retainer being a very competent gillie and said as much. 'Ye couldnae be more wrong, hen. When the old bugger's in a good mood, ask him to tell you about how handy he is with a twelve-bore; the sawn-off variety, ken?'

Henri regarded her, puzzle: *twelve-bore? Sawn-off?* However, she was keen to bring the conversation back to the MacKenzies. Lachlan's tale could wait for another day. 'So, Alice, I've shared my troubles with you. Tell me your story.'

Alice put the TV remote on the small side table next to her. 'Aye, right enough, I did promise ye chapter and verse; ask away.' Henri took a few moments to think which question to ask first.

'Lady MacKenzie is . . . was your sister?' She wasn't quite sure which tense to use.

'Was. She died over thurty years ago.' Her expression was thoughtful as she stared into the fire.

'Thurty—I mean, thirty years ago? Keir must have been a child when she passed away?' she added, almost as an aside.

'Aye, he was six years old, to the day.' *To the day?* Henri wondered why that was significant. 'And she didnae pass away, lassie, she was drown't. Oot there, in the loch.' Her expansive gesture took in the loch, flowing and eddying round the castle in the darkness. 'Along wi' Keir's brother.'

Henri sat bolt upright—Keir MacKenzie had a *brother*? A brother who drowned?

'A brother?' she repeated, for want of something better to say.

'Aye, Maol Choluim—wee Malchy, as we called him; Himself's son and heir. He was ten years old and a bonnie laddie, full of promise and . . .' She sighed, picked up her hot chocolate and took a deep drink. 'But I must tell you everything in order, or you won't understand.'

'Please. If you can bear to.' Following her lead, Henri drank her chocolate, cupping her hands round the mug for warmth and comfort.

'It was the summer of 1976, we were living above our parents' bakery in Motherwell, getting shouted at for playing the transistor too loud as we served the customers. I was twenty-five and Mary was twenty; she was a bonnie thing—had good looks and brains, just like you. I was the big sister who looked after her; should've looked after her.' It was clear, from her expression that in some way she blamed herself for what happened to Mary Dougal. 'We were young, bored and up for an adventure. We didnae wah-nt to serve in a cake shop for the rest of our days. One day, a customer came in with a copy of the *Daily Record* under his arm and left without it.'

'*Daily Record?* I'm guessing that's a newspaper?'

'Och, I keep forgetting that you're a Sassenach,' she used the word jokingly. 'Mary saw it first—the advert,' she added, catching Henri's puzzled look. '*Help needed to run tea rooms in the Highlands for the summer season, while owner recuperates after operation. Full training given.* We took one look at each other and decided that was our summer taken care of—a free holiday in the Heilans o' Scotland. *Pack the midge cream, Alice; we're on our way,* Mary said; and that's what we did. We'd grown up used to helping Mammy and Daddy—baking fresh bread and rolls in the wee small hours, waiting tables and so on. The only difference, as we saw it, was that we'd be far away from Motherwell and have the mountains and lochs to look at instead of high-rise flats. And we'd be serving tourists and Highlanders instead of men coming off their shift at the Ravenscraig.'

'Ravenscraig? Oh, yes, the steel mill. Go on,' she urged. Alice seemed happy to comply, reliving the moment in her mind's eye—remembering . . .

'I was *old*. I mean, in those days, at twenty-five I shoulda bin married to a steel worker or a miner, living in Bellshill wi' a couple of weans. But Mammy, Daddy and Mary needed me, so I kept putting it off, putting it off. I had offers, ah can tell ye.' Henriette didn't doubt it. At sixty-five, Alice Dougal was a handsome woman; slim, enviable complexion and careful how she looked and dressed. Back in the day, any man would've been lucky to marry her.

These days, no one considered that at twenty-eight years she should be married with a couple of kids. In the academic circles she and her parents moved in, a gap year or two, followed by studying for a BA, MA and then a PhD took up most of one's twenties; add another ten years to establish yourself in your chosen field and—well, if you didn't time it *just* right, the moment for marriage and children could pass you by. Much as it had done, she guessed, with Professor Hallam.

Aware that she'd zoned out, Henri focused and encouraged Alice to continue.

'So, you came up here and . . ?'

'. . . and, we were fair scunnered after a week. It was so different to Motherwell.' At that statement of the obvious, they both laughed. 'I know. I know. These days we would have Googled the place and thought: no way! God, it was so quiet in the evenings, never dark enough to get a good night's sleep; eaten alive by midges, no shops, cinemas or dance halls within walking distance. Not what we were used to. We were longing to go back tae Motherwell, but . . .'

'You'd bigged it up to your friends and couldn't go back without losing face?'

Alice nodded. 'We did consider it. Then—' levering herself out of her chair, she went over to the grate and put a few more logs on the fire. More, Henri suspected, to hide her expression than because it needed tending. Containing her exasperation and sensing that the story was about to take a twist, Henri waited until Alice sat down again, ready to continue.

'Then?'

'Himself met Mary and that was *that*.'

'That?'

'They were married in the wee church on the far side of the loch and I went home without her.' It was obvious from her tone, that she felt if she'd stayed, kept an eye on things, the drowning might never have happened.

'I get that your sister was beautiful, but what made—'She paused, not quite sure how to phrase the next bit.

'What made a Highland laird marry a wee lassie frae Motherwell? Four cousins who worked at the Ravenscraig and were built like brick outhouses, that's what.' Alice gave a dry laugh, evidently remembering something, which at the time, hadn't been amusing at all. 'Let's just say that Himself didn't so much *walk* to the altar as made a dash for it, closely followed by oor male cousins in case he changed his mind. Probably the ugliest set of bridesmaids ever to have set foot in that wee kirk. Mary was . . .'

'Pregnant with young Maol Choluim?' Henri guessed, wanting to give Alice time to collect herself.

'Aye, she'd found her way out of Motherwell and Himself had found a way of *not* marrying his cousin, Miss MacKenzie-Grieves, that following Christmas. That's Ciorstaidh and Alexander's mother, in case yer wondering.'

Ah, so that's why she was so keen to let me know there was no impediment to her and Keir marrying . . .

Henri glanced at Alice, she looked drawn and there were high spots of colour in her cheeks. 'Here endeth the lesson?' she suggested, gently. 'Part one, at any rate.'

Alice threw back her tartan comforter, laid her hands flat on her knees and pushed herself to her feet. 'Ah'm away tae my bed, Henri. You stay and watch your movie. I'll tell you the rest of the story another time. All I will say is, dinnae go mentioning *treasure* in Keir's hearing. It brings back memories; memories we'd all rather forget.'

Henri fixed a smile on her face, not wanting Alice to know that her warning had come too late. Hadn't she just spent the best part of that afternoon lecturing Keir MacKenzie on what did, or did not, constitute *treasure*? Now she understood his strained look, the bleakness behind his eyes she'd noticed when his guard was down. He'd lost his mother and brother when he was barely out of the infant class. The connection between his mother, brother, himself and treasure was harder to figure out.

More information was needed.

Alice stopped by her chair, stroked Henri's hair and then dropped a kiss on her head. 'Yer a good lassie, I see that. And if—that is, I hope that it's you, who . . .' Then she stopped herself, as if she was saying too much. 'Night, hen.'

'Night, Alice.' Henri replied and then added in a thick accent, as if she had been born in Motherwell. 'See ye the morrah, eh?'

'Not if I see ye first,' Alice laughed, and closed the door quietly behind her.

Henri stared into the fire and drank the last of her hot chocolate. All she could think of was the dark waters of the loch closing over Keir's mother and brother's heads, them gasping for breath until they could no longer keep their head above the water. Her heart felt as if it was breaking and her eyes filled with tears for a man she barely knew and for a family almost wiped out in one single, tragic moment. She now understood why Sir Malcolm could not bear to be in the castle—it must seem empty without his wife and heir. No wonder he spent most of his time at the MacKenzie-Grieveses'. Although why he was estranged from Keir and appeared to be running the castle into the ground, was harder to fathom.

Picking up the remote from the side table, Henri pressed the 'play' button, freeing Kate Winslet from 'freeze frame' prison. But as her favourite movie played out and Eli Wallach explained the meet-cute to Kate Winslet, for once it didn't hold her attention.

Chapter Seventeen
Across the Loch

Henri didn't usually work weekends, but today she made an exception. She was keen to empty the last remaining bookcase and re-categorise the books stacked on the tables and floors. After that, she'd make a list of those books worth saving and ask Lachlan to take her over to the post office where she could email the list to Maddie Hallam. It was down to Maddie to get in touch with academics, antiquarians and auction houses, to bring the content of the library to their attention.

On a separate matter, she wanted to ask Maddie to find out why HR hadn't chosen a date for the hearing yet, or forwarded the relevant documents to her, as promised.

Sitting on the bottom rung of the library steps, face cupped in her hands, Henri sighed. Her time in the castle was drawing to a close and she'd be sad to leave because, strange as it may seem, it was beginning to feel like home. So far, she'd only seen a fraction of it—kitchen, Great Hall, bedrooms, bathrooms, Alice's study, the Laird's sitting room and those rooms used for storage. She was keen to explore the rest, with Himself's permission, of course. Above all, she'd love a *wee keek,* as Alice would say, inside Keir MacKenzie's rooms, which were kept dusted and aired for the rare occasion when he stayed over.

She hadn't seen the Master of Mountgarrie since last week and she wondered if she'd imagined the growing sense of connection between them? Now she knew more of his backstory she understood his mercurial moods, his melancholy and unwillingness to stay in the castle. If only she could help.

She couldn't rid herself of the niggling feeling that, apart from discovering the *MacKenzie Papers* and the miniature, she'd only done half a job.

There was something in the library, in the castle, waiting to be discovered. She felt it in her water! If that was true, she'd better get a move on. Time was running out.

Half an hour later, Alice entered the library carrying a pile of old blankets.

'Come on, lassie, no time for daydreaming. Keir's on his way and we've got to get the manuscripts down three flights of stairs and oot o' the castle before Lachlan returns. Sir Malcolm's taken his E-Type for a spin, and Lachlan'll be back tae watch the afternoon racing on the telly, signal permitting; not tae mention getting under my feet.'

At the mention of Keir's name Henri tingled all over, but feigned indifference.

'Wouldn't it make more sense to wait until Lachlan gets back and ask for his help?'

'Lachlan MacKenzie? The biggest clype this side o' the Cairngorms? Ah dinnae think so.'

'Clype?' That was a new one on Henri.

'A snitch. A stoolpigeon. Everything you tell him, goes straight back to Himself. Castle Tèarmannair disnae need the internet; not with Lachlan MacKenzie around. Och, come *oah-n*, Henri; look lively!' She threw blankets on the floor by Henri's feet and tutted. Taking the hint, Henri rolled up her sleeves and set to with a will.

Soon the large leather volumes containing all the estate rolls and records were swathed in individual blankets. Next, Alice produced bubble wrap, scissors and a roll of sticky tape to wrap the chests containing the Bonnie Prince Charlie miniature, marriage lines, baptism papers, death certificates, deeds of transfer, and tenancy agreements stretching back hundreds of years. They took extra care not to break the wax seals dangling from ribbons on some of the older documents, because that would affect their provenance and value.

Pausing briefly, Alice picked a marriage certificate out of the last box— that of her sister to Sir Malcolm. Tears welled up in her eyes as she glanced over it, remembering. Before Henri could utter any words of comfort, she closed the lid of the chest with a decisive snap. As if to underline that there was no time for sentiment today.

'Ready?' She scooped up one of the largest volumes and tried to tuck it under her arm.

Henri removed the book from her grasp and gave her a chest to carry instead. The last thing she needed was Alice pinned down under one of the massive tomes, lying at the foot of a spiral staircase with a broken hip, or worse.

'No arguments, Alice. I'm the expert, here. Remember?'

'Aye, lassie; ah havnae forgot. Lead on, *Doctor* Bruar.'

By the time they made their way through the undercroft with the first load, Henri was out of breath. The large volumes were unwieldy and she was forced to carry them sideways-on, arms opened wide, pressed back against the stone walls of the spiral staircase for balance. She descended a step at a time, using a crab-like gait to negotiate the twist in the staircase. She wished that Lachlan *was* there, stoolpigeon or not, to help with the lifting. At this rate, it would take ages to get everything into Keir's boat.

Time they simply didn't have.

Keir was waiting on the jetty. Upon seeing her, he rushed forward, took the book out of her hands as if it weighed no more than a paperback, and carried it down the castle's external stairs. Standing at the top of the steep flight, Henri pushed her hands into the small of her back and straightened as Keir put the book in the cabin of his motor boat, double checking that it was securely wrapped against the threatening rain. In time, her breathing returned to normal and her pulse slowed to a steadier beat and Keir relieved Alice of her precious cargo and stowed it away. Just as she was readying herself for another trip, Keir re-emerged from the cabin.

Raising his hand to shield his eyes against the low autumn sun, he sent her a considering look, as if something was perplexing him and he had to figure it out. The sexy narrowing of his eyes as he squinted up at her against the light, made conserving an important primary source seem suddenly unimportant. Henri wondered how it would feel to have him look at her like *that* for entirely different reasons. Not because he found her an enigma but because he found her sexy and provocative. Henri acknowledged that her timing was rotten, her life was a mess and her career was in tatters. Quite honestly, there was no place in it for a man like Keir MacKenzie. It was pointless, harbouring thoughts about him or imagining scenarios which started with—*what if.*

His card was marked, he was practically engaged to his cousin. Added to which, she'd be leaving after the Samhain festivities and that would sever her connection with Castle Tèarmannair and those who lived there, including Keir MacKenzie. He didn't look like the kind of man who wanted, or needed, a pen pal.

Thank God neither Keir nor Alice were aware of the thoughts whirling through her mind, making her giddy. However, in spite of her good intentions not to think of Keir MacKenzie in *that way,* her hormones had other ideas. Holding onto the castle wall, she pretended to look across the loch for Lachlan, hoping that being in the shadow of the castle her wild thoughts were hidden from them.

'Are ye a'right, Henri? I hope ye are nae over doin' it. You've gone awfu' pale, hen, although—wait a minute, your cheeks are flushed.' Beckoning her down the steps, Alice laid the back of her hand against Henri's brow and checked her temperature. 'Keir, what do ye think? Does Henri not look a wee bit . . .'

However, Keir didn't respond to his aunt's words. He was still regarding Henri in that same, steady way, making her feel very conscious—of him, of herself, and the electricity crackling between them.

'Alice, I'm f-fine,' Henri asserted, although she stumbled over the words. 'Can we just get on? Please?'

'Aye, verra well. But there must be a reason for ye looking so flushed. Should I get a doctor's appointment for ye, for after the weekend?' Henri caught Alice's knowing wink, and in return sent her a pointed: *will you behave?* look.

'Are you sure, Henri, you've been working for days without a break. Maybe I should—' Keir came forward, treating her as if she was an elderly academic and not the woman who'd scored two goals at the shinty match.

'Please, stop fussing; both of you. We're on a mission here, let's move, people.' Automatically, they glanced over at the farther shore where Lachlan's orange dinghy was moored by the jetty. No sign of him—yet, thank goodness. Galvanised, aware that the clock was ticking, they retraced their steps and, with Keir sharing the burden, emptied the library of its prized cargo in double quick time.

After the last trip Alice joined Henri and Keir on the jetty, carrying a large, tea-towel-draped wicker basket. She regarded her nephew with a mix of asperity and wry affection.

'Ah'm guessing ye havnae been shopping, Keir MacKenzie. And that ye expect this poor lassie to starve to death while she sorts through the books at the Beach House?' Keir had the grace to look sheepish. Henri ran her hands surreptitiously over her waist and hips, knowing that she'd gained weight, a direct result of Alice's delicious home-cooked meals and cake-laden afternoon tea trays.

Anyone less likely to starve to death in the next couple of hours was hard to imagine.

'Guilty as charged, m'lud.' Henri blushed as he gave her curves a quick onceover. 'I planned to nip to the post office and get a few provisions while Henri checked everything survived the trip across the loch. Although,' again, the smile which made Henri's stomach flip over, 'you're right. It wouldn't do to expect my guest to share my iron rations.'

He didn't elaborate what those might be, leaving Henri to suspect that he ate cold beans out of a tin, washed down with spring water collected from one of the icy streams which fed into the loch.

'Well, you can keep your *road kill* sandwiches for another time,' Alice quipped, 'there's enough food here to last you a couple of days. Not that I'm expecting the job to take *that* long; I want Henri back before Malcolm notices she's gone.'

'Yes, ma'am,' Keir saluted.

'What about Lachlan? Won't he realise I've gone AWOL?' Henri enquired.

'Och, you leave him to me. He'll be so busy reading the racing pages and drinking the laird's whisky that he won't notice you're not around. Afterwards he'll be crabbit because he's lost all his money and'll sulk in his bedroom until supper, by which time you'll be back. Now, off youse go. Have fun and,' she gave Keir a warning look, wagging a finger at him, 'play nicely, children.'

'Yes, Auntie Alice,' he said, making light of her concern.

'Ye'r never too old for a skelp't arse, Keir MacKenzie, so less of it.' She laughed to take the sting out of her words and accompanied them to the end of the jetty. She waited until Henri was safely on board and then handed her the basket of food. Giving Alice a bone-crushing hug, Keir leapt on board, fired up the engine and steered his boat straight up the loch, like a homing bird.

'Put this life jacket on and get below deck,' Keir commanded Henri. 'We don't want Lachlan, or anyone else, catching a glimpse of you from the shore.' He put his free hand lightly on the top of Henri's head as she ducked into the wheel house, evidently concerned that she might knock herself out. 'Once we round the next bend I'll hug the shore and we'll be out of sight of the castle. Then it'll be safe for you join me on deck.' Hunkered down in the wheelhouse and with her back towards the prow of the boat, Henri nodded, even though he couldn't see her.

But she could see *him*—and had a very good view at that. With his dark hair, navy blue eyes, long legs, tight rear and broad shoulders, he was a fine looking man. And she was a young woman with blood running through her veins, not ink. Naturally, she wondered what it would feel like to have him make love to her. She dismissed the idea as crazy and advised herself to get a grip, blaming these wayward thoughts on the sudden flood of oxygen into her lungs after being holed up in Castle Tèarmannair.

'Okay, it's safe to come out.' Keir MacKenzie thrust his hand into the cabin. After a moment's hesitation she took it, allowing him to pull her upright. 'Come and stand by me, that way you'll get the best view of the Beach House when it heaves into view.' Henri hung back, unsure of *how* close to stand next to him. Suffering no such reservations, Keir put his arm round her waist and drew her closer, to steady her. 'Put your hands there, on the wheel house, it'll keep you balanced.'

It was as though the scorching look they'd exchanged on the jetty had never happened and he was more concerned about her safety than trying it on. Taking control of the wheel, he concentrated on steering the boat up the loch and long seconds passed during which neither of them spoke. Feeling it was incumbent for her to say something, anything, Henri chose the stunning scenery as a suitable topic for conversation.

'I spent my gap year travelling the world, but nothing comes close to *this*. The way the light shifts and changes, how the weather alters in the blink of an eye, catching you unawares. When the mist comes down and otters create a wake, you can almost imagine it's one of Lachlan's water horses following us.' Encompassing the loch, mountains and hills in one expansive gesture she temporarily lost her balance. 'Whoops,' she laughed, leaning backwards to right herself. Keir, one hand on the wheel, caught her and pulled her into his side, much as he'd done earlier.

Only, this time, he didn't let her go.

The way he held her was nonthreatening and seemed to be all about her safety, nothing more. Henri relaxed and blew her hair out of her eyes with a small breath. How like her to misread the signs! He was simply being friendly, doing his best to help her forget their disastrous first meeting, and make her feel at ease. There was nothing sexual or inappropriate in his light touch.

They were partners in crime—yes, that was it. If it wasn't for the *MacKenzie Papers* she wouldn't be on his boat, he wouldn't be steadying her with his arm and . . .

'It's so wild and untouched,' he broke into her thoughts. Slipping on a pair of sunglasses against the glare of the low sun, he pulled his baseball cap lower over his eyes, turned to her and smiled. 'Everything okay with you, Henri?'

'F—fine. Never better.' The way he looked at her, even though he was wearing shades, sent a jolt of sexual awareness zipping through Henri's veins. She turned away and indicated the stunning scenery with a sweep of her arm. 'It's all down,' she said and gulped in a steadying breath, 'to big earth movements.'

'*Big earth movements*?' Keir laughed, giving her arm a friendly squeeze. 'That's one way to describe it, certainly. I studied geology at St Andrews and I've explored every inch of the loch and its shore. You should visit Assynt in the north-west corner of the Highlands, if the opportunity arises. The scenery is almost surreal, it takes your breath away—mountains, lochs, ruined castles, white sand beaches. My favourite feature, after the mountains, are the small lochans which are covered with water lilies in the summer.'

'You seem to know it well,' she ventured, enjoying learning about this other side to him. Not wanting to force the pace, she let him do the talking.

'I spend many days in the pouring rain, with students from the Geology Department, logging the different types of lichen found there.' Turning his head, he looked down on her and gave a self-deprecating smile, as though counting lichen didn't quite fit in with his image. 'Manly pursuit—*not.*'

'Well, those lichen won't count themselves now, will they?' she said, like a severe schoolmarm—and he laughed at her joke. The feeling that their relationship was moving forward inch by inch made Henri excited and apprehensive in equal measure, but more alive than she'd felt in years.

'But there were compensations. If you ever go to Durness, travel on to Balnakeil where they serve the best hot chocolate in the world, at Cocoa Mountain. There's a memorial garden to John Lennon there. Apparently, he had relatives in Durness and used to holiday there with Yoko and the kids, back in the day. The Smoo Caves are well worth a look-see, the Vikings used them as dry dock for their longboats during the winter.'

'I'll make a note of that.' She pretended to scribble it down in the palm of her hand. 'Vikings. Dry dock. Hot chocolate.'

'Can you take a second, unmanly confession?' he asked.

'I'm steeling myself—go on.'

'I'm a total chocaholic.'

'Me, too!' Then, to trump his information about lichen, John Lennon and caves, she added, 'chocolate is loaded with dopamine—they call it the *love drug;* it causes your pulse rate to quicken, resulting in a similar feeling to being in love . . .' Oh, God, where had *that* come from?

'Thanks. I'll remember that, next time I eat a Mars bar,' was his dry response. Then he laughed at her discomfiture, in an open, friendly manner.

They sailed on without speaking and then, to redeem herself, Henri gestured to the magnificent scenery. 'There's a softness to the hills and the shore line which even a dyed-in-the-wool cynic would find romantic. A—a majesty to the mountains, as if each side of the loch was designed by a different hand.'

There was another pause, during which he weighed up her statement. 'I'm guessing you're a romantic.' Piloting the boat up the loch, he never once looked anywhere other than straight ahead. Nor did he rush to release her although, by now, she was steady on her feet.

'I'm drawn to history for the romance of the subject, seeing people behind the facts and figures, dates and important events. But, if you ever tell anyone I admitted to being a romantic, I'll deny it. I am a *serious* historian,' she said, using a mock-scholarly tone.

'Then, as a dyed-in-the-wool, closet romantic you've come to the right place,' Keir said, his face softening. 'Here is the most romantic, stunning place on earth, and anyone who can't appreciate that, has no poetry in their soul.'

There being nothing more to be said, they continued their journey in a companionable silence, Keir occasionally moving his arm into a more comfortable position. And, as they rounded another bend in the loch, the water stretched out before them—navy blue in places where the sun didn't reach it and almost aquamarine where it did. Now they were on a straight section of the loch, the wind was like a slap in the face. Henri rocked on her heels at the force of it, clinging to the wheel house for dear life.

Keir laughed. 'That wind has a mind of its own; sometimes, coming from the south —warm and gentle. Other times swinging round from the northeast, whipping up waves on the loch so that you can almost imagine yourself at sea. In times like that, I stay as close to shore as the boat's draught allows. I never venture onto the loch in adverse weather conditions.'

His face darkened, as a memory took him to another place, a place he'd rather forget. Henri remembered what Alice had said about Keir's mother and brother drowning; how he'd survived. Maybe, if they got to know each other better she could probe him for more details. Then she shook her head—who was she kidding? Keir MacKenzie was a man who kept his own counsel.

Buffeted by the rising wind, she lost her footing and brushed against MacKenzie's shoulder. 'Sorry,' they said simultaneously, and then laughed—but this time their laughter was forced and tinged with awkwardness.

'Look.' Keir pointed to where a spit of white sand curved round a small bay on their right. Trees came all the way down to the water's edge and, where the beach ended, the gentle slope of the hills began. On their left, were mountains; dark, craggy and veined with snow on the highest peaks.

'The Beach House,' he announced, his voice full of pride, as if he was showing her something special.

The Beach House, a former Victorian hunting lodge, was built of granite and stood four square against the wind. Henri recalled the huntin', shootin', fishin' paraphernalia stored in the undercroft, as if waiting for those times to return. As they drew closer, a substantial boat house became visible, its wooden jetty poking into the loch, like a tongue. Keir moved Henri to one side with a polite *excuse me*, and killed the engine. Then, coiled rope in hand, he leapt out of the boat and moored up, glancing anxiously in the direction from which they had just come.

He pointed and Henri turned to look, seeing slanting rain clouds on the western hills. 'Rain on the way. Come on, let's shift this lot while we have the chance.'

He held out his hand and Henri took it.

'You, okay? You look very . . . fierce.'

'Just anxious to get everything safely stowed away,' she said.

Now it was his turn to look serious as he helped her onto the jetty. Once he was sure she was safe, he jumped back onto the boat, making it rock at its moorings. Then he ducked into the wheelhouse and brought out the first of the large volumes of estate records, securing the blanket before passing it up to her. He returned for another which he also handed up to her, and then he clambered out of the boat and was at her side.

'This way.'

Carrying a volume each they followed a pebble and shingle path round to the back of the Beach House. Keir led the way into an open-sided porch, fished under a plant pot for the key to the back door, kicked the door open and brought Henri into a large, square kitchen. He put his volume of the *MacKenzie Papers* on a cloth-covered table and indicated that Henri should do likewise. Then he straightened and flexed his back.

'Up for another trip?' Henri nodded, keen to get the job done and back in the castle before her absence was noted. And before the weather worsened. She knew, from growing up around a lake, albeit in the Swiss Alps, that bad weather had a tendency to circle lakes, returning with a vengeance when you thought it'd done its worst.

She followed Keir back to the boat and they repeated the trip until all the manuscripts and bubble-wrapped boxes were in the warm, dry kitchen. Only then did she allow herself to relax, taking a seat at the table and watching Keir as he raised the lid on a small Aga in an alcove and slid the kettle over onto its hotplate. It was all reassuringly domestic and once she had a coffee in front of her, refusing the slug of whisky he put in his, she relaxed further.

Glowering rain clouds swept towards the Beach House and the wind, which had been on the keen side on their trip over, gathered pace and whooshed towards them like a banshee. Keir stood in front of a large window overlooking the loch, nursing his coffee, giving Henri a chance to observe his profile as she drank her coffee.

Turning back from the window he drained his mug of coffee and set it on the draining board. 'We just made it in the nick of time,' he observed, seemingly in an attempt to fill the silence which had descended on them. The feeling of a common purpose, which had united them on their way across the loch, was disappearing fast.

'Where are you going to store the manuscripts and boxes? Can I see?' Henri asked, thinking it was time to assert her academic credentials.

'I thought in the damp cellar, through the door there,' Keir answered, poker-faced.

'Wh—what?'

'Just kidding! You looked so anxious sitting there, I thought I'd better make a joke.'

'I'm fine; just worried about storing these precious documents safely.' She hoped he didn't see her as some sort of virginal, Victorian blue-stocking who would faint if a man got within three feet of her. 'Nothing more.'

'Okay, drink up and I'll show you the space I've cleared. I hope it meets your exacting standards, *Dr Bruar*.' Taking his teasing in good part, she placed her mug on the corner of the Aga and followed him into the hall. She suppressed a smile at thinking for one moment that the beach huts at Wells-next-the-Sea had anything in common with this substantial dwelling. None of the former could boast a panelled hall complete with carved mahogany staircase—although there were too many antlers and deer heads for her taste—or a tartan carpet which covered the hall, stairs and landing. Light slanted through a large stained glass window showing the MacKenzie coat of arms. It cast a pool of light at Henri's feet and helped to illuminate the mid-afternoon gloom in the shadowy hall. Keir led her under the cantilevered staircase and into a small room which housed empty, glass fronted cabinets. It smelled musty, like the vestry in an old church and when he switched on the electric lights, Henri noticed that the windows were shuttered and barred.

'What is this?' Henri asked, blinking in the unforgiving, fluorescent brightness.

'The old gun room,' he gestured towards the empty cabinets. 'I'm into conservation, not blasting everything that moves. Although some would argue, my father among them, that breeding game birds for sport has kept certain species alive.'

'I don't know enough about the subject to comment, although I'm against shooting animals for sport, as a matter of principle. What?' she demanded, catching his sideways, amused look.

'You. Not knowing something.'

'I never said I knew *everything*, just most things.' They both laughed at her bold assertion. 'Back to business, we need to move everything in here before anyone notices I'm missing.'

'No need; I can make everything secure once you're back at the castle. Okay, I'm guessing from your look that you don't quite think I'm up to carrying everything through here, locking the door and swallowing the key?'

'I—' She wasn't sure if he was joking.

'Okay, let's do it together and then I'll take you back. Although, Alice won't be very happy if I don't share at least some of the basket of food with you,' he called over his shoulder as they went back into the kitchen. Moving everything into the gun room didn't take long and Henri was soon warming her derriere against the Aga as he unpacked Alice's goodies. 'Enough here to feed an army. What we don't use, I'll freeze. So, what comes next?'

'Well, I'm ravenous and could eat—oh, you mean with the documents?' Henri blushed and then pulled herself together. 'I'll contact Maddie Hallam, she's got contacts in all the right places. It's her I'll be emailing with the list of books I think are worth selling.' Now it was her turn to slant him a look. 'You seem to have accepted the inevitable, regarding the library, I mean. After our first . . .' she paused, searching for the right words.

'Dramatic meeting?' He glanced over his shoulder as he put food in a large, serviceable fridge and then removed something foil-wrapped from the basket and transferred it to his back pocket. Next, he removed a bottle of white wine in an insulated sleeve, held it up and looked at her enquiringly. When she nodded, he poured two glasses and handed one to her. 'Budge up,' he said, taking up position next to her, leaning against Aga for warmth.

Their hips and thighs touched and they both stared straight ahead, sipping their wine as if this close, physical contact was nothing out of the ordinary. Another lengthy silence which Keir eventually broke with, 'Did I ever apologise? For throwing you on the chesterfield?'

Henri pretended to give his question serious thought. 'You know, I don't think you did.'

'Ok-ay,' he drew out the syllables. 'In view of our partnership, I offer an apology and an explanation. I'd just got off a long haul flight from British Columbia, we'd been held up by a baggage handling dispute. When I reached MacKenzie's Halt and Castle Tèarmannair,'—Henri noticed that he didn't say *home*, and found that telling—'I was brought over from the far side by Lachlan. He took great delight in telling me that Father had installed another of his *wimmen* in the castle. Another so-called personal assistant.'

'I'm guessing that most of your father's PA's could only type one-fingered and thought that shorthand is what people used on their phones before auto-correct was invented.'

Keir laughed. 'Not to mention the ones Alice chased out of her kitchen with a sweeping brush and told to 'get dressed', when they wandered down to breakfast scantily clad.'

'So, Lachlan thought I was one of those? No wonder he was so rude and practically refused to take me over to the castle. He still looks at me askance, as though he expects me to revert to type.'

'When I found you lying on top of my father and then learned that you'd been called in to asset strip the library, you can imagine how I felt.'

'Quite.' Henri sipped her wine, wondering how she could bring the conversation round to the subject of his mother and brother. They were getting on and didn't want to risk a setback, so, she settled on what she hoped was a less personal question. 'Why were you in British Columbia?'

'I have MacKenzie cousins who own and manage a profitable timber business there. I'd like to set one up on our estate, one day; I've spent time there, over the years, learning the necessary skills. One of my cousins is very keen to come over here and help. However—' He moved away from the Aga and walked over to the window. Standing with his back to her and looking out into the approaching squall, he continued, 'It won't be easy.'

'How so?'

'Father's rented out our land and, apart from the few acres the Beach House stands on, I have nothing. No money. No land. Whenever I'm home for any length of time I have to get casual work in Fort William, or farther afield.' He gave a self-deprecating shrug. 'Most of the work is cash in hand—delivery driving, order picking at a large warehouse in Fort William. I go under the name of James Dougal, my maternal grandfather's name, it wouldn't do to let employers know that Sir Malcolm is my father, or that I live in a castle.'

'I get that,' she said slowly, enjoying the warmth from the Aga spreading across her buttocks and the wine working its way into her bloodstream. She was caught off guard when he turned to her, and asked,

'What brings Dr Henriette Bruar to MacKenzie's Halt?'

'I'm here thanks to Maddie Hallam. Sir Malcolm wanted the library catalogued and sold—and I, for my sins, have been commissioned to do just that. Sorry.'

She could tell by his raised eyebrow that he wasn't buying her story and she began to feel uncomfortable. It wasn't the fact that she'd smashed up the Dean's television set which made her reluctant to tell Keir everything. It was more that the incident reflected badly on her, making her appear less like the academic she professed to being and more like a deranged bunny boiler.

'Very well.' Keir didn't seem in the least put out by her reticence. 'Castle Tèarmannair is a good place to hide away from the world; it keeps its secrets.'

Again, the slight hesitation, as if memories crowded in on him. Then, he rubbed his hands together and moved the conversation along. 'While I make us something to eat, you can tell me where we go next, regarding the *MacKenzie Papers*. Deal?'

'Deal,' she replied, watching him make his way round the kitchen preparing their late lunch. She hoped that she was capable of doing the best for the archive and that it would, in some small way, go towards restoring the fortunes of the MacKenzies.

Chapter Eighteen
The Curse of MacKenzie's Gold

Perhaps Keir didn't like being watched while he carried out his duties as a host, because after a few minutes he ushered Henri into a sitting room situated across the hall, and told her to make herself comfortable. Waving a hand, he indicated a large roll-top bureau housing his laptop and a rather ancient telephone.

'The connection's not brilliant, but feel free to make use of both. I'll call you when lunch is ready.' With that he left, closing the door behind him.

As soon as Henri moved closer to the router, the iPhone in her bag starting 'pinging'. Whilst living in the castle, it had suited her purposes to 'go dark'. However, she knew that the time had come to raise her head above the parapet and rejoin the real world.

She and her parents had exchanged letters, and she'd sent postcards of the castle—found at the back of Sir Malcolm's secretaire bookcase and dating from the days when visitors paid fifty pence to be shown round Castle Tèarmannair by old Lady MacKenzie. In them she'd written *I'm happy and safe. On an assignment for Professor Hallam. No internet or phone signal. Will be in touch via snail mail as soon as possible.*

She hadn't told her parents about the close encounter with the Dean's television. Time for that when she saw them at Christmas, by which time the disciplinary hearing would be over and everything would be resolved—one way or another. She missed her parents and would have loved to speak to them, but decided that an international call in the middle of the day might be stretching Keir's hospitality too far.

She settled instead for ringing Maddie Hallam at St Guthlac. She picked up straightaway.

'Henriette, my dear girl, how are you?' Maddie had the husky voice of a forty-a-day chain smoker and Henri could imagine her brushing ash off her desk as she spoke. 'How's that old reprobate, Malcolm? Keeping his hands to himself, I hope.'

'No worries on that score, Maddie,' Henri laughed and then cut to the chase. 'Listen, I'm in Keir MacKenzie's Beach House and this is my only chance to phone you. I've made an amazing discovery.' She went on to describe the *MacKenzie Papers* and the miniature of The Young Pretender.

'Clever girl to realise their worth. Treasure isn't only gold and silver.'

'That's what I told Keir,' Henri asserted proudly. 'Where do we go from here? It's Keir's wish—my wish—that the papers stay together as a complete archive. We're worried that Sir Malcolm will sell them off, lot by lot at auction, if he learns of them. They deserve better than that.'

'Agreed. I'll start making discreet enquiries. I'm sure that a well-endowed university would be willing to pay a fair price for such an archive. If we can get a bidding war going, why the sky's the limit. I wish St Guthlac could afford to keep them,' she said, wistfully. 'But the coffers are empty. Okay, I'm getting ahead of myself. Well done you, and . . .' another pause, 'about *the other business*. Finding the *MacKenzie Papers* will stand you in good stead at the hearing—paint you as a serious academic, not a—'

'Suitable case for treatment?' Henri finished off the sentence. Maddie laughed and her lungs rattled. Henri knew it was useless to ask her to give up cigarettes. Maddie's philosophy was that she'd reached seventy and, after living a full life, any additional years were a bonus. 'Look, I'd better go, Keir's making lunch.'

'How are you two getting on? Go easy on him. He's had a hard life, even if he is the son of a laird and will inherit a romantic castle in the middle of a loch.' The last was said with heavy irony as she was aware the estate was running on empty. 'I'm sure he'd trade it all to have his mother and brother, safe and well. You know the whole story, I'm assuming?'

'No, Alice was going to tell me but somehow we've never found the right moment.'

'The redoubtable Alice. Oh my God, she rang me from the post office and gave me a total bollocking over the trick I played—'

'Trick?'

'Sending you, instead of your alter ego—Dr Henry Brewer, moustachioed and hairy of chest, to catalogue the library. I knew she'd never condone a female academic, thanks to Malcolm's reputation. But I knew you could handle the old goat.' She laughed again. 'She's forgiven me since then and says she's going to miss you when you leave. Although, why she stays in that damp pile of stone and puts up with Malc's behaviour, I'll never know. Look, it's not for me to tell the tale of Keir's tragic past. Ply Keir with whisky, get him to drop his defences . . .'

'That'll take some doing.' Henri pulled a face.

'. . . Then you'll understand everything.'

'Before you go, Maddie, could you chase HR up? I'm still waiting for the date of my disciplinary hearing and—'

'Well, of course I will. It's been half-term here and everything's ground to a halt. On top of which, they are understaffed and, I suspect, working to rule to make their case for more funding. Not for nothing are they referred to as Human Remains.' She laughed at the joke. 'I thought you wouldn't be in any rush to leave the castle and the gorgeous Keir behind, so I haven't pushed things this end.'

'I simply want things settled.'

'Of course. And how's the dissertation coming along?'

'Don't ask. I've hardly had a moment to myself since I got here.'

Another phone rang in Maddie's office. 'Damn. Look; gotta go. Leave everything with me. And well done, that girl. Laters?'

'Laters.' Just when 'laters' might be, Henri had no idea.

'That was delicious.' Henri pushed her plate away. 'Where did you learn to cook like that?'

Keir laughed. 'To be honest, most of it is down to Alice. She keeps me supplied with home-cooked meals while I'm at the Beach House. If I don't go over to the castle for a few days, she sends Lachlan, over with fresh provisions. Although he moans that he's not paid to be at *her* beck and call, he's the laird's man. Not that we take a lot of notice, he's never happier than when he's moaning. But, I do owe him a debt of gratitude.' As he leaned forward to fill up Henri's glass, a shadow passed across his face.

'This wine is exceptional. Cheers.' She encouraged him to top up his own glass, remembering what Maddie had said earlier about plying him with drink. Henri looked at him over the rim of her glass; he was keeping his intake to a minimum because he had to take her back to the castle after lunch.

Commendable, to be sure—but also frustrating.

'Father had a lottery win a few years ago and instead of using the money to effect a few repairs to the castle, he stocked up his wine cellar. He's living in the past—back in the days when the MacKenzies' had money and influence. Alice takes it upon herself to stow away a few bottles along with the homemade flans and cakes she packs up for me. It might turn out to be my only inheritance, the way things are going.' He raised his glass to his lips, and stared through the window into the middle distance out over the loch. 'Pudding?'

It took Henri a moment to follow his line of thought. 'I'll pass, if that's okay. It's looking pretty choppy on the loch and I wouldn't like to be sick over the side of the boat. Sorry,' she laughed, 'not so romantic.'

'All part of Doctor Bruar's charm, I would say.' He regarded her, poker-faced, although there was banked-down humour in his eyes.

'Not everyone appreciates it.'

'That, I can believe.'

Getting to his feet he cleared the table, brushing aside Henri's offer of help. She watched him load an ancient dishwasher which was rusty round the edges and had knobs and push buttons in place of digital controls. Glancing round the old kitchen with its ancient Aga, stone butler's sink and painted, free-standing kitchen units, she could imagine the parties held here, back in the day . . . Guests spilling out of the house, onto the gardens and down to the beach. They'd enjoy the long summer twilight, barbequing fish caught in the river which fed the loch and game shot in the hills. In her mind's eye she could see them bringing an old gramophone out of the house and setting it on a table, dancing to scratchy tunes from another era.

She shook her head free of the seductive images and focused her attention on Keir, instead. She'd thought that being in the Beach House with him would result in awkward silences interspersed by polite conversation. Instead they'd discussed every topic under the sun and she wondered where he'd developed his easy-going manner—Scotland, or Canada? Were confidence and assurance in his DNA, a direct result of knowing this was his land and these were his people? He seemed far removed from the Old Testament Prophet who'd burst into the library and thrown her over his shoulder.

'Coffee?' he asked, crossing over to an old-fashioned Cona coffee machine on the counter. Fascinated, Henri watched as he set a glass jug containing water over a methylated spirit burner and left it to heat up. After grinding coffee beans, he put them into a second glass jug which he suspended over the first by means of a mechanical arm. As the water boiled, it was syphoned up into the top jug via a long glass tube and mixed with the coffee grounds.

'Wow,' she said.

'My party trick. Shazam!' He passed his hands over the coffee machine, as though commanding coffee-making imps to do his bidding. 'The magic isn't over, yet. Behold.' Another magician-like flourish and the freshly-brewed coffee went back down the filter rod and into the first jug, after which he put a small cap over the burner, extinguishing the flame.

'We could have had a Nescafé,' she joked.

'You have no soul.' Taking the jug off the stand, he poured them each a mug of coffee. 'I normally get a round of applause from my audience,' he said, pretending hurt and disappointment. Obligingly, Henri clapped her hands, wondering who exactly made up his 'audience'. Ciòrstaidh Mackenzie-Grieves? Other women? No one would know who was staying in the Beach House unless they made the effort to cross the loch, walk along the jetty and knock on the front door. Why did the thought that he'd shown this trick with the coffee pot to other women make her feel edgy and uncomfortable?

'My parents are scientists,' she informed him. 'I was brought up on this kind of 'magic'.' Getting up, she moved away from the table and looked out of the window. 'The wind's getting up,' she commented. He left the coffee on the counter and joined her at the window. Standing at her shoulder, he leaned forward and peered into the gathering storm gloom. As Henri breathed in the clean, scent of him—a slight male muskiness undercut by fabric conditioner and a light, tangy aftershave—her feeling of unease intensified.

What game was he playing? Was it *like father, like son*—was Keir MacKenzie a serial womaniser like the laird?

'I thought it would have settled down by now, but I think it's actually getting worse. Let's have coffee, give it half an hour to make its mind up. If it's safe, I'll take you back to the castle.'

'And, if it isn't? Safe, I mean . . .' Biting her bottom lip, she half-turned to face him.

'We'll sit it out. It'll have calmed down by the morning.' He spoke as if her staying overnight in the Beach House was no big deal.

'The *morning*!' Her voice rose an octave. 'What is this? The Highland equivalent of running out of petrol in the middle of nowhere and having to spend the night in the car?'

'There's plenty of room here—'

'Alice will be worried to death—'

'Alice knows I have more sense than to take the boat out in a squall. We've got enough food to feed an army, the house has survived two hundred years of the worst the weather can throw at it. I don't see a problem.' He walked back to the counter and asked, 'Sugar?'

'Sugar? Are you mad? What will your father and Lachlan think?'

'No worries on that score. They'll assume—rightly, that we're two adults, and—'

'What happens in the Beach House, stays in the Beach House?' she fumed.

'Why? What do you think is going to happen?' He turned, two mugs of coffee in his hand and grinned, evidently enjoying her discomfiture.

'Why—why, that is—*you* might—*I* might.'

'Yes? What *might* you do, Doctor Bruar? Is my virtue at risk?'

She raised her head, caught the amused light in his eyes and then let out a long breath.

'Sorry; bit of an overreaction. It's simply that, quite recently, I—I had the carpet pulled from under me in spectacular fashion, and I don't want to repeat the experience. No one's putting *this* Baby in the corner—ever, again.' Pointing back at herself with her thumb, she sent him a warning look.

'That isn't going to happen. Door . . .' It took Henri a few seconds to realise that she was required to open the kitchen door. Soon they were back in the sitting room and seated on either side of the wood burner. 'No central heating but the Aga and the wood burner keeps downstairs pretty warm,' he said, dismissing her fears. 'No need for us to huddle together for warmth, in case you're wondering. Unless you want to, of course?' He sent her a quizzical look and then laughed at her expression. 'Relax. On really cold nights, I sleep on the sofa over there. Compared to winters in British Columbia, it's sub-tropical here.' He reached down by the side of his chair, retrieved a bottle of whisky and held it in front of him. 'Fancy a wee dram?'

'No thanks,' Henri replied, more primly than intended. She quickly calculated how many units of alcohol he'd consumed since their arrival at the Beach House. What were the rules governing how many units you could knock back before you were considered unfit to sail a boat?

'Don't worry,' he said, reading her mind, 'I never take risks where the loch's concerned. There,' he cocked his head on the side and gave her another amused look, 'the thought doesn't seem so shocking, not now you've got used to it. Does it?'

'No, no it doesn't.' She drank her coffee, annoyed with herself for overreacting.

He must think her some dry as academic who'd never had sex and wanted to go to her grave untouched and unsullied. She'd had boyfriends, of course she had, fellow students and, latterly, fellow academics. But none of them had made her want to set her ambitions aside for domesticity, babies and all that entailed. She wanted to conquer the world, and if she had a man at her side, she would be his equal, not his slave.

Keir stretched his long legs out in front of him and gazed at the flames through the wood burner's glass doors. It was all very relaxed and companionable and she felt rather foolish for implying earlier in the kitchen that he was about to jump her bones. She'd lay even money that Keir MacKenzie had never coerced any woman into his bed, and the reverse was nearer the mark.

After a while he spoke. 'Maddie Hallam, was she excited by your find?'

'Very. She thought it might help to—' She paused.

'Help to?'

Outside, rain threw itself at the window, the wind strengthened, the light faded and an early October dusk descended on the Beach House. It felt safe and warm in the room, cocooned from the elements and the world beyond. Encouraged, Henri took a deep breath and told him everything about the scrap of manuscript she'd discovered, foolishly trusting the Dean, the damage she'd wrought to his television. How everyone at the university now thought she was psycho.

'Bruar-the-bunny-boiler,' she added, glumly. 'Rather trips off the tongue, doesn't it?'

He sipped his whisky and then replied, 'Who wouldn't have done the same in the circumstances? And you're hoping that the *MacKenzie Papers* might help restore the balance?'

'Exactly.'

'Which would be—what?' He looked at her for clarification.

'That they make good on their promise of junior lectureship which was on the cards before this happened.'

'I see. But why would you want to be part of an establishment where your word counts for so little?' Finishing his whisky, he put the glass on the granite hearth. Henri took a deep breath and explained.

'You have to understand the pecking order in a university department. Hierarchy, tenure, the latest piece of ground-breaking research, a change in historical interpretation backed up by primary sources—those things matter. The wheeling and dealing that goes on behind the scenes in a university department makes *Game of Thrones* look like *The Archers*.' She managed a weak joke.

'You don't have to explain the concept of hierarchy to the son of a Highland laird.'

'I suppose not.'

'And that's what you want for yourself?'

'More than anything.' However, even as she said it, a little worm of doubt wriggled in her brain. 'I mean—don't get me wrong; I've loved my time here. The castle's provided a bolt hole, a Highland hideaway, if you like; but it's time for me to hand everything over to the experts. I need to go home.' Her voice quavered as she said *home*, making her wonder if she was as ready to leave Castle Tèarmannair as she made out.

'Where is home?' Keir asked.

'Where the heart is,' she quipped, deflecting his interest. He smiled but wasn't letting her off the hook that easily; he nodded, encouraging her to elaborate.

'My parents' home in Switzerland, I have my own small annexe there and come and go as I please. They work long hours so I have to amuse myself. But that's okay, I'm used to it. During the long summer holidays from boarding school they'd enrol me into mind-improving or athletically challenging summer camps. I used to *long* for a holiday on the beach, like other families. But their work was too important for them to take more than a long weekend away from the lab. If I'm driven and single-minded, it's down to them.' She laughed, but looking back at her childhood and adolescence she realised that she'd missed out on the simpler things in life.

'I'm guessing that you don't commute from Switzerland every day,' he joked. 'Do you live on the university campus?'

'Yes; I have grace-and-favour accommodation in return for mentoring post-grads studying for their Master's. Very plain, ultra-modern and utilitarian, nothing like Castle Tèarmannair.' Feeling she'd talked enough about herself, she asked a direct question. 'So, how about you? Where is *your* home? It's plain that you can't bear to live in the castle; and how do you come to be at loggerheads with your father?'

Keir fed the wood burner to give himself time to consider his response. 'What has Alice told you?'

'How she and her sister came to work in the local café, how your mother met Sir Malcolm and they married. That your mother and brother drowned. But she didn't tell me anything about the accident, saying that was down to you …'

Keir looked so bleak that Henri wished she'd never brought up the subject. But there was no going back so she sat quietly and waited for him to begin.

'It was the morning of my sixth birthday and, along with my brother, I'd been pestering Mother, Father, Lachlan—anyone who would listen—to take me out onto the loch, so we could look for MacKenzie's Gold.'

'MacKenzie's Gold?'

'A cache of arms and chests of gold allegedly shipped over from Spain to finance the 1719 Jacobite rebellion. According to legend, some rowing boats split off from the main armada, sailed up the loch at dead of night, unloaded the so-called treasure and hid it one of the caves. The rebellion was quickly quashed at the Battle of Glen Shiel and . . . well, you're a historian, you know the rest. My ancestor was arrested, his estates sequestered and he narrowly missed losing his head, thanks to the Grieveses' intervention.'

'I'm guessing from your tone that you believe the Grieveses might have betrayed your ancestor and had ulterior motives for saving him from the block?'

'They gained access to the castle and our title through marriage to my ancestor.' The thought that Ciorstaidh was out to make sure history repeated itself hung in the air between them. 'The rebellion was over so quickly that the Spanish gold and cache of arms were never put to good use. The men responsible for hiding it, so the story goes, were either killed at the battle, hanged as traitors or sent to the West Indies as indentured servants.'

'Slaves, in other words,' she said, almost to herself.

'Exactly. As a child, Malchy and I were intrigued by the idea of treasure—what child isn't? Mother finally caved, agreeing to spend the morning of my sixth birthday on the loch, with Malchy and me. We were to have a *brief look*, she'd said, because there was my birthday party organised for the afternoon—and she had lots to do.'

'Go on,' she prompted.

'The plan was to anchor off-shore, take a small dinghy over to one of the beaches, have a picnic and then explore every cave and inlet we could find. It was a fine summer's day when we set out, but . . .'

Henri could see where this was going, but held her peace.

'. . . a summer squall blew up. On the way back to the boat, the dinghy was flipped over by a freak wave and we were thrown into the loch. I was the only one wearing a life jacket.' He rubbed a weary hand over his eyes. 'I know; I know. Stupid. Foolish. Reprehensible. However, thirty years ago people weren't so aware of health and safety. Nowadays there would be risk assessment forms to complete in triplicate before we set out. So, under-prepared, and without another adult to help her, Mother sailed up the loch without checking we'd got enough life jackets on board.'

'No-oh,' Henri managed to breathe out, her hand covering her mouth.

'I remember the water closing over my head, choking for breath, being dragged down as my wellingtons filled up. Mother and Malchy were trying to swim to the boat because the dinghy had been whisked out of reach by the wind. If they'd reached the dinghy, the outcome would have been different.' His voice faltered and he was no longer in the room, he was out in the middle of the loch, six years old and fighting for his life. 'The last I saw of them, they were trying to kick themselves free of their wellingtons and swim for the shore. In quiet moments, I can still hear my mother calling out: Keir . . . *Keir!*'

The only sound in the room was the hissing of the logs as they burned and the rain battering at the windows. And then a sob, as Henri thought of how much he'd suffered that day, and subsequently. Instinctively, she longed to cross the space between them, put her arms around him and tell him it would all be okay. Instead, she knelt at his feet and put one hand on his knee, not caring if her touch was unwelcome, too intimate. She wanted to show compassion and this was the only way she knew how.

'When my father found out that we were out on the loch, alone, he sent Lachlan after us. He found the boat, but no sign of the dinghy—'

'Oh, no . . .'

'He fished me out of the loch, unconscious. Malchy and Mother had disappeared without a trace.' His voice trailed off and he rolled the whisky tumbler round in his hands, staring down deep into the amber liquid as though it was the peaty waters of the loch.

'Did—did they find them?' Henri dragged him out of his dream by squeezing his knee gently, urging him to finish the story.

'A few days later, yes. Washed up along the beach, not far from here. They're buried in the village churchyard.' He drank deeply from his glass and then cradled the empty tumbler in his hands until Henri removed it. 'My father—' He faltered.

'Yes?'

'Blamed me. Said I'd badgered Mother into taking us out.'

'You were a *child* for God's sake,' she interjected, but Keir wasn't listening.

'Said he'd rather I'd been the one who'd drowned, that Malchy had survived. He was the heir, I was the spare. Oh, I don't blame him, he was half-mad with grief. After that, he kinda lost the plot. I was parcelled off to boarding school as soon as I was old enough and he set about systematically running the estate into the ground. Almost as if it was his way of punishing me—for what I'd done. As far as he was concerned, with Malcolm and Mother gone, there was no point in preserving the estate, let alone passing it on to me. He wanted to be the last MacKenzie to live in Tèarmannair.' Shrugging away the guilt and pain, he shuffled around in his chair but didn't shake off her hand. 'After a couple of miserable terms, I refused to go back to boarding school—so Alice, lovely Auntie Alice, was shipped in from Motherwell to act as surrogate mother, chief cook, bottle washer and castle chatelaine. Until I was old enough to give boarding a second try.' He smiled at that, raised his head and looked at her, his eyes desolate. 'Know what the worst part is?'

'No,' she whispered.

'I can't really remember what Mother looked like. Father had every photograph of her and Malchy taken down when they died, as though he couldn't bear to be reminded of what he'd lost.'

Henri was indignant on his behalf.

'How about what *you'd* lost? Mother, brother *and* father—' Up until then, she'd thought of Sir Malcolm as a harmless, penniless landowner, trying to relive his youth. Now she saw there was a darker purpose behind his eccentricities, a cruelty. He was denying Keir his birth right as a punishment for those two deaths. She wasn't sure if she'd be able to exchange a civil word next time they met. Keir looked down at her hand on his knee as though seeing it for the first time. His put his hand over hers and kept it there. Henri felt there was more to learn so she squeezed his fingers encouragingly.

'What do you remember of your mother?'

'Nothing tangible; just a *feeling* of her. When I was tiny, she used to hold me in the crook of her arm, wrap us in a tartan shawl and knot it over her hip, as her mother and grandmother had done before her. Then she'd sing to me, nonsensical, crooning songs . . . I remember her smell; her hair brushing my face.' He smiled sombrely, remembering. 'At night, she'd sit me on her knee and Malchy would sit on Father's, and she'd read to us or tell us stories she'd made up about Jacobites and treasure and . . . remind us to always be proud of our lineage. Both as Highlanders and as the descendants of men and women who'd worked hard to earn their living.' He reached down for the whisky and topped up his glass. 'Then it was gone, and I was alone—until Alice came to stay.'

'Keir, I'm so sorry . . .' Her voice caught in her throat and tears filled her eyes at what he'd suffered. What they'd all suffered. Sir Malcolm, widowed; Alice, dedicating her life to bringing up her nephew; even old Lachlan, fishing Mary and Malcolm's bodies out of the loch. A single tear rolled down her cheek.

Keir brushed it away with the underside of his thumb. 'Och, dinnae fash yersel' lassie,' he said in a broad Scots accent to make her smile and to break the mood. 'It all happened a long time ago, it's water under the bridge—sorry, bad choice of words. But now you know why I can't bear to be in the castle while *he's* there. Why I can't stay and watch the last of my inheritance going 'doon the stank', as Alice would put it.'

Any residual guilt she'd felt at removing the *MacKenzie Papers* from the castle without Sir Malcolm's knowledge, vanished. She vowed, on her knees, to do her everything in her power to preserve what was left of Keir's inheritance. Then she was struck by the realisation that he'd listened patiently to her story about smashing up the Dean's television and the internecine squabbles of a university faculty. She groaned, and then covered her face with her hands to hide her shame.

'What's this about?' he asked, leaning forward and removing her hands so he could see her face.

'You must think me a self-obsessed idiot. I'm so sorry for inflicting my *pathetic* story on you.'

'Hey—now we know where we're both coming from. If we're to be partners in crime, that's important.' Henri nodded, pushed herself up from her kneeling position and sat back in her chair.

'You know, I think I will have that drink after all.' He fetched another glass and poured her a thimbleful of uisge beatha.

'*Slainte Mhath*, partner.'

'*Slainte*,' she toasted back. Emboldened by the whisky, she asked one last question. 'And the treasure? What became of that?'

'No one has ever found it. Hardly surprising, as I think it only exists in legend . . .'

Once, Henriette had thought of herself as a cross between Indiana Jones and the Relic Hunter. The notion of a lost treasure awakened that half-forgotten dream. 'What would you do if you found the treasure?'

'I'd rebuild the castle, restore the estate to its former glory and bring employment to my tenants. I'd replant the timber plantations, diversify—have weddings at the castle, guided tours, anything which brought in people with money to spend. Pass something down to future generations of MacKenzies, in memory of Mother and Malchy.'

Now that she knew the full story, Henri forgot all her qualms about spending the night in the Beach House. She nodded and when he leaned over to top up her glass, she didn't protest but sank lower into the comfortable armchair and prepared to sit out the storm with him.

Chapter Nineteen
An Unwise Decision

The next morning Henri awoke to find Keir kneeling in front of the wood burner, nursing it back to life. Last night, he'd insisted in making a bed up for her on the large sofa, declaring he'd sleep in one of the upstairs bedrooms. Too late—just as she was drifting off to sleep, Henri remembered him mentioning there was no central heating in the Beach House and that *he* usually slept on the sofa. He'd laid open his heart, and she'd stolen his bed! However, after drawing up the terms of their newly founded partnership over several more glasses of uisge beatha, Henri had thought it unwise to invite him downstairs to spend the night in the armchair.

Mixed messages and all that.

Instead, she'd said nothing—reminding herself that, according to Keir, *Argyll was almost tropical compared to British Columbia.* Not that she believed him for one second. Guilt at stealing his 'bed' resulted in her spending the night tossing and turning on the sofa, thumping a rather lumpy pillow into shape. If sleep eluded her, it was simply a result of sleeping in an unfamiliar bunk. It had nothing to do with the image of them huddled together for warmth in a cold, unaired bed upstairs as he'd jokingly suggested in the kitchen.

An image she couldn't get out of her head once it had taken up residence.

'You do that a lot, don't you?' He'd stopped riddling the ashes of the wood burner and regarded her quizzically over his shoulder whilst hunkered down in front of the log basket.

'Do what?'

'Zone out; stare into space; daydream.'

'Sometimes, daydreams are all we have,' she said, simply. 'I warned you, back on the boat that I was a romantic.'

'True.' He turned round, threw a firelighter and some dry logs onto the smouldering remains of last night's fire and coaxed it into life. 'You forget to mention *how* romantic, however.'

'I'll ignore that.' She seized the opportunity of his back being towards her, to get dressed. By the time he turned round again, she had stripped the sofa and the bedclothes were neatly folded on a wooden captain's chair next to the roll-top bureau. 'I'll take these over to the castle and have them washed.'

He was on his feet and laid a hand on her arm. 'No need. You only slept in them one night and, besides . . .' She suspected he was about to say something chivalrous and probably wholly inappropriate about her leaving a trail of her scent on the covers, because he stopped himself. 'Breakfast,' he substituted. Walking past her, he pulled the heavy curtains open and let in the daylight.

Henri rushed over to the window to look out. The storm had washed everything clean and a bright blue sky, criss-crossed by vapour trails, heralded a fine late-autumn morning. The gloriousness of the view was further enhanced by the deciduous trees which fringed the margins of the loch shedding burnt ochre leaves in the reflecting pool of the water. Henri sighed, part of her wanted to return to the library and finish her task, but she also longed to stay in the Beach House and savour its air of tranquillity a little longer.

Making her choice, she headed for the kitchen.

'Breakfast,' she agreed. 'But this time, I do the cooking and you can go and—oh, I don't know—do something *manly*, until it's ready.' She smiled, to show she was teasing.

'I see you're in a provocative mood this morning, Doctor Bruar. I suspect that's because you had a better night's sleep than I did.' He followed her across the hall and into the kitchen which, thanks to the Aga, was warm as toast. Henri wondered if it'd simply been the cold which had disturbed his night or if he'd shared her crazy thoughts . . . the cold linen sheets slowly reaching blood heat from their entwined limbs, their breaths mingling in the cold air, the eiderdown becoming too heavy and restrictive when they became warm enough to . . .

'Sorry? What did you say?'

'I said, I like my eggs sunny side up, two rashers of bacon, fried tinned tomatoes, toast with marmalade and strong, black coffee.' He sat on a straight-backed Windsor chair by the Aga, shook out yesterday's newspaper and started to read.

'I don't class *that* as manly activity,' Henri protested, indicating the newspaper.

'Au contraire, Doctor Bruar, it is very fitting that a man read the paper while his—while the lady of the house makes breakfast.' Henri suspected that he'd about to say, *wife,* but checked himself.

'Indeed? *Now,* who's being provocative? Very well.' She pretended to be annoyed at his presumption. 'But if you think for one moment I'm wrestling with that coffee machine which is straight out of the *Ark*. Think again.'

'You make the breakfast and I'll lay the table—and make the coffee. Deal?'

'Deal,' she laughed, suddenly very light-hearted. She knew this was just an interlude, a step away from the problems confronting her, but it felt good to be in the Beach House with Keir MacKenzie on this glorious morning, when the castle and all the unhappy memories associated with it seemed miles away.

After breakfast, Keir refused to let Henri load the dishwasher. Instead, piling the dirty dishes in the sink, he opened the back door and seemed in a hurry to leave. Disappointed, Henri put on her coat and wrapped her pashmina around her neck and over her ears. She was in no hurry; there were things she needed to discuss further with him and she would have liked an opportunity to use the internet for a half an hour.

Leaving via the back porch she turned left to head for the jetty.

'This way,' Keir said, putting his hand in the small of her back and steering her in the opposite direction.

'Aren't we going back to the castle?'

Keir shook his head. 'Not immediately. There's something I want to show you; people I want you to meet.'

'O-kay,' Henri drew out the syllables, wondering what he had in mind. Keir never did anything without a reason, without considering the effect of his actions. That much she knew of him.

Taking her by the hand, he led her through a small plantation of Scots Pine and up a steep slope, finally coming to rest on a flat, concrete space where a Land Rover was parked. He opened the door and Henri climbed in, enjoying the air of mystery attached to their journey. Soon they were out on the main road and driving along with the loch on their right hand side. Sitting beside Keir in the close confines of the old Land Rover was deliciously intimate. She liked the way his thigh muscles flexed and contracted as he changed into a lower gear or braked, the way his arm brushed against hers as he steered round the steep bends, or slowed down to avoid sheep cropping grass on the road side.

Henri spotted one of the *beware of feral goats* signs.

'Did you know that feral goats in Scotland were protected by an act passed by The Bruce, himself? I read about it in a guide book I found in the library. '

'I thought they'd escaped from the circus, or something else completely ludicrous,' he laughed. 'Sorry, Doctor Bruar—do tell me more.'

'He was being hunted by soldiers and hid in a cave, a herd of goats arrived and started grazing by the mouth of the cave. When the soldiers arrived, The Bruce heard them discussing whether or not it was worth searching the cave for him. One of them proclaimed that if there was anyone in there, the goats wouldn't have hung around, so they continued their search elsewhere. The Bruce, on gaining power, forbade anyone to harm the wild goats.'

Keir laughed. 'If history is correct, he spent more time in caves with spiders and goats than he did ruling the country.'

'Do you doubt the veracity of my research?' Henri pretended affront.

'I wouldn't dare!'

Before long, they pulled into an open-all-hours store with petrol pumps, café and post office. The signage, in English and Gaelic, informed that it also offered free internet and sold coal, logs and peat briquettes from its forecourt.

'Come on,' Keir smiled at her. 'I need milk and flowers.'

Flowers for whom, Henri wondered?

Jumping down from the Land Rover, she followed Keir into the store. Everyone seemed pleased to see him and greeted him like a long lost friend. He shook hands with staff and customers, permitted elderly ladies to kiss him on the cheek and make a fuss over him. It amused Henri to see him being treated like royalty which, she supposed, he was in their eyes. She was less amused when *she* became the centre of attention and Keir drew her forward, introducing her as Doctor Bruar, academic and historian. Her fame appeared to have preceded her, for they all knew about her dismantling the library—they sent Keir a sympathetic look—and that she'd been helping Alice to get ready for the Samhain celebrations. If she hadn't returned to England by then.

She exchanged a brief, wry look with Keir. No guessing where they got their information from! Lachlan. She'd learned from Alice that the old grouch spent most of his time in the café located at the back of the shop, drinking lattes, spreading gossip and complaining about life in general, instead of doing any real work. That is, when he wasn't ferrying the laird between Castle Tèarmannair and the shore. What Lachlan couldn't tell them about the goings-on in the castle, Young Lachy was able to provide when he fetched the papers each morning. Happily filling in the gaps regarding Doctor Bruar, the Master of Mountgarrie, and if the laird was up to his 'old tricks'.

'Ye'll be sad to return to England, I'm after thinking,' one elderly customer smiled at Henri. This encouraged the others to add their two pennyworth, in rapid Gaelic, which she couldn't follow. She was surprised when Keir joined in the conversation, speaking Gaelic, too. How little she knew about him and his culture—and how little time she had left to find out.

'Very sad,' she replied, speaking from her heart and not from a desire to curry favour with them. 'Will you excuse me? I have to . . .'

There was a small section at the back of the store where guide books, teach yourself Gaelic pamphlets and gifts could be purchased. There was also a computer connected to the internet designated for community use. Henri used the excuse of using the internet to escape the friendly inquisition, fielding a few final questions as she segued towards the rack of postcards. As she thumbed through the postcards, she smiled inwardly; if only she'd thought to venture across the water to the store, she'd have learned everything she needed to know about the family.

'Ready?' Keir appeared at her elbow with a couple of pints of milk, packets of biscuits and a tired-looking bouquet of flowers.

'Just let me pay for these and I'm good to go.' She walked over to the counter with her purchases, including a slim pamphlet—*Teach Yourself Everyday Gaelic Phrases*. She might not have time to master more than *Good Morning* and *Thank you* before she left, but she felt it was worth making the effort. Once back in the Land Rover, it was onwards and downhill towards the village of MacKenzie and the station at MacKenzie's Halt where her adventure had begun. After indicating left, Keir swung the Land Rover across the road and parked in a layby which offered a wonderful view of the loch, Castle Tèarmannair and the mountains beyond.

Neither of them spoke as they looked down on the granite-grey castle, sitting on its grass covered island in the middle of the loch; proud of its history and as immovable as the mountains around it. It had guarded the land and its people against Viking invaders, now it was down to Henri and Keir to save it, if they could.

'I love this place with all my heart and being,' Keir declared passionately after a few moments, as if reading her mind. 'I'll do everything in my power to keep Father from destroying it.' He gripped the steering wheel so tightly that his knuckles turned white.

Henri wondered if that included marrying Ciorstaidh MacKenzie-Grieves.

Ciorstaidh becoming Lady MacKenzie and future chatelaine of Castle Tèarmannair would solve their financial problems in an instant. Goose bumps pricked her skin and her stomach churned at the thought of Keir sacrificing himself to save the castle. Then her analytical mind, born of years of reading and interpreting statistics and primary source material, kicked in. Marrying for love was a very recent concept in the circles Keir moved in. Him speaking Gaelic and the reception he'd received in the store really brought home to her just *who* he was and the responsibilities he carried on his shoulders. He might have been born as the *spare*, but he was definitely regarded by all who knew him as the *heir*.

Having got that straight in her mind, she glanced over at him, but he was deep in thought and staring moodily at the castle. He made her think of a poem she'd learned at school, Keats's *La Belle Dame Sans Merci*.

Oh what can ail thee knight at arms,
Alone and palely loitering?
The sedge has withered from the lake
And no birds sing.

Now she understood why he often looked burdened with sorrow and responsibilities. She suspected that, when he really was at low ebb, he actually believed he was responsible for his mother and brother's death. Emboldened by the fact that they were getting on so well, she leaned across and squeezed his arm. Her touch drew Keir back to the present, reminding him that he wasn't alone; he had a friend, if he ever needed one.

Apparently appreciating the gesture, he put his hand on top of hers, turned his head and smiled. As their eyes met and his moved lower and stayed on her lips, something short-circuited in Henri's heart. However, even as she returned his smile, she reminded herself that forming an attachment to Keir MacKenzie was ill-advised, given the state of her life at that moment. When he appeared in no hurry to remove his hand, she repeated her father's pet saying, 'Onwards and upwards,' and moved hers.

Keir turned over the ignition, slipped the car into gear and headed on down the hill, leaving Henri to look over her shoulder until the castle disappeared round the bend in the road.

After some time, Keir pulled up in front of imposing wrought iron gates, supported by two columns surmounted by carved stags. 'Oh my God, it's Skyfall!' Henri quipped, trying to lighten the heavy mood which had settled on them, following her breaking physical contact with him.

Keir laughed at her reference to James Bond's Highland home. 'They think so. It's the Glen Shiel House, the MacKenzie-Grieveses' residence. They practically live on our doorstep. The loch protects us from them, much as the Channel has protected England from invasion for the last thousand years.'

Now it was Henri's turn to smile. 'You can't see much from the road.'

'Let's keep it like that, shall we? The house is the usual mix of Scottish baronial—granite, whitewashed walls, turrets and stepped gables. They do have a long, tree-lined drive, which we cannot boast of.'

'Peacocks on the lawn?'

'I'm afraid so.'

'Don't be too cast down, you have Lachlan.' Keir let out another bark of laughter and they exchanged a look of empathy regarding the laird's faithful retainer. Having lightened the mood, Henri continued. 'Sounds a bit . . . tame and domestic to me; gimme a castle every time.'

'With rising damp, no internet, a leaking roof and chain-rattling ghost?'

'Wait. There's a chain-rattling ghost—how did I miss that?'

'I might have made up that last part,' he slanted her a flirty, sideways look, encouraging her to continue the nonsensical conversation.

'Might?'

'Okay—*did*!'

'Mind you.' Now it was Henri's turn to look pensive. 'I have thought . . . upon occasion . . . that —no, I can't tell you. It's too fanciful.'

'Now *I'm* intrigued. Go on.'

'I thought . . . several times, I've heard a piper playing a lament. Once, on the train out of Fort William, then in the library—and also the day I discovered the *MacKenzie Papers*,' she declared in a rush. Then she waved the thought away as if it was too absurd.

Keir's unblinking regard made cold fingers trail along the archipelago of her spine. He didn't appear fazed or surprised by her revelation, in fact he looked as if was seeing everything more clearly. He'd been born and bred in a land shrouded by mist, old legends, and thousands of years of remembered history, and lived in a castle in the middle of a loch supposedly inhabited by a water horse. Of course he believed in other-worldly things: buried treasure, ghostly ancestors and phantom pipers.

'I see, then, you . . .' Plainly, he wanted to say more but in the end decided to hold his peace. Maybe he didn't want to frighten her?

To restore everything to normal, Henri said with a kind of desperate jollity, 'Here's where my adventure began.' She pointed towards the sign: Station —MacKenzie's Halt.

And, here's where it will end, she thought, hiding her dismay.

'Come on, I have something to show you.' Keir parked in front of the station, retrieved the flowers from the back seat, climbed out of the vehicle and waited for her to join him. Skirting the station, they went through a small gate and turned sharp left. Soon they came upon a whitewashed kirk where Keir walked up to a polished granite headstone and stood before it. Handing Henri the bouquet, he picked up a vase of dying flowers by the headstone, took it over to a compost heap and threw the flowers away. Walking over to a standpipe he rinsed out the vase and filled it with fresh water before returning to the graveside.

Obviously not caring if he got his trousers muddy, he knelt by the grave and held out his hand for Henri to pass each bloom to him. Watching him placing the flowers on his mother's grave with exaggerated care affected Henri deeply. She blinked away the tears and swallowed hard to stop a sob escaping from her raw, tight throat. Overwhelmed by the need to lay her hand on his bowed, dark head and tell him everything was going to work out, she resisted the urge and stuck her hands in her pockets instead.

'I always visit when I'm home. In between times, Alice and—despite everything we've said about him—Lachlan, keep the flowers fresh.'

'Sir Malcolm?'

'What do you think?' he asked, his voice bitter.

Henri read the inscription on the headstone.

Mary, Lady MacKenzie and Maol Choluim MacKenzie—Master of Mountgarrie

Henri was so used to thinking of Keir as the Master of Mountgarrie that it came as a shock to realise that he'd inherited the courtesy title on his brother's death.

Keir screwed up the cellophane and coloured paper which had wrapped the flowers. 'Know how to kill the mood, stone dead, don't I?' he asked, but his eyes asked for her understanding.

Henri was quick to give it.

'Now I know everything. Thank you.' Walking over to a rose bush which had a few blooms as yet untouched by the early autumn frosts, she twisted off a few stems and put them on the grass in front of the headstone. Keir touched the headstone, tracing his fingers over the gold lettering, his face sombre. Seemingly, he'd spent the last thirty years trying to make sense of his mother and brother's tragic deaths, the fact that they lay in the cold earth, under his feet; so close, yet so far away. And, if his father's distorted view of the tragedy was to be believed, he'd put them there. Henri felt his pain, the rawness of it—even after all these years. She twined her fingers through his and gave his hand a supportive squeeze.

'We'd better get back or Alice will send out a search party.'

'Agreed.'

Walking side by side up the narrow path, still holding hands, Keir on the grass and Henri on the gravel path, they left the graveyard and climbed into the Land Rover in thoughtful mood.

Chapter Twenty
How Very Dare You?

Henri leaned back against the deck rail as the Beach House disappeared from view round the curve of the loch. She was glad she had the 'excuse' of the MacKenzie Papers and the pretext of using the house's internet connection to return, and didn't need to wait for Keir's invitation. Glancing at him as he steered the boat into deeper water, she sensed that the sombre mood hadn't left him. She felt privileged that he'd taken her to the family grave and hoped it was because he wanted her to understand him better. It was also, she conjectured, his way of explaining how he felt towards his father, the castle, Alice—and yes, even Lachlan.

'You know, I've really enjoyed having company at the Beach House; your company,' he said, breaking into her reverie. 'Most of the time, here or at my cousin's place in BC, I live a solitary life. I spend too much time thinking, brooding over the past. It isn't healthy. I'd almost forgotten how it feels to live in the moment, to share food, wine and laughter with another human being. No, strike that—to share my house and my food with an intelligent woman. And to answer Sandy M-G's impertinent question from lunch the other week: yes; I do find clever women a *turn on*, as it happens.'

That made Henri blush and come over all unnecessary. 'Why, thank you, kind sir,' she curtseyed, making light of his remark.

'No, *thank you*, Henri. For dragging me out of my introspection—and for reminding me that there's a world out there and I should take a greater part in it.'

Henri mumbled something along the lines of, 'It's my pleasure.' Maintaining a neutral expression, she concealed that she was secretly pleased he valued her intelligence above her physical attributes. Too often people saw no further than her height, long blonde hair and vivid green eyes and completely glossed over her academic qualities and capabilities.

The Dean for one.

Shaking her head, she took Keir's lead and stopped brooding over what couldn't be changed.

'I hear that old Lachlan threatened to feed you to the water horse the first time he took you over to the castle?' Keir changed the subject.

'The first and only time,' Henri corrected. 'I wouldn't get in the dinghy with him again for love nor money. He was quite vile.' Then she added, hoping she didn't offend Keir, 'He is a horrible old man.' There, she'd said it. 'What's the connection between him and your father? I can almost imagine him sleeping across the across the laird's door, sgain-dubh in his hand to make sure that none disturb him.'

'That would probably have been true in the olden days, for Lachlan *is* the laird's man.' There was a pause, which hinted there was a good reason for Lachlan's devotion.

'You can't stop there! You have to tell me the whole story.'

'Very well, Lachlan's version is that he was arrested, charged and put away in the Bar-L for parking on double yellow lines.'

'The Bar-L?'

'Her Majesty's Prison, Barlinnie. Or, as it's often described—*the big hoose in the east end.*'

'East end of —?'

'Glasgow. It's a maximum security prison.'

'Oh.' A slight pause as she marshalled the facts in order. 'And Lachlan was put in there for parking on double yellow lines?'

'I told you that was *Lachlan's* version of the story.' Keir was clearly teasing her and drew out the explanation.

'And the official version?'

'He *was* parked on double yellow lines—outside a bank in Sauchiehall Street in a getaway car with the engine running, while his cousins—Glasgow *keelies*, to a man—were inside robbing the bank. He was having a wee holiday at the time and staying with them in Springburn. When they asked him to drive them into Glasgow, as a favour, he had no idea what he was letting himself in for.'

Henri remembered something Alice had said. 'When the old bugger's in a good mood, which might be never, ask him to tell you about how handy he is with a twelve-bore; the sawn-off variety.'

'He was sent down, then?'

'This was in 1970. He was charged under the Firearms Act of 1968 with *possession of firearm with intent to endanger life*—which carried a life sentence. Father hired a QC to defend Lachlan and his offence was commuted to *shortening a shotgun; conversion of a firearm*. He got ten years in the Bar-L alongside his cousins, who got a much longer sentence. At the end of it, Father fetched him home and here he has remained ever since.'

'When did all this take place?'

'He was released in 1978, when he was thirty-five years old.'

'Did your father fight his corner because he's a MacKenzie? Clan loyalty and so on?'

'Partly, but also because we're second cousins, twice removed—or something like that. The links between Highland families are labyrinthine, to say the least.'

Which also meant he was related to the MacKenzie-Grieveses. Henri supressed a smile. She'd bet anything that Ciorstaidh only shared *that* little pearl on a need to know basis. She felt a pang of sympathy for Lachlan MacKenzie, and the laird was partly restored in her good graces for remaining loyal to the old villain.

'Can I ask another question? Why is your boat called *The Saucy Nancy*? I thought she would have been named after some Scottish Hero—Rob Roy, Lochinvar, The Wallace, or The Bruce.'

'The name was my mother's idea. She said that sailing to the Beach House for picnics in *The Saucy Nancy* reminded her of the holidays she'd taken as a child 'doon the watter' with her family in Largs, Ayr and Dunoon. Father bought her the boat as a wedding present and Lachlan taught her to sail. Father believed that if you lived on a loch you should learn to sail on it. Although he's never said as much, I know he believes that if he'd never given her the boat, she and Malchy would still be alive.'

There was no answering that, so Henri gave out a heavy sigh instead.

'I wish that every time one met new people, someone would hand out a crib sheet, bringing one up to speed on their history. It would avoid pitfalls and unintentional gaffes.'

'You mean, as in—*new readers start here?*'

'Exactly that.'

'But then, it would take the fun out of. And I wouldn't have the pleasure of telling you family history—' he pulled a face.

'—and you'd miss hearing, first hand, what a total cock-up I've made of my career.' Henri tried to keep her tone light but her voice broke in spite of her attempt to remain upbeat. 'I just hope that . . .' Her next words were lost as two fighter jets shot across *The Saucy Nancy's* bow and then disappeared as suddenly as they had appeared, leaving noise and confusion in their wake. 'Holy fuck,' Henri exclaimed, jumping out of her skin and straight into Keir's arms at the unexpectedness of it. Her legs were shaking, her nerves shot to pieces and she could feel her breast bone reverberating from the noise of the engines. Instinctively, she buried her face in Keir's shoulder, clutching at his Arran sweater to steady herself until her breathing returned to normal.

Laughing, Keir put one arm round her, pulling her into his side. The smell of warm, slightly damp wool and his rubbery life-jacket filled Henri's nostrils as he steered the boat with his free hand. He smelled so uniquely *Keir;* so reassuringly strong and dependable that Henri was reluctant to leave the safety of his arms.

'I meant to warn you that this part of Scotland is classed as a TTA.'

'Which means?' she asked, her voice muffled by his Arran.

'A Tactical Training Area. The jets are permitted to fly as low as a hundred feet along this corridor. They use Castle Tèarmannair as a marker; in the summer, it's fun to sit on the battlements with a couple of beers and watch them coming up the loch towards you. As if they're on a bombing run. There'll be another along in a few minutes, so brace yourself.' Raising her head off his shoulder she looked up at him, her limbs still shaking. 'Seriously, are you okay?' He put his hand under her chin, tilting her face upwards so he could read her expression.

'Just about—'

'Poor Henri. Now I feel really bad . . . taking you to see my family's grave and then scaring the bejeezus out of you. If this was a first date, I doubt there'd be a second.'

'Oh, I don't know . . .'

Now her limbs were trembling because of the way he held her, looked at her. She tried to convey how she felt about him without using actual words. Keir glanced down at her and frowned, as if wanting to make sure he was reading her correctly. Deciding it was one of those times when actions did speak louder than words, Henri raised her hand and traced the line of his jaw. Now it was his turn to shudder, to experience those feelings which rocked Henri to her core. To know how it felt when your knees crumpled under your weight because your bones had turned to water. Then he smiled, and the sombre mood which had hung over them since visiting the grave, vanished. Wordlessly he released her, and then spun her through one hundred and eighty degrees until she was facing the wheel house. Without speaking, he spread her arms wide along the roof of the wheel house and prised her legs open with his knees.

'Wh—what are you doing?' she asked, half-laughing, half-frightened by his intentions.

'You'll see, lady.' Laughing, he frisked her as professionally as an undercover cop. 'I'm checking that you aren't carrying your hockey stick. I don't want to suffer the same fate as the Dean's television.' Turning her round, he sent her a look which turned her insides molten. The light in his eyes reflected the blue waters of the loch and the clear sky above, drawing colour from both.

She had to say something, anything, before she lost the power of speech.

'H-hockey stick?' Ignoring her question, he raised her chin a little higher and then lowered his head towards her.

'I've been wanting to kiss you, all morning. And most of last night, too. Hell, I've wanted to kiss you since you set foot on the *Nancy*.' Placing his hand in the hollow of her back, he drew her to him. His kiss was warm and sweet against her cold lips and her stomach turned cartwheels at the unfamiliarity of the sensation. Then, contravening every health and safety rule governing the sailing of boats in open water, Keir took his hands off the wheel, his eye off the course and deepened the kiss.

With a groan of longing, Henri grabbed his Arran sweater and pulled his head closer. When his tongue gently pushed her lips open, and he whispered something in Gaelic against her lips, Henri was lost. Then, demonstrating commendable control and detachment he pulled away, and returned to steering the boat towards the castle which lay dead ahead.

Face burning, thinking that maybe she'd reacted—overacted?—a little rashly, Henri found her voice. 'You didn't learn to kiss like that in the backwoods of British Columbia.'

'And I'm guessing that you didn't learn to kiss like *that* in a university library, Dr Bruar.' He arched his eyebrow and Henri bit back a very unromantic snort of laughter. 'Now, hold yer wheesht wumman, and let me sail mah boat in peace, fur the love o' God.' Channelling Lachlan, Keir navigated up to Castle Tèarmannair's wooden jetty and moored up, alongside Lachlan's boat, the one which had transported Henri across the loch and brought her to this magical, otherworldly place.

When they burst into the kitchen, laughing and breathless from the exertion of climbing the stairs—stopping frequently to kiss, they found Alice and Lachlan in the middle of a full-blown argument.

'Ye durty wee clype!' Alice waved a wooden spoon at Lachlan, looking as if it would give her the greatest pleasure to beat him round the head with it.

'Shut up, old wumman, ye cannae tell *me* what to do. Only Himself can do that.' Lachlan was sitting in his favourite chair by the Aga, arms folded and sporting a mutinous expression. At least, as mutinous as he dared, in the face of Alice's fury.

'What's going on?' Keir inquired.

Slamming the spoon on the table, Alice addressed her nephew, hands on hips. 'This yin here,' she jerked a thumb over her shoulder at Lachlan, 'has been telling tales oot'a school. He's dobbed ye's in to Sir Malcolm.' Anger made her accent more pronounced and Henri had a job following what she was saying.

'Dobbed us in? You mean, Lachlan has told Father that Dr Bruar and I spent the night in the Beach House?' Now it was Keir's turn to glare at the hapless Lachlan who pulled his greasy cap further down over his ears in a vain attempt to shut them out.

'Pull yon awful, greasy bunnet down as far as ye like Lachlan MacKenzie, it'll make no difference, for Keir will make himself heard.'

'Why, Lachlan?' Keir asked.

'A castle is no place for a wee lassie. I told youse no good would come of it.' He sank lower in his chair to escape Keir's wrath, but found a few shreds of courage to defend his actions. 'Ah'm the laird's man. Mah furst duty is to Himself and the estate. Like it or lump it.' He pushed out his bottom lip, like a mutinous teenager—albeit one with hair sprouting out of ears and nostrils. Giving a final harrumph, he refused to concede that he'd done anything wrong.

'Oh, so, ye'r the *laird's man* are ye, Lachlan MacKenzie? And when, in the fullness of time, Keir becomes laird, will ye serve him, or sit greetin' by Himself's grave over in the churchyard, like Greyfriars-feckin'-Bobby? Ye deceitful wee baucle. Get oota ma sight—or I'll swing for ye. Scunner that you are.' At that point, she picked up a large kitchen knife off the table and looked as if she was about to fillet him.

Henri only caught one word in three but she could tell that Alice was disgusted by Lachlan's deceitful behaviour. Alice was Keir's auntie, being the laird's sister-in-law came a very poor second to that. Henri didn't quite get why Sir Malcolm's knowing that she and Keir had spent the night (innocently) together in the Beach House should present a problem. Measured against *his* reprehensible behaviour in the South of France, his son had behaved like a perfect gentleman. And, her lips reminded her, the kiss on the boat had been mutual, and no one other than a pilot flying at Mach speed had witnessed it.

'Ah was thinking o' the castle; o' the family,' Lachlan asserted with a noble air, once he was sure that Alice wasn't going to shish-kebab him. 'If Miss Mackenzie-Grieves finds out whit Keir and Dr Bruar have been up tae, she'll never marry him; without her money the castle will fall down round our ears and we'll all end our days in an old folks' home in Fort William.' For dramatic effect, he blew his nose into the disgusting-looking rag covered in engine oil which passed for his hanky.

Then for added effect, he examined the contents.

'*You* might,' Alice corrected him. 'But I have family in Motherwell who will gladly have me.'

Now Henri understood Lachlan's aversion to wee lassies in the castle, and her in particular. She was putting his plans for a comfortable old age in jeopardy by making Keir have second thoughts about a dynastic marriage to Ciorstaidh Mac-G.

'And whit makes *you* think Herself will have a disgusting old toe-rag like you at her table when her smart friends come visiting? Or, indeed, that Keir will lose all sense and marry her?'

Evidently deciding that the discussion was going off-piste, Keir moved Alice away from the knives and addressed Lachlan. 'Where is Father?'

'He's here!' Sir Malcolm answered, coming through from the direction of the library and Great Hall. 'Ah, I see the prodigals have returned. I'd like a word with you in my sitting room, Keir.'

'Would you, now? I think whatever you have to say, can just as easily be said here. As you may have gathered, the topic is already under discussion and all the interested parties are present.' At that, Keir scraped a chair away from the table and sat down.

'We don't want to discuss family matters in front of Dr Bruar.'

'Bit late to worry about that. Lachlan has already been pointing out the error of my ways—*our* ways.'

'At least he has some sense. What were you thinking of, spending the night alone with Henriette in the Beach House?'

'I hardly think that putting the boat out in last night's storm was a sensible course of action. Two drownings in a generation is quite enough, wouldn't you say?' The teasing light in his eyes disappeared and in its place was the dark melancholy which Henri had hoped had gone forever. But, clearly, it would take more than a few stolen kisses to sort out years of despair and his relationship with his father.

'If I might interject, Sir Malcolm,' she said coolly, although furious at Lachlan's meddling and the laird's cynical take on the matter. 'Nothing happened between us at the Beach House last night. I slept on the sofa and Keir in one of the bedrooms.' Sir Malcolm looked between Henri and Keir, and shook his head at what he evidently perceived to be a missed opportunity on Keir's part.

'That's not the point, Doctor Bruar. The fact is it *could* have. Who's going to believe that any man with red blood coursing through his veins would be able to spend the night in the same house as you, and *not* try it on?' Henri shuddered at the way he gave her the onceover. 'As Lachlan has pointed out, this could ruin Keir's chances with Ciorstaidh.'

'Humph,' Lachlan put in as an aside, the laird having justified his actions.

'I have no *chance* with Ciorstaidh. I want no chance with Ciorstaidh—now, or at any time in the future. Talking of which,' Keir glowered at his father, 'why didn't you marry her mother, as was arranged forty years ago? The MacKenzie-Grieveses would have got the title, the land and the castle and you could have burned your way through their money instead.'

'Fat chance of that happening. Her father and his lawyers had got it all sewn up. At best, all I would have received for my pains was a plain wife, and a monthly stipend which wouldn't have kept me wine, or petrol for the E-Type.'

'A prenup?' Henri said below her breath, but apparently the laird heard her.

'Yes; before they'd ever been invented. That lawyer was years ahead of his time.' Admiration for the canny lawyer crept into his voice.

'She's been widowed many a long year and her father's been pushing up the daisies in the kirk yard for even longer.' Alice entered the argument, walking over and standing behind Keir's chair. 'Why don't *you* marry her, you auld foo-ul? The money's *all* hers now.'

'Alice, have a heart. Once, she was just plain; now she's plain *and* old. No amount of money would compensate for waking up each morning next to *that* face,' Sir Malcolm said, with brutal honesty. Then he turned and addressed Keir. 'You might not believe this, but there has only ever been one woman for me, and that was your mother.' Henri's heart squeezed in compassion at the look father and son exchanged. Neither had achieved closure over the drowning and the wounds were still raw. Both were in mourning, each dealing with it in their own way—Sir Malcolm living out his years in Cannes, and Keir staying with his Canadian cousins until Castle Tèarmannair was his.

Whatever remained of it.

Henri wanted to give them all a shake, tell them to put the past behind them. Get professional help to cope with the hurt and pain, try to move on.

'Well, if Keir disnae wah-nt to spend the rest o' his life with Ciorstaidh, no one can make him. We'll have to think of another way to raise money to save the castle.' Alice, the fight having gone out of her, moved over to the stove to stir a saucepan simmering away on the hob. Surreptitiously, she wiped her eye with the corner of her apron and Henri's heart was wrung afresh—after all, it was her sister and nephew they were talking about.

Evidently intent on having the last word, Sir Malcolm rounded on Keir. 'And why, for the love of God, did you go parading Henriette in front of all the old biddies in the village store? We might have been able to carry out some damage limitation with the MacKenzie-Grieveses, but now everyone's seen you two buying milk and flowers, will put two and two together and get—five.'

'I wasn't paraded in front of anyone, as you so delicately put it, Sir Malcolm. Keir bought flowers in the store and then took me to see his mother's grave. I have every right to live my life as I see fit, without either the approval of the MacKenzie-Grieveses or you; and I believe that Keir should be extended the same courtesy. Now, if you'll all excuse me, I have a library to deal with. Let's hope the last bookcase yields something of value, and the buckets lining the corridors to catch rain water become a thing of the past.'

With that she headed for the sanctuary of the library and closed the door quietly behind her.

Chapter Twenty-One
Cooking up a Storm

The morning after the family-conference-from-hell, Henri lay in bed drinking the cup of tea Alice brought her every day before breakfast, her ears ringing with echoes of the angry words exchanged in the kitchen yesterday. She felt sick in the pit of her stomach as she remembered the laird's tone when speaking to her and Keir. She didn't know if she could face Himself over the cornflakes this morning without having Keir there as backup.

Unused to family drama, she'd been left unsettled by the toxic atmosphere in the kitchen. Her parents never argued in front of her and any disagreements they might have had were discussed in the privacy of their bedroom. Doubtless in the same calm voice they used when speaking to her. Try as she might, she couldn't shrug off the feeling that she was partly to blame for yesterday's argument. She should have insisted Keir brought her back to the castle before anyone had noticed she was missing.

She frowned; but then she wouldn't have learned all about the tragedy which had befallen his mother and brother. Wouldn't have taken a giant step forward in understanding what made him tick.

Deciding that she couldn't stay in bed all day, she dressed and went downstairs to breakfast. Much to her relief, the laird had decamped to the MacKenzie-Grieveses' house for a few days to carry out *damage limitation*, as promised. Evidently he hadn't given up all hope that Keir and Ciorstaidh would make it to the altar. That thought made Henri feel sicker than ever.

She was less than pleased to discover Lachlan seated at the breakfast table, chewing a lamb chop with all the finesse of one of Sir Malcolm's dogs. He glared at her and she glared back. Evidently, he'd returned to the castle after dropping Sir Malcolm off and had no intention of shifting himself, despite Alice dropping large hints. Henri swore she could see his ears turning this way and that, like radar dishes, hoping to catch some juicy titbits to go running to the laird with.

She hoped that Alice would send him over to his sister's for a couple of days, or at least until the laird was ready to return to the castle. That way, everything could get back on an even keel.

Later that morning in the library, Henri rolled up her sleeves ready to tackle the 'last man standing', a large Georgian secretaire bookcase. Hopefully, that would take her mind off everything for a couple of hours.

Straightening her shoulders, she set about clearing the shelf of books behind the secretaire's glass-fronted doors. At her request, Sir Malcolm had removed his personal correspondence from the bookcase a couple of days ago, pushing everything into a Morrison's carrier bag to be *gone over later*, as he put it. Just as well she wasn't hoping for his cooperation today; she suspected that he'd probably refuse, point blank. Sighing, she removed the last book from the shelf and then sat down on a once-beautiful Sheraton chair in front of the writing desk. Its horse hair and wool stuffing spilled out through the split seat covering and pricked her when she moved. To amuse herself, Henri-the-daydreamer struck a pose, imagining how it would feel to be lady of the house—writing letters, issuing orders to her housekeeper, and filing away her notes in one of the many pigeon holes and small drawers at the back of the writing desk.

Cheered up a little by her play acting, she picked up the novel and turned it over in her hands. It was a first edition of Sir Walter Scott's *Waverly*. He'd been inspired to write it after hearing tales from veterans of the 1745 rebellion and Henri felt as though she was holding a piece of history in her hands. Something which connected her to Charles Edward Stuart and the aftermath of his defeat at Culloden. A turbulent time in Scottish history, when the wearing of tartan was prohibited, an offence punishable by six months' imprisonment. Or, for a second offence, transportation to His Majesty's plantations beyond the seas.

Then a thought struck her. She'd never seen Keir in a kilt other than at the shinty match, or sporting the tartan trews, Sir Malcolm wore ninety percent of the time. Doubtless it was all tied in with him knowing he was the *spare* who'd become the *heir*, by default.

Soon there would be hundreds of miles between her and Keir and the only legitimate reason she'd have for keeping in touch would the eventual sale of the *MacKenzie Papers*. Having 'found' Keir, how could she bear to let him go? The thought filled her with despair.

Tracing Sir Walter's signature on the flyleaf of the novel with careful fingers, Henri became aware of a heavy silence wrapping itself around her and the library. Up until now, the only discernible sound had been the rustle of paper as she turned the pages of the book. Now there was *another* sound, one which seemed to come from a long way off. It started as a faint buzzing in her ears, then changed tone and grew into the lament she'd heard on the train out of Fort William. Plangent, mournful, heart-breaking. As if it was trying to speak to *her*; tell her that she was going nowhere until she did her best to bring this family together and make them whole, again.

Thoroughly unnerved, yet at the same time strangely calm, she closed the copy of *Waverly* and stood up, glancing behind her, half expecting to see the piper. She laughed at the fanciful thought and that seemed to break the spell. The tune faded, replaced by other sounds —her breathing, the fire roaring up the chimney, the slow ticking of the clock on the mantelpiece. Standing alone in the library she felt marooned in time, stranded somewhere between reality and the dream world she lived in more and more.

Drawn over to the window, she knelt up on the cushioned seat and looked down over the loch towards the hills shrouded in mist and rain. From her vantage point, no pylons, telegraph poles or electric lights were visible. It was easy to imagine she was back in those dangerous times, waiting for her lover to return from supporting the Bonnie Prince, a price on his head.

In her mind that lover was Keir MacKenzie, his kilt secured by a wide belt, the upper half of his fly plaid draped over the left shoulder of his dress coat and fastened there by his clan badge. His hair would be much longer and tied back in a queue under his Highland bonnet. The wide cuffs of the coat turned back and filled with lace, as befitted his status as MacKenzie of MacKenzie. Then, giving her imagination free rein, she pictured him hiding from the redcoats in the heather, his kilt doubling as his blanket, his face reddened by the wind and frost—his hands and legs covered in battle scars.

From a great distance she heard Alice call out, 'Henri. Are you ready?'

'R—ready?' As she turned away from the window, the connection with the past was broken. 'Ready for what?'

'To skelp the clootie dumpling's erse.'

'The *what?*'

Laughing Alice beckoned Henri to follow her down the long corridor to the kitchen.

It'd been a strange day, full of conflicting emotions; daydreams, angst brought on by yesterday's argument, the rush at finding the *Waverley* novels, and hearing the piper again.

Now she was being invited to *skelp the clootie dumpling's erse.*

Once she left Castle Tèarmannair life would never be the same.

The kitchen, was warm, steamy and smelled like Christmas. Henri breathed in the spice-scented air, and glanced over at the table where a large wet linen cloth, liberally dusted with flour had been spread out. Sitting in the middle of the cloth, looking like Jabba the Hutt, was a huge Quatermass experiment of a pudding.

'What *is* it?' Henri asked.

'Behold the clootie dumpling,' Alice announced, laughing. 'Come on, come closer and skelp its erse. When I was a wean growing up in Motherwell, making clootie dumpling was a great event. We all took turns to stir the mixture . . .'

'What's *in* it?' Henri eyed the large mass in the middle of the cloth.

'Suet, plain flour, oatmeal, dried fruit, golden syrup, ginger, cinnamon, baking powder and a tablespoon of milk,' Alice reeled off the ingredients. 'It's Keir's favourite and a bit of a tradition at Samhain, in this family at least.' She pulled a face when she said *family*, because anything less like a family was hard to imagine. 'Come oh-an, dinnae be feart, it won't bite you.'

Following her lead, Henri skelped the dumpling on its large, round bottom. 'What now?' she queried, comparing its mottled surface to cellulite on an odalisque's thighs.

'We-ll,' Alice drew out her answer, obviously relishing her part. 'You could make a wish, help to tie it up in the cloot and then put the dumpling in the pot.' Henri made a wish and when she opened her eyes, Alice was regarding her in a knowing fashion. 'All done?'

'Done.'

'Have you made a wish, Alice?'

'Yes, and it's already come true because Lachlan has gone to stay with his sister for a few days.'

'Phew.' Henri wiped her forehead with the back of her hand in an exaggerated fashion. With the castle's *mole* out of the way, they could both relax.

Gathering the corners of the cloot, they secured it at the neck with thick, hairy string, leaving just enough room for the mixture to expand. Next, Alice placed an upside down saucer at the bottom of a deep saucepan of boiling water to act as a trivet, then together they carefully lowered the dumpling onto it. Straight away the water went off the boil and Alice made sure that a kettle of hot water was kept simmering on the Aga's hotplate to top up the saucepan when required.

'How long will it take?' Henri enquired.

'The dumpling? Och, about three hours, give or take. I have a recipe for making it in the microwave, but sometimes I like tae do things the auld way.'

Glancing at the kitchen clock and then at the door, she smiled. 'Your wish? That will take slightly less time.' Henri sent her a baffled look, but all was made clear when the door opened and Keir walked in.

To use Alice's phrase, he looked *braw* in a hand-knitted Arran sweater, tartan scarf tied like a muffler at his neck, dark jeans and a yellow waterproof jacket. Even the beanie pulled down over his ears to ward off the cutting wind could not detract from the overall effect.

'Oh no,' he said in mock despair. 'I'm too late to skelp the dumpling's erse.'

'Aye, ye are that, laddie,' Alice said, exiting the kitchen via the other door with the knowing air of a matchmaker. 'Ahm away tae catch up on mah soaps,' she said, and then added her usual rider, 'now, play nicely for Auntie Alice, children.'

Then they were alone.

Chapter Twenty-Two
Partners in Crime

Henri was amazed that she hadn't gone into cardiac arrest the moment Keir entered the kitchen.

Her heart was leaping around in her chest like a wild thing. For several long moments, as the dumpling pot came to a rolling boil, she stood transfixed. Her first instinct was to run towards Keir, tell him how much she'd missed him, and demand to be kissed. Just like he had done on the *Saucy Nancy*. Her head, however, reminded her that her time here was coming to an end and that any course of action which resulted in her laying her cards on the table, only to have them swept aside and her heart broken, would be foolish in the extreme.

Keir, however, had no such reservations

Crossing the kitchen, he took her in his arms and without a moment's hesitation, kissed her and declared, 'God, I've missed you.'

Henri managed a stammered response. 'M-me, too. Missed *you*, I mean. I haven't missed myself, because that would be—mmph.'

Her words were cut short as Keir kissed her again, his lips curving against hers in a smile. Then his smile faded and he became serious, as though it was important to him to get their embryonic relationship off on the right foot. It would be *so* easy to get it wrong. Then he kissed her again, deepening and intensifying the kiss and demanding a matching response. For a moment, Henri was unsure if she was on fire as a result of his ardent courtship, or the steamy atmosphere in the kitchen was making her feel overheated as her blood reached boiling point.

Emboldened by Keir's declaration and deciding to go for broke, she pushed her hands under his jumper, teased the t-shirt out of his jeans and touched his warm skin. Splaying out her fingers, she traced the musculature of his back where it dipped in above his waist. Gratifyingly, he shivered at her touch. Emboldened and enjoying her mastery over him, she grabbed his belt and pulled him into a deeper clinch, as though she couldn't get enough of him and wanted to climb inside his very skin. When Keir's hand crept upwards and found the curve of her breast, his fingers curling round it in possession, she gave out a gasp of shock and delight. Her reaction seemed to please Keir because he pressed her back against the edge of the table and moulded his body into hers, leaving her in no doubt as to how aroused he was.

At that point, caution overruled passion and Henri thought it prudent to call a halt to their lovemaking. Alice might be watching the omnibus edition of *Coronation Street*—signal permitting—or her boxset of *Take the High Road*, but it wouldn't look good if she found them in a passionate clinch while her precious dumpling boiled dry.

'Now what's made you smile?' Keir inquired. Standing back, he crossed his arms over his chest and regarded Henri with mock severity.

'I skelp't the dumpling's arse—or, as Alice would say, *erse*—made a wish, and it came true.'

'Alice and her traditions.' Laughing, he threw back his head. There was a light-hearted gleam in his eyes, a carefreeness which was so far removed from his anger towards his father yesterday that Henri relaxed. Everything was going to be alright. 'I assure you, however, that I was on my way over before you conjured me up.'

'How do you know my wish was about you?' Pretending hauteur, she went over to the Aga to check the water level in the dumpling pot. Not from any desire to appear on *The Great British Bake Off*, but more from a breathing space in which to regain her sense of balance and plan a more considered response to his kisses.

Keir showed no such reserve. 'Wasn't it? Because I've thought of nothing else for the last twenty-four hours.'

'What? Smacking a large pudding's bottom?'

'You know what I mean.' The passionate tenor of his voice set her pulse racing, again.

'Do I?' she asked, over her shoulder.

'We both do.'

Walking over, he put his arms round her waist and pulled her back against his chest. Dipping his head, he buried his face in the nape of her neck, breathing in her scent. Then he spun her round so that she was facing him and then pressed her back against the Aga rail—from which a very unromantic tea-towel and a scorched oven glove dangled. Putting one arm round her, he drew her into his body.ABandoning all pretence, they kissed passionately, hungrily, as though they wanted to shut out the world and all its attendant problems and responsibilities. Those nagging voices which wanted to know where this was leading; insidious whispers which warned her that things could never work out between them.

How could they?

Once her disciplinary hearing was over, she'd be head down, working hard to restore her professional standing, if St Guthlac allowed her to stay on. He'd return to self-imposed exile in British Columbia, waiting to inherit a ramshackle castle upon his father's death. Maybe even marrying Ciorstaidh, in spite of his protestations, because he felt obliged to restore the MacKenzie fortunes and could no longer withstand pressure from both families.

So, they shut them out because they didn't want to hear; didn't want to consider if things would work—*could* work out, between them. They wanted to live in the moment, especially if the moment was as glorious as this. Experiencing a feeling of weightlessness, as though she could take flight, Henri forced herself to think rationally.

Breaking free, she twisted out from his arms.

'I've got a surprise for you.' Walking over to the door which led to the corridor and the library at the end of it, she held out her hand and waited.

'Better than this?' He looked unconvinced as he removed his beanie and weatherproof jacket, threw them on the flour-covered table and took her hand.

'Not better. Different.' Eyes bright with mischief and with a sense of what she was about to show him, Henri led him into the library.

It was odd how kissing in the steamy kitchen felt real and looking down at the *Waverly* novels felt illusory, unimportant. But the novels *were* important and she had to emphasise their value to Keir before Sir Malcolm saw them. It would then be up to Keir what happened next—show them to antiquarians or hide them in the Beach House along with the *MacKenzie Papers,* for another day.

'I've found a complete set of Walter Scott's Waverly Novels, the first dating from 1814. The books are in their original binding—by James Ballantyne, Canongate in Edinburgh, and have hardly been touched by age or damp.' She handed him one of the books to examine. Keir turned it over in his hands and then looked up at her for further enlightenment. 'Some of the volumes, *Waverley, Rob Roy* and *The Bride of Lammermoor* have been signed. I'm thinking—if we could find the bill of sale among the *MacKenzie Papers* it would provide provenance and increase their value to a collector. Maybe,' she said, full of enthusiasm, 'the castle will have that new roof, after all.'

'Providing we can persuade my father to spend the money as it should be spent.'

'A big ask?' Henri inquired, although she already knew the answer.

'Huge.'

'Oh.' Her face clouded over. Keir replaced the book on the arm of the chesterfield and, sitting on one corner of the wide fender with his back to the fire, patted his knee, inviting her to join him.

'Och dinnae look like that, lassie, you've done a great job. Wi' the library, the estate papers and—aye—wi' me, too, ken?' His faux Lowland accent made Henri laugh. Reaching out, he guided her onto his knee, pulled her close and whispered into her ear. 'Okay, so the library isn't worth as much as Father, or I, might have wished. I half suspected that would be the case. The estate's bankrupt,' he shrugged. 'End of. Let's concentrate on getting the *Makenzie Papers* valued, ensure that Father doesn't split up this valuable collection of Walter Scott novels to sell piecemeal, and let that be enough. For now.'

'Unless—' she began and then faltered.

'Unless?'

'Unless I find something else of value,' she said, as Keir kissed her. Part of her was swept away by his lovemaking, the other half believing that there was more to this old castle than she'd discovered so far. The spectral piper, the legend of MacKenzie's Gold, the atmosphere of times gone by, and the air of romance and mystery contained in its very fabric, convinced her of it.

And, if that was true, she—Henriette Bruar, would find it.

Chapter Twenty-Three
A Conundrum

Alice and Henri stood in the Great Hall helping with the preparations for the Samhain feast.

In the middle of the hall, a long table covered with serviceable white sheets and embroidered runners bearing thistles, saltires and the MacKenzie coat of arms, took pride of place. In the centre of the table there was a ram's head complete with glassy eyes, a wig of white hair and curling silver-tipped horns. On top of the thinning wig, it sported a gilt crown with a hinged lid. Henri had wrinkled her nose on first seeing the ram's head which did not appear to add anything to the ambiance in the ancient hall. Laughing, Alice had explained that the ram was part and parcel of the myth of The Bruce, the goats who'd saved him from the English—and another legend involving MacKenzie of MacKenzie hiding from the redcoats after the Battle of Glen Shiel, the gist of which no one seemed to remember.

'It's also possible that the head was some kind o' snuff box, when the laird's great-great grandfather was a wee boy.'

'Gruesome,' Henri commented. 'Ah, I see my tables are being put to good use.'

She gestured at the trestles pushed up against the long sides of the hall. In place of books, they held an assortment of glasses from the cash and carry in Fort William, free with the meagre wine order which Alice had paid for, Sir Malcolm's credit card having been declined long ago. Next to them, in sad juxtaposition, was a motley collection of the castle's glassware, some of it precious, but most of it chipped, or dull from being through the dishwasher too many times. In place of the customary champagne which had graced Castle Tèarmannair's tables in the past, there was sparkling wine and cheap prosecco. This was ranged on the steps of the spiral staircase at the far end of the hall to keep it cool and conceal its less than noble vintage.

At that end of the hall, two fireplaces situated side by side belted out a furnace blast of heat, but it was too early in the day for the warmth to reach Henri's end of the hall. Tending the fires was down to Lachlan, who'd spent most of the morning complaining loudly that he would end up with a hernia from lugging coal, peat turves and logs up and down the stairs. He had Young Lachy to help him, but appeared to do little actual work apart from ordering his hapless nephew about. Behind Henri, two carved screens concealed the entrance to the Buttery where, once, the Samhain feast would have been prepared and relayed to the guests by uniformed staff. .

'This is an amazing space—so old . . .' Henri enthused, taking it all in.

'Och, you should have seen it when my sister was alive. The walls were hung with tapestries, there were flowers everywhere, great vases o' lilies and Birds o' Paradise. And, in the court cupboard there was heirloom glass, china and silver—handed down through the generations. It was her pride and joy. But Himself sold it off to the MacKenzie-Grieveses and now Keir's heirlooms are *theirs*. All we have left are some crested silver serving spoons and serving dishes, which I've hidden under my bed. Otherwise the puir boy wid hae nothing tae inherit when the auld fou-ull dies—most likely of a heart attack, chasing a floozy half his age roond the bedroom.'

How like the MacKenzie-Grieveses to buy up Keir's inheritance, Henri fumed. It was a no-brainer where they were concerned, as all goods and chattels would return to the castle when Ciorstaidh became Lady MacKenzie. Being charitable, she wondered if that was Sir Malcolm's reason for selling Keir's inheritance to them. He appeared to attach no sentimental value to pieces which had been in his family for hundreds of years. In fact, he seemed to derive a kind of warped pleasure in selling them off.

Henri shook her head, sad that this once great family had come to this pass and that the castle had little of its history left, apart from bricks and mortar. The hall appeared to share her sadness and had a rather forlorn air. Its granite walls, stripped of their tapestries, were grey and unwelcoming and little natural light came through the tall windows cut six feet deep into the walls. Where once Murano chandeliers had hung from the rafters, there were now light fittings constructed from deer antlers, festooned in outdoor lights in an array of bright colours, purchased from the local garden centre.

'Aye, look at them. Like a coconut shy at Portobello Fair,' Alice remarked, following Henri's eye. 'There used to be fine paintings on the walls: Van Dykes, a Turner, and a Landseer. But they were sold off to pay the old laird's death duties. Keir, me and—aye, even Auld Lachlan, have tried tae make the place look like a proper castle with what little's left, but—'

Her sweeping gesture encompassed the leather targes and claymores on the walls, a couple of lethal looking blunderbusses, and a rusty suit of armour—the helmet of which was set at a rakish angle. As though, like Sir Malcolm, its former inhabitant was a bit too fond of a wee 'drap o' the swally'. The hall had the look of *Monty Python and the Holy Grail*, crossed with *Carry On Up the Castle*. That depressed Henri and crushed her romantic soul.

There were some incongruous touches, too. In one corner there was an early seventeenth-century court cupboard which had probably survived because it was too heavy to move. Henri hoped that even Himself wouldn't hack it to bits in order to get it down the stairs, like an Ikea flat pack chest of drawers.

'Aye, nae doot that'll be next to go,' Alice opined. 'Along with those.' She pointed at a fine set of late Stuart dining chairs, complete with two beautiful carvers.

'Such a shame,' Henri agreed, and then winced as she looked up at the Minstrels Gallery. It was completely out of a place, a Victorian affectation no doubt inspired by Sir Walter Scott's novels and Queen Victorian's obsession with all things Scottish. It looked bolted-on, and detracted from fine roof beams supported by corbels, sporting a range of gurning faces. Seeing the dejected slump to Alice's shoulders, Henri put her arm round them and gave her a hug.

'Food?' she asked, changing the subject.

That had the effect of making Alice look even more crestfallen. Another deep sigh. 'Everyone is tae bring 'something on a plate'. Can you believe it? *Something on a plate!* Ciorstaidh has coordinated that end of things, so we should be well catered for.' Her cheeks burned at the shame of it. 'In my sister's day, Castle Tèarmannair was famous for its hospitality. Oh, Henri, you should have seen us *then*. This is all a sham. A sham.'

'So why continue to hold the feast here? I'm guessing the M-G's would be more than happy to take that over, too.'

'Ye shouldnae need to ask, lassie. It's to do with tradition and pride—foolish pride in Malcolm's case; and besides, Keir wouldnae let the tradition of reciting *Tam O' Shanter* at Samhain be handed over to the MacKenzie-Grieveses without a fight.'

Without a fight.

Henri was back at the shinty match, recalling the transforming moment when she understood *who* Keir Mackenzie was; had seen him as a warrior, a man out of his time, tied to the land and its people by history and right of inheritance. There was more to him than simply being the second son of a bankrupt laird. The thought of leaving her Highland hideaway was hard to bear and the thought of leaving Keir made it harder still, because she knew, deep in her heart, that if time and opportunity allowed, they could go the distance.

'Och, lassie, I dinnae think you've heard a word I've spoken to ye.'

'I have,' Henri protested, but then grinned because she knew she was lying. 'Just to make sure, what did you say?'

'I said, here's a luckenbooth, a brooch to help you pin the plaid to your shoulder and to ward off the evil eye.' Henri shivered, although she could see that Alice was joking.

'Evil eye?'

'That should be evil eyes, plural—Ciorstaidh and her mother.' She crossed herself then, laughing at her joke, pulled Henri towards the arched doorway leading to the staircase. Carefully negotiating the twists and turns, trying hard not to kick over any bottles of faux champagne, they made their way up to Henri's bedroom. There, laid out on her bed, was a long skirt in MacKenzie tartan, a high-necked blouse and a stole, also in MacKenzie plaid. Turning, Henri gave Alice a quizzical look.

'We all dress up for Samhain, Henri. I ken't fine you wouldnae have an outfit of your own, so I've provided ye with wa-hn.' Henri picked up the skirt and held it against her; it was a little short but looked as if it would fit. The blouse was made from white silk, but was yellow with age. The large wrap was of the finest cashmere and when Henri held it against her face it smelled of roses and something spicy, like cedar wood—possibly to ward off the moths.

'Am I entitled to wear this?' Henri was worried that she might offend someone by wearing clothes which weren't hers and a tartan she had no right to. It had been her intention to simply 'look in' on the festivities, hear Keir recite *Tam O'Shanter* and then retire to the library where she had one or two last tasks to perform. 'Who did they belong to?' Alice's expression said it all. 'Your sister? Oh, Alice, I couldn't. Really . . .'

'Aye, ye *could*, hen. It's all been lying in its cardboard box amongst scented tissue paper for years. She ordered it for Samhain that year, but didnae— didnae—' Her voice faltered. She swallowed. 'Didn't live long enough to wear it.'

Both women sat down on the edge of the bed, overwhelmed by sadness; Alice for her sister and Henri for a woman she would never know. She felt pain, real pain at the thought of how Keir and Alice had suffered, still suffered, because they'd been denied the closure which would make them whole. They stared into the flames of the fire, lost in thought. At last, Henri spoke, her voice husky: 'Won't Keir, or Sir Malcolm, be upset to see me wearing the late Lady MacKenzie's things?'

'No. They have no idea that I've kept them. When Mary and Wee Malchy drowned, Himself ordered every last trace of them be removed from the castle. He couldnae bear to see any of it. But I've kept back a few pieces, for Keir; for his wife, when the time comes.' She sent Henri a telling look, making plain her hopes and plans for her nephew.

'Oh, Alice.' Henri put her hand over the housekeeper's. 'In that case . . . leave the things where they are. If I feel uncomfortable wearing them, I'll wear a dress of my own but with the stole over the top. It's so beautiful and soft, even after all these years.' Alice nodded, leaving the final decision to Henri. 'Now, explain to me about Keir reciting *Tam O' Shanter*.'

Glancing at her watch hours later, Henri realised that if she left the room now, she'd be in danger of joining Keir, Sir Malcolm, Alice and the MacKenzie-Grieveses in the Great Hall before the other guests arrived. She had no intention of standing by their side as meeting and greeting took place. She wasn't family and it wasn't appropriate. She planned to be as inconspicuous as possible, sneaking into the back of the hall when the party was in full swing and hope that no one noticed her. To which end, she'd put away her heels and was wearing ballet flats (so as not to accentuate her height) and had settled on wearing a simple black dress with the MacKenzie shawl. She'd piled her hair on top of her head in a careless knot, teasing out long strands to frame her face and touch the silver caman necklace Keir had given to her. She didn't want it to appear as if she'd tried too hard. She could do without Ciorstaidh, her mother and the whiskery aunts sending looks which implied she was no more than a Sassenach strumpet who'd set her cap at the Master of Mountgarrie.

With time to kill, she lay on top of the bed, settled two pillows behind her head and allowed her mind to wander. After some time, she focused on the marble-topped dressing table which doubled as her desk. It held an untidy jumble of objects: her laptop which, in the absence of an internet signal, had been relegated to the position of 'very expensive typewriter'; research books; handwritten post-it notes on the key points of her thesis, arranged around edges of the three-sided mirror. It all looked very industrious though, in truth, the post-it notes were little more than scribbled bullet points which had never been expanded upon. However, they made her feel as if she'd made a start on her magnum opus—*The Highland Clearances—ethnic cleansing or economic reality?* Next to her laptop lay her redundant iPhone, waiting like the princess in the tower to be awoken from its long sleep. Vodafone, in this case, standing in for Prince Charming.

That made her smile and her survey of the room ended with one last sweep which took in the tartan skirt, shawl and silk blouse draped over the foot board. The scent of apple wood from the fire mingled pleasantly with her perfume, waxed, ancient floorboards and the dusty, faded bed hangings. After she left the castle those ancient scents would linger on, while her perfume disappeared after time, leaving no record of her stay.

Sitting higher up in the bed she checked her watch again, ten minutes to wait. After then, it would be safe to venture downstairs, sneak into the Great Hall, and stand quietly in the shadows, unremarked upon, unnoticed. Her gaze wandered round the room a second time, but stopped when it encountered the door in the right-hand corner. She frowned; there was something about the layout of that side of the room: door, wall and floor which, when combined with the shifting shadows cast by the fire, puzzled her. Since day one, the room had presented her with a conundrum; as though it was a cryptic clue, pointing to something else. A cypher she couldn't crack, no matter how hard she tried. Her father had taught her how to complete *The Times Cryptic Crossword*, saying it honed her reasoning skills and focused her too-romantic mind. She smiled—remembering the riddle her father had used as a starting point, teaching her think outside the box.

when is a door not a door? The answer to that was simple, *when it's a-jar*.

If only the riddle of *this* door, wall and floor was as easy to crack.

Each time she climbed the spiral staircase from the floor below, walked along the corridor and entered her room, she was beset by a feeling that she was missing something. Something important, something tantalisingly close, yet out of reach. All it needed, was for her to hear the phantom piper playing the lament in her bedroom and she'd convince herself that the room held a mystery.

One which only she could solve.

So far he'd proved elusive, or unwilling to help out.

Swinging her legs off the bed, she reached for the plaid shawl, and the luckenbooth on her bedside table. Folding the shawl into a long rectangle, she arranged it over her left shoulder and pinned it to her dress and then rearranged the pleats. There; that made it appear fairly inconspicuous, but the act of her wearing it would please Alice. She wasn't looking forward to the Samhain celebrations, as the memory of the argument in the kitchen was still raw and caused her anguish every time she thought of it. The MacKenzie family was dysfunctional, to say the very least. Merely by smiling on the wrong side of her face tonight she would offend someone. However, needs must. She hadn't seen Keir since yesterday and was missing him so badly it was like a physical pain.

Recalling a line from Macbeth, 'Lay on, Macduff, and damned be him who first cries 'Hold! Enough,' she closed the bedroom door behind her. If anyone wanted a piece of her tonight, they'd better be prepared for the consequences!

Chapter Twenty-Four
Tam O'Shanter

When Henri entered the Great Hall, it had been completely transformed by the purple gloaming outside the windows, strategically placed candles and the roaring twin fires. A harpist was playing a selection of melodies on a clarsach, and in another corner, children were dookin' for apples in a barrel of water, supervised by nannies or older siblings. The young *guisers,* dressed as ghouls, spirits or favourite super heroes, took great delight in frightening the grown-ups with turnip lanterns dangling from sticks and fake Dracula fangs.

If Henri had dressed so as not to draw attention to herself, the other guests showed no such restraint. They were celebrating Samhain in style; the men in kilts, 'Bonnie Prince Charlie' jackets over matching waistcoats, dress shirts, black tie, and brogues. The women in long plaid skirts/kilts, silk blouses with lacy jabots or, like herself, in simple black dresses worn with clan tartan in the form of a shawl or a sash. Clearly, this was an evening for showing off, because heirloom tiaras, necklaces and bracelets had been taken out of the bank vault. The jewels caught the candlelight and added extra glamour to the evening.

A knot of men stood at the far end of the hall, warming themselves by the fires. Amidst good natured joshing, backslapping, man hugs and hearty laughter, they knocked back drams of uisge beatha, topping up their glasses from the fine malts ranged on the court cupboard. No doubt provided by the MacKenzie-Grieveses.

One man stood apart from the rest, and it took several seconds before Henri realised that it was Keir. She'd never seen the Master of Mountgarrie other than in his work clothes. But *this* Keir, wearing full Highland dress with unconscious grace and style was every inch the laird she'd dreamed about in the library. Grasping her silver caman for good luck, she stepped out of the shadows and into the hall.

Seemingly sensing her presence, Keir slowly turned towards her. Had this been a scene in a movie, they would have been the only two in focus, the rest of the guests drifting past like smoky-grey shadows. Their matching MacKenzie plaids would provide the only colour in the shot and Henri's rapid breathing, underscored by the lilting tune played on the clarsach, would have been the only sound. Keir said Henri's name below his breath and looked at her wonderingly, as if unable to comprehend how quickly their relationship was moving forward; how time had seemed to speed up since that kiss on the boat. Henri whispered his name, too, mirroring his actions, and that released Keir from being held in a freeze-frame shot, as though this really was a movie.

After the moment of stillness, which had lasted no more than a few seconds, his purposeful stride towards Henri's end of the hall alerted guests that something unusual and dramatic was happening right in front of their eyes. The electricity between Keir and Henri was palpable and when he reached Henri, Keir took both her hands in his own and twined their fingers. Then he pulled her close and kissed her on both cheeks. Superficially, the embrace seemed no more than the polite double-kiss one might exchange with a relative, or close friend. However, as Keir kissed first her right cheek and then her left, his lips brushed across her mouth, tantalisingly.

Henri's gasp was audible and the guests looked on, transfixed. They were, for the main part, family and friends of longstanding and knew Keir's tragic history and had him marked down as a man who kept his feelings and emotions under tight rein. But *this* Keir, the one standing before them and holding a woman's hand as though he'd never let her go, was a revelation. Henri knew that she was responsible for the sea-change in this proud, private man and experienced elation and terror in equal measure. Keir's boyish, self-deprecating smile as he looked at her, showed that he knew he was behaving like a moon-struck calf in front of friends, family and clan.

But he didn't give a damn.

'Dr Bruar,' Keir bowed over her hand.

'Keir,' she acknowledged, graciously inclining her head.

Putting his arm around her waist, he turned towards the assembled guests with the air of a man about to make an important announcement. 'My friends, this is Doctor Henriette Bruar of St Guthlac University, our guest at Castle Tèarmannair, commissioned with the task of cataloguing the library.' Henri was grateful that he didn't say *dismantling and selling off our library to the highest bidder*, as he might have done a few weeks earlier. 'However, I want everyone here tonight to know that she —'

Demonstrating an agility which belied his age, Sir Malcolm bounded across the hall towards them, kilt swinging around his knees. He cut Keir off in mid speech and then led Henri into the centre of the hall by the hand, as if about to partner her in a reel.

'Thank you, Keir. Allow me, as laird, to put your sentiments into words,' he said, giving Keir little choice in the matter. 'Dear friends, as Keir was about to say—the time has come to bid farewell to the lovely *and* talented Dr Bruar. Her task of cataloguing the library is complete and the world of academe beckons her. We cannot expect her to stay on indefinitely, however much we would like to. We cannot be that selfish.'

Flashing Henri an apologetic *sorry, but you've left me no alternative* look, he glanced down the hall towards the MacKenzie-Grieveses who were listening, boot-faced, to his speech. Pulling himself up to his full height, he struck an aristocratic pose and took control. For, in spite of everything, he was Sir Malcolm MacKenzie of that Ilk, descendant of a long line of MacKenzies, and held the title of baronet. An honour bestowed upon his family by no less a personage than King James VI of Scotland.

A wee lassie from a second rate university in the north of England came a poor second to that. And if his son was enamoured of her, he'd soon forget her when she was back where she belonged, and he was in British Columbia.

'Well, I—' Henri began, but was cut off mid-sentence.

'I ask you to charge your glasses my friends in honour of Doctor Bruar. After that, the Master of Mountgarrie will recite *Tam O' Shanter* to usher in Samhain.' This was greeted by a muted groan as, clearly, the partygoers had made a connection between the Master and the Doctor of Letters and were in the mood for romance. A poem, recited in broad Scots, concerning a demonic ceilidh in Alloway Kirk where the devil plays the bagpipes, wasn't going to quite cut it. 'Keir—'

Clapping his hands, Sir Malcolm summoned his son forward.

Left with little option but to comply, or publically disobey and humiliate his father, Keir stepped up to the mark. Arranging his fly plaid more securely on his shoulder, he signalled the harpist to play a refrain in the background. Then, with one last smouldering glance at Henri he rolled out his party piece —

When chapmen billies leave the street,
And drouthy neibors, neibors meet,
As market days are wearing late,
An' folk begin to tak the gate;'

Henri was unsure what to do next. Much as she wanted to stay and listen to Keir reciting the poem, she felt scorched at being publically dismissed from her post by Sir Malcolm, however charmingly expressed.

The distaff members of the MacKenzie-Grieveses were standing so close to Keir in the middle of the Great Hall that they could have doubled for his backing group. Their inimical stares made it plain that, if looks had the power to kill, she'd be wearing a wooden overcoat bearing a brass plaque with her name on it! All at once, the press of people, their curious stares and prurient interest in her and Keir felt suffocating. Backing out of the hall while everyone's eyes were on Keir, Henri headed for the only place she felt safe—the library.

When she reached there, she closed the door firmly behind her and claimed sanctuary, in a ritual as old as Christianity itself. St Guthlac, after whom her university was named, would have been proud.

Chapter Twenty-Five
An te a bhreab nead na gasbaid

Being in the library was so calming that, after a few minutes, Henri's equanimity was restored. This was her domain, she had full control over it—let no one lose sight of that. However, despite that brave assertion, her confidence wavered; who was she kidding? She'd just been given her marching orders albeit in the nicest possible way, but Sir Malcolm was right. It was time for her to leave Castle Tèarmannair. Even if that meant taking a cart load of what-ifs with her and leaving things, half-finished, unsaid.

There were issues which had to be settled before she could move on with her life. Burning looks and scorching kisses were all very well, but they didn't help resolve the mess she'd left behind in Hexham. The thought of leaving the castle filled her with sadness, while the thought of leaving Keir filled her with despair. But what was the alternative?

At that point, the library door creaked open and Alexander MacKenzie-Grieves walked in.

In no mood for his puerile games, she snapped out: 'What the bloody hell do you want? Shouldn't you be in the Great Hall listening to the words of the Ploughman Poet?'

'Or *Rabid* Burns, as we nicknamed him at school.' Closing the door he moved closer and, hand on heart, belted out: *My Love is Like a Red, Red Rose* in a fine baritone, altering the words to—*My Love Has Got a Big Red Nose*. He laughed and then adopted a droll, crushed expression at Henri's less-than-amused glare. 'Sadly, listening to my esteemed cousin reciting all of the verses of *Tam O' Shanter*, in Scottish patois, holds no allure for me. Or for you, either, apparently?'

Ignoring the leading question, Henri countered with: 'Aren't you proud of your culture?'

'Up to a point, but the Ayrshire dialect?' he shuddered. 'Not so much. Nanny spoke with a Glaswegian accent, which meant I did too, up until the age of seven when I was sent to boarding school to have it eradicated. If a gentleman and landowner speaks with a Scottish accent, it had better come from Edinburgh. Not so much *See, you Jimmy?* as *Catch you later, Torquil?* However, if it's Gaelic you want, the true language of Scotland, then I'm your man.' He tapped himself on the chest, took a step backwards and executed an elaborate bow, which wasn't easy given he was as drunk as a skunk.

'Really? *Really?*' Henri repeated, to show she wasn't impressed.

'Yes; really. I believe in giving honour where honour is due—so, respect to Dr Bruar—*An te a bhreab nead na gasbaid.*' His next bow was accompanied by an elaborate hand gesture where he touched his heart and then his forehead, in turn. It owed more to Ali Baba and the Forty Thieves than Rob Roy and, in spite of herself, Henri laughed. She quickly suppressed her amusement because she knew it didn't take much to encourage him.

'The *what?*'

'*The Girl Who Kicked the Hornets' Nest.* Like the book title?'

'Stieg Larsson? Oh, I get it. Look—' She tried to side-step him but he anticipated her move and barred the way. 'I'm really not in the mood, so make your point and get out.'

'Tut, tut, Dr Bruar,' he continued, as if she hadn't spoken. 'What *were* you thinking? Kicking the hornets' nest and then hightailing it back to the Beach House, leaving gossip and speculation behind? Parading yourselves in front of the geriatrics in the village store, buying milk and flowers at *that time in the morning*. Making it plain to anyone with half a brain that you and Keir had spent the night together—having hot, monkey sex, like as not.'

'Hot monkey, *what?*'

Obviously intrigued by the idea of Keir and her having sex—monkey, hot, or otherwise —Alexander lost his train of thought. Then, gaining control over his whisky-dulled senses, he continued.

'Aye, neither of youse spared a thought for puir wee Ciorstaidh, or the heirloom china she threw at the wa' after she overheard our cleaning lady—who got it from Cook—telling the gardener, that she'd seen youse in the local Spar.' The sentence, delivered in broad Scots, despite what he'd said earlier about Robert Burns, seemed to overtax him. He paused and tried to marshal his thoughts. 'Where was I?'

Henri was about to say: *hot monkey sex*, but thought better of it.

Instead, she brushed down her dress and levelled a cold stare at him. 'Time you returned to the party, I think.'

'Just one more thing—' His tone ensured that she stopped and listened to him. 'I do hope Keir isn't using you to make the point to my beloved sister that she will never be mistress of this old heap. Mind you—' Catching her arm, he tripped and ended up pushing her back against the low side arm of the chesterfield, 'Ciorstaidh is a pragmatist and would be prepared to overlook Keir's latest *peccadillo,* if her dream came true. And it will, given that you're heading back to the land of the Sassenachs and we'll never hear from you again.'

Henri turned her head away from his whisky-fume breath.

Although his analysis was spot on, her haughty expression implied that he didn't have full command of the facts. Putting her hands on his chest, she gave him a less-than-gentle push towards the door, sending him teetering backwards.

'I might have known you'd like it rough,' he said, struggling to regain his balance. Once he'd righted himself, he dusted down his jacket and pulled down his waistcoat and jacket to cover his midriff. 'Lucky old Keir.'

'I'll thank you to get out of my library.' She pointed towards the door with all the hauteur she could muster.

'Oh, it's *your* library now, is it? Not *quite* what Himself implied in the Great Hall. He can't get you on the train to Fort William fast enough, and

Ciorstaidh installed in the castle with a ring on her finger before Keir returns to the wilds of Canada.' Henri shook her head, denying his assessment of the situation, sorry that she ever thought him in the least bit amusing. He was a poisonous serpent, like the rest of his family. But he hadn't finished. Reaching out, he caught the end of the shawl fastened to her shoulder with the luckenbooth and rubbed it against his cheek, suggestively. 'I see you've been given MacKenzie tartan to wear. Alice's idea, I'll bet. Clever Auld Alice, using you as a pawn, parading you as 'a MacKenzie', for all to see. A bit below the sporran, wouldn't you say, rubbing salt into puir wee Ciorstaidh's wounds like that?'

'I have the feeling that *puir wee Ciorstaidh* is more than capable of looking after herself. Now stand to one side, ye wee bauchle, before I hit you over the head with that axe on the wall.'

'Wee bauchle, is it? Ha! Alice has taught you well. Of course, it's only to be expected that she sanctions her beloved nephew's actions. She'd rather he married the woman who sells the *Big Issue*, than my sister. Alice knows once Ciorstaidh is Keir's wife, the first thing she'll do is get rid of *her*—and the malodorous Lachlan. After that, she'll give Himself enough money to live out his days in the South of France, where cirrhosis of the liver or hardened arteries will send him to meet his ancestors.'

'Don't *you* realise once she's achieved that, she'll stop funding your louche lifestyle? And deservedly, too. Apart from Keir, what I've seen of MacKenzie men has not impressed me.'

'Ouch, that hurt, darling—and maybe you're right. However, I'll have my own trust fund by then, and she can go hang. As for Alice Dougal; can you see her going home to the wee cake shop in Motherwell after years of playing lady-in-the-castle?' Falling into his trap, Henri let her inner turmoil show in her face.

'Are you implying that Keir taking me into the store to buy milk and flowers, and Alice giving me this plaid to wear, is nothing more than *stage management?*'

'I think she's got it,' he said, channelling Professor Higgins. 'I've got to admit, Ciorstaidh's deranged belief that she will one day be Lady MacKenzie suffered a serious setback this evening seeing you in MacKenzie colours. I'm guessing she'll have a few words to say to Keir after his rendition of the poem. But dinnae fash yersel', hen; if it disnae work out between you and my angst-ridden cousin, I'll gladly step into the breach. You look like a girl who knows how to have a good time.'

'Why you—you—'

'Time the Master of Mountgarrie found a good therapist; time he moved on and gave us all a break. All that angst and guilt . . . enough already; we get it. Oh, wait, he's a taciturn Highlander and doesn't show his feelings to anyone outside his circle of trust.'

That idea that she was included in Keir's circle of trust made Henri's heart swell. 'That's where you're wrong,' she said, and then clammed up. He didn't need to know about her relationship with Keir or what they'd shared in the Beach House the night of the storm.

'Whatever,' he shrugged. 'I just wanted you to know that good old S-shandy's on hand to pick up the pie-shes, when he dumps-sh you. For dump you he will, in favour of restoring the castle and the family fortunes—even if it means sleeping with my shrew of a sister for the rest of his life.' It was a good speech, given how drunk he was—in vino veritas, and all that—*if* one ignored the part where he called himself *Shandy*, tried to tap the side of his nose and poked himself in the eye.

'I'd rather spend the night with Lachlan,' Henri declared.

He laughed at that, he really was quite uncrushable. Furious, Henri walked over to the library door and held it open, wordlessly. Taking the hint, Alexander MacKenzie-Grieves left the library—kissing her roughly on the mouth as a parting shot. Henri wiped the back of her hand across her lips to eradicate the taste of him and he lurched drunkenly down the corridor towards the Great Hall, leaving mocking laughter in his wake.

Ten minutes later, sitting on the fender, chin in hand and gazing into the fire, Henri wondered if anyone would miss her if she didn't return to the party. Then she thought, damn it—that'd be playing right into the MacKenzie-Grieveses' hands. Making her move, she stood in front of the mottled mirror over the fireplace and pinched colour into her cheeks and bit her lips to bring blood flowing back to them. Then she smoothed down her shawl, squirming slightly as she remembered Alexander brushing the fringe against his cheek.

Dismissing the image, she straightened her shoulders and made for the door, a warlike glint in her eye. However, before she reached it, Keir walked in. All the poison Alexander MacKenzie-Grieves had poured in her ear was forgotten as she threw herself into Keir's arms. He held her so tightly that the clan badge fastening his fly plaid to his shoulder pressed into the soft skin of her décolletage. But she didn't care. She *wanted* to be marked out as his woman. Keir tightened his hold, as if he wanted to fuse every last inch of his body with hers: bone, sinew, tissue, blood. Then, in complete contrast to his fierce embrace, he whispered something soft and sibilant in her ear, in a language she didn't understand. However, she knew, instinctively, that his words had nothing to do with Rabbie Burns, hornets, or their nests.

He was opening his heart to her -

'*Tha thu a' coimhead brèagha. Tha gaol agam ort.*' He trailed light kisses across her collarbone and then the swell of her breasts above the shawl collar of her dress. Each kiss drew a shuddering response and she tilted her head back, offering herself up to him; encouraging him to explore lower—much lower. Finally releasing her, he held her at arm's length. 'You look beautiful. I love you,' he translated the Gaelic phrase, simply and without pretence.

It took a moment for Henri to realise what he'd said; what it meant.

Her half-stammered Anglo-Saxon, *I—I love you, t-too*, was no match for the poetry of the Gaelic. In spite of that, her words appeared to have magical qualities, for Keir's haunted look vanished, as though he'd confronted his demons and reached the conclusion that his mother and brother's drowning was not his fault. He smiled down at her, and Henri sensed in doing so, the last remnants of guilt had left him

It hadn't taken an army of therapists to 'cure' him, as Sandy MacKenzie-Grieves had so snarkily suggested, simply the love of a good woman. Her love.

'Seeing you in the hall, wearing MacKenzie tartan fastened to your shoulder by my mother's luckenbooth, looking so slender and beautiful, I nearly turned my back on tradition and told them to get someone else to read *Tam O-bloody-Shanter*. All I could think of, all I can think of *now*, is taking you upstairs to my bedroom and making love to you, all night long. And damn what anyone else has to say about it.'

More used to a closed-off, shuttered Keir who weighed up his words before uttering them, Henri was knocked off kilter by his passionate speech. She liked the idea of his bedroom, his plan to tell the world to leave them alone, and that they might spend the night together. She was forced to dismiss the beguiling image because she detected a *however* hovering in the air.

'However . . .' she prompted,

'*However*, first we have to play Sardines.'

'Sardines?'

'You don't mean the children's game—*sardines*, do you?'

'That's exactly what I mean.'

'What—I mean, for the love of God—why?'

Leaving her side, Keir sat down on the leather chesterfield and then invited her to join him. Once she was settled firmly under his arm and tucked into his side, he explained.

'Back in the bad old days,' Henri sensed, rather than saw, the face he pulled at the expression, 'it was customary after the Samhain Feast for guests to pair off. The parties at Castle Tèarmannair had a reputation for being wild and uninhibited. We're talking Edwardian times—when people of my class married to safeguard inheritances and/or to preserve the bloodline, rather than for love. Once an heir-and-a-spare had been produced, aristos were free to pursue their own *interests*. Word reached London and no less a personage than the future king, Edward VII, travelled all the way up here with a couple of mistresses in tow for a—'

'Sleepover?' Henri supplied.

'And the shooting and fishing, of course.'

'I'm guessing the royal sleepovers didn't entail braiding hair, practising makeup techniques, listening to boy bands and spending the night on the floor in a sleeping bag?'

'Exactly. Although our brief association with royalty, movers and shakers did stand us in good stead.'

'In what way?'

Positioning himself so that his head was resting back against the side of the chesterfield and his feet stretched out towards the other end, Keir twisted Henri round so that she lay between him and the long, low back of the sofa. Propped up on one elbow, he traced a line from her forehead to her lips with his forefinger, dropping teasing little kisses on her skin as he told the full story.

'Politicians, royalty and millionaires wanted to stay over at Castle Tèarmannair, for the shooting, the fishing, hospitality and the—'

'Wife swapping?'

' —and so, MacKenzie's Halt escaped the swingeing cuts which affected other branch lines without, shall we say, friends in high places?' Henri found all this fascinating, however, given that his trailing fingers were moving ever lower and doing delicious things to her, she wanted Keir to action his promise of carrying her upstairs to his bedroom and . . .

'Sardines?' she prompted, a little impatiently.

'I'm getting there.' Finding the zip at the back of her dress, he slid it down several inches and then pushed her dress off her left shoulder. Her skin glowed in the firelight as he kissed along her collarbone.

'Get there quicker,' she begged, breathless. Keir laughed, then obliged— carrying on with his story, and lowering her zip further.

'The arrival of my mother as a young bride put paid to all of those shenanigans. Corridor creeping was no longer acceptable but guests still wanted the fun of it. So . . . sardines—once the wee ones had been put to bed in the sitting room with their nannies. Then, at midnight, on Hallowe'en when spirits are said to roam the castle at will, everyone crosses the loch in a flotilla of boats, decked out with lanterns. Those the worse for wear, sleep it off in the sitting room until morning.'

'It all sounds very romantic.'

'It is.'

'Much better than squeezing into dark, tight spaces with people you hardly know. Not sure that I fancy being in a confined space with your cousin, Alexander, or any of his drinking companions.' She pulled a face and shuddered.

'Sandy gives upper-class twits a bad name.' Keir stopped kissing her shoulder, pulled his head back and looked at her, pointedly. 'Has he behaved inappropriately towards you?' Henri thought it best not to share her recent conversation with Alexander, or mention the rough kiss he'd planted on her lips.

'No, nothing like that. It's just—he's a bit of an idiot, and tonight I'm not in the mood for idiots.'

Keir looked at her for a few moments and then appeared to reach a decision. Quickly pulling up her zipper, he rearranged the neck of her dress and stood up. Holding out his hand, he pulled her to her feet and led her towards the door. After checking the corridor, he turned, put his finger on his lips and whispered. 'You can hide in my room. The others will be so drunk, they won't notice you're missing.'

Henri had a crazy notion that Ciorstaidh had slipped a homing device into her handbag when she wasn't looking and was tracking her movements round the castle. That made her giggle and when Keir looked at her curiously she shook her head to signify that it would take too long to explain why she felt light as air and wonderfully carefree. Reaching the end of the corridor they paused before ascending the stone stairs to the next level. The sounds of merriment had tailed off and the wistful strains of a tune played on the pipes reached them—plangent, haunting.

Henri stopped, frozen to the spot. 'Wh-what *is* that tune?' she asked, relieved that Keir heard it, too.

'A lament, composed by the MacKenzies' piper for those clansmen who lost their lives at the Battle of Glen Shiel in—'

'1719,' she put in impatiently and then gripped his arm. 'Do you remember I told you, back in the library that I kept hearing a lament? Well, it's that *one*.' She jabbed the air with a forefinger, feeling vindicated. She hadn't imagined it, after all.

'It's an old tune, and this is an ancient castle. The tune is probably woven into the stones of the building. ' He stated it matter-of-factly, as though it was nothing out of the ordinary, and that he believed it himself. Then he tugged her hand. 'Come on, upstairs before anyone sees us.'

But Henri was listening to the lament, eyes big as saucers. 'Yes; but what does it all *mean*?'

'Mean? No one's heard it in years -'

'But that's just the point—*I have*. The morning after I stayed at the Beach House, I mentioned it to you and you looked at me strangely.'

'That's because I was still wishing I'd joined you on the sofa the previous evening,'

'Be serious.'

'I am being serious—oh, about the piper you mean?' They listened to the mournful skirl of the pipes as the lament drifted up the staircase, the old stone walls amplifying the sound. A draught sprung up from nowhere, and blew across Henri's low neckline, making her feel as though she'd been plunged into a bath of ice cold water. A convulsive shiver travelled her length and her legs lost the ability to function and the power to support her weight. All colour drained from her cheeks, as if she'd received a shock, or bad news.

'Henri, your reaction is the reason I didn't elaborate about the piper on the other day. Imaginative, sensitive people like you, don't need to know that—'

'Know *what*? You can't stop there!'

Keir, sighed in a resigned fashion. 'You're not going to let this drop, are you?' She shook her head and compelled him to explain. 'I was about to say

—don't need to know that the piper is only heard at significant moments in the family's history. They say . . . but no, I don't want to go there. Not tonight, not on Samhain, when spirits are alleged to return to visit their loved ones.'

His last sentence made her skin break out in goose bumps.

'Go on,' she urged, taking in a large gulp of air and clutching his arm for support.

'They say,' he acted as though the words were being pulled out of him, 'that when my mother and brother drowned, the lament was heard. However, that night, everyone was in such a state that the Bay City Rollers could have been playing a medley of their greatest hits on the battlements and no one would have known the difference.' Henri knew he was trying to dismiss her fears by referencing the Bay City Rollers, however she couldn't let it drop, she had to *know*—even if it meant making him revisit that dreadful day.

He started towards the next flight of stone steps which led to the floor where his room was situated. She hung back. 'It's just—'

'Just?' He paused, one foot on the bottom tread and then turned to face her. Folding his arms across his chest, he leaned back against the wall, his expression resigned, knowing that she wouldn't let the subject drop until it'd been discussed, properly.

'It's just—I can't shake off the feeling that I haven't done my job thoroughly. That there's something . . . something important I've overlooked. In the library,' her expansive gesture took in the castle in its entirety, 'my bedroom, the Great Hall. Somewhere. Anywhere. I have a feeling that some . . . some*thing* is waiting for me to find it. *That's* what the piper is trying to tell me.'

Having got that off her chest she half-expected him to think she was mad, fey or both. Instead, his steady regard didn't miss a beat and after a few moments, he delivered his considered response.

'Henri.' Reaching out, he took her hands in his, as though he wanted to show he was speaking from the heart. 'You've found the *MacKenzie Papers* and the first edition *Waverley* novels. It won't be enough to keep the wolf from the door, but you've done enough to gain us a breathing space. To stop Castle

Tèarmannair from falling down round our ears. It's time for you to stand down.'

Her chest tightened. Did he mean it was *time for her to leave?* Is that what he was saying? Suddenly, going to his room didn't seem such a good idea after all, she wanted more from Keir MacKenzie than a quick tumble in his bed and a ticket back to England. Reading her expression and evidently knowing exactly what she was thinking, Keir shook his head. Pushing himself away from the wall, he took her in his arms and raised her face to his.

'How can you doubt me, or my intentions? Didn't you hear what I said to you in the library? *Tha gaol agam ort.*' He whispered it against her hair again. 'How many women do you think I've said that to?'

'I—I don't know . . .'

'You're the first, and you'll be the last woman I will ever love, *mo chridhe.*' *More* Gaelic! Was he trying to make her swoon with his passionate words? 'Do you understand me?'

'Y-yes,' was her tremulous response. 'You had me at . . .' she frowned, trying to remember the phrase: *'Tha thu a' . . .'*

Keir laughed. 'Well, I'm very thrilled that you think I'm beautiful, but—' Henri joined in with his laughter and that released the tension.

'Upstairs?' she suggested, dismissing pipers, premonitions, the feeling of a job half-done, unquiet spirits and everything that was part and parcel of Samhain. Keir nodded and started up the spiral staircase in front of her, sidestepping as he wouldn't release her hand and the narrowness of the stairs prevented them from walking side by side.

Soon they reached the corridor which lay directly above her own and walked to the far end where Keir's bedroom lay. Earlier, she'd helped Alice change his bed and had heard her threaten Lachlan with dire consequences if the fire wasn't kept burning. She'd thought at the time that Alice had gone to extraordinary lengths to make Keir stay the night, and not risk sailing up the loch in the pitch black—fresh flowers, the best Egyptian cotton sheets and pillowcases which had been part of the late Lady MacKenzie's trousseau.

Now she understood that Alice was giving them her blessing.

Ever-present tears filled her eyes and, after taking a steadying breath she laughed.

'What?' Keir inquired.

'I wondered why Alice removed some of the scented candles from the main bathroom and put them in yours. Such a romantic . . .'

'She's been anticipating, and planning, this moment ever since I took you over to the Beach House with the *MacKenzie Papers*. She even—no, I can't bring myself to tell you . . .' Now he was laughing and his eyes shone with love as he closed the heavy bedroom door, turned the key, and locked out the world.

'Go on. Nothing Alice does would surprise me—'

'When I unpacked the basket of food, I found that she'd included a packet of condoms next to the wine . . .'

'I *thought* you removed something and put it into your pocket. Alice—what is she like?'

'She doesn't want history repeating itself, I guess. She wants us to have time to get to know each other, before events overtake us, I guess.' An event such as an unplanned pregnancy, Henri realised.

After that, there was nothing else to say so Keir changed the subject, kissing her so thoroughly and passionately that her heart momentarily forgot its rhythm. Once his kisses stopped, he backed her towards the bed and sat her on the edge while he knelt at her feet. Raising his head, he took her hands in his and kissed their palms.

'Henri—I can't just walk away from the feast, I have things to attend to.' His expression was serious and Henri felt she had to make one thing clear.

'If it's about what Himself said in the Great Hall earlier, giving me my P45 and all that. It doesn't matter. I know I have to leave and . . .'

'It isn't that,' Keir forestalled her, 'although he was bang out of order.' There was a glint of steel in his eyes and his expression hardened. 'No; I have something to do, something I should have done years ago.' Henri held her breath, not knowing what he was referring to, but feeling it wasn't her place to ask. However, Keir seemed to have no such reservations. 'I have to make it perfectly clear, using words of one syllable—so there can be no mistake—that I have no intention of marrying Ciorstaidh. Not now. Nor at any time in the future, no matter what my father has promised.'

'I see.'

'Once that's established you and I can go forward. Tonight is about putting the past behind me and looking to the future. And then—'

'Then?'

'Then I shall return and—'

'And?' she teased.

'What d'you think?'

Their exchanged look was hot enough to melt the brass candlesticks on the sills of the thick window embrasures. Raising her feet off the carpet, he removed her ballet flats and laid her on the bed. Next, he settled a couple of large square cushions behind her head and cupped her cheek, briefly, in his right hand. 'I'll return with champagne. Not that gut-rot Father ordered from the cash and carry, proper stuff. Alice stashed a bottle of the MacKenzie-Grieveses' Pol Roger in the fridge, hiding it the one place Father would never think to look—behind the fruit and veg. He never touches the stuff, convinced it'll shorten his life.'

Henri laughed, thinking of the amount of booze Sir Malcolm put away and his penchant for big fat cigars, *when* he could afford them.

'Interesting theory. I'll have to run it past my parents some time.' She wondered what they would make of everything which had befallen her since she rang the bell on the far side, less than two months ago. Less than pleased, she guessed. They were fixated on her rising to the top of her profession and hadn't factored in her falling in love with the son of a penniless Highland laird.

'I won't be long. Promise. You can lock the door behind me if you like—although, no one would dare to set foot in my room uninvited. Not even Himself.' Henri caught a glimpse of the laird Keir would one day become: firm, fair but standing no nonsense from anyone. 'I'll make up the fire before I go.' Bending down on one knee he added a few peat turves from the small basket by the tiled hearth. Henri observed the pleasing way the pleats of his kilt fanned out over his bent knee, how his short jacket emphasised his broad shoulders and slim waist, the curl of his hair over the collar of his dress shirt. A moue of desire escaped her. Hearing it, Keir pushed his fly plaid out of his way with an impatient gesture and glanced round sharply. 'You okay, Henri?' he asked, misinterpreting the reason for her wistful sigh.

'More than okay,' she smiled. 'Hurry back.'

Standing, he brushed down his kilt and dusted his hands. 'Wings on my heels,' he grinned. Then, walking over to the bed, bent his head and kissed her again. Their tongues touched and, grasping the lapels of his jacket, Henri drew his head down level with hers, taking the initiative and kissing him in a manner which made it plain how much she wanted him.

Pulling back from the kiss, albeit reluctantly, Keir drew the quilt folded at the foot of the bed over her knees. All his earlier resolve seemed to falter at the thought of leaving her, forcing Henri to push him away with a laughing, 'Go. Go! The sooner you leave, the sooner you'll return.'

And they both knew what that meant.

'Roger that.' A final salute and he was gone.

Pulling the quilt up to her chin, Henri let out a long, slow breath, looked up at the ceiling, unromantically counting the damp patches where the rain came in, and waited for her heartbeat to return to the regulation number of beats per minute. Then she rested back against the large cushions and allowed her gaze to wander around his room, unable to comprehend that she was actually in Keir's bed.

To calm her nerves and to pass the time, she made a careful inventory of his room—from the faded Turkish rug by the small grate, to the large window which opened directly onto the battlements. As Keir had said, no one was allowed in this room without his permission and, as a result, it had everything her room lacked—tapestries, paintings, a bookcase with an assortment of novels, the half-tester bed with new hangings (Alice's touch, no doubt); a marble-topped dressing table much like her own, and fine oak furniture which even Himself hadn't had the effrontery to sell behind Keir's back.

There were two lopsided Airfix Spitfires on the bookcase, faded photos of first elevens and rugby teams in an assortment of frames, alongside those of dogs and ponies long since departed. But no photo of his mother or brother. It was as he'd said, they'd been airbrushed from history. Thank God the *MacKenzie Papers* had given them a common goal which had led—well, had led to him trusting her—and finally, to *this*.

What *this* was, she wasn't quite sure. She'd take it one stage at a time and allow things to unfold at their own pace.

In spite of the heat coming from the fire, she shivered and her arms were pricked all over with goose bumps. She'd lovers, of course she had; however, despite her age, she was sexually naïve. She hoped that wouldn't show when—

Gah! Listen to her. Now was not the moment to start thinking like that, it was certain to give her pre-performance nerves! Wasn't it supposed to be like riding a bicycle?

She pulled a face at the banality of the phrase and then, in order to make time pass, returned to comparing Keir's room with her own. Hers was directly below and had more or less the same layout: door in the right-hand corner, windows along the left-hand side looking across the loch to the shore where Lachlan had picked her up that fateful evening. Door—wall—windows; all identical. The only discernible difference being the length of their corridors from the spiral staircase to the end wall, hers being a good six feet shorter. Then she reminded herself that the castle was hundreds of years old and not constructed to an exact design. The corridors, doubtless built during Victorian/Edwardian times to accommodate bedroom swapping in the middle of the night, were bound to be of varying length.

She couldn't fathom why that bothered her. But, bother her it did.

Phantom pipers, uneven corridors, walls, windows, doors. She yawned, wishing Keir would hurry up with the champagne. Shadows danced on the ceiling and, as the wind whistled around the castle, rattling the ill-fitting windows and making the peat turves hiss in the fireplace, her eyelids grew heavier.

She was, if the truth be told, bone weary. The business in the hall, her encounter with Sandy MacKenzie-Grieves in the library, even the passionate kisses she'd exchanged with Keir had taken their toll.

Surely it wouldn't hurt to close her eyes for a moment?

Soon her breathing settled into a deeper, more rhythmic pattern and she was fast asleep.

Chapter Twenty-Six
And So to Bed

Henri awoke with a start, wondering where she was. The room looked exactly like her room, but it most certainly *wasn't* her room. Neither was this her bed! Then she remembered—the Samhain feast, the conversation with Alexander in the library, Keir leaving to 'take care of something.' It felt as if she'd been asleep for a hundred years.

'Keir—' she murmured, disorientated.

'Yes?'

He was sitting on a low armchair by the dying fire, hand cradling his cheek, stockinged-feet stretched towards the fire for warmth. Mortified that she'd fallen asleep—*how romantic*—instead of keeping watch and waiting for his return, Henri pushed the coverlet off her knees and swung her feet onto the floor. Trust her to fall asleep and ruin the moment—another Henriette Bruar #epicfail.

If she could find her bloody shoes, she could leave with her dignity intact.

'Looking for these?' Keir pushed the ballet flats towards her with his toe. Judging by his grim expression, he'd surmised she was having second thoughts and couldn't get out his bedroom fast enough.

'Yes. I—I—Keir, I am *so* sorry. Falling fast asleep when I should have been . . .' she trailed off, unable to find the right words.

'Waiting for me with open—not to say, eager—arms?' A faint smile.

'Don't make it worse than it already is, please.' Her voice was muffled as she put her shoes back on. Straightening, she did a double take as her sleep-befuddled brain registered that Keir had a pack of frozen peas pressed against his cheek. 'Oh my God—what happened to you?'

Keir removed the makeshift icepack, to reveal the beginnings of a large swelling and a real shiner. 'Oh, this?' He dismissed the injury with a nonchalant shrug. 'Safe to say, things did not go as planned . . .'

In a flash Henri was at his side, full of anxiety. 'Did Sir Malcolm do that to you—or, Alexander?' It seemed unlikely, but she had to ask. Removing the pack of frozen peas from his face, she gasped at the extent of his injury. Plainly, someone's knuckle had grazed his cheekbone and, as a coup de grace, clocked the outer orbit of his left eye. 'I'll wrap the peas in something, the packet shouldn't be in direct contact with your skin, you'll get frost burn.' To make up for not spotting his injury straightaway, she diligently stripped a pillowcase off the bed and wrapped it round the frozen peas. 'Here, that should feel better.'

Full of concern, she handed the cold compress back him.

'Thank you.' He pressed the pillowcase against his face. Struggling to contain her curiosity, Henri sat back on the bed, desperate to learn what had happened. Now wasn't the time to start asking a hundred and one questions. Keir would reveal everything in his own good time.

'You're welcome,' she replied in automatic response. Then she noticed a crimson stain spreading across the front of his dress shirt, like a Rorschach blot. The last vestiges of sleep vanished as she rushed over and pressed the flat of her hand against his chest to check for injuries, and to stem the flow of blood. 'Keir. You're hurt!'

'It's not quite what it seems,' he dismissed her concern. 'Trust me.' When Henri removed her hand and sniffed, she was relieved to discover that the crimson stain was in fact red wine.

'Wine? I'll take *that*, and your black eye, as a sign that things did not go well?'

'You could say that.' Wincing, he settled the ice pack more comfortably against his cheek and explained. 'When I returned to the hall, Ciorstaidh was in full flow, organising the game of Sardines. When she spotted me, she headed for me like a heat-seeking missile. Demanded to know where I'd been. What I'd been doing. Where *you* were. The game, she explained, couldn't begin without *you*. I was a bit puzzled by that comment, until I realised that Sandy had been commissioned to keep you out of the way while we—Ciorstaidh and I, as designated joint 'hiders', squeezed ourselves into some dark nook or cranny until a 'seeker' found us—and climbed in beside us.'

Her and Sandy MacKenzie-Grieves? *Exactly like the shinty match!*

The image of Keir crushed up against the MacKenzie heiress in an intimate, dark space, did nothing to improve Henri's shattered nerves. The castle was vast and had so many hidden places that they could have been stuck in a hidey hole for *hours*. Sickness rose in her throat and a physical sensation, akin to a length of barbed wire being dragged through her innards, rocked her to her core. She was quick to recognise it for what it was—jealousy. An emotion she'd hitherto never experienced with any man.

However, Keir MacKenzie wasn't just any man.

Reining in the green-eyed monster, she urged him to continue.

'When I told her *exactly* where you were . . . in my bed, waiting for me to return, she totally lost it. Shrieked—called me a double-dealing bastard; drew her arm back and landed a right hook on the side of my head. I swear, my eyes rolled in their sockets and my teeth rattled. Then she carried on screaming and shrieking—calling me everything from a pig to a dog, while the whole room watched on in stunned silence. Then her mother, apparently getting a handle on what was unfolding, picked up a glass of red wine—a fine Montepulciano, by the taste of it, tossed it in my face and joined in with Ciorstaidh's screaming fit. For an elderly lady she had a fine stock of swear words.' He smiled weakly at his joke. Henri put her hands over her mouth in horror, not knowing what to say, but finally managed a distressed—*Oh, Keir.* 'My father, not to be left out, denounced me as unworthy of the MacKenzie name and how, if he had his way, he'd disinherit me in favour of—oh, I don't know, Lachlan, or possibly one of the dogs.'

Although he made light of it, Henri could tell he was perturbed by the turn of events. What had started out as a 'quiet word' with Ciorstaidh and his intention of doing the right thing, had ended up in an unseemly slanging match. And where had she been? Snoring her head off in his bed, oblivious.

Kneeling, Henri placed her hands on Keir's kilted thighs and looked up at him with troubled green eyes. 'Keir, I—I'm lost for words -'

'I never thought I'd hear you say that. Now I know the world has gone mad.' His sense of humour slowly returned and his mouth quirked in a half-smile. Putting the cold compress down on the hearth, he covered her hands with his own. 'No worries; I've been threatened with disinheritance dozens of times over the years. The main thing is that the *Keir-and-Ciorstaidh-will-marry-one-day* roadshow has come off the rails. I should have put her straight years ago; however, by foolishly trying to spare her feelings I've managed to hurt her more.' A knife twisted in Henri's stomach at his show of concern for his cousin. Then she gave herself a severe mental scolding. Keir was an honourable man, how could he not feel guilt and remorse over what had happened in the Great Hall?

'Go on,' she urged, sensing he had more to say.

'Every time I came home from Canada, I hoped they'd given up on the plan to marry us off. I hoped that she'd forget me; but each time we've met over the intervening years she seemed more determined to have her way. To have *me*. To keep the peace I remained silent, hoping she'd outgrow her ambition to become Lady MacKenzie.'

Did he really have no idea of his own attractiveness, Henri wondered? As Ciorstaidh had said in the library when Henri had stated Keir wasn't her type: *Have you seen him? He's every woman's type.*

'Oh, Keir.' Unsure whether to laugh or cry, she gave his hands a reassuring squeeze. What a night!

Ciorstaidh using foul language in front of the guests and then placing a well-aimed punch to the side of his head. Stiff, proper Mrs MacKenzie-Grieves anointing him with wine, no doubt with the aunts rolling up their sleeves and standing in line to deliver the sucker-punch while he was down. His father, disowning him for the *nth* time as penury and bankruptcy loomed ever closer. Now everyone—guests, aunts, tiny tots and faithful retainers—

would know how things stood between the Master of Mountgarrie and Dr Henriette Bruar. Before morning it would be common knowledge that she was in his bedroom waiting for him. The news would spread outwards from the village store (courtesy of Lachlan, no doubt), across the loch to MacKenzie tenants and then, growing in the telling, recounted to anyone with half an interest in the families.

If the spirits of the dead had any sense this Samhain, they'd return to the underworld where life was more tranquil. Next year, instead of Trick or Treat and pumpkin heads, she'd dream of *guising,* neep lanterns, clootie dumplings and a harpist playing Celtic tunes.

Henri felt a grudging respect for Ciorstaidh MacKenzie-Grieves. She knew what she wanted and went all out to get it. Whereas she wavered between wanting to remain in Castle Tèarmannair, and returning to St Guthlac to defend her name and reputation.

'Why didn't you wake me?' she asked, returning to the present.

'I was more concerned with barricading the door to my bedroom in case Sandy MacKenzie-Grieves came demanding satisfaction because I'd slighted his sister. Or my father got Lachlan to set about me with one of the Lochaber axes hanging up in the hall.'

'Are you taking any of this seriously?' she asked, not quite understanding why he so looked relieved.

'I'm putting a positive spin on things. Don't you see, Henri, at last I'm free; free to embrace the future on my own terms.' The meaningful look he shot her from beneath straight black brows, indicated that his future involved her. 'A black eye and a wine stain down the front of my shirt is small price to pay for being spared an unhappy marriage. The charade is over; even father knows that, in spite of his bluster. Added to which, *mo chridhe,* you looked so beautiful lying there asleep, that I didn't have the heart to wake you.'

'Beautiful? I'm sure I was snoring—and drooling.' She dismissed his words with the throwaway remark, to hide how much they affected her.

'Well, maybe a little bit of drool—just there.' Raising a forefinger, he pointed to the corner of her mouth. Mortified, Henri drew back—but when he leaned forward and kissed her on the spot, she realised he was joking.

'Why you—'

Slipping his hands beneath hers, he took hold of her wrists, and pulled her onto his knee. Tipping her back, he cradled her in his arms and looked down on her face. 'I'd go five rounds with the late, great Mohammed Ali, if it meant having you in my bed, lassie.' Then he kissed her and, there being nothing else for it, Henri kissed him back. Desire banished second thoughts, regrets and what-ifs. All they had was the moment; however long that 'moment' lasted.

Let that be enough.

Pulling back, she touched the side of his face where Ciorstaidh's right hook had landed. He winced slightly as she planted feather-light kisses on the bruise, running her free hand through his wine-sticky hair. Keir let out a breath and closed his eyes, as though her light, caring touch was all he needed to make him whole. Then he slid his hand along her leg and under the stiff material of her dress, until he reached the lacy top of her sheer stockings. They both stopped breathing at that point and Henri's cheeks flamed as the intimate touch went higher, ever higher. Almost on automatic pilot, she unfastened the buttons of his ruined dress shirt. When her fingers trailed across the firm planes of his chest, Keir groaned and scooped her up, carrying her over to the bed where he laid her amongst the monogrammed pillows.

Walking over to the door, he turned the key in the lock. 'Just to be sure we aren't disturbed. I intend taking my time making love to you, Henriette Bruar. For you are a pleasure not to be rushed.'

'Oh—' was her inadequate response to this passionate speech.

At that moment, far below them on the jetty overlooking the loch, a piper played a lively tune.

'Put that thought on hold, *mo chridhe*. This is something you must see.'

Leading her over to the window, Keir opened it, stepped through on to the battlements and beckoned her to follow. Once out in the cold October air, he slipped off his fly plaid and wrapped it round her to keep her warm. Henri found his concern for her welfare more affecting than heart-stopping kisses and romantic declarations.

'Look,' he commanded, 'down there.'

Below them, a flotilla of small boats, decked with lights and rocking at their moorings filled up with departing guests. Above them, a hunter's moon, bright as a searchlight, lit the way across the loch to the far side. Then, as the piper squeezed his bag, took in a good lungful of cold Highland air and changed key, Lachlan and young Lachy set off fireworks. Rockets shot into the air, exploding like giant chrysanthemums and were reflected on the waters of the loch. Manoeuvring Henri so that she was in front of him, he shielded her from the wind by positioning her behind one of the battlements.

Wordlessly, they watched each boat cover the short distance between castle and shore where waiting cars and taxis were parked. After setting off the last firework, Lachlan, his nephew, the piper and Sir Malcolm travelled the short distance across the loch by boat, too; Lachlan to his sister's house and Sir Malcolm, obviously having no concept of shame, to stay with the MacKenzie-Grieveses.

Keir and Henri stood until they'd all departed and the surface of the loch was free of the wakes created by outboard motors. Then Keir pulled Henri back against him and kissed the top of her head

'And so to bed?' His voice was husky as he kissed the nape of her neck.

Nodding, Henri shivered; the tremor had nothing to do with the wind blowing off the loch and everything to do with her feelings for this man. Taking a step away from him, she unwrapped herself from his plaid and, taking his hand, led them through the window, into his room and the sanctuary of the ancient, half-tester bed.

Chapter Twenty-Seven
Next Morning . . .

Henri was woken by Keir twirling a loose feather from one of the goose-down pillows over her collarbone and then between her breasts. Discarding the feather, he rained light, teasing kisses in its wake until his mouth found her nipple and latched on, making her gasp. Last night, he'd declared her a pleasure not to be rushed, and had been true to his word. Each time they made love surpassed the time before as they explored each other's bodies, discovering what pleased them and taking pleasure to new heights.

Henri's reservations about appearing sexually gauche had vanished when Keir took command of their lovemaking and then encouraged her to take the initiative. Gaining in confidence she'd pushed him over onto his back and done things which had made him call out her name as they climaxed. Now, as she arched her back, pushing her breast closer to his questing tongue, cradling his head there, a cry of pleasure escaped her. When his hand slid between her thighs and her body remembered his touch, it called out for more.

It took them a few seconds to register that someone was knocking on the door. Ignoring the rat-a-tat-tat, Keir raised his head and traced a line from Henri's breast to just above her bikini line with tiny kisses. Henri tried to ignore the knocking, too, but in the end she was forced to wriggle out from under him.

'Find out who it is.' She pushed him over to his side of the bed. 'Then get rid of them.'

'Who's there?' Keir asked in a mock-cheerful voice, adding in a whisper, 'because, whoever you are, I'm going to kill you.'

'It's Alice, with a cup of tea for you and Henri.'

Keir sent Henri a helpless *what is she like?* look of inquiry. Nodding, Henri indicated that he should unlock the door. Then she pointed to their clothes scattered all over the floor and signalled that he should restore some order to his bedroom before admitting his aunt. It looked as if they'd ripped each other's clothes off their backs last night in their hurry to get into bed. Which is exactly what had happened—however, she didn't want Alice to know that! Giving another mock-resigned sigh, Keir got out of bed, picked up their clothes and threw them over the foot of the bed. That made everything look a little bit more respectable, until he tied his fly plaid around his hips like a tartan sarong, walked over to the door and unlocked it. Opening the door, he ushered in his aunt with a mocking little bow and a sweep of his hand.

'Why don't you come in, Auntie Alice,' he said, as Henri pulled the duvet up to her chin to hide her nakedness. But she guessed it was all rather academic. She didn't suppose that worldly Alice Dougal, who'd put up with a succession of Himself's *wee lassies* parading round the castle in their under things, imagined for one moment they'd spent the night in the Master of Mountgarrie's bed playing Pictionary.

'I will. Morning, Henri.' Alice entered bearing a tray laden with breakfast: teapot, milk, sugar, hot buttered toast (now rapidly cooling), a pot of homemade marmalade and *three* teacups.

'Morning, Alice. Tea and toast I see, for *three*.' If Alice detected irony in Henri's voice, she gave no indication.

'Aye, well, I thought I'd bring breakfast and share it with youse. You'll be hungry after—well, I just thought you'd be hungry.' She didn't quite meet Henri's eye, so Henri's blushes were spared.

'Here, you sit on the end of the bed, Alice, while I get the fire going,' Keir suggested. Alice did just that, laying the tray flat on the bed and pouring out three cups of builders' tea, nothing as refined as Earl Grey or Darjeeling on offer this morning. She held a cup out to Henri, but was forced to repeat her name because Henri was admiring how the muscles on Keir's back expanded and contracted as he manipulated an ancient set of hand-bellows. Once the flames were leaping round the rolled up newspaper, he added kindling and a firelighter. Then he hopped back into bed, removed his plaid and dropped it on the floor by his aunt's feet. Smiling, he took the cup and saucer Alice proffered, holding it in his hand as delicate as a bishop at a tea party.

'Well, this,' he said, looking between both women and sticking his pinkie out as he sipped his tea, 'is verra nice.'

His dry delivery and the extended pinkie had Henri giggling and she had to nibble on her toast to gain control of herself. In that instant, she was reminded of the romantic pot-boilers she'd devoured at boarding school. The ones where the family of the virgin heroine demanded evidence the morning after the wedding night that the marriage had been consummated. She hoped Alice wouldn't go that far, although, one was never quite sure with her. Keeping her thoughts private, she let Keir and Alice do the talking as she savoured the moment.

'Och, will you look at yer eye, Keir, it's a fine mess. Ah'll away and fetch the arnica and dispose of the defrosted peas, once we've drunk our tea. Last night—what a to-do, ah didnae think wee Ku-rsty had it in her. Anyone would think she'd been in training, the way she delivered that right hook. The wee besom. And,' she bent down and picked Keir's dress shirt off the floor, 'will ye just *look* at your best shirt; I'll never get that stain oot in a month o' Sundays. Not even if I use a whole bucket of stain remover and put it through the boil-wash—twice.'

The fact that she was lying next to Alice's nephew, naked, while Alice discussed the boil wash, was enough to set Henri off again. Her cup rattled in her saucer as she convulsed with laughter. For a moment Alice regarded her severely, as if a ruined hand-made shirt was no laughing matter. Then she, too, saw the funny side of them taking breakfast together the morning after her nephew and the castle archivist had become lovers.

'Let's go mad and throw the shirt away?' Keir suggested, putting his cup on the side table, slipping his free arm around Henri's shoulders and drawing her into his side. 'I declare today a holiday. It feels like the first day of the rest of my life.' He kissed the side of Henri's head while his aunt looked on approvingly. 'I'm guessing Father spent the night at Glen Shiel House?'

'Aye, for he has n-oh shame. Now you've made it plain that Ciorstaidh'll never be mistress o' this castle, they'll have no further use for the auld foo-ul. He'll be as welcome as a drunk at a Methodist tea. The sooner he returns to France, the better, for all concerned.'

'You don't think he'll make an offer for Ciorstaidh's mother, then?' Alice's expression was grim as she considered Henri's question. Things were about to change at Castle Tèarmannair, and not for the better. Without Ciorstaidh's money, Keir's inheritance was doomed, even if his emotional well-being was safeguarded.

'Not even he's that stoo-pit,' Alice replied, shaking her head.

'Don't be so sure,' Keir interjected and then gave a start as Henri kicked his leg and regarded him with wide, *what-are-you-saying*, green eyes. If she and Maddie had worked out that Alice had carried a torch for the laird all these years—why else would she stay in this draughty, damp castle?—surely his son should have picked up on it, too. Men. Honestly. Keir looked at her, mystified, then the penny dropped and he tried to cover up his gaff. 'Mind you, after last night's exhibition, I doubt he'd give her a second thought. She swore like a trouper, I think even Sandy was appalled at her vocabulary.' Then he steered the subject onto safer ground. 'I don't know how you carried that tray up two sets of spiral stairs, Alice. Leave everything where it is and I'll bring everything down—later.'

'Later? Oh, of course.' Taking the hint, she got to her feet and scooped Keir's dress shirt off the end of the bed. 'The clocks went back last night, so you'll get an extra hour in bed. Now, take as long as youse like, to . . .' Tenderly touching their intertwined limbs, she straightened the duvet as she took her leave. 'There's no one in the castle but me and the dogs. Just me and the dogs.' Her whole body sagged and, fleetingly, she looked her age. It was as if, seeing the two of them in bed, glowing and sated after a night's lovemaking, reminded her of what she'd given up to act as surrogate mother to Keir and unpaid housekeeper to the laird.

'Tell you what, Alice,' Henri began, 'if you're up for it, why don't you start on one of your legendary steak pies? We'll join you later and help clear the Great Hall?'

Alice saw through Henri's offer but was evidently happy to play along. 'Ye'r a good lassie, Henri, and that's a capital idea. I'll ring Lachlan and get him back to lend a hand; lazy, good-for-nothing layabout, that he is. I'll no have him sitting in the post office café drinking lattes and giving a blow-by-blow account of last night's drama. We dinnae wah-nt our dirty washing hung out in public.'

'Not even my dress shirt?' Keir teased.

'No; not even that,' she grinned, more her old self. Then she left them alone, closing the bedroom door quietly behind her after with a last, longing look. 'Now,' Keir leaned up on his elbow and looked down on her, 'where were we, Dr Bruar?'

'I think you had one hand *here*, and your other hand was about *there*.' She guided them into position. 'And I believe you were about to—mmph.'

Having no further need for her help, Keir rolled her under him and kissed her, driving all thoughts of steak pies, dirty laundry and post-party clear ups from her mind.

Chapter Twenty-Eight
A Eureka Moment

Some hours later, Henri made her way down the spiral staircase towards her room on the floor below. Minutes earlier Alice had called through Keir's bedroom door that she'd run Henri a bath and was doing the same for him. Apparently, there was masses of hot water bubbling in the ancient plumbing system, thanks to last night's fires in the Great Hall and she didn't want it going to waste. Plainly, *that* was Alice's *un*subtle way of reminding them it was early afternoon and time they made good on their promise to help clear the Great Hall.

Although loath to leave Keir's warm bed, Henri relished the thought of washing her hair and putting on something more suitable than her black dress and hold up stockings. As she made her way along the lower corridor she smiled, remembering how, every time she'd attempted to get out bed, Keir had pulled her back for *one last kiss*. One kiss had led to many more until she'd been forced to retrieve her clothes from the chair and leave the room without a backward glance, in case her resolve weakened.

What a difference a day makes.

Grinning like a jackanapes and well pleased at how things had turned out, she was determined to live in the moment. Who knew what tomorrow would bring?

Entering her room, she found Lachlan stoking the fire. 'Oh,' she exclaimed, pulling the edges of Keir's borrowed dressing gown together in order to shield her nakedness. 'Good morning, Lachlan.'

'Afternoon, mair liker it,' he hissed, clattering the coal bucket to express his displeasure. Struggling to his feet, he shook off her proffered hand, his arthritic bones creaking as he straightened. Then he shot her another sour look. 'Have ye no shame, lassie, spending the night in the Master's bed, getting up tae goodness knows what?'

Henri was tempted to tell him that goodness didn't come into it, but resisted the impulse. There was no need to stoop to his level or to antagonise him further. 'I really don't see what business it is of yours what Keir and I get up to . . .'

'Are ye glaekit?' Henri recoiled as he stepped towards her, brandishing a small coal shovel like a weapon. 'Well, let me explain it tae ye, seeing as ye *dinnae get it*.' He said the last as if she was slow-witted. 'Thanks to *you*, Himself will be away back tae France as soon as he can—leaving *me* high and dry. Mah sister's had enough of me staying in her spare room and ah'm getting too old to cart buckets of coal up and down stairs a' day long, so ah'll doubtless be let go, by *her* in the kitchen. I'm for the knacker's yard, d'ye no ken that? If Himself was coming back here tae live it'd be different, he'd never throw me oot. I'd have a home for life.'

'Keir would never throw you out; you know that, Lachlan MacKenzie.' Henri was fierce in her defence of her lover. 'You're his clan, and his blood, he'll always look after you.' But he refused to be mollified and seemed affronted that she should concern herself with MacKenzie business.

'It was a bad day's work when I brought ye over from the far side. Ah shoulda drowned ye like—like an unwanted kitten, while I had the chance. Now, oot'a mah way, Auld Alice has a list o' jobs for me, which'll take me maist o' the day—should the Guid Lord be kind enough tae spare me.' Pointing the shovel in her direction once more, he left the room, banging the door behind him so forcefully that the fire belched out black smoke.

'Bugger.'

Dropping her dirty clothes on the floor, Henri collapsed backwards onto the bed. Evidently, she was the villainess of the piece, the upsetter of apple carts. The wee lassie who'd brought bad luck to the castle and ruined all their dreams. Letting out a huff of dismay, she lay on her back staring up at the ceiling, long legs dangling over the side of the bed, toes touching the floor.

The encounter with Lachlan had pricked her bubble of happiness.

After a few minutes, she pushed herself upright, determined not to let him rain on her parade. Collecting everything necessary for her bath, she left the room, smoking fire and Lachlan's rather pungent odour behind, anxious not to spend any more time than was necessary away from the Master of Mountgarrie. Or his bed.

After Alice's signature dish—peppery steak pie cooked beneath a puff pastry crust, carrots, neeps and tatties, followed by a slice of microwaved clootie dumpling and double cream—Henri returned to the library. Now the Great Hall was clear and the trestle tables were back in place, each book had to be transferred from the floor back onto its designated place. Only she was qualified to do that, so she'd left Keir stacking the dishwasher and Alice making the coffee in the kitchen. The library shelves were now empty, including the secretaire bookcase and, in spite of the roaring fire, cold air wafted round her ankles. She glanced round the echoing library and felt sad.

'I don't want to leave,' she declared to the empty room. 'I *never* want to leave.'

The books, however, had no words of wisdom to offer and the spectral piper was evidently on his coffee break. Shaking her head, she cursed Lachlan, all five feet three of him, for implying they were *all* on borrowed time and the castle was about to be sold from under them.

The door opened and Keir entered carrying a tray of coffee. Her heart gave a glad leap and her stomach flipped over as she experienced the heady rush of falling in love. Every inch of her skin remembered last night—his touch, his kisses, his tender lovemaking. Then reality kicked in, like a douche of cold water. Where would it end? Any invitation to stay on at Castle Tèarmannair or the Beach House had to come from Keir, much as she might wish it otherwise. And that didn't sit easy with her. She liked being in control, mistress of her destiny . . . hell, she didn't even know whose bed she'd be sleeping in tonight.

'Coffee? I'm desperate for a cup.' Hiding her turmoil behind a bright smile she took the tray from Keir and placed it on the low table between the two chesterfields. Turning, she glanced up at him through lowered eyelashes and, in spite of all her best intentions to stay level-headed, a lance of desire stabbed her clean through her heart. Hands shaking, she spilled coffee into the china saucers. Was he aware of the effect he had on her? Did he know that with just one look he could turn her bones to water and make her forget the world beyond the castle walls, her life back at the university and her dream of becoming a university teacher?

'Alice'll be along in a minute. I was given my marching orders because according to my beloved aunt, I was stacking the dishwasher like a love-struck teenager. And whose fault is that?' He sent her a long, burning look from beneath straight black brows and her cup rattled in the saucer all the more. If she was agitated—in the nicest possible way, as a result of last night's love-making—Keir appeared to be handling the situation more adroitly.

'M-mine?' she stammered.

'Ach, will you look at you standing there, backlit by the fire—your hair all tumbling round your face, like an angel? Don't just stand there, wumman; come and kiss me.'

The contrast between Keir's first sentence and the way the second was delivered in a gruff, Highland accent made Henri laugh. Forgetting all her qualms, she ran into his arms with such enthusiasm that he was knocked back on his heels by the force of it. Then she did as commanded, kissing him with fierce passion. One kiss led to another until hearts beating in unison and unwilling to release each other for even a second, they shuffled over to the chesterfield, as though tied together for the three-legged race at the village sports day. The low back pressed against Henri's knees and Keir exerted just enough force to ensure that she rolled over it, taking him with her.

They landed in a heap with their limbs entwined and laughing in delight at the ridiculousness of it all. Keir rolled Henri under him and she revelled in the weight of his body on hers, how he pressed her down onto the sofa, long legs ranged against her own, hard chest muscles crushing her softer breasts. It was all so deliciously arousing that she could do no more than close her eyes and revel in the moment.

'What've you been doing since we last met?' Keir asked, pushing her hair out of her eyes and trailing little kisses along her nose and cheekbones.

'Thinking about you; about us.'

'I meant in an academic sense, Dr Bruar.' Taking his weight on his elbows, Keir pretended disapproval at her lax attitude towards the books.

She sent him a straight look.

'I feel light as air but—at the same time, full of dread . . . because I don't want to ruin things . . .'

'How could you ruin things? You, Dr Bruar, are *perfect* . . .'

A lump began to form in Henri's throat and tears misted her eyes—really, she was turning into an emotional wreck. She took in a shuddering breath. God, she so wanted it to work between them, but she'd made a mess of every one of her previous relationships for one reason or another: academic ambitions, pickiness, lack of enthusiasm for the man in question, incompatibility.

Would history repeat itself?

'I'd never let that happen; know that?' There was an honesty in his expression and a clear light in his eyes which dazzled her. As he waited for her answer, his hand slid under her thick jersey, and his watch snagged on her silk, thermal vest. 'Hello, what have we here?' He pushed her jumper higher so he could give her practical, but very *un-sexy* choice of underwear, a more thorough examination. 'I'm sure, in the circles you mix in, such garments are regarded as alluring. However, I promise, once the war's over and clothes come off rationing, I'll take you to Edinburgh to buy something more suited to getting my pulse racing.'

Laughing, Henri slapped his hand away, pulled down her jumper and settled deeper into his arms. 'I think,' she said, pressing her ears up to his heart, 'that your pulse is racing fast enough. Besides, my choice of undergarments is very much in vogue with female academics. Designed to keep us warm in freezing cold libraries and ancient castles, and for no other reason.'

'Not for the titillation of the heir of said castle?'

'Certainly not!'

'Then, may I suggest, that you reconsider your choice, Dr Bruar?'

'Of lairds or underwear?'

'Underwear.'

'Otherwise?'

'Otherwise, I'll have to do this—' He pushed aside the jumper and thermal vest, revealing her lacy bra. 'Then this.' He pushed his hand between the edge of her bra and her skin. 'And possibly, this.' His mouth replaced his hand and he sucked hard through the lacy material. Henri cried out, her womb contracting in response to his sure touch. Wrapping one long leg around his buttocks, she drew him in closer until she felt his arousal pressing up against her pelvic bone. After that, her love-drugged brain was capable of only one thought.

It didn't matter whose bed she slept in that night, as long as Keir was by her side.

There was a discreet cough at the door and Alice entered. Eyes averted, she polished the corner of the rosewood piano with her pinny until Henri's clothes were rearranged and she and Keir were sitting upright on the chesterfield.

'Merely checking that Dr Bruar is correctly attired for the northern wastes and is wearing a simmet. That's a *vest*, to the uninitiated,' Keir quipped, earning a dig in the ribs from Henri.

Alice flashed him a reproving look and settled herself on the sofa opposite.

'You got the books back on the tables in record time, Henri,' she commented, ignoring her nephew. 'Now, down to business; I've got what you asked for. Ah'm no feart to go into Himself's sitting room without permission.' She passed a large rolled-up chart across the table to Henri. 'This is the oldest floor plan of the castle I could find . . . '

'Thank you, Alice.'

'I don't suppose anyone has looked at it in years. I only know it's there because I move it every week when I do the dusting and empty his disgusting ashtray.'

'Still smoking those cigars?' Keir asked, frowning.

'Aye, when he can afford them.'

'Perfect!'

Ignoring them, Henri unrolled an ancient floorplan of Castle Tèarmannair and placed a coffee cup on each of the three corners and a cut glass paperweight on the other.

'I don't understand why an old map of the castle should be of such interest to you. Is it valuable?' Keir asked, kneeling beside her and looking over her shoulder.

'Yes—and no. Sorry—here's the thing; earlier, when I was having my bath, I had a Eureka moment. Like Archimedes?' Bright-eyed with enthusiasm, she looked up, and encountered two puzzled faces. 'You know the story— Archimedes was in his bath when he discovered the principle of water displacement and exclaimed, Eureka! Eureka! I have it. Then he ran through the streets of Syracuse, naked, to share his discovery.'

Keir appeared to give the idea serious thought. 'I'm not sure that running naked through MacKenzie's Halt at this time of year is a good idea—'

'Stop teasing the lassie and let her continue.'

'Thank you, Alice.' Reminding herself that she wasn't giving a lecture on ancient Greek mathematicians, Henri cut to the chase. 'Something about my room has been puzzling me since I arrived at the castle. I couldn't quite put my finger on it until,' she looked down at the ancient map to hide her blushes, 'until I woke up in Keir's bed this morning.'

'Another Eureka moment?' he inquired, straight-faced, only to receive another chastising look from his aunt. 'Okay, I'll behave. Go on, *mo muirnín*.' Engrossed in her explanation, Henri failed to notice Keir's use of the Gaelic endearment—*my darling*.

'Your room is roughly the same size as mine, yet the corridor outside my room is about five feet *shorter* than your corridor. I needed to check a castle plan to confirm my hunch, before I got too excited.' Shuffling on her knees, she crouched in front of the long side of the plans of the castle and explained. 'You see, corridors weren't introduced in grand houses until well after the 1820s, and then not universally. Blenheim and Castle Howard had corridors installed much earlier, in the late seventeenth, early eighteenth century, but are the exception rather than the rule. So, I got to thinking—how long had my corridor *been there*? There's no sign of it on the 1715 plans, yet it appears on *this* plan which is dated,' she looked sideways at the map, '1745.'

'Let me see.' Keir was checked the plans. '1745—and yes, there's your corridor.'

'It doesn't say when my corridor was built, but I'm guessing between 1715 —the first major Jacobite Rebellion, and 1745, the last. Your corridor, Keir, isn't on either set of plans, which leads me to believe it was a much later addition; mid-nineteenth century, possibly. Which would make perfect sense.'

Looking up from the plans, she moved away and sat on the fender, buzzing with excitement, and waited for their reaction.

Keir was first to break the silence. 'You love all this, don't you, Henri?' His expansive gesture took in the library, the plans and her flushed, excited face. 'History; finding things; breaking new ground.'

'It's what I'm good at. It's what I do.'

'And you miss it, don't you?'

'In some ways—yes. But that doesn't mean I don't love it here. That I don't love *you*.'

Henri was anxious to make Keir understand that although she did miss aspects of her old life, she'd give it up in a heartbeat. For what could equal what she'd found in Castle Tèarmannair—happiness, contentment, the man she wanted to spend the rest of her life with?

Evidently deciding that they needed time alone, Alice made her excuses. 'I've got to—there's a *thing* in the kitchen—I have tae—catch you later.' With that she left the library.

For long seconds neither of them spoke and Henri, knowing she'd said the wrong thing, stared into the fire trying to find the right words to explain her feelings to Keir. When she raised her head, he was standing by one of the far windows looking over the loch towards the lights on the shore; all brooding and silent. On the face of it, it must seem as though she was putting her love of history and her ambitions first. However, nothing was further from the truth. Everything she did was for him—for *them*. Joining him at the window, Henri pressed her cheek against his back and put her arms around his waist. Her heart gave an anxious lurch when he didn't respond.

'Keir, I've expressed myself badly. Give me chance to explain—'

'Maps, corridors, MacKenzie's Gold,' he said after a pause. 'You've heard that damned piper again, haven't you?' His throwaway remark sounded forced, clumsy, a feeble attempt to lighten the mood. He gave her hands an encouraging squeeze but remained apart from her, staring out into the November gloom. 'Go on, explain.'

It was clear from his tone that Henri had one chance to get it right. Taking a deep breath, she began.

'What if—and, run with me on this one—what if my corridor is *just* as long as yours? That it doesn't finish at the far wall. What if the end wall was erected sometime after the 1715, thus creating a void—a *space* behind it. Making my corridor shorter than yours by about six feet.' Henri gave him time to evaluate the evidence. After all, she'd had a whole afternoon to give her theory serious consideration.

'A space?' He turned round, his curiosity aroused and looked down on her.

'Yes!' Henri had one chance to make him understand *why* she was so thrilled about the apparent difference in the length between the two corridors. She grabbed it with both hands.

'And what would be in that space, exactly?' he asked, keeping his enthusiasm in check and allowing her to explain further.

'It—it's only conjecture on my part—but, what if the legend of MacKenzie's Gold is more than a myth. What if the treasure—lost when the

Spanish Fleet carrying arms, men and money foundered in the great storm of 1719—is simply waiting to be found?'

'It's possible,' he allowed. 'Go on.'

'And, what if the treasure was taken into safekeeping by your family until the time was right to launch another Jacobite uprising?'

'Surely someone would have remembered hiding a cache of arms and gold?'

'I don't think the men who hid the treasure ever forgot about it. I believe they were overtaken by events. Think about it,' she went on. 'Your MacKenzie ancestor escaped the executioner's axe by a whisker and was compelled to marry the Grieves heiress, whose family was firmly on the side of the Hanoverians. He would hardly go round shouting from the battlements that he had treasure in the castle and was keeping it safe until it was needed to restore the Stuarts to the throne.'

'Okay, I'll buy that,' he conceded, leaning back against the sloping window embrasure. 'But why didn't they bring it out thirty years later when Bonnie Prince Charlie raised his standard at Glenfinnan?'

Henri looked at him, pleased that he giving her the chance to explain why her excitement for history had—momentarily—made her forget everything else; including her love for him. 'I have a theory about that.'

'I thought you might,' he said, his face softening. 'Go on, Dr Bruar, convince me.'

Henri was happy to do so. This was what she was good at, putting forward theories which challenged the accepted view of history. Debating, changing hearts and minds and, more often than not, winning the argument.

'You read all the time about Saxon and Viking hoards buried in fields and then forgotten. Only to be stumbled across thousands of years later, by a farmer or detectorist. What if—' Then she grinned, 'Sorry, I keep using that phrase . . .'

'Go, on, you've brought us this far.' Henri was encouraged by his use of 'us'.

'What if—the same applies to MacKenzie's Gold?'

'Which you think lies beyond the wall at the end of your corridor?'

'It's certainly a possibility, and one well worth exploring. I learned, through reading *The MacKenzie Papers* one wet afternoon, that your ancestor who escaped execution after the Battle of Glen Shiel, died before the '45 Rebellion. Died,' she grasped his arm with both hands, willing him to trust her judgement, 'before he could use the gold to help the *Young Chevalier* regain his throne.'

'It's possible.'

'I think that those who helped him conceal the treasure—men like Lachlan and women like Alice—loyal to the bitter end, had probably passed on, too. Taking the secret to the grave with them. Don't forget, in those days, you were considered middle-aged at thirty-five, and lucky if you made it to fifty without disease or illness seeing you off.'

'Henri, *mo chridhe*, I admire your enthusiasm. However, it was belief in MacKenzie's Gold which cost my mother and brother their lives, and has brought the castle and estates to the brink of ruin. MacKenzie's Gold, even if it does exist, is cursed; it brings only bad luck to those who go searching for it. Forget it, Henri, concentrate on returning to university, clearing your name and getting on with your life.'

Henri felt his dismissal as acutely as a slap in the face. She watched, downcast, as he walked over to the fire, put one foot on the fender and stretched his hands out towards the flames. Heart in mouth, she walked over and stood before him, arms folded. She wasn't prepared to give up on her theory about the treasure. Or on him, on *them*.

Didn't he realise the implications if she was right?

'I was thinking, if we could remove one of the stones which makes up the so-called false wall . . . have a look-see if there's a void there . . . perhaps shine a torch in, and—well—' She left him to him to fill in the gaps.

'You've thought this through, haven't you?' A smile softened his features, giving her hope.

'I *have*. And I believe it's worth a punt.'

'Wouldn't removing a stone wall bring the castle down round our ears?'

'Not if, as I believe, it's a partition wall; not a supporting one. What do you think?' Unfolding her arms, she made him sit on the fender and then plonked herself down on his knee. Resting her head on his shoulder, she repeated the question, playing with the buttons on his shirt in a provocative manner. 'What do you think?'

'It's difficult *to* think with you on my knee. Sit over there,' he commanded, pointing to the chesterfield and trying to look fierce. 'Don't move until I say so.' Henri did as commanded, putting her knees together, folding her hands in her lap and feigning a look of contrition. Keir returned to staring into the fire, seemingly mulling over everything she'd told him. Then he took her hand, swung her onto her feet and headed for the library door.

Oh my God, he's going to throw me out of the castle, bag and baggage—and make me find my own way back to England.

'Where are we going?' she demanded, digging her heels into the carpet and refusing to budge. Keir looked at her as if she was a mad woman, but a mad woman that he loved.

'*You*, to fetch Alice; *me*, to fetch tools from the undercroft. We'll meet at the wall. If you're right, Henri, I—' The light was back in his eyes, chasing away the demons which haunted him, and which were waiting in the wings for a chance to destroy his happiness; *their* happiness.

'Sh.' Henri stopped his mouth with a kiss. 'Don't jinx it. Not yet.'

'You're right. There's too much at stake. Go—'

He dispatched her towards the kitchen with a playful tap on her bottom and then headed for the spiral staircase and the undercroft, taking the steps three at a time.

Chapter Twenty-Nine
Romancing the Stone

They reconvened at the far end of Henri's corridor—Keir, armed with tool kit and an aluminium stepladder, Henri carrying a large torch and Alice a dustpan and brush. They'd been delayed because Alice had advised them to wait until Lachlan finished for the day and headed for the other side of the loch to his sister's house. He couldn't be trusted to keep a secret and they couldn't risk the laird finding out what was going on. So, with the light fading behind the arrow slits along the right hand wall, they stood ready to remove the first stone.

'Wait, let me . . .' Alice switched on the light bulb dangling from a frayed cord at the far end of the corridor, but it did little to disperse the gloom. Impatient to begin, Henri swept the torch beam over the ancient wall, but nothing out of the ordinary was revealed. Glancing over his shoulder, Keir pulled a 'here goes nothing' face, flexed his shoulders and started to tap the centre stone with his chisel. Henri was so hyped up that she had trouble keeping the beam of light steady on the stone as Keir dug out a line of mortar.

'Wh—where's the phantom p-piper when you r-really need him?' she quipped, teeth chattering.

Thank goodness it was November the first, All Saint's Day, and not Hallowe'en, otherwise her knees would be knocking like castanets at the enormity of their undertaking. Demolishing a centuries-old wall which probably had a preservation order on it, disturbing ancient spirits and inviting bad karma down on their heads. All for a treasure which, in all likelihood, did not exist.

She felt less like an academic and more like a tomb raider.

'Phantom piper?' Alice whispered, the magnitude of their enterprise clearly having an effect on her, too.

'Henri's heard the piper,' Keir confirmed almost as an aside as he tapped along one side of the stone. 'Many times.'

'Well, a few,' Henri amended, giving Alice an embarrassed half-smile. 'Hasn't everyone?'

'I havnae, for one.' Alice sent her a strange look, as if she now believed Henri had *the sight,* and her hunch about the treasure should be respected. Being a pragmatic Lowlander, Alice habitually dismissed the thing most Highlanders held dear—a belief that supernatural, mythical and spiritual worlds co-existed alongside the ordinary. However, she was intelligent enough to respect those things she couldn't understand, or which couldn't be readily explained. To her mind, simply because she hadn't heard the piper, didn't mean he didn't exist.

Tutting, she laid her dustpan and brush on the floor, and removed the torch from Henri's slack hands with a *gei'us it here, lassie,* and directed its beam at the wall. Henri gave out a huff of annoyance, not so much at Alice's interference but more because she was acting like . . . like a complete *girl*. And so out of character. However, she had a lot riding on this; if her hunch was wrong, it could have a negative impact on her and Keir's relationship.

Which was the last thing she wanted.

When she raised her head, Keir had chiselled the mortar away from the long side of the stone. She and Alice watched in silence as he worked on, his chisel striking sparks when it slipped out of his grasp. At one point, it fell on the floor and clattered on the stone flags. The sound was amplified in the eerie silence which had descended on them, making them glance over their shoulders, feeling they were being watched.

'Last bit,' Keir said.

Although it was freezing cold in the corridor, perspiration beaded his forehead and he wiped it away with his sleeve. As if choreographed, Alice and Henri shuffled closer and looked up at the stone, as though it could reveal what lay behind the wall. The stone, however, had other ideas. It remained stubbornly in its place despite Keir's best efforts to dislodge it. Henri experienced a crushing sense of anti-climax.

To temper their collective disappointment, Keir attempted a feeble joke. 'What—no chain-rattling ghosts, spectral pipers, or the sound of MacKenzies spinning in their graves? Maybe this is the wrong wall? What we need is a sign that we're on the right track . . .'

At that moment, the light at the end of the corridor flickered and the bulb exploded, showering glass everywhere. As one, they leapt out of their skins, and Henri and Alice grabbed Keir's arm. Then, an old-fashioned telephone bell rang out from the floor below and made them jump again.

'Holyshmoly!' Henri exclaimed.

'Och, for the love o' God; will ye just look at us?' Alice said, common sense reasserting itself. 'It's the phone in the kitchen. Not the ghost of Flora-bluddy-MacDonald, or her granny. I'd better go and answer it, most likely it's Himself asking where Lachlan is. We dinnae wah-nt him speculating where we are, whit we're up to, or returning to the castle afore we're finished. Don't wait, Keir—get that stone oot'a the wall and put Henri, all of us, oot of our misery.' With that, she ran along the corridor and descended the spiral staircase in the dark, with the ease of someone who knew the castle like the back of her hand.

Obeying his aunt's command, Keir thumped the centre of the stone with his mallet and stood back to survey the result. Zilch. Nothing. The stone didn't budge. Frustrated, Henri bent down and selected a larger mallet from the tool bag at their feet.

'Stand back,' she said, pushing up her sleeves.

She had too much riding on this to give up so easily.

'Henri, I really don't think—' Keir protested. When Henri swung the much heavier mallet, it slipped and skittered across the surface of the stone, almost kneecapping her when it swung back against her legs. 'Och, will ye gei it here, wumman,' Keir said, in mock-disparaging tones. Spitting on his palms in a workman-like fashion, he picked up the chisel and set about loosening the last of the mortar holding the stone in place.

Sensing that whatever happened next would seal the fate of generations of MacKenzies to come, neither of them spoke. Instead, taking a deep breath they looked at each other and then nodded, conveying their willingness to see this through to the end; whatever the outcome.

Turning, Keir stared long and hard at the wall, evidently reluctant to remove the stone and have Henri's hopes dashed for good. 'Don't get too excited, Henri. It could just be a—a hole in the wall,' he said, without turning round. 'Nothing more.'

'I know.' Glad that he couldn't see her, Henri let the corners of her mouth droop and her shoulders sag. Remaining upbeat, yet keeping hope and enthusiasm banked down in case there really *was* nothing to be discovered, was taking its toll on her. She'd had a sleepless night —for all the right reasons, and was now dog tired. In spite of that, she felt—no, *knew*—that her instinct about the treasure was right. All that lay between her and confirmation of her theory was one ancient stone. 'Well, go on; take the stone out of the wall. Put me out of my misery.'

He turned and looked down at her. 'Shouldn't we wait for Alice?'

'Of course!' What was she thinking? She smacked her forehead with the palm of her hand. Putting down his tools, Keir sent Henri a steady look which lasted for several beats. 'Partners?'

Aware that the partnership he was referring to had nothing to do with Jacobite gold, Henri nodded, relieved that she hadn't blown it. 'Partners.'

Taking her hand in his, Keir uncurled her fingers, bent his dark head and kissed her wrist where the blue veins were visible below the sleeve of her jumper. Then he traced a line of kisses to the centre of her palm, never once taking his eyes off her face, and her heart somersaulted in response. All the skills and knowledge she'd amassed over the years, all the clever words she had at her command, counted for nothing when compared to the feeling of raking her fingers through his thick, dark hair and how it sprang back after her touch.

'Partners for ever, Henri? Even if we find nothing?' he murmured against her hand. In the shadowy corridor, lit only by the torch balanced on the stepladders, Henri saw hope for the future—their future—written in his face.

'Ah, Keir . . . Dear God; we've found each other, and that's treasure enough for me.'

She swallowed hard and then nodded her agreement, trying hard not to think about how their story could've ended. Closing her eyes she took a deep, steadying breath and she knew that if he asked to make love to her right now on this stone cold floor covered in mortar dust, she would forget all about the treasure, university—everything—and say yes.

'I love you, Dr Henriette Bruar—and, whatever lies beyond that wall, be it Spanish doubloons or an empty space, my love for you will never falter. I give you my word.' It was an unlikely speech, delivered not down on one knee, as the poets had it but in a place where the temperature was so cold that their breaths coalesced and the tips of their noses were turning a very unromantic shade of blue.

'I love you, Keir MacKenzie. I want you to—'

Her sentence was cut short as Alice came along the corridor twisting the corner of her pinny into a corkscrew in an agitated fashion, breathless from the exertion of climbing the stairs,.

'Alice?' They chorused, sensing something was wrong.

'Oh, Keir—Henri . . . my dears.' Pushing herself between them, unaware that she had joined them at an inappropriate moment, she reached up and put her hands on Keir's shoulders. 'It's Malcolm. The silly auld bugger's only went and crashed his E-Type on the far side of the loch. That was Ciorstaidh, ringing to say he's being airlifted to Inverness and we should get over there as soon as possible. In case—in case he disnae make it through the night. Have I no tol't him, over and over, that he's too auld to drive that car? It's no as if he's a daft teenager anymore, is it? But, he widnae listen tae *me*. I'm nothing more than his housekeeper; that's all I've ever been in his eyes; all I'll ever be.' Although she tutted and pretended annoyance with Himself, her hurt was palpable. 'If he dies, he'll never know . . . never know . . .'

She trailed off, covering her face with her pinny and leaving them to speculate how that sentence would have ended. Immediately, Keir took command of the situation.

'Get your coats, we'll take my boat over to the Beach House and fetch the Land Rover. I'll ring Lachlan and tell him to meet us there. We'll go to Inverness, together.' Reaching out, he enfolded both women in his arms and kissed first one, then the other. 'Right?'

Henri looked over at the abandoned tool bag at their feet and then at the immovable stone above Keir's head. She felt like crying in frustration but swallowed her disappointment. Sir Malcolm came first, of course he did. If there was treasure to be found, it had lain undiscovered for hundreds of years. Another twenty-four hours wouldn't make any difference.

'We'd better remove the evidence.' She pointed to the foot of the wall.

'Clever gurl.' Automatically, Alice set to sweeping up the dislodged mortar and Keir picked up the ladder and tool bag. Torch in hand, Henri moved towards her bedroom and then, sensing Keir had more to say, paused.

'I think we should each pack an overnight case. We have no idea how long we'll be at the hospital—best to be prepared for . . . well, best to be prepared.' At that, a heart-rending sob escaped Alice and Keir took her in his arms and gave her another fierce hug. 'Och, wheesht now, Auntie Alice. He's a tough old bugger and besides, I need you to keep it together to help me cope with Lachlan. Despite his gruff exterior, he's a big wean at heart and his devotion to my father knows no bounds. We'll meet in the kitchen in fifteen. I'll collect a few things from my bedroom, the rest I'll get from the Beach House and then we'll be on our way.'

'Aye, yer right, laddie. It's the best we can do, for now.' Alice wiped her eyes with the back of her hand.

Keir's expression as he walked past Henri summed up their mixed emotions.

It seemed as if the Curse of MacKenzie's Gold had returned to cast a dark shadow over the castle once more. Only, this time, the blame for disturbing the ghosts and spirits of the past, could be laid squarely at Henri's door.

Chapter Thirty
Cas-ual-ity

Henri listened in resigned fashion to Lachlan bad-mouthing her from the back of the Land Rover. According to him, things had gone downhill since her arrival at Castle Tèarmannair. He even went as far as to suggest that the laird's accident was a result of the bad luck Henri had apparently brought with her.

Initially, Alice and Keir cut him some slack because of his age and devotion to the laird. However, when his tirade showed no signs of ending, Alice rounded on him.

'Lachlan MacKenzie, if ye dinnae hold yer wheesht I'll skite mah hand aff yer lugs. And, I promise ye, when we get to Inverness, you'll be joining Himself in cas-u-ality to have yer bunnet surgically removed from yer napper. Because ah'll have pulled it down past yer nose, and stapped up yer foul gob wi' it. Ya wee scunner, ye.' Then, apparently remembering that she was the laird's sister-in-law and chatelaine of Castle Tèarmannair, she continued in a more reasoned tone. 'Henri's the best thing to cross the loch since Keir's mother, and ah'll thank you to remember it.'

Keir added a terse sentence of his own in Gaelic and then switched to English for Henri's benefit. 'Lachlan MacKenzie, if I hear one more word, I'll put you out on the road and you can hitch your way to Inverness. Got it?'

'Aye, I've *got it,* a'right,' he muttered mutinously. 'Seems like a man cannae say whit's on his mind these days.'

'You'd do well to remember which side your bread is buttered.' Keir's tone brooked no defiance. 'Now, settle down, man, we have things on our mind other than your opinion of Dr Bruar and me.'

Lachlan gave a derisive snort but *held his wheesht*, as directed.

Reaching across for Henri's hand, Keir gave it a reassuring squeeze. Her heart contracted in silent response and she held his hand in her lap, stroking his thumb almost absentmindedly as she gazed into the November darkness.

'Loch Ness is somewhere out there in the darkness,' Keir informed her, trying to lighten the atmosphere. 'But it lies well below the level of the road and there's no moon, so you won't be able to see it tonight.'

'You'll have to settle for the sight of Lachlan in your vanity mirror, in place of the monster,' Alice couldn't resist one last jibe.

'Alice, behave.' Removing his hand from Henri's grasp, Keir pointed ahead. 'You'll see the lights of Inverness soon. Once there, I'll park and we'll see how things are.' Although he sounded composed and self-possessed he swallowed hard, as though his throat was constricted. Henri realised that, in spite of everything which had passed between Keir and his father, blood really was thicker than water. Crossing her fingers, she prayed that Sir Malcolm's injuries weren't life-threatening and that father and son would be given a chance to put the past behind them.

When they arrived at the hospital they found Alexander and Ciorstaidh MacKenzie-Grieves in the A&E waiting room, scrolling through their mobile phones. Via Alexander, they learned that Sir Malcolm was still in theatre. After that, God willing, he would be transferred to the ICU where they'd reassess him, once he regained consciousness. The family—or at least, Keir—would be allowed to see him, briefly, if and when his condition stabilised.

Henri hung back, conscious she was a very recent addition to the family and didn't want to get in the way. Ciorstaidh had no such reservations. When she saw Keir, she launched herself at him, almost bowling him over as she threw her arms around his neck. Then she touched his black eye and when he winced, declared in a husky, attractive voice—'*I am so sorry, I am so sorry.*' For dramatic effect she burst into pretty tears.

'Uncle Malcolm,' she managed to gasp out, 'poor Uncle Malcolm.' Burying her head in Keir's chest she tightened her grip on his jacket, leaving Keir no option but to stand there until her crying jag was over—or physically prise her from him, finger by finger.

'And the Oscar for *most distraught cousin, twice removed*, goes to Ciorstaidh MacKenzie-Grieves for her excellent performance in, *Raigmore Cas-ual-ity Department—the Movie.*' Alexander MacKenzie-Grieves whispered in Henri's ear, seemingly so unconcerned about the laird's condition that he could make a joke at his sister's expense.

'You really are . . .'

'Oh, c'mon, Henri, look at her; sobs, but no actual tears. We wouldn't want to ruin our makeup, now would we? Not after we've spent half an hour painting it on, in anticipation of Keir's arrival. Mind you, I think she was hoping for the hero to arrive, without supporting cast: Auld Lachlan, scary Auntie Alice and the beautiful Dr Bruar. Who, judging by her frosty demeanour, has not forgiven me for stealing a wee kiss in the library.' He tilted his head to one side and regarded her with mocking eyes.

'She has *not*,' was Henri's icy reply, as she looked past him to Ciorstaidh who was still clinging, limpet-like, to Keir.

'No?' He pulled an *I don't believe you* face. 'Didn't you enjoy it, just a tad? I'd bet anything that I'm a better kisser than Keir.' The conversation was so inappropriate given the circumstances, that Henri was lost for words. 'Am I?' he prompted.

'No, you are not.' Annoyed at answering such a leading question, she niftily side-stepped him and walked over to Keir. 'Go *boil yer heid*, Alexander MacKenzie-Grieves.'

He laughed. 'Tut, tut. Alice's lingo is perfectly acceptable in Motherwell, but not *quite* the thing for the Master of Mountgarrie's lady. Mind you, you ladies are full of surprises—turns out, my mother can swear like a trooper and my sister can deliver a right hook with all the skill of a bantamweight.

Who knew?' Furious that he was continuing to make jokes, Henri glared at him.

'Keir?' she queried, walking over to him.

He looked glad of an excuse to put Ciorstaidh aside, without appearing brusque. 'It seems we'll be playing a waiting game for the next few hours, at least. Sandy—' he turned his attention to his cousin. 'What happened?'

'Malc wanted to take the Jag for a spin along the loch road. It'd been coughing and spluttering all week and he felt something was fundamentally wrong with it, so . . .'

'Had he been drinking?' Keir cut in.

'What do you think?'

'Why didn't someone take the keys off him?'

'Off *Himself—Sir Malcolm MacKenzie of that Ilk*? Come on . . . only you or Alice would dare.' Keir regarded his cousins as though they were a pair of idiots. Ciorstaidh had the grace to look chastened but Alexander continued to stare Keir down. Henri realised that, in spite of having everything he wanted, Alexander was jealous of Keir and coveted what little he had: a stack of unpaid bills, final demands from creditors, a decaying castle and a courtesy title passed down through his father.

But, more than anything—he wanted *her*.

Unconsciously, she slipped her hand through Keir's and they locked fingers. Then he raised her hand to his lips and kissed it, adding loud enough for everyone to hear, 'I'm glad you're here, Henri.'

'So am I.' She moved closer to him and the cousins took one step back. Boundaries were redrawn and, in the absence of Sir Malcolm, Keir was acknowledged as the most senior member of the family and their branch of the clan.

'Here ye go.' Returning from the machine, Alice and Lachlan handed out six cups of coffee and civility was restored. After wiping his nose along the length of his grubby sleeve, Lachlan brought a half bottle of whisky out of his pocket and added some to his coffee. He offered the bottle to Keir and then to the MacKenzie-Grieveses as if it was the laird's finest malt and not a bottle of supermarket whisky. However, considering the possible cause of Sir Malcolm's accident, and the filthy state of the bottle, they declined. Ciorstaidh wrinkling up her nose and Alexander, although plainly fancying a wee nip, not daring to accept under Keir's fierce gaze.

'Shall we?' Keir gestured towards the plastic chairs and they made their way over. 'It's going to be a long night. I don't see the point in us all losing sleep. However, if Sandy and Ciorstaidh want to go home, I quite understand.'

'We're family; we're staying,' Ciorstaidh declared, sending Henri a bold look.

'That's settled then.' Alexander plonked himself down on a bright orange chair and began checking his phone for messages, prompting Henri to check her phone, too. It'd been over a week since she'd switched it on, feeling there was little point in running down the battery when there was no signal at the castle. The phone gave a little chirrup of delight at being woken up and started downloading texts and voice messages via 4G.

Scrolling through, Henri dismissed all of them but the last. 'Oh,' she exclaimed.

Keir was at her side in an instant. 'Henri? Everything okay?'

'I-I need a moment . . .'

Turning away, she opened the email from the HR department. It required a direct response, in writing, stating her intention to attend the disciplinary hearing, in two days' time. In addition, there were three PDF attachments for her to download, print off and read prior to appearing before the Disciplinary Panel.

'Bloody idiots. Don't they realise . . .'

Plainly, the letter she'd sent explaining that high speed, fibre optic broadband was not universally available in the western Highlands and informing them that they'd have to communicate via snail mail, had gone astray. Or, more likely, was sitting in someone's *pending tray*, unread. She remembered Maddie saying, during their phone call at the Beach House, that the department was on a go-slow, and everything had shut down for half-term.

'Henri, what is it?' Henri passed her phone to Keir without a word; quickly, he assessed the situation and came up with a solution. 'Not a problem—when we leave the hospital, we can call in at the Beach House and you can email the university asking for a postponement, following it up with a phone call, tomorrow. You'd be well within your rights to cite mitigating circumstances. You need time to print off the attachments, go through them carefully, present your case . . .'

Henri shook her head and replaced the phone in her bag. 'Keir, I know *exactly* what I'm going to say. I've thought of little else since I set foot in the castle. I don't want a postponement, I want it over and done with.'

Taking a deep breath, Keir reasoned in a quiet voice. 'You don't have to go, Henri. Your future is *here*, with me; with us. Not in a world where it's considered acceptable to pass someone's research off as your own; to accept the kudos for discovering an important manuscript, with no sense of shame.'

He was right; of course he was, but this was something she had to see through to the end. No matter how bitter that end might be.

'I know all that, Keir. However, I can't leave things unresolved, any longer. I have to put the record straight. I found the manuscript, and I want full recognition of the fact. I need to hear the Dean admit he's a cheat and a liar, and what he did was morally wrong. I want my day in court.'

The Dean's smug face swam before her eyes, stiffening her resolve. The dream-like bubble she'd lived in since setting foot in MacKenzie's Halt burst, and the scales fell from her eyes. She blinked under the harsh overhead lights and it was as though she was seeing Keir, the MacKenzie-Grieveses, Alice and Lachlan for the first time. 'I-I,' she stammered, searching for the words which would make Keir understand her reasons for returning to university when it was plain that he thought she belonged here, with him; with all of them. That the world she wanted to return to, wasn't worth a hill of beans.

Keir tried to reason with her. 'Henri, you owe them nothing; *nothing*. Believe me, I understand the importance of having a dream, seeing it through.' He bent his head and whispered so softly that she struggled to hear. 'Don't you understand? I'm worried that, once you return to your academic comfort zone, you'll forget all about Castle Tèarmannair, Alice, Lachlan. Me. No don't say another word.' Turning on his heel, he joined the others who were aware that some kind of discussion was taking place and regarding them curiously.

Henri longed to call him back, to explain this wasn't so much about following a dream as gaining closure.

'Mr MacKenzie?' A triage nurse called Keir over to the desk. 'Your father's out of theatre but it will be a while before you'll be allowed to see him. I suggest you all go home, have a good night's sleep and return in the morning. He's in good hands and we'll contact you if anything changes.'

Shame washed over Henri. *This* was the real world; a world containing love and pain in equal measure. Keir had so much to shoulder and she'd inadvertently added to his burden. She tried to catch his eye, to mutely communicate everything she was feeling to him. However, when Keir finished speaking to the nurse and turned to face her, he was a stranger—Sir Malcolm MacKenzie's son and heir, the Master of Mountgarrie; not the tender lover whose bed she'd left only hours before.

She saw the way the nurse looked at him, how her professional persona slipped fleetingly when she checked him out. 'Oh, your eye,' she commented, seeing Keir's shiner. 'Were you in the accident, too? Do you need me to look at it for you?' She looked as if that would give her pleasure and make a long night shift pass quickly.

'I'm fine, thank you, *Anne*.' Keir checked out her name badge and smiled down at her. Blushing to the roots of her fair hair, *Anne* almost melted in front of him. It was a small thing, but it was enough to bring home to Henri that, if she didn't want him, there would be plenty of women who did. 'Returning to the subject of my father—'

'Of course.'

'I prefer to stay until he's conscious at least. The telephone in the castle is very unreliable and we can't get a mobile signal once we leave the main road.'

He gave a self-deprecating shrug, aware that the busy nurse didn't need to know chapter and verse of their communication problems.

'Ah'll stay with you, son,' Alice said, standing shoulder to shoulder with him.

'Me, an' all,' Lachlan added, putting his bottle back in his pocket and stepping up to the plate. 'Himself deserves nothing less.'

'I'm here for you, Keir,' Ciorstaidh added. Tears misted her grey-blue eyes, but when she turned to look at Henri, they were as hard as flint.

'Group hug?' Alexander suggested, holding his arms wide. When no one took him up on it, he returned to scrolling through his mobile phone adding, 'Thought not.'

'Henri?' Alice beckoned her over. Henri wasn't sure how much they'd overheard, how much they knew. She was about to bring them up to speed when Keir forestalled her.

'Henri has to leave. She's been recalled to her university and will be gone some time.'

'Some time?' Alice interjected. 'But she's needed *here* . . .'

'Alice, I have *that matter* to attend to. The one we discussed, *remember?*' It was important that Alice understood she wasn't simply walking out on them.

'Aye, I do, pet. But surely . . .' She jerked her head towards Keir, and then, Ciorstaidh. Her meaning was plain; in returning to university, Henri was leaving the way open for Ciorstaidh to insinuate herself into Keir's good graces—in spite of everything that had happened in the Great Hall on Hallowe'en.

Once Henri left, it would be a case of—the queen is dead; long live the queen.

'I'd better . . .' Henri picked up her overnight bag and walked over to the noticeboard to check out the number of a local taxi firm. Much better to spend her time in Inverness railway station until the first train to Edinburgh pulled in, than to endure recriminating looks from Alice and, yes—even Lachlan. Clearly they thought she was deserting them in their hour of need.

And, in one sense, she was. She could hardly read the notices for tears blurring her eyes.

In the end, it was Alexander who came to her rescue. Removing her overnight bag from her slack fingers and, apparently understanding that she couldn't/wouldn't ask Keir for a ride, he inquired in a faux-Cockney accent: 'Taxi to the station, lay-dee?'

'Thanks, Sandy.'

'The first train to Edinburgh leaves at 4.53, I've caught it myself, many times when I couldn't be arsed to catch the late train back after the weekend. It gets in for about half-past nine . . . give or take.' Henri was only half-listening as she was busy searching the internet for the connection from Edinburgh to Newcastle.

'If I catch the ten o'clock, I can be back in Newcastle by 11.28,' she said, almost to herself. 'Then I can get a taxi to Hexham.' That would leave her the whole afternoon to download the attachments, read them through and start making the case for the defence.

'I'll keep you company until the station opens—if you want me to, that is. And if Keir allows it?' He pulled a wry face and glanced over at his cousin who was engaged in conversation with Alice, making practical arrangements for their stay in Inverness.

It was on the tip of Henri's tongue to say that she didn't need Keir's permission. Not anymore. Instead she said, 'If you behave, yes,' and used humour to hide her aching heart.

'I'll behave. Scouts' honour.' He gave the three-fingered scouts' salute, trying to cheer her up. They stood around uncertainly for a couple of minutes, waiting to inform Keir of their intentions. However, his conversation with Alice and Lachlan showed no signs of drawing to a close and Henri, not wishing to prolong the agony, turned on her heel and made for the exit. Much to her amazement, Ciorstaidh rushed after her, hugged her and then kissed her on both cheeks.

'Make sure this is goodbye and not *au revoir*, Sassenach,' she hissed, gripping Henri by the upper arms. Then she patted her on the shoulder in sisterly fashion and sent her on her way with a none-too-gentle push towards the door. 'Off you go, Sandy. I'll stay here with Keir.'

'I bet you will,' Alexander grimaced. 'Ready, Henri?'

'Ready.'

She followed Alexander out of the building, knowing that if she looked back in Keir's direction, her hard-won resolve would crumble.

Chapter Thirty-One
Academe

The taxi dropped Henri off at St Guthlac University next to Jarrow Hall where her study-cum-bedroom was situated. Exchanging freezing corridors, grey walls, dim light and studded oak doors for plate glass, exposed steel girders and blond wood was disorientating. A blast of the centrally heated air greeted Henri as the double doors parted to admit her to Jarrow Hall and almost bowled her over.

Her muddled brain, the part not fixated on Keir MacKenzie, struggled to make sense of students and lecturers strolling around in bright t-shirts and light clothing. It was the third of November and Henri was dressed for the arctic, or at least, life in an eleventh century castle—thick sweater, Uggs, woollen leggings, gloves and pashmina. Adapting to living and working in a centrally heated environment would take some getting used to.

But that was the least of her problems.

Pausing by the fountain in the middle of the main atrium, all she could think of was yesterday morning and waking up beside the man she loved. A wave of heart-sickness and longing assailed her, leaving her feeling bereft and disorientated in this once-familiar place. She *had* to get Keir out of her head; she needed to be firing on all cylinders to answer the charges brought against her. She had to be exonerated of all wrongdoing, otherwise leaving Keir and Castle Tèarmannair would be the worst decision she'd ever made.

'Doctor Bruar—Henri, you're back!'

A knot of students joined her by the fountain as the clock reached the top of the hour and together they watched as a water-powered sculpture rose from its depths and unfolded its bronze petals. The petals caught the last of the sunlight streaming into the atrium and sent a kaleidoscope of colour bouncing off the walls. It was a clever conceit, but compared to the shifting light on the loch, or the brooding majesty of the hills and mountains beyond Castle Tèarmannair, it was mere sleight of hand.

The display came to an end, the sculpture descended back into the water and the students demanded Henri's attention.

'We've missed you.'

'How have you been? Have you finished your research?'

'I can't wait to read your next paper.'

'A sabbatical? Lucky you. We're bogged down in mid-term exams.'

'The hockey team's lost every match since you left . . .'

Hockey team.

Shinty match.

Henri touched the silver caman round her neck and muttered something vague about having to unpack. Then she made her way towards the lifts where another group of students travelled up to the tenth floor with her. It was there that she learned that the official reason given for her absence was the sabbatical she'd taken to research her dissertation on the Highland Clearances. That, seemingly, being the university's attempt at damage limitation and quashing the rumours circulating about the incident in the Dean's sitting room. Like all universities, St Guthlac had to attract students, funding and research grants. It could ill afford scandal getting out regarding academics who'd 'gone rogue'. Or Deans who claimed the glory and kudos for something which wasn't rightfully theirs.

'Will you be attending the official dedication of The Venerable Bede manuscript at the end of term?' one student inquired. 'It's going to be quite an event—reuniting the book with the piece of manuscript the Dean discovered.'

Grinding her teeth, Henri nevertheless managed to smile and mutter something noncommittal as they travelled upwards in the lift. 'Apparently, experts from the British Museum, the V and A, and some of the TV historians have been invited to the ceremony.'

'The Duke and Duchess of Northumberland are guests of honour.'

'It's going to be televised—'

'A second documentary has been commissioned, bringing the story up to date.'

'I wouldn't miss it for the world,' was all Henri said.

She waited for the lift to empty and then pressed the button for the tenth floor. That floor was reserved for Deans of Faculty and those with higher doctorates who were granted free accommodation and a small sinecure, in return for making their research available to others, mentoring undergrads, and teaching small groups of postgrads in their given subject.

The downside of living on the tenth floor was the close proximity of the Dean of History's office and study to her rooms. There were too many bad memories for Henri to feel entirely at ease as she walked past with her heavy rucksack. The wooden slider had been drawn across the nameplate on the Dean's door, signifying that he was *out of office*. Henri felt like kicking the door as she passed by, but refrained. Better to channel all her anger and aggression into preparing for the disciplinary hearing in two days' time.

Cool, calm and collected would win the day—not more hot-headedness.

Unlocking the door to her room, she entered. The room smelled musty and unused, and was just as she'd left it: bed unmade, clothes and books all over the floor. It was testament to the frame of mind she'd been in when she'd left Hexham for MacKenzie's Halt. Dropping her bags on the floor and her keys on the desk, she walked over to the windows and rolled up the blinds to catch the last of the light. Ignoring the sweep of hills towards Hadrian's Wall to the east, and the sun setting over Carlisle and the Solway Firth in the west, she pressed her forehead against the glass and looked northwards to Scotland; where her heart lay.

She recalled an advert from years ago where a hungry model was shown with a gaping hole in the middle of her body, demanding for it to be filled by some low-calorie snack biscuit. That's exactly how she felt; hollow, sunken and running on empty. Turning her back on the window, she connected her phone to the air printer and started printing off the files emailed to her by Human Resources.

When the phone rang two days later, displaying UNKNOWN CALLER. Henri paused before answering it. If this was some firm cold-calling about PPI or 'a recent accident', they'd get short shrift.

'Doctor Bruar.'

'Hello, hen.'

'Alice!'

'Y'okay, pet?'

'No bad,' she said, adopting a Scottish brogue as she flopped onto her desk chair 'Alice—you're on a mobile. How come?'

'I'm ringing from the hospital café. One thing about being in Inverness, you can get a mobile signal and internet at any time o' the day. Ah didnae realise whit ah was missing at the castle. Almost worth that silly auld bugger running himself off the road, just so's I could experience it.'

Henri laughed, although it sounded hollow and forced. 'Talking of which—how is Himself?'

'Lying in bed like a rajah and giving orders, as per. I'm cutting him some slack at the moment because he's high on morphine, but he'd dae well not to push his luck wi' me. Just aboot every bone in his right leg has been replaced with metal and it's going to be months before he can walk without help. We're talking about him, me and Lachlan moving in tae the Beach House because he willnae be able to manage the stairs at the castle.'

Henri pictured Keir alone in the castle. What if he hated living there on his own? What if he decided to cut his losses and return to British Columbia before she had a chance to make things right?

Aware that Alice was waiting for a response, she pulled herself together. 'You'll have your hands full if that happens.'

'That's right. Keir says I've got tae ask one of the wee lassies from the village to come in twice a week, if we can afford it. He's been trying to flirt with the nurses like he's twenty-one again.' Henri's blood ran cold and an adrenaline rush sent pins and needles shooting up her arms. 'Bloody auld fo-oul.'

'Oh, I thought for a moment you were talking about Keir.'

'As if,' Alice snorted. 'Mind you, he is awful worrit—'

'Worrit? I mean, worried—about his father?'

'Henriette Bruar, for an educated woman ye'r awful glaekit at times.'

'So what is Keir worrit about?'

'You, lassie, *you*. He's worrit that you won't return. That you'll ring up and ask me to forward the rest of your stuff to your university—and that'll be an end of it.'

'Oh,' Henri looked out of the window. 'So, why hasn't he called?'

'Think aboot it. He wants you to make up your own mind; he disnae wahnt to put pressure on you.'

'So, why—'

'Am I putting pressure on you?' Alice laughed. 'Because you're the best thing to have happened to my nephew—to us—in years. He needs you and,' she took a deep breath and rushed on, 'you need him, *too*. Can ye no see that? Hell, even that useless scunner Lachlan can see it. Over the last few days, sitting at Himself's bedside like a faithful dug, he's had time to think things over—especially since I took the whisky bottle aff him.' They both laughed at that. 'He's come to realise that if he wants to be part of life at Castle Tèarmannair, he'd better mend his ways. Be nicer to you, for starters.'

'Lachlan? Nice to me? Now that would be a shock,' Henri laughed, but her voice trembled with emotion. 'Alice, it's lovely to hear your voice, especially today—'

She glanced over at her wardrobe where her doctor's robes hung on the back of the door. The black cassock-like gown with its row of bright red buttons down the front—denoting she'd attained a higher-level doctorate requiring a substantial body of research, a thesis and a *viva voce* examination in front of two examiners—had once been her pride and joy.

Now she'd gladly swap it for the shawl and luckenbooth she'd worn at the Samhain party.

'Och, Henri, is it today that you're facing the firing squad?' Alice broke into her reverie.

'Firing squad? That about sums it up. Yes, it is, but I'm not going down without a fight.' Swinging her desk chair round, she glanced over at her bed where her doctor's bonnet or round cap lay. The bright red cord round the brim exactly matched the red silk lining of her fur-trimmed academic hood. 'I want the chance to put the record straight, and then, after that, I'll decide what's best for me.'

'You'll do great, Henri, I know ye will. Let me know how it goes? You'll be able to get through to me on the castle phone. Keir's taking me back there to get some things for Himself. Lachlan wants me to leave my mobile with him. *Dream on*, I said, *knowing you, it'd probably end up down the lavvy pan*. The eejit.'

They laughed at the thought of Lachlan mastering modern technology. Then, Professor Maddie Hallam entered the room and Henri ended the conversation.

'Hope I'm not intruding?' Maddie's bright eyes ranged over Henri's face, as if trying to gauge her mood.

'Come in, Maddie. That was Alice on the phone.'

'How is Alice? I haven't seen her since last summer. But she phones me when she can make it over to the post office, or when Malc pays the arrears on his phone bill.' She pulled a face at Himself's lack of financial acumen.

'She's fine, thanks.'

'How's Himself? On the mend? Chasing nurses round the room with his Zimmer frame?' She rolled her eyes at the ceiling.

'Not quite up to that, as yet. But, knowing Malcolm, very soon in all likelihood.'

'And Keir?' Henri shrugged, as though Keir not being in touch was of no interest to her. 'Good man; he knows you need a clear head to present your case. Plenty of time for romance once this ordeal is over,' she said briskly, getting a bright red lipstick out of her pocket and applying a fresh slick in front of the mirror.

Then she fetched Henri's academic gown and helped her into it, lowering the fur trimmed hood over her head and fastening the small loop around Henri's shirt button, so it wouldn't slip backwards. Finally, she handed Henri the soft, rounded Tudor bonnet and straightened the tassel on that too.

'Lippy,' she commanded. Henri applied a fresh coat of lipstick and took the shine off her nose with pressed powder. 'Attagirl. War paint is necessary; it's your armour against the collective misogyny of the panel you're about to face. It's still a man's world; never forget that.'

'As if I could!'

Henri was allowed a representative to help her present her case and respond to the allegations on file. Smashing the television set, accusing the Dean of misappropriating her research and claiming credit for finding the scrap of manuscript, were deemed as misconduct and warranted a Level 3—First and Final Written Warning being brought against her. Henri knew that she could have no better advocate than Maddie Hallam.

Professor Hallam was as famous for her signature Chanel lipstick, austere Mary Quant geometric haircut and designer trouser suits as she was for her seminal work: *Speenhamland-English Poor Law in the Eighteenth Century*. It was a look she'd adopted in the mid-Sixties and saw no point in changing at her age. And if she had taken to dyeing her hair jet-black, it was a sign she hadn't given up on life, and was as formidable as ever. She knew everything about Sir Malcolm, Keir, Alice and Castle Tèarmannair, talking to her was almost as good as being there.

Maddie adjusted the angle of Henri's cap and rested her hands on Henri's taut shoulders. 'One final thing?' Frowning, Maddie gave her own professor's robes a dissatisfied onceover in the mirror and then sighed, seemingly accepting they were what they were—hideous, and in no way flattering—or, was that the point?

'Yes?'

'The Chair of the Disciplinary Panel? Professor John Gwyeth —I've known him for years and, should the need arise, I might remember *exactly* where he was the night the Chancellor's car was smeared with cow dung during Rag Week, when Malcolm and I were undergrads.'

'Blackmail?'

'Nothing so crude, sweetie. Just a knowing wink and a bit of arm-twisting in the Senior Common Room over a couple of G and T's last night. Believe me, he has no love for the Dean, and is not above using your disciplinary as an opportunity to settle old scores.'

'I told someone recently that the higher echelons of academic life was a snake pit.' Sandy M-G's face swam before her the day of the shinty match. 'I was right.'

'Forget all that. Focus. Come on, kid; show 'em what you're made of.'

Chapter Thirty-Two
Choices

Maddie curled Henri's fingers round a heavy, Waterford crystal glass and told her to knock the contents back in one. Sitting in Maddie's vintage Eames chair with her feet up on its matching footstool, Henri looked as if she'd been struck by lightning.

'Wh—what just happened in there?' she asked.

'Well,' Maddie took a large slug of *Gin and It* and regarded Henri indulgently. 'From what I can make out, three things. One, you were let off with a warning concerning the smashing of the Dean's TV, ordered to replace the television and pay a fine. *Two*, it was accepted that there had been a little misunderstanding over your research and who it actually belonged to; it was accepted that it was your intellectual property, but you graciously offered it to the history department. Nice touch.' She clinked her glass against Henri's. 'And, *three*, the small matter of who had actually discovered the missing piece of manuscript has been finally settled and you will be given full credit, with the Dean receiving a commendation for recognising its importance and safeguarding it for the university.'

'But—I was the one who recognised its importance—' Henri knocked back the lethal G and T and almost choked.

'I know, Henri; however, he couldn't be allowed to lose face entirely. Not with the ceremony taking place at the end of term. Let it go. You've won, your name's been cleared and, besides, everyone now knows the truth. I suspect the Dean will be side-lined and, after a suitable period of time, offered early retirement. The Chancellor will be glad to see the back of him before any sexual harassment cases are brought to his attention. The Dean's oh-so-not-funny joke that having nubile researchers *under* him, was like having 'tottie on tap', is not so funny anymore.' Pulling back the ring pull on a small can of tonic water, Maddie diluted the lethal concoction in Henri's glass. 'Bloody idiot, acting like he was Howard Kirk in that book by Malcolm Bradbury—'

'*The History Man*?' Henri supplied.

'That's the one. And,' Maddie went on, pushing a dish of nuts towards Henri, 'the icing on the cake. You've been offered a junior lectureship, starting next term. You're a great teacher, Henri. The work you've done with the MA students has been outstanding,' Turning her head on the side, she awaited a response. 'So what's bugging you?'

Henri put her glass on the floor and then leaned forward. 'You know the old saying—*be careful what you wish for*?'

'Uh-huh.'

'That.'

'I don't understand, didn't you want to be exonerated of all wrongdoing?'

'Of course I did—and I'm glad to have my reputation restored. It's simply that—oh, I don't know, it all feels *flat*, somehow.'

'Flat?'

'Yes; as though there should be *more*. That I should feel m-more elated. I'm not explaining myself very well.'

'Henri Bruar, for as long as I've known you, you've been goal orientated—BA with first class honours, MA, PhD, making your name in a crowded academic field—your determination to become a university teacher. Now, it's within your grasp it's almost as if . . .'

'I as if I no longer wanted it? I thought that a junior lectureship *was* the be-all and end-all; but now I find—'

'Go on.'

'That what I really want is—'

'A castle in a loch? The son of a bankrupt laird, who's all kinds of gorgeous but doesn't have a bean to his name?'

'How did you guess?' Henri picked her glass up off the floor and had a second attempt at drinking the contents.

'I saw the stars in your eyes when you returned to university. They sure as hell weren't there when you headed for Scotland.'

'How did you know? Ah—Alice?' The penny dropped.

'We've been friends for years and she keeps me in the loop. It *is* Keir—isn't it?' Maddie persisted

'Keir, Alice, Himself and, yes, even grumpy old Lachlan. Freezing cold mornings when the mist settles on the loch and you feel like you're floating on a cloud. The battlements outside my bedroom, etched against the sunset. No internet, a phone that rarely works. A phantom piper who—'

Maddie held up her hands. 'I get the picture. So why are you sitting here, drinking my poisonous G and T's when you should be looking up train times and packing your bags?'

'Precisely for all the reasons you mentioned earlier. I'd hate to be like those girls at boarding school who, after gaining a place at university, gave it up for some boyfriend or other—and settled for less.'

'Henri—look at me, seventy-two and travelling the world raising funds for a mediocre university which, not so long ago, was a mediocre polytechnic, and before that a theological college which only survived after the Great War because they admitted women to improve its deplorable academic standards. I mean, Jesus—no disrespect, *come on*. Not exactly first rate, are we?'

'Maddie, I had no idea you felt this way.'

'Well, I do. I'd trade it all in tomorrow for the love of a good man and the children I never had. I was part of the sexual revolution in the Sixties and believed that we could have it all—career, family, a happy life. However, in the end, hard choices had to be made.'

'You sound as though you made the wrong ones.' Henri saw the spark leave Maddie's kohl-rimmed eyes.

'Maybe I did. I turned down an offer of marriage because it would have meant me taking a career break, as they now call it. I was worried that they wouldn't have me back; and, at that point in my life, my academic research meant more to me than anything. My lover was a proud man and took my rejection hard; he never asked me again. If I had it to do over, I'd do it differently.'

'Oh, Maddie.' Henri reached out and touched Maddie's hand.

'We think we have tomorrow, but all we really have is today.'

'I've worked so hard, I'd be giving up so much. Wouldn't I? Even to her own ears, her excuses sounded feeble.

'Academically, you're very gifted. The faculty's poster girl. You'd spend a couple of years at St Guthlac, max, then you'd be headhunted by one of the Russell Group Universities. Eventually you'd receive an offer from an Oxbridge college and, in the fullness of time, you'd be Professor Bruar. But it would come at a price. Listen to your heart, follow your instincts.'

'I don't know what to *think* anymore.' Henri started to tease out the French plait which was pulling at her temples and giving her a headache.

'Nowadays, employment laws ensure that you can work part-time, should you choose to. With the internet, you can carry out research from the desk in your study whilst rocking some adorable infant in a bassinet with your foot. It would only take a couple of trips a year to the British Library, or wherever, to finish your thesis on the Highland Clearance. You can self-publish in the unlikely event of no academic publishing house showing interest. Your career needn't stop, it can simply take a change of direction. I'm guessing they have universities in Scotland, too?'

She arched her eyebrow, making Henri laugh, 'Apparently.' Then she sobered. 'It all comes down to choices in the end, doesn't it?'

'It does, my darling, it does. Chin-chin,' she said as they clinked glasses.

'Slainte Mhath,' Henri responded in Gaelic.

Maddie grinned. 'See? You're halfway to becoming a Scot, it's in your DNA, lassie. Why not go the full hog? Marry a laird's son.'

'*If* that's on offer . . .'

'From what Alice tells me, I'd say it was.'

'Alice?'

'I'll probably be hung, drawn and quartered for this, but what the hell. . .'

Henri steeled herself for what was coming next. 'Alice and I have been friends since Malcolm married her sister. She keeps me up to speed regarding Malcolm, the castle, the MacKenzies. It's my own private soap opera,' she laughed. 'When you were in trouble I saw a chance to help them *and* you—so, I took it, sending you to catalogue the library when any auction house would have done.'

'I did wonder!'

'I thought . . . you and Keir would be perfect for each other. And, it turns out I'm right, doesn't it?' Henri blushed and bowed her head over her glass, her unplaited hair hiding her expression. 'Alice really did think that a *Doctor Henry Brewer* was coming to stay, I thought it was best to use a little subterfuge because I know her feelings about sexy young things turning up at the castle, unannounced. She would have rejected Henriette Bruar out of hand.'

'Maddie. You schemer.'

'Once Alice got to know you, she did her best to bring the two of you together.'

Henri raised her head and smiled. 'That's what Alexander M-G intimated.'

'He's a card, isn't he? Good looking but feckless. I would *not* have been happy to see you with him.' Getting to her feet, she took the glass out of Henri's hand, indicating that their heart-to-heart was over and she should be packing.

Henri regarded Maddie with wry affection. 'What hope did Keir and I have against a couple of *shadchans* like you and Alice?'

'Jewish matchmakers, hmm? Now, there's an alternative career for me to consider. C'mere, you.' She held out her arms and Henri allowed herself to be embraced, breathing in some expensive perfume which Maddie, doubtless, had specially blended in Grasse.

'It'll take me ages to pack, to see the Chancellor, to inform the department—'

'Leave all that to me. I don't think the Chancellor will stand in your way. He owes me, big time.' Henri recognised the combative light in her eye, Alice had it too. It declared that they were women of a certain age, and knew how things worked; they did not suffer fools gladly and if anyone was unwise enough to put that to the test—let them try.

'Thanks, Maddie, I won't forget what you and Alice have done for me. One day, I'll repay your kindness, you'll see.'

'Och, away with ye, lassie,' Maddie said in a faultless accent. 'Be happy. Bring happiness into the lives of those in Castle Tèarmannair and MacKenzie's Halt. That'll be payment enough.'

After one last hug, Henri flew out of the door as though she had wings on her heels. She was going home.

Home to Castle Tèarmannair.

Henri parked her hired car at Raigmore Hospital, Inverness and made her way up to Ward 3A, with only half an hour's visiting time remaining. Although she was desperate to get to MacKenzie's Halt, she felt she couldn't drive past the hospital without calling in on Sir Malcolm. Walking between the ward's curtained-off bays, she took a deep breath. It wasn't concern over Sir Malcolm's condition making her hyperventilate, it was the thought of seeing Keir—and what they would say to each other.

How would he react? What if he'd changed his mind and no longer wanted her? Heart thumping, palms sweating, she tiptoed up to Bay 6 and pushed back the curtains. There she found Sir Malcolm sitting up in bed, arms on top of the bedcovers, and with his left leg in traction. He was hooked up to an IV drip and his blood pressure was being monitored via a cuff connected to a machine. Alice was on one side of the bed and Lachlan on the other, each holding his hand, as if possession of Himself's fingers gave one superiority over the other.

'And ah say—if Himself wah-nts a wee drap o' the swally, he should have it.' Lachlan tugged on Sir Malcolm's hand with each syllable of *he-should-have-it*, almost yanking him out of the bed.

'Oh, aye, and remind me—exactly *when* did you pass your doctor's exams, Lachlan MacKenzie?'

'Never you mind that, auld wumman, Himself's lucky to be alive and you're denying him a wee dram? Have ye no heart?'

'Can ye no see he's on morphine? Ye cannae mix alcohol with morphine—ya numpty.'

'I'd be willing to give it a try,' Sir Malcolm added, smiling weakly. 'I've been dry for almost a week. If the hospital food doesn't kill me, my liver will give up the ghost at being denied uisge beatha. It's my right as a Highlander to have a wee dram every now and then.'

'*Now and then?*' Alice repeated, releasing his hand as a sign of her displeasure.

Defeated, he flopped back on the pillows, looking far from his usual bullish self. However, when Henri stepped into the bay, his face lit up and he held both hands out to her. 'Henri, darling girl; get me out of this place.'

'Good evening, Sir Malcolm, I've called in on my way back to the castle. I've hired a car so I'll be able to return tomorrow for a longer visit and bring you anything you want . . .' Sir Malcolm's eyes lit up.

'Within reason,' Alice added.

'Within reason,' Henri agreed.

'I want to go home,' he said in a piteous voice. 'However, Keir won't hear of it.'

Alice pursed her lips, obviously about to make some stinging retort, when Henri stepped in. 'It's hardly up to Keir, now is it? You've survived a RTA, be grateful that you're still alive."

'That's what I've been telling him; bluddy auld fou-ull. Even if they let you home the morrah, which is extremely unlikely, you won't be able to return to the castle. It'll be the Beach House and a bed in the sitting room, until you can manage stairs. That's what's been agreed,' she said to Henri. 'Himself, me and Lachlan living there for the foreseeable future.'

'Not that anyone asked *me,*' Lachlan put it, aggrieved, but openly pleased that he would be living with Himself and Alice on a permanent basis. Henri surmised that Lachlan's sister would be pleased with the arrangements, too! 'Nah; poor auld Lachlan just goes alang wi' everything. And, for the record, ah dinnae like the sounds o' it. Mister Sandy tol't me the Beach House would be like a menagerie, with the three of us living there. But ah dinnae quite understand whit he meant. ' Removing his greasy bunnet, he scratched his head.

'A menagerie?' Henri questioned.

'Och, it's just Sandy pulling his leg. He meant a *ménage a trois*, knowing Malcolm dreams of being trapped between two young beauties. Is that no right, Malc?' Alice laughed, her humour restored. Henri could well imagine Alexander MacKenzie-Grieves winding up the unsophisticated Lachlan.

'It might yet come to pass,' was Malcolm's stiff reply.

'Dream on, pal. You've got me as your nurse and Lachlan as your orderly until yer over the worst of it. What more could a man ask?'

Sir Malcolm looked as though he was about to tell her *exactly* what he wanted, but held his wheesht. 'Humph,' was all he said, folding his arms as best he could with the blood pressure monitor and IV drip being attached.

'Humph.' Apparently the feeling was shared by Lachlan.

Henri looked down at them and her heart swelled. These people were beginning to feel like her dear friends, if not exactly family—at least, not yet. She smiled to herself, hoping she wasn't turning into one of those women who imbued everything with a rosy glow when in love. Next thing, she'd be bursting into song on the castle ramparts and inviting small birds to perch on her finger and feed from her hand.

'Something's made ye smile, lassie. And I'm glad of it,' Alice whispered when Malcolm and Lachlan were otherwise engaged, arguing over the last toffee. 'Good news from England, perhaps?'

'Very good news, Alice. I—I can't wait to share it with K-keir.'

'Well, off you go, visiting's nearly over. Lachlan and me are staying at the Travelodge and visiting Malcolm twice a day while Keir gets the Beach House ready. So,' she adopted an innocent expression. 'You'll have the castle all to yourselves. Is that no romantic?'

Henri's confidence faltered. Romantic? She wasn't so sure.

Keir had said: *Partners for ever, Henri? Even if we find nothing behind the wall?* And she'd replied: *We've found each other, that's treasure enough for me.*

It all seemed so long ago; so much had happened over the last few days that it was little surprise that she felt giddy, sick and off her food. She needed to see Keir. Find out where she stood, and if she'd been right to give up everything for passionate words exchanged in a cold, dank corridor.

'Are you still here?' Alice asked, laughing, waving a hand in front of Henri's face. 'Go! You'll know no peace until you've seen Keir. Neither will we.' Henri realised that Alice was intimating that all their futures: hers, Himself, Lachlan's and even the MacKenzie-Grieveses', were subject to what happened between her and Keir tonight.

It was a good two-hour drive on an unfamiliar road from Inverness to Fort William and another half hour after that before she reached MacKenzie's Halt.

Alice was right; it was time for her to leave.

Parking her hired car in front of the station, Henri made her way over to the ticket office. As expected, everything was locked and deserted with only an old-fashioned lamp over the doorway lighting the November darkness. Henri cursed the impulse which had made her drive all the way to MacKenzie's Halt at this late hour. She had no idea if Keir was in the castle, or over at the Beach House, preparing it for his father's return.

It would have been more sensible to stay overnight in the Travelodge and drive over in the morning. However, she felt far from sensible. She longed to see Keir—to be held in his arms, breathe in the scent of him and rub her cheek against the rough wool of his jumper. There would be no rest for her until she did. Hefting her rucksack over her shoulders, she crossed over the wrought iron bridge and down the other side towards the loch.

Once she left the station light behind she became aware of how dark it really was.

Pulling a torch out of her coat pocket, she switched it on and edged her way along the slippery path to the jetty. When she reached the shore of the loch she was enveloped in a dead silence. Nothing stirred, not even water fowl settling down for the night. When her senses became more attuned, she made out the shape of the Castle Tèarmannair, outlined against the faint luminosity of the Milky Way. Putting the torch back in her pocket, she made her way over to the mini bell tower and tugged on the rope three times.

The sound was preternaturally loud and shattered the silence before fading with a dying fall. She remembered the first time she'd rung the bell; Lachlan's less than enthusiastic welcome and the shock on Alice's face when she'd realised the castle archivist was, in fact, Dr *Henriette* Bruar.

What a clever trick Maddie had played on them all. How long ago that now seemed. Making herself focus, she looked straight ahead at the castle and saw that it was in total darkness. Ringing the bell for a second time, she waited for a response. Then realisation dawned on her.

No one was coming for her.

No one wanted her.

She was on her own.

Chapter Thirty-Three
Pyrotechnics

Turning, she trudged back up the path to her parked her car. It was all so different to how she'd imagined her homecoming that tears pricked her eyes and her chest tightened in misery. Swallowing her hurt and disappointment, Henri took several calming breaths and considered what to do next.

'You've travelled the world on your own, Henriette Bruar, you're more than capable of figuring this out. If the worst comes to the worst, you can ask the MacKenzie-Grieveses to put you up for the night.' She paused in mid-thought; if the worst did come to the worst, she was prepared to sleep in her car or the boat house. Even if the latter smelled disgustingly of rotting fish, a reminder of the family of otters who'd taken up residence there, last summer.

A frosty welcome at the MacKenzie-Grieveses or a stinking shed?

It was a no-brainer.

The very idea of asking Ciorstaidh MacKenzie-Grieves for a bed for the night made Henri falter. She slipped on the muddy path, landed on her hands and knees, and was dragged sideways by her heavy rucksack as it slipped off her shoulder. Shocked but unhurt, she clambered to her feet. Feeling very sorry for herself, she ran her hands over her clothes and was unsurprised when they came away, wet and slimy with mud.

'This is what happens when you hitch your wagon to someone else's star,' she declared.

Sitting on the edge of the jetty she stared blindly at the light flashing on and off at the end of it. She felt as if it was speaking to her—

Go-

Stay-

Go-

Stay-

telling her to give it one last shot.

In her heart of hearts, she couldn't believe that Keir would let her down. Yet, what other conclusion was she to draw from his nonappearance? Spending the night in her car was beginning to look an attractive alternative when a solution came to mind. She'd drive to the Beach House. She knew where he kept the key. If he wasn't there, she might be able to pick up a clue as to his whereabouts, use the telephone or even sleep on the sofa, like last time. Feeling more optimistic, she settled her rucksack on her shoulders and started off up the path for a second time.

Then she heard it—the faint, but unmistakable sound of a boat travelling at speed across the loch in the darkness. Turning, she raced to the water's edge just as the boat rounded the corner. The light on top of the wheel house threw a sheet of molten gold on the face of the dark water, all the way to her muddy feet. For one surreal moment she felt imbued with the power to walk across the beam of light and meet the boat, halfway. Instead, she used the time to compose herself so when she came face-to-face with Keir, she didn't act like a giddy schoolgirl on a first date. Because that's how he made her feel, brand new; each response unrehearsed and spontaneous, as thought she was learning to live all over again.

She could barely look at him as he leapt onto the jetty and secured the boat, in case her feelings showed in her face. Her body trembled with nerves as he walked up from the jetty and stopped two paces from her. As though in a dream, she watched him strip off his gloves in that purposeful way of his, stuff them in his pockets and then give her a sweeping inspection which took in muddy clothes, the long strands of blonde hair which had escaped from her beret, and her tentative, half-smile.

Then her smile faded. He had the look of a man who had a speech to deliver, one he'd spent all afternoon rehearsing. Henri's hopes sank and she steeled herself for the worst. Stony-faced, Keir regarded her for some time, and when he spoke, his voice was hoarse.

'Henri, you're covered in mud,' he said, in lieu of a greeting.

'I fell over,' she explained somewhat unnecessarily, and searched his expression for some clue to what he was about to say. Momentarily, he covered his face with both hands as though composing himself, searching for the exact expression. Dropping his hands, he regarded Henri with some deliberation and then delivered his speech.

'God knows, Henri, I've played this scene over and over in my head since you walked out of the hospital with Sandy. Promising myself that I'd act cool and detached when we met again. Not let you know that I've spent every waking moment hoping—praying—that you'd come back to me. To *us*. Although, in reality, I've thought of little else . . .' His voice cracked again and, abandoning all attempts at diffidence, he cupped her cold face in his hands and looked into her green eyes, as though searching for a clue to how *she* felt.

'Keir, I'm s-so—sorry . . .' Her stammered reply seemed inadequate compared to his impassioned speech. She covered his hands with hers, wanting to keep them there forever. Then she looked up into his face and a sob of relief escaped her.

Apparently finding it easier to express his feelings in Gaelic, Keir dismissed her stammered apology, declaring, '*Tha thu a' coimhead brèagha. Tha gaol agam ort; mar a tha mo chridhe.* You look beautiful. I love you, my heart.' Henri's breath snagged at the tenderness in his voice and a fat tear rolled down her cheek, unchecked. Not because she was sad, but because she'd doubted him—and she should have known better.

Keir brushed away her tear with his thumb.

'I -I—thought there was no one in the castle. I thought that you wouldn't c-come.'

'How could you doubt me, even for a second?' Keir asked. Resting his hands on her shoulders, he gave her a gentle shake. 'I'll never let you down.'

'Because I th-thought you might hate me. I left you—*all* of you, when you needed me.'

'Henri, you had to draw a line under your old life. You had scores to settle, and needed space to work out if your future was here with me, or in some dusty library where your beauty and spirit would wither with the passing years.' His words echoed what Maddie had said, almost to the letter. 'Selfishly, I made that choice difficult for you, and I'm sorry.'

'You didn't even look at me as I left. You let me to g-go with Sandy, without a b-backward glance.'

Now she really *was* crying as all the hurt and pain she'd bottled up spilled out. Keir folded her in his arms and whispered against her ear. 'Don't you realise that if I'd turned round I would have been undone? I'd have fallen on my knees and begged you not to go. I took the coward's way out, turned away and used every ounce of my self-control not to look back. The decision to stay or go was yours to make, I didn't want to play on your emotions, that wouldn't have been fair.'

Henri loved him all the more for that. 'Oh, Keir,' she breathed.

'I'm guessing that you've made your choice?' His voice rose at the end of the sentence and, holding her from him, he studied her face in the light from his boat.

'I have. With Maddie's help.'

'She's a good woman—and, once, I thought Himself would marry her. But she was too clever and independent to take him on.'

'Probably for the best,' Henri sniffed and raised her head. 'Alice is the woman for him, *when* he grows up and is ready to admit it.' Keir brushed the thought away, as though he didn't want to talk about other people.

Only *they* mattered; only *she* mattered.

'In case you're wondering, I'm not looking for a housekeeper, or a friend. I want you as my lover, my wife and the mother of my children; the chatelaine of my castle, for as long as it stands. I'm hoping that's what you want, too, Henri.'

'Yes. A thousand times, yes.'

She threw her arms around his neck and kissed him with such passion that the last vestiges of awkwardness disappeared. Keir returned the kiss with interest, sweeping away the demons of indecision and regret which had been Henri's constant companions over the last few days. His lips were warm on her cold face, his tongue gentle and probing, as he reminded himself of how her kiss tasted. Then he undid the zip on her jacket, put one arm round her waist and drew her close. His free hand found her breast and their heartfelt sighs synched, acknowledging that the flame of their passion burned as brightly as before.

'Welcome home,' Keir said.

When, after some time, he managed to stop kissing her, Henri declared: 'I thought you weren't going to show . . .' There. She'd said it.

'There was some confusion about when you would arrive. Alice rang me from the hospital and told me you were on your way. I was delayed; there was something scheduled for tonight. Something I couldn't easily get out of. Luckily, Ciorstaidh was only too happy to deputise for me. And— here I am.'

'Here you are,' she agreed, ignoring the dart of jealousy which pierced her heart at the mention of his cousin's name. He'd declared his intentions towards her: lover, wife, mother of his children. Let that be enough.

'Come on, Dr Bruar, I have something to show you.' Taking her by the hand, he led her onto the boat, slipped a lifejacket over her head and cast off. Once they were in the middle of the loch he cut the engine and dropped anchor.

'What?' she regarded him, quizzically.

'Wait.' Glancing at his watch he pointed towards Castle Tèarmannair. Leaning back against the side of the boat he put his arms around her waist and drew her back against him, kissing the nape of her neck. 'Any second now . . .'

Henri leapt out of her skin as the first rocket shot up into the night sky and then fell to earth, screaming as it did so. Pyrotechnic chrysanthemums of all hues burst around them; shooting stars of iridescent green and yellow carving a path through the darkness.

'What is this?' Laughing, Henri turned round to face him.

'It's your welcome home party, Dr Bruar.'

'Really?' She shot him a disbelieving look.

'Okay, so you're sharing it with the MacKenzie Shinty Club Bonfire Party. But it's the same thing.'

'I think you'll find,' she sent him the chastising look of an academic for whom such things mattered, 'that it is not.'

'Och, hold yer wheesht, wumman, and kiss me again.' When they drew apart, he tapped himself on the chest and explained. 'You are looking at the man who usually *lights the blue touch paper and stands well back*. Or, if not me, then my father. It's tradition. But tonight I thought, bugger tradition, the love of my life is standing in the cold and dark, waiting for me to take her home.'

Henri's spine tingled at, *to take her home*—and she squeezed his hand. For several minutes they watched the fireworks in silence, then she turned to Keir and grinned mischievously.

'What?' he asked.

'*This*. The absurdity of being on a boat in the middle of a loch, watching a firework display celebrating the trial and execution of a Catholic terrorist—Guido Fawkes—four hundred years ago, for attempting to blow up a Scottish king in an English parliament.'

'It *does* sound romantic when you put it that way.' They both laughed. 'Now, Dr Bruar, put that clever mind of yours to solving a rather more pressing problem.'

'Such as?'

'My place—or, *my* place?' he asked, subverting the old chestnut. 'Castle or Beach House?'

'The castle has always felt like my home,' Henri replied.

'I'd love you for that, alone.' Pulling her closer, Keir kissed her with such fervour that the boat's wooden planks were in danger of spontaneously combusting.

When next they looked, the firework display had ended and the loch was in darkness.

Henri laid her head on his chest. 'Take me home, Keir. To the castle, to your bed. For nothing else matters.' Nodding his agreement, Keir raised the anchor and set the boat for Castle Tèarmannair.

They didn't so much climb the stairs as take them two at a time, breathless and laughing as they clung onto the rope bannisters and rounded each turn and twist. Through the kitchen, past the library and the Great Hall, up another flight and then another before reaching the top floor and Keir's bedroom. Flinging the door back on its hinges with scant regard for its age or provenance, Henri tossed her rucksack on the floor and pushed Keir onto the bed.

For a few moments, they were incapable of doing more than lying back and looking at the ornate plasterwork on the ceiling while their laboured breathing returned to normal.

'Know what?' Keir managed to say, at last.

'What?'

'I have a newfound respect for Auld Lachlan.'

'You have?' Henri raised herself up on one elbow and looked down on him. Then she started to pull down the zip on his Belstaff jacket.

'God, yes. I've had to keep the fires burning in my bedroom, yours and the library, tend the Aga in the kitchen—once that goes out, it's the devil to light. Not to mention trying to get the Beach House warm enough for when Father, or in the first instance, Alice and Lachlan set up camp there.

Completely knackering.' He let out a long breath. 'I don't know how Lachlan does it, at his age I mean.'

'Poor baby. I hope you're not too worn out,' Henri continued on a solicitous tone, opening the front of his jacket and starting on the buttons of his shirt.

'It has been hard work, lugging buckets of coal and baskets of wood and peat up and down the stairs. Let me tell you *that*.' Then, catching her drift, he pushed her onto her back and straddled her. 'Why, you—' Stripping off his jacket, he threw it on the floor and laughed: 'It'll take more than a few buckets of coal to keep me from your bed, lassie.'

'That's alright then,' Henri responded. 'You had me worried for a few moments, there.'

'No fears in that direction,' he reassured, removing her coat and slipping it from under her. Then he drew her higher up in the bed so they could lie together without their legs dangling off the end. 'You know, I need to find a shorter girlfriend or buy a longer bed.'

'*Girlfriend?*' Henri pretended affront. 'Really?'

'Lover?'

'Better.'

'Fiancée?'

'I'll settle for that—and a longer bed. Although, most beds of this age reflect the lack of height in the general population at the—mmph.' Henri's treatise on nineteenth-century Scottish beds was cut short as Keir slipped his hands under her buttocks and pressed his full length against her. Plainly, schlepping coal, wood and peat up three spiral staircases had neither sapped his energy nor dulled his ardour.

'You are caked in mud, Dr Bruar. I cannot risk having this heritage quilt spoiled so I must relieve you of your outer garments.' His tone was solicitous as he pulled off her boots and removed her mud-caked skinny jeans. 'Och, and will ye look at your blouse, lassie; I'll never get the stains oot.' Channelling Alice, he slipped off Henri's blouse and then, kneeling over her, removed his shirt and threw it on the floor, too. Henri giggled, but acknowledged that this absurd role playing was necessary to return them to the easy relationship they'd had before the phone rang three nights ago and everything had gone pear-shaped.

'Why, thank you, kind sir,' she said, using a demure tone.

'Ah, the thermal vest; how could I forget. But, thank *you* for reminding me, Dr Bruar.' He pulled it over her head and draped it across the foot board.

'My turn.'

Clad only in her underwear, Henri slid out from under him and, with some help, slipped off his heavy boots, closely followed by an old pair of salopettes, complete with jazzy braces, that he'd donned to keep out the chill wind on the loch. The pockets, full of manly detritus—loose change, screw drivers, fuses, bits of string and so on—emptied their contents over the carpet when the salopettes were upended. When she turned back, Keir had shrugged off his shirt and wearing only his boxer shorts, draped himself across the bed in the manner of a male model. Giggling afresh, Henri climbed onto the bed and scrambled under the covers which Keir pulled back with a gallant gesture.

When he joined her, his skin touching hers, rough chest hair lightly grazing the swell of her breasts, all playfulness left them. Suddenly serious, Keir pushed her hair off her face.

'I never want this to end—my wanting you.'

'It never will,' Henri vowed, lost in the depths of his dark blue eyes. Opening her front-fastening bra, she offered herself to him and was lost as their lovemaking gathered pace. Soon, only the crackling of the fire and the sound of their breathing could be heard until a voice, sounding so like her own, yet unfamiliar to her, cried out: 'Now, Keir. For God's sake. *Now.*'

With one final, deep thrust he called out her name, then clung to her like a drowning man.

Later, waking and seeing bright stars through the windows and knowing that there would be a hard frost, Keir got up to tend to the fire. The temperature in the room would soon plummet and it would take some effort to get it warm again. Naked apart from the coverlet draped over his shoulders, he looked down on Henri's sleeping form: flushed face, sex-tousled hair, arm tucked under the pillow, long limbs reaching towards the foot of the too-short bed. Every part of him wanted her, wanted to bury himself deep inside her and make love until they were too exhausted to think.

The very thought made the blood thrum in his ears and his skin tingle in anticipation.

Building up the fire he felt at peace, content and sat back on his heels savouring the moment. Then, unexpectedly, he was swamped by another emotion. One so unfamiliar that he couldn't immediately identify it. On autopilot, he stacked turves of peat next to the coal scuttle until the word revealed itself. To his surprise, the word which eventually sprang to mind was, *happy*. He sat back on his heels; the last time he'd felt truly happy—truly happy—was the morning of his sixth birthday, hours before his mother and brother had drowned in the loch.

Stunned, he stopped tending the fire as another truth revealed itself to him—their deaths truly weren't his fault. He'd been a child at the time, how *could* their deaths be down to him? It was a tragic accident. Alice and Henri were right, it was time he stopped beating himself up over what couldn't be undone. He let out a long breath and a great weight lifted off his shoulders. The shackles of the past fell away, taking with them the guilt and despair which had dogged his waking moments for the last thirty years. Intoxicated by the endorphins flooding his body, he stood up and looked down on the woman who'd brought him back to life. Oblivious to his moment of epiphany, she slept on until he whispered: 'I love you, Dr Henriette Bruar,' and the soft cadence in his voice penetrated her sleep.

'Keir? Where are you?' Eyes closed, Henri's left hand swept over the still-warm bed, searching for him. 'I'm cold. Come to bed and warm me up.'

No longer shackled by memories of that dreadful day, and the certain knowledge that his father was hell-bent on handing a bankrupt estate down to him, the Master of Mountgarrie swung the coverlet off his shoulders and climbed into bed. With this woman by his side he had riches enough and he could live anywhere—a one bedroom flat in Fort William, a shack in British Columbia if it meant they could be together.

That was all that mattered.

Chapter Thirty-Four
Romancing the Stone —take #2

Henri awoke to the sound of cups rattling in their saucers and a heavy knife falling onto the floor. It was so reminiscent of the morning when Alice had brought them tea and toast in bed, that she was temporarily disorientated. Then her sleep-befuddled brain cleared and, opening her eyes, she saw Keir place the breakfast tray on a side table.

'Not quite up to Auntie Alice's standards, I'm afraid, but I'll have to do,' he grinned.

'Well, you have other skills, which make up for your deficiencies as a breakfast chef.' Taking the cup and saucer from him, Henri sent him a bold look over the rim of her cup.

Playing along, Keir climbed into bed beside her. 'And what might those be?'

'If I told you *that*, it would only encourage you to form an even higher opinion of yourself.' Laughing to take the sting out of her words she pointed at the breakfast tray. 'Toast, please, and be quick about it. I have an enormous appetite this morning.'

'I wonder why.'

'I'm guessing that it's somehow connected to the aforementioned *skills*.'

'I am pleased to see that you have a high regard for the niceties of language, Dr Bruar.'

Henri slid as far down in the bed as she could without spilling her tea. Balancing the plate of toast on her chest she added, 'Among other things.'

'You are a great tease, Dr Bruar, and will be shown the error of your ways, after breakfast.'

'After breakfast?' she said through a mouthful of crumbs. 'Do we have to wait that long?' They looked at each other, desire sublimating everything else. Taking the teacup, saucer and plate from Henri, Keir propped himself up on his elbow and looked down on her, eyes full of light and laughter.

'Here beginneth the lesson.' As he pulled her on top of him, they greeted the morning and their new relationship with a long, lingering kiss.

Later Henri was preparing lunch as best she could, given that Keir kept pulling her onto his knee and kissing her every time she passed the kitchen table, where he was sorting through the post. When the phone rang, he ignored it until Henri flicked him with the tea-towel and gestured that he should answer it.

'Castle Tèarmannair, MacKenzie speaking. Oh, Alice—how're things?' Henri stopped and listened to the one-sided conversation. 'That's good. No, give yourself and Lachlan a breather, you don't have to visit him twice a day. We'll draw up some kind of rota and make things easier for you. Don't wear yourself out—yes, it's going to be some time before he's allowed home. I'm sure he wants visitors twice a day, but he can't always get what he wants. You can tell him that, from me. I've got the Beach House to sort out, and . . .' Although he was mellowing towards his father, it was apparent he had no intention of spending every waking hour at Himself's bedside, when he was being looked after perfectly well by the nurses and doctors of Raigmore Hospital. 'Yes—Henri's here. Henri . . .' He pulled her onto his knee and passed her the ancient handset.

'Hello, Alice,' she said, coiling the cord round her finger like a ringlet.

'Aw'right, hen?'

'Yes; Keir's looking after me.' She bit her lip to stop herself smiling at the simple pleasure those words afforded her.

'I'm driving me and Lachlan home, later on. Himself needs clean pyjamas, his electric razor and—oh, a whole list of things. Most of them forbidden.

Dream on, Malc, I said to him when he mentioned whisky, again.' Henri imagined the satisfaction Alice would derive from denying Sir Malcolm what he wanted.

'It'll be lovely to see you back in the castle, Alice. However, it might be better if you waited at the Beach House after you drop Lachlan off. We're returning my rented car to Oban after lunch, it being closer than Inverness. There will be no one to bring you over to the castle until later.'

'Okay. I'll pick up some food on the way over and we can eat withoot Lachlan. There's only so much of him—and Sir Malcolm—a body can stand. It'll be just the three of us and I want to hear *all* about what happened in England. On top of that, I want to hear you say that you're staying with us forever.' She spoke in a gruff voice to hide her emotions.

'I—hope I will.' Glancing down, Henri traced a pattern on the table.

'Okay, laters,' Alice said, as if she was twenty-something.

'Laters.' Henri returned the phone to its charger on the wall and then paused, her back to Keir.

'Everything okay?' Keir questioned, evidently sensing that something was bothering her.

'Yes.' Turning and leaning back against the sink, Henri took a deep breath and said in a rush, 'Keir—how come the phone's working perfectly well now?'

'Ah, that.' He gave an embarrassed cough and stroked the side of his nose with his forefinger, a tell-tale show of embarrassment.

'Yes; that.'

'When you first arrived, Alice was too ashamed to let you know that the phone had been disconnected because Father couldn't pay the bill, so she pretended that the phone didn't work. Faces were saved. Not that it worried Father, he has full access to the MacKenzie-Grieveses' phone and, as far as he was concerned, the rest of us could go hang—or, use the phone in the post office. Failing that, we could drive halfway to Oban and pick up the mobile signal; or schlep all the way over to the Beach House and use my phone.'

'I see.' Small wonder the university hadn't been able to reach her. If she hadn't spoken to Maddie at the Beach House that day, she would have been totally in the dark concerning the timetable for her disciplinary hearing. She looked over at Keir and sensed there was more. 'And . . .' she prompted.

'I knew how important it was for you to have access to your university, so I offered to pay the phone arrears in instalments to the phone company, with the proviso that they reconnected the phone immediately. Just as well they agreed, otherwise . . .'

'Otherwise, we wouldn't have learned of the laird's accident until later the following day when Sandy or Ciorstaidh brought the news over to the castle. I wouldn't have found the email in my inbox summoning me to the disciplinary hearing. If I'd been late, or had ignored the summons, the university might have interpreted that as disinterest or arrogance on my part, and things might not have turned out so well.' Giving a superstitious shiver, she acknowledged that there were subtle forces at work in this ancient castle. Forces which wanted her and Keir to be together and had been working towards that end from the moment she'd set foot on the train and heard the piper.

Or was that too fanciful?

She shook her head.

No; here, in this mystical, magical place—anything was possible. She totally bought into *that*. Releasing her, Keir walked over to the table and returned to sorting through the letters, bills and such like which Sir Malcolm had shoved in the dresser drawer and forgotten, as though they were of no significance.

'What is it?' she asked, seeing a shadow cross his face.

'It's worse than I thought. The bank's threatening to foreclose because Father hasn't made any repayments on his loans for almost six months. They're demanding that assets be seized and liquidised to meet his debts—including farmland which has been in the MacKenzie family for almost a thousand years, and the Beach House.'

'Oh, Keir, I'm so sorry. But, I don't get it—don't *you* own the Beach House?'

'Yes—and, no. It's complicated, and governed by the rules of primogeniture where the eldest son inherits everything. The Master of

Mountgarrie, my courtesy title, and the Beach House are part of Father's 'gift' to me. I have them on 'loan', as it were, until the day I become laird and inherit the baronetcy, estate, castle, Beach House, everything—including the debts secured against the estate. Until then, Father can dispose of it all as he sees fit. Now you know why I spend most of the year in Canada. I can't bear to see him running the estate into the ground.'

'I'm guessing this is constantly playing on your mind?'

'You could say that. But you made me forget all about it, for a night at least.'

'What can you do?'

'I've persuaded Father to allow *me* to deal with the bank manager while he's in hospital. Maybe I'll be able persuade the bank to defer any decisions until he's well enough to leave hospital and move into the Beach House.'

'How likely is that?'

'Not very. Banks are there to make money, not help out feckless lairds who've defaulted on their loan repayments.' Then he gave himself a shake, as if to blot out the image of a sale board being hammered into the garden of the Beach House.

'Keir, what can I do?'

'You can follow me to Oban to drop off your car. Then we'll meet Alice at the Beach House, bring her back here and enjoy a quiet dinner together. Let's have one more night of laughter and love before reality bites—tomorrow.'

That wasn't exactly what she meant and she would have liked to have said more. However, common sense told her that now wasn't the time. Returning to the sink, she continued with lunch preparations and thought long and hard about a solution to Keir's financial problems as he, head in hands, tried to make sense of his father's filing system.

Alice's sitting room and adjacent bedroom were nice and toasty, thanks to the fires lit earlier and the fan heater blasting out hot air. Time to worry about the electricity bill when it arrived, Keir had said. Another bill they couldn't pay . . .

Too depressing for words.

'So, I said to Ant and Dec, that I'd love tae take part in the next series of *I'm a Laird—Get Me Oot'a Here,* providing Lachlan came along to repel the insects. They agreed, because—get this—they want a Scottish vibe on their next show.' There was a pause, as Alice waited for their reaction.

Henri blinked a couple of times, as though being pulled out of a dream. Keir stared into the fire deep in thought, his arm round her as though he couldn't bear to let her out of his sight.

Alice tried again. 'So—with that in mind, ah thought I'd get in training for the Bush Tucker Trial by cooking up locusts and serving them with neeps and tatties for dinner. That okay?'

'Perfect.'

'Great idea, Alice.'

'Of course,' Alice continued, 'Himself will struggle with conditions in the rain forest, but once his plaster comes off, he should manage to hack back the jungle with the aid of his Zimmer frame, nae bother. The insects won't worry him, he's been eaten alive by midges for more summers than either of us care to remember.' Getting to her feet she coughed and then stood, hands on hips until they acknowledged her presence.

'You're going to be on *I'm a Celebrity*?' Keir said at last.

Picking up a small cushion, Alice threw it at his head. 'No, ah'm not, I just wanted to check if you were listening.'

Grinning, Keir put the cushion behind his head. 'The lights *are* on, but no one's at home. Sorry, Auntie Alice.'

'I can see that.' Alice looked between them and then smiled, indulgently.

'Sorry, Alice, are we being too self-absorbed?' Henri moved along the sofa, putting space between her and the Master of Mountgarrie. The only way to ensure she could resist him.

'Aye; a wee bit, maybe.' Alice walked over to the sideboard and then paused. 'I thought we'd agreed to look at the old photo albums this evening? I've got them all ready. Do you wah-nt to give it a miss?'

'No way! I'm dying to see the ones featuring Keir on a sheepskin rug wearing nothing but a smile.'

'Aye, he was a bonnie baby. Him and Wee Malchy. So different, like chalk and cheese. Malcolm was fair, like his mother and father—but Keir came out with a head of dark hair and a cross face; a typical Highlander.' She passed the albums over to Henri who balanced one on her knee and flicked through the pages while Keir looked over her shoulder. Once, interleaving sheets had held the photos in place, but over the years they'd lost their adhesiveness and photos kept slipping onto the floor.

'Oh, Alice,' she let out a breath, 'you and your sister were beauties. All that Farrah Fawcett hair—those side flicks; wow!' She smoothed out a cracked photo showing the blonde Dougal sisters serving behind the counter of a local café.

'Mary and me were obsessed with *Charlie's Angels*,' Alice laughed. 'But the nearest we got to the west coast of America was Wester Ross and a wee café on the side of a loch. Och, will ye look at that. We're wearing the high-waisted flares and cheesecloth smocks we bought at the Glasgow Barras on our way to catch the train to Fort William. Thought we were the bees' knees. And there's Malc in his safari suit, look how *thin* he was. We all were.' They all looked at Sir Malcolm sporting double-denim and a fine head of thick blond hair beneath a baker boy cap, set at a jaunty angle.

Henri couldn't help but laugh at Himself looking so on-trend. She apologised, but then Keir and Alice joined in.

'Who's *that*?' She pointed at a slight figure in platform boots, wearing the widest flares imaginable and a knitted tank top over a bare torso. 'Oh, tell me it isn't. Lachlan?'

'Aye, it's Lachlan a'right. Fresh out of a ten-year stretch at Barlinnie and wearing some of Malc's old clothes. They just about drowned him, him being a wee baucle. He had nothing of his own and his family didnae wah-nt to know him. The first time I met him, he came across as a bit of a sleaze-ball, whining to me and my sister that he'd missed out on *free love* whilst in prison—and that all the bonnie lassies were taken. Hint. Hint.'

'Lachlan? Free love? Eww—can't imagine that.'

'Wedding photos next?' Alice asked, her anxious look intimating that Keir hadn't enjoyed looking at them in the past.

'Why not?' he shrugged. 'Time we all moved on and gained closure. Dreadful word, but it sums it up.' He drew Henri back into his side and kissed her temple, emphasising that she was responsible for this sea change.

'How beautiful Lady MacKenzie looks,' Henri sighed.

For a few moments no one spoke, looking instead at the photo of a young woman in a simple high-waisted gown, inset with lace, and tight sleeves which came to a point over her ring finger. Alice took the photo out of the album and kissed it, looking sad.

'We bought the Butterick dress pattern and the material for our dresses in Inverness. Malc drove us there in his Land Rover, I remember feeling every bump in the road because I sat in the back. Afterwards, he took us for a slap up lunch and we hurried home to make a start on the dresses. Mary and me had great fun making them—in this very room, on a sewing machine borrowed from—I forget who, exactly. Malcolm was the very devil, kept popping his head round the door trying to catch a glimpse of the frocks. Oh, how happy we were.'

Her voice caught and Henri gave her hand a reassuring squeeze.

'Look at your father, Keir. Those sideboards!' Henri laughed, chasing away the sadder memories trying to crowd in. 'What a dude.'

'He was great back then, such a laugh; so anxious that Mary and me would fit in and be happy. Old Lady MacKenzie, on the other hand, was a right old cow. She wouldn't let Mary borrow the family veil or tiara because she was set on Malc marrying his cousin. Malcolm told her to go to the devil, and so I made Mary's bouquet and headdress myself, with some help from the village ladies. We didn't bother with a veil, Malc said that he loved her long, blonde hair too much to see it covered.' She raised her hand to her own short style, as if remembering how thick and luxurious it had been.

'My grandmother *was* a bit of an old witch,' Keir agreed.

'Ach, well. It was all about the money, you see, even then.'

'And who are they?' Henri pointed to four men in ill-fitting suits, flanking Sir Malcolm.

'Our cousins: Billy, Danny, Johnny and Frankie. They finished their shift at the Ravenscraig, packed their cases and caught the same train to Fort William—in case Malcolm changed his mind and left Mary at the altar, with a baby on the way. But there was never any danger of that. He loved her and she'd saved him from a fate worse than death.'

Her last word hovered in the air and they all shivered, in spite of the blazing coal fire. Alice opened another album and as she did so, a large coin slid from between the pages and landed on the floorboards by Keir's foot. Bending down, he picked it up, turned it over in his hands without saying a word, and then he glanced at his aunt.

'My Spanish doubloon. I can't believe you've kept it all these years.' He spoke so softly that Henri could barely hear him.

'Aye, son, your pirate gold.' Pulling up a small stool, Alice sat at their feet. 'It was in your pocket when I stripped off your wet clothes, the day of the accident. I was going to return it to you, but Himself said that your head was full of enough nonsense about treasure and Jacobite gold—and I was to throw it away. I couldnae do that, I know how you loved that coin. I've always meant to give it back to you, but—' She shrugged away over thirty years of pain and grief, her face ashen and her blue eyes dull as she remembered that awful day. 'Afterwards, I forgot all aboot it.'

'I'd forgotten all about it, too,' Keir admitted.

'Can I see?' Henri held out her hand and Keir dropped the coin into it. She wandered over to the table lamp to gain more light.

At first glance, the coin looked exactly like the kind of chocolate coin children find at the bottom of their stockings on Christmas morning. However, as Henri examined it closer, and felt the weight of it in her hands, she knew it was more than that. On one side there was a bust of Queen Anne—surrounded by the words *Anna Dei Gratia*. Under her left 'shoulder' a name was imprinted: VIGO. As she ran her thumb over the name, her hands tingled and a feeling of presentiment washed over her, making her shiver.

'Henri? Are you okay, lassie—you've gone awfu' pale.'

'Oh,' she mouthed, faintly.

'Henri, what is it?' Taking took the coin out of her slack fingers, Keir examined it more closely.

'How did it come into Keir's possession?' Henri asked Alice.

'The floor in your bedroom had a touch of dry rot, and many years ago several of the boards had to be replaced . . .'

'Which floorboards?'

'The ones closest to the corridor wall.' Alice's brow puckered as she remembered. 'The coin was discovered when the floorboards were lifted. Knowing Keir's fascination with pirates, Mary gave it to him, tae play with—'

'Henri, what's the matter? It's just an old coin with a sad history. Come here, mo chridhe.'

Taking a calming breath, Henri re-joined Keir on the sofa, glad of the opportunity to sit down.

'Th -this coin,' she stammered and then coughed, clearing her voice. 'This coin was minted over three hundred years ago from gold seized off Franco-Spanish ships returning from Havana, Cuba. Earlier, the British Navy had made an abortive attempt to capture Cadiz, and so, to deflect attention from this failure, much was made of this haul of treasure. The gold and silver was received at the Royal Mint by—' At this point, her tongue cleaved to the roof of her suddenly dry mouth.

'Give her a drink, Keir. For the love o' God, Henri, ye cannae stop there.'

'The treasure was received b-by Sir Isaac Newton who was Master of the Mint,' Henri finished in a rush, wondering if the first person to touch the newly minted coin had been the great scientist.

'Sir Isaac Newton? The one sitting under the tree when the apple fell on his head and he invented gravity?'

'*Discovered* gravity, Alice,' Henri laughed.

'So what does the name signify?' Keir held the coin closer to the light.

'*Vigo*, stands for Vigo Bay where the Spanish were unloading the treasure when the Brits attacked them. Queen Anne issued a directive that the gold and silver seized should be used to make new English coins, bearing the name of the 'victory', *Vigo*. Only twenty gold coins were minted; fifteen of them have been rediscovered, which means . . .'

'There are still five out there, waiting to be found.' Keir's voice was hoarse. 'And you think—'

'This is one of them? Yes!'

'It looks too new for that,' Alice said, hardly daring to believe Henri.

'That's because it's pure gold. If you buried it in the ground and dug it up in a thousand years, it would look exactly the same.'

'A coin as rare as that, would be worth—what?' Now it was Keir's turn to hold his breath.

'About two hundred and fifty thousand pounds.' Henri had the pleasure of seeing Alice and Keir's jaws drop as they took in the enormity of the find.

'A quarter of a million pounds?' Keir let out a slow whistle. 'How do you know all this?'

Eyes shining, Henri replied, 'Trust me. I'm a doctor.' At that, they all laughed, then sobered as the enormity of the find dawned on them.

'For God's sake, don't tell, Malc,' Alice advised.

'We won't—at least, not until it's been verified.' Alice and Keir nodded, acknowledging that Henri was the expert. 'We don't want the press getting hold of the story. Sir Malcom's creditors would come out of the woodwork.'

'Once he's paid off his debts, there might be enough left over to fix the roof and buy me a new fridge' Alice clasped her hands together, as if in prayer.

'Install a stair lift in the Beach House—' Keir added.

Henri dismissed all that with an impatient flick of her hand. 'You're both missing the point.'

'Which is?' Keir and Alice looked at this new, bossier Henri with respect.

'The coin was found in my bedroom, under the floorboards butting up to the corridor. The corridor which, I believed—*still* believe—has a false wall. Remember the night of Malcolm's accident? We were about to remove one of the stones and put my theory to the test? I must admit, since then, I've felt quite embarrassed about the whole thing . . . I got carried away that night; stopped being logical, analytical Doctor Bruar and *totally* bought into the legend of MacKenzie's Gold. To be honest, so much has happened since then, that I'd quite forgotten about the treasure—until now.'

'Now?' Keir repeated, not quite following her train of thought.

'This coin changes everything. What if the treasure was stored in my bedroom and, at dead of night, a handful of trusted servants built the wall? Let's imagine that, when the treasure was moved, this coin rolled onto the floor and, in the candlelit darkness, slipped between a gap in the floorboards, unnoticed.'

'And remained there until Mother found it and gave it to me?' Keir sounded choked as the realisation dawned that, maybe, he and his mother had found treasure after all.

'Now what, Henri? Will you take a photo of it and email it to Maddie in the morning?'

'No.'

'No?' they both chorused.

'Tonight,' she palmed the coin and held her fist above her head, in triumph, 'The Hole in the Wall Gang are going on a treasure hunt.' With that she headed into the corridor, leaving Keir and Alice behind, in stunned silence. Then she stuck her head around the door and asked in a thick accent, 'Ahm ah on mah oh-an, or are youse two comin'?'

'Right ahint, ye lassie,' Alice's responded.

'You're going nowhere without *me*,' Keir added. 'Lead on, Dr Bruar, we're right behind you.'

Chapter Thirty-Five
Is There a Doctor in the House?

This time, they were fully prepared: aluminium stepladder, electric lamp on an extension cable, Lachlan's tool kit, dustpan, brush, and a fully charged mobile phone. Henri wanted to record this moment for posterity—this was her find, and she wasn't prepared to risk any repetition of the 'illuminated manuscript' fiasco. Not that Keir would cheat her out of her moment of glory, he was too honourable for that. Apart from which, she was fully aware that anything found there belonged to the MacKenzies—treasure trove laws permitting.

She was there in the capacity of an expert, nothing more.

All fired up, she skidded to a halt outside her bedroom door, the extension lead curled round her arm and shoulder, Indiana Jones style. Plugging in the lead, she retrieved her mobile from the dressing table and then joined the other two in the corridor, the light from the extension lamp unnaturally bright in the semi-darkness.

The three treasure hunters high-fived each other and then, with the MacKenzie battle cry, *'Tulach Ard!'* ringing in their ears, got down to it. Standing still for a moment, Henri committed the scene to memory—Keir, mounting the rickety stepladder, buoyed up with hope—so different from the disillusioned, self-contained man he'd been when they'd first met. Alice, as excited as a child on Christmas Day, knowing the impact this discovery would have on the family, and future generations of MacKenzies.

As for herself . . . crossing her fingers behind her back, she offered up a silent prayer —*please, God, let me be right about this. I couldn't bear to see Keir have his hopes dashed twice in a lifetime.*

'Hold the light steady, Henri.' Keir's commanding tones brought her back to the present. 'Alice, same tools as before, please.' Running his hand over the stone he'd loosened the night his father was taken into hospital, he proceeded to scrape away the remaining mortar. Pausing, he looked back at Henri for advice.

'Should I push the stone through into the gap, or try and lift it out in one piece?'

'One piece, if possible,' Henri said in a rush. 'We don't know what's on the other side of the wall and we don't want the stone to land on anything precious.' Nodding, Keir flexed his shoulders and started to work it loose. 'Wait!' Henri passed the extension lamp to Alice, raised her mobile and started videoing. 'Okay, go ahead.'

As Keir wrestled with the large stone, the temperature in the corridor dropped and Henri's ears filled with the now-familiar buzzing which heralded the spectral piper. Her hands shook as cold air from the spiral staircase rushed towards them, wrapping itself round her like an icy blanket. This was followed by a gut-wrenching keening sound which chilled her blood. Forgetting all about the videoing the excavation, Henri fastened her arms around Keir's knees and buried her face in the back of his thighs. When the noise stopped, Henri raised her head to find Keir and Alice regarding her with some amusement.

'Oh my God. Wh-wh-at *was* that?'

'Och, I must have forgotten close the door which leads from the kitchen to the foot of the staircase. When that happens, a muckle great draught comes whirling roond the corner and chills ye to the bone. What's the matter, Henri? Ye didnae think it was the ghost of long dead MacKenzies coming to claim back whit is rightfully theirs?'

Although that's *exactly* what Henri thought, she dismissed the preposterous idea with an airy wave of her hand. Well, as airy as she could, given that she was still clasping Keir's knees. 'Duh. 'Course not; just a bad case of nerves and an overdeveloped imagination.'

Laughing, Keir addressed his aunt. 'Academics, eh Alice? Henri, *mo chridhe*, once this job is finished you can hold me as tightly as you like, but for now . . . can I please have my legs back?'

Feeling a very foolish academic indeed, Henri released Keir's legs, stepped back and raised her mobile. 'Okay—Alice; lights, camera, action. Keir—*you're on.*'

Grunting, Keir dislodged one side of the stone and, after much rocking and manoeuvring, managed to swivel it backwards and forwards until it was half out of the hole. Then he slid his hand along the stone and reached into the void behind it. With one final effort, he pulled the stone out of the space.

For several moments no one spoke . . .

Henri continued filming.

Alice held the lamp steady.

Keir cradled the stone as thought it was his first-born, regarding Henri with respect for her leap of faith. Then he dropped the stone at their feet and broke the spell. 'Lamp, Alice,' he said, turning back to the wall.

'What can you see?'

'What's there?' Henri asked, as he poked the lamp into the void.

'A bloody great space,' he said laughing, half crying. 'As you predicted—my lovely, clever Dr Bruar.'

'Anything else?'

'I'll have to take out a few more stones. Hold this.'

Passing back the lamp, he removed two further stones—with greater ease this time, now the original stone was no longer in place. Then, holding the lamp, he shoved his whole arm into the space, right up to his shoulder. After a few moments of twisting his head and squinting into the gap, he turned round, his face serious. Expressionless, he hooked the extension lead on his belt, descended the stepladder, and stood in front of Henri, dusting off his hands. A feeling of crushing disappointment washed over her and she felt like bursting into tears.

How *could* she have got it so wrong?

Standing before her, Keir unhooked the lamp from his belt and handed it to her, indicating that she should climb the ladder and take a look.

'This moment belong to you, Henri. Don't you agree, Alice?'

'Aye. Honour where honour is due.'

'Well, go on,' Keir said, grinning and holding the ladder steady.

Taking a shaky breath, Henri climbed to the top of the ladder and, copying Keir's actions thrust her arm into the void as far as it would go. Turning her head sideways to get a better look, she exclaimed in a muffled voice—

'Oh my God, Keir—swords, pistols, muskets and—three chests, one large and two smaller ones. Can it be? Is it possible that the legend of MacKenzie's Gold is true, after all?'

'It certainly looks that way,' Keir said, trying but failing to keep his excitement in check. 'Come on, Auntie Alice, this moment belongs to you, too.' Henri stepped down off the ladder and he helped his diminutive aunt to look into the void.

'I'm hoping that what's been hidden in those chests for almost three hundred years will make the *Vigo* coin look like pocket money. Once word gets round, museums and collectors will be queuing up to buy the swords, muskets and pistols—especially as they come with bona fide provenance proclaiming them Jacobite treasure.' They looked at her in amazement as she morphed from the Master of Mountgarrie's lover and Castle Tèarmannair's temporary archivist into Doctor Henriette Bruar PhD.

As the significance of the find dawned on them, Keir let out a warrior cry that his MacKenzie ancestors would have been proud of, gave Alice a massive hug and swung her round a couple of times.

Then he drew Henri into his arms. 'We have you to thank for this—' he said, his mouth against hers.

Henri took a step back and, still in full academic mode, held up her hand. 'Slow down, Keir. There are things we need to do—like, contact the coroner.

No, wait; the law governing treasure trove is different in Scotland, no surprises there.' She sent them a dry look and then continued. 'I'll need access to the internet. I want to do this right—no comebacks.'

'You *will* do it right, hen. We know that.' Alice laid a hand on Henri's arm and gave it a reassuring squeeze.

'Agreed. But I'm afraid you'll have to wait until morning, Henri, when I can take you over to the post office, or the Beach House to get onto the internet,' Keir added.

'The Beach House, definitely. We don't want everyone knowing our business. I might also get in touch with Maddie Hallam. If this hoard is as significant as I *think* it is, it wouldn't hurt to have another expert on board. She could also help with cataloguing the MacKenzie Papers and finishing off the library. Although, those will be small fry in comparison.' It was clear from her expression that she was already mentally planning meetings with officials, valuers and experts.

As she'd remarked to Keir—this was what she did; this was what she was good at.

'What is it, Henri?' Alice asked as Henri smiled at them and her face lit up.

'My parents won't be able to say that I made the wrong decision in leaving St Guthlac. And, I'm guessing that next winter Castle Tèarmannair will be watertight and centrally heated. This discovery is going to be *massive*. I feel it in my bones.' Clapping her hands, she executed a happy dance, forgetting her earlier resolution to remain professional and detached, as an academic should.

'Okay, there's nothing we can do tonight. Or, is there?' A mischievous look crossed Keir's face. 'It wouldn't hurt to remove a few more stones, would it, Dr Bruar?'

'Probably not.'

'Or to open one of the chests?'

'Possibly not.'

'And take a wee keek?' Alice added.

'Let's do it,' Henri declared. 'I'll make a video and take photos of everything we do. And the order we do it in.'

That being decided, Keir started to demolish the wall, handing the stones back to Alice and Henri. When the hole was big enough for one of them to pass through, he paused and then stood back.

'You should go first, Henri, it's your find.'

'It's your heritage, Keir. You should go first.'

'It's only right that the Master of Mountgarrie should be the first MacKenzie to enter the hole, in almost three hundred years,' Alice agreed. Obeying, Keir disappeared into the void and Alice passed the lamp in after him. She squeezed Henri's hand as, standing shoulder to shoulder in the freezing cold corridor, they both felt the weight of history pressing down on them.

When Keir stuck his head through the gap and beckoned them forward, they nearly jumped out of their skins. 'There's room for a warhorse in here, never mind a pony,' he quipped. 'Join me, but watch you don't trip over the ledge.'

'Youse go ahead. Ah'm away to put the kettle on, I'm bluddy perished.' Alice rubbed her hands together and then winked at Henri, indicating that they should have this moment alone.

'Come on, Henri,' Keir said, poking his head back through the gap.

Hardly able to contain her excitement, Henri climbed into the dark space alongside Keir, clutching her mobile as if her life depended on it. 'Oh,' was all she could manage, as the extension lamp illuminated a great pile of arms: basket hilted swords, targes, biodags (long, pointed knives), Lochaber axes, muskets, pistols and drawstring leather bags containing musket balls.

Tracing the engraving and silver inlay on a fine pair of flintlock pistols in a silk-lined, mahogany box, Henri could hardly speak for excitement. 'These could be worth over forty thousand pounds, on their own,' she said as she took another photo. 'And this, too.' Ignoring all her training, she picked up a heavy basket-hilted sword, its hand guard exquisitely wrought in silver. 'Look, the protective padding is still intact. A conservative estimate would put this at between four and six thousand pounds. Oh, Keir—I know we said we'd only remove the stones, but could we have a *wee keek*, inside one of the chests, too?'

Smiling, Keir cradled her cheek in one hand, letting her know that she was more precious to him than anything they might find here, tonight. Henri covered his hand with hers and then turned her face into it and kissed his palm, before hunkering down in front of the smallest of the three chests. Glancing up at Keir, she whispered. 'Think—the last person to touch this chest could have been your ancestor—Mackenzie of MacKenzie, or the Master of Mountgarrie.' Letting out a long breath, she undid the clasp and opened the lid. The harsh electric light revealed a chest full of coins, precious metal and jewellery. 'I'm guessing,' Henri said in a breathless whisper, 'this is Spanish gold from the New World, and that your ancestor was commissioned to keep it safe until . . .'

'The Jacobites had need of it?'

'Exactly. See,' she brought the lamp closer, 'the coins are irregular in shape, have no milled edge and are stamped with the coat of arms of Philip V of Spain. That helps us date the collection to sometime after 1702, but no later than 1745, when he died.'

'A year before Culloden; prophetic. However, Dr Bruar, time to call a halt, methinks, Your hands are like blocks of ice. Let's join Alice in the kitchen.' Shutting the lid of the casket, he guided her back through the hole and into the corridor. They stood before the stepladders, pile of stones and the gaping hole in the wall.

Keir watched as Henri took some last photos.

'I'm so excited,' she said, putting the phone in her pocket. 'I won't be able to sleep tonight.' She turned and looked at him, bright eyed, innocent of what she'd said.

'I won't either,' Keir responded poker-faced. 'Maybe we should keep each other company, during the wee small hours? What do you say?'

'What do I say—oh.' The penny finally dropped. 'I say, jolly good idea. I could bring my book of coins with me and we could research and date some of the coins in the chest.' Henri adopted an innocent expression to counter Keir's passionate regard.

'We *could*,' Keir agreed, leading her along the corridor by the hand, 'but should that prove to be just *too* exciting?'

'We could discuss which holes in the roof to have mended first.'

'Or simply spend the whole night making love?' Keir suggested with a nonchalant shrug, as though her answer was of no concern to him.

'If we must,' she sighed. Then she laughed and ran to the end of the corridor and threw him a catch-me-if-you-can look over her shoulder. Today was the best day of her life and she could think of no better way of ending it than in the arms of the Master of Mountgarrie.

Chapter Thirty-Six
Playing the Waiting Game

'I've just about had it up tae here,' Alice fumed in the kitchen, a month later. 'Since Himself's been moved from hospital to the Beach House, he thinks I've been put on this earth to wait on him, hand and foot while he recuperates. Just because he cannae climb the stairs tae the bathroom and has to use a commode—which Lachlan empties, thank the Lord—disnae mean I have to be his slave.'

'I'll have words with him, Alice.' Keir attempted to mollify his aunt, but she brushed him aside; she was on a roll and had more to say.

'And—get this—that wee scunner, Lachlan, has brought a china bell over fae his sister's and given it to Himself to ring whenever he wants anything. Which is every five minutes, by-the-by. Ah've already tol't him, if he doesn't get rid o' the bell, they'll be air-lifting him *back* to hospital tae have it surgically removed from his—'

Just in time, Henri stopped her tirade and put her arms round Alice's stiff shoulders. 'Without meaning to, we've taken you for granted and that's wrong.' She indicted, via a few sharp head movements, that Keir and Maddie Hallam should make similar soothing noises.

'You've borne the brunt of the nursing, Auntie—sorry; we'll be able to help from now on,' Keir agreed.

Then Maddie Hallam added her piece. 'We've been so focused with cataloguing the finds, contacting the Treasure Trove Unit, visiting the Queen's and Lord Treasurer's Remembrancer offices in Edinburgh regarding ownership, that we've overlooked what's been happening outside the bubble.

Again, sorry, darling Alice.' Following Henri's example, she walked over to Alice and hugged her.

Now it was Alice's turn to apologise. 'Och, I know you've all been busy getting everything moved out of the castle before Malcolm realises what's going on. It's just—every now and then, I need tae let off steam and have a guid auld moan.'

'Alice, you're entitled; I know, first hand, how exasperating Father can be. If you want to brain him with his bedpan, don't hold back on my account,' Keir said, only half-joking.

'It'd take more than a disposable bedpan to dent his thick skull,' Alice added, her sense of humour returning. 'And, FYI, I leave *that side of things* to Lachlan. Mind you, I'll be glad when Malc's plaster cast comes off and he can get around without help.'

'Malcolm's always been incredibly spoiled.' Maddie Hallam said, walking over and sitting on the armchair next to the Aga. 'Old Lady MacKenzie doted on him—bigging-him-up, giving him an overinflated sense of his own importance. In common with many of the upper-class boys who came to St Guthlac straight from boarding school, university wasn't quite what they expected. Academic rigour, having to think for themselves, no one spoon-feeding them information. Malcolm caved pretty early on—and then spent most of his time smoking weed, chasing girls and driving his E-Type at death-defying speed round the villages, before dropping out completely.'

'Well, the E-Type's a write-off. As for chasing lassies, walking to the front door's more than he can manage at present,' Alice informed, with a degree of relish.

'Can I speak frankly?' Maddie asked Keir.

'You and Alice aren't known for holding back—go ahead.'

'The only good thing about Malc being *hors de combat*, is that it's kept him out of the way. If he'd been discharged from hospital earlier, he would have caught us red-handed, transporting everything over to the Beach House and then into Keir's Land Rover. MacKenzie's Gold is safe in Edinburgh with the Remembrancer, now. It'll be at least a month before we hear from them regarding ownership and provenance, longer possibly, with Christmas and Hogmanay being just weeks away.'

'We've been given a breathing space,' Henri agreed. 'Let's make the most of it—replace the stones, tidy up the corridor and finish sorting through the books in the library. I'm guessing you won't be selling them, now?'

'Probably not; at least, not the ones worth saving. After all your hard work, too, mo chridhe.'

'I don't mind. The books are what brought me here, after all. Let's make the most of the quiet before the storm to have everything in place for when the Remembrancer's Office gets back in touch.' Leaving Alice's side, she walked over and sat on Keir's knee.

'Henri's right,' Maddie pronounced. 'Once news of MacKenzie's Gold gets out, Castle Tèarmannair will be in the spotlight, whether we like it or not.'

'So—are we all agreed there's no point involving Father until we know how much the find is worth and where we stand regarding ownership?'

'Aye, if he knew what's been going on, he'd hack his way out of the plaster cast with a bread knife and demand that Lachlan brings him back to the castle. Malc can smell money a mile off.'

'You've done a great job, Alice. Now it's time for you to stand down. I should be able to persuade the bank to extend our overdraft until the provenance of the treasure has been verified. I'll organise a couple of women from the village to call in at the Beach House every day to do the housework and cooking, and so on. There might even be enough money to pay for a qualified nurse during his convalescence, if you think it necessary.'

'No one too beautiful,' Maddie joked. 'I wouldn't put it past Malcolm to chase them round the sitting room on crutches.'

'Now I've let off steam, I'll go back to the Beach House and help Lachlan out. However, once the new staff are bedded in, Keir, I'd like tae move back intae the castle. Will that be alright with you and Henri?' Alice cast them an anxious look and Henri's heart went out to her. Castle Tèarmannair had been her home for over thirty years and she obviously felt the wind of change sweeping through the castle, touching every dusty corner, nook and cranny. Nothing would ever be the same—for any of them. It was a testament to Keir's love for his aunt that he picked up on her fears straightaway and was able to reassure her that Castle Tèarmannair would always be her home.

'Actually, I was going to ask you to move back in, Auntie Alice. We really could do with you running the castle, as per usual. With everything else that's going on, Henri, Maddie and I will be pretty much tied up sorting out the other business.'

'Aw'right,' she said, tying on her apron and cheerfully reassuming the role of chatelaine. Getting up from Keir's knee, Henri went over to the fridge in order to prepare lunch.

'I'll do that,' Keir offered. 'You and Maddie have more important matters to get on with.' Knowing that he was prepared to share the cooking, shopping and other duties with his aunt, only made Henri love him more.

'Professor Hallam.' Henri walked over to the door kitchen door and held it open, eyes bright with laughter. 'Are you free?'

'I am free, Doctor Bruar,' she responded in time-honoured fashion.

Arms linked, they headed for the library to work on cataloguing the *MacKenzie Papers* which had been brought back to the castle, now that the treasure had been found.

Two weeks later, they were all on tenterhooks waiting to hear from the Remembrancer's office. To make the waiting more bearable, Maddie and Alice planned a trip to Fort William to start on their Christmas shopping, promising to call in on the Beach House on their return journey. Alice had found two local matrons to help with most of the nursing duties, and cooking and cleaning. Things were very much at the 'suck it and see' stage, however the women appeared thrilled at helping out the laird. It was typical of Malcolm that he was charm personified in their company, but saved his complaints for Alice and Lachlan on the women's day off.

After dropping Maddie and Alice on the far side where Maddie kept her car, Keir joined Henri in the library. Stretched out on the leather chesterfield, hands behind his head, he watched as she replaced those books they'd decided to keep. Henri planned to restock the library, should there be any money left once more urgent calls upon it had been answered. Although it seemed as if all her hard work had all been for nothing, the enterprise had been far from pointless. It had brought her and Keir together, the library was now professionally catalogued and some priceless books had been rediscovered.

Job done.

'Comfortable?' Henri looked at Keir, her snarky tone implying that a cup of coffee was long overdue, and he should be the one to make it.

'Very,' he grinned.

'Good, but—'

'I was thinking,' he mused, 'of erecting a plaque. There. Above the fireplace.' He framed the space with his hands.

'A plaque? About the treasure?'

'No. One which reads: *In this ancient place, did the Master of Mountgarrie find the love of his life.*' Dropping his hands, he sent Henri an ardent look which demanded one in return.

'What?' she asked.

'I've missed *this*. Us.'

'Me, too.'

'Prove it. Join me on the chesterfield.'

Laughing, Henri allowed herself to be pulled on top of him, touching every inch of him with her body. Burying her face in his neck, she breathed in his essence: clean clothes, fabric conditioner, lemony aftershave, and the sharp tang of male. She let out a contented sigh and began kissing along the line of his jaw until their lips met and the serious kissing began. 'I'm assuming,' Keir said after some time, 'that your duties are at an end for the day, Dr Bruar?'

'They are.'

'In which case, would a *quickie* be out of the question?'

'It most certainly would,' Henri replied, feigning shock. 'However, in view of the fact that we are alone in the castle for the first time in *weeks*, I think a *long-ie* would be more appropriate. Don't you?'

'A *long-ie?*' Keir feigned not to understand.

'Yes; the opposite of a quickie? Need I fetch the thesaurus, Master MacKenzie?'

'I think you need to fetch proof of your qualifications,' he responded, straight-faced. 'I'm sure that no such word exists in the English language, Dr Bruar.'

'I beg to differ,' Henri said, getting to her feet and extending her hands to him. 'However, if you wish to check my credentials, might I suggest that we go somewhere warmer and more comfortable in order for you to do so?'

'Such as?'

'Your room. Your bed. Your—'

'Manly arms?' Keir asked, pushing himself upright and flexing his biceps in the manner of a circus strongman.

'The same.'

'And before mah two aunties come home wi' the messages,' Keir added, staying in role.

That made them sound like amorous teenagers, up to no good while the grown-ups were out—not the future laird of MacKenzie and his highly qualified fiancée. Henri couldn't keep the laughter out of her voice, or hide the love she felt for him. Her eyes shone and her lips curled in a soft smile when she saw the same love-light mirrored in his eyes.

'C'm'ohn, lassie.' Keir led her out of the library by the hand. Henri gave a delicious shiver and something deep within her tightened with anticipation at spending a dreich December afternoon in the arms of the man she loved. With that, they headed towards the spiral staircase at the end of the corridor—books, treasure, and ancient history all forgotten in a haze of love, desire and happiness.

Keir brought Alice and Maddie back over to the castle around about quarter past six. The women dumped their shopping bags on the table and, without removing their coats, headed for the door at the far end of the kitchen.

'Alice's room, Henri,' Keir said without preamble.

'Why? What's happened?'

Henri looked at Keir for clarification, but he shook his head and, grim-faced, guided her up the stairs to Alice's quarters instead, his hand resting lightly on the small of her back. The little bubble of happiness which had surrounded her as she'd waited for Keir to return from the far shore, burst, leaving her feeling anxious.

Once in her sitting room, Alice switched on the television. Luckily, they were able to pick up the signal, although the sound quality was poor and the image kept pixilating.

'What is it?' Henri asked, dry-mouthed.

'We're busted,' Keir answered.

'Watch,' Alice and Maddie said in unison.

The usual *Highlands and Islands* news stories unfolded on the screen: Christmas concerts in tiny village primary schools, bad weather affecting the ferries to the more remote islands, a minor celebrity switching on the Christmas lights. Once this was out of the way, the rest of the programme was given over to BREAKING NEWS.

'*And, in other news today, a treasure—hidden in a castle in Argyll for over three hundred years, has been unearthed and sent to Edinburgh for verification . . .*'

'How on earth . . .' Henri began.

'Sh,' Alice held up her hand.

Next, a shot of Sir Malcolm in his wheel chair filled the screen. 'You must be thrilled by the discovery of the treasure, Sir Malcolm,' the reporter gushed, holding a microphone towards him.

'Not so much thrilled as *surprised*,' Malcolm replied, looking directly at the camera—directly, it seemed, at the four conspirators holed up in *his* castle and keeping secrets from him.

'No-oh . . .' Henri covered her eyes with her hands.

'The discovery was made by my personal archivist, Dr Henriette Bruar,' Sir Malcolm explained, without batting an eye, 'the result of research undertaken, at my instigation, concerning the pivotal role the MacKenzies played at the battle of Glen Shiel.'

'News to me,' muttered Henri, thinking of the hours she'd spent in the freezing cold library prising damp pages apart in the hope of finding something salvageable.

'She was recommended by Professor Maddie Hallam, who attended the same alma mater as Dr Bruar and myself—St Guthlac, Northumberland. You may have seen a documentary recently concerning a piece of manuscript uncovered in the university library? *That* was Dr Bruar's find, too. Clever girl, Brilliant academic.' Henri's jaw dropped in surprise, and she glanced over at the others, who were too transfixed to comment.

'Aye, she is that.' The camera panned round to reveal Lachlan, hair slicked down like an otter, wearing his best shirt and one of the laird's ties—looking mighty pleased with himself. 'I tol't Himself that the wee las—Dr Bruar, that is—would bring good luck to the castle. And I wus right.' He flashed startling white false teeth at the camera, almost blinding the interviewer.

'Oh. My. God,' Alice exclaimed, 'I haven't seen him with his teeth in, for *years*. It looks like he's had them whitened—and he's taken his bunnet aff. Those ladies helping Himself had better watch out, Lachlan's on the hunt for a wife!'

'And, is that *my* jacket he's wearing?' Keir questioned, far from pleased at the thought of Lachlan rifling through his wardrobe.

Henri thought they were missing the point. The laird knew all about the treasure and all they could talk about was Lachlan's false teeth and him wearing borrowed clothing. Then, as the interview came to an end, the reporter turned to back to the laird.

'I hope, Sir Malcolm, when everything is settled, that you will share the story of Dr Bruar's amazing find with us? And perhaps outline its implications for the local community, the estate, and your family?'

'Not to mention his floozies in the South of France,' Alice added, in a bitter aside.

'It will be a pleasure. As you can imagine, I have much to discuss with my family at this juncture.' Again, that long look into the camera lens, no doubt intended to bore into their double-dealing hearts.

'Thank you, Sir Malcolm—and now, back the studio . . .'

Reaching for the remote, Keir switched off the television.

'Will someone *please* tell me what's going on?' she demanded. They all started speaking at once, starting and finishing each other's sentences.

'On our way back from Fort William, we thought we'd drop in and check on things -

'Of course, we expected Malcolm to be having a massive sulk because Alice wasn't at his beck and call any longer—'

'So, we bought him some stem ginger, and Lachlan his favourite boiled sweets.'

'When we got to the Beach House—'

'He was uncharacteristically nice to us. Asked the woman to make us all a pot of tea and open a packet of biscuits. Everything went swimmingly until—'

'She left, then all hell broke loose.'

'He called us everything from a pig to a dog and demanded that you and Keir be summoned to the Beach House this very evening, to—'

'Explain yourselves.'

'Crikey,' Henri exclaimed. 'How did he find out? Did someone see us loading the treasure at the Beach House?' She frowned, that didn't seem likely. They'd transported everything across the loch in the pre-dawn darkness, and from there straight to Edinburgh.

Keir shook his head. 'The Remembrancer's Office tried to ring us at the castle, yesterday, but no one answered. So they tried my mobile and left a message which I didn't receive because of the signal. Then, some bright spark had the idea of looking up *Sir Malcolm MacKenzie of MacKenzie* in the phone book, found an entry for the Beach House, and rang him there.'

Maddie took up the story. 'Imagine his surprise when they started talking about the treasure. With more presence of mind than I thought he possessed, he acted as if he was in the loop and said he'd get back to them. In the meantime, he called in a few favours, and a hasty television interview was arranged, filmed and put out on the news tonight.'

'The sleekit auld bugger,' Alice said. This was followed by a lengthy silence during which no one could think of anything useful to say.

'Fait accompli—how clever.' Henri was first to break the silence. 'Now what?'

'I'm going straight over to the Beach House to lay it on the line; to make sure he understands that any money raised from the sale of the treasure will be used to pay off his debts and then ploughed back into the estate. No argument.'

'Good luck with that,' Maddie said, pulling a face.

'Go now, Keir, before he's had too long to think about it,' Alice advised. 'And if he starts digging his heels in, tell him that he owes me thirty years' salary, and I want all the money I've ever loaned him, repaid—with compound interest. I'll make those pay day loan companies look charitable, by comparison.'

'You're right,' Keir said, already halfway to the door. 'This discussion is long overdue. We found the treasure, so we'll be calling the shots; I'm going to make that perfectly clear to him. Our futures are at stake here.' There was a steel behind his eyes and a stubborn set to his jaw. Henri could only imagine the scene which would take place at the Beach House later. The old stag locking antlers with a younger, more virile buck.

Once they were on the jetty, their coats pulled round them and their scarves up to their ears, Keir took Henri in his arms. His fierce expression was abandoned as he pulled her scarf down below her chin and sought her mouth. He kissed her, pulling her into a tight clinch which made it almost impossible for her to breathe. That kiss carried a weight of meaning and for a moment their love for each other was all that mattered. When Henri pulled away and looked up at him, more stars than she'd ever seen in her whole life wheeled round his head, and a bright Christmas moon illuminated the castle and the loch, like a searchlight.

'You aren't sailing all the way to the Beach House, are you?' she questioned, mindful of the dark loch, strong currents and the temperature which was dropping by the minute.

'No. Just as far as the other side. I'll drive the rest of the way.'

'Good. I—I couldn't bear it if anything happened to you. Stay safe.' Her voice snagged and her view of the boat blurred as her eyes teared over. 'You are my future, Keir.'

'As you are mine, bonnie lass.' Although his tone was light, there was a wealth of emotion in his voice, too. Henri gave him one last kiss and then released him, watching as his boat edged away from the jetty and towards the shore.

Glancing up at the stars, she gave a superstitious shiver. Whatever happened tonight between Keir and Sir Malcolm would seal all their fates. When her gaze returned to the loch, Keir was already halfway across, seemingly keen to get this interview over with. Pulling her coat around her, Henri started up the three sets of spiral stairs and back to Alice's room where, doubtless, they'd sit the night out, waiting for Keir's return.

Chapter Thirty-Seven
Na Fir Chlis

Sitting alone in bed three hours later, Henri mulled over the discussion in Alice's room earlier regarding the treasure 'windfall', and how it could benefit the estate.

Ever the historian, Maddie, had said, 'People will come from miles around to see where the treasure was found. Funds raised from the sale of the treasure will enable Keir to refurbish the castle and grounds—'

'. . . pay off Himself's creditors; fix up the tenants' cottages, and replace the trees sold to the paper mills,' Alice put in.

'The Beach House would make a great holiday cottage. We could get the castle licenced for weddings—'

'Starting with yours and Keir's,' Alice said, laughing as Henri blushed.

' . . . convert some of the rooms on the ground floor as an education/visitors' centre. Henri and I could organise that between us—'

'I'd love to run a café in the castle during the summer months—'

'They'd come from miles around to experience your cooking, Alice. You could run a cookery school; a kind of Great Scottish Bake-Off.'

'Count me in,' Maddie added. 'I'm up for anything, and I do mean *anything*, which means I'll never again have to travel the world raising funds for Grotty Guthlac.' They shuddered in sympathy at the humiliations Professor Hallam had experienced on her fundraising lecture tours over the years.

'Poor Maddie.' Henri had given her a kiss.

Holding Henri at arm's length, Maddie had given her an unyielding look. 'You, Dr Bruar, have a book on the Highland Clearances to write. Don't think I've forgotten.'

'No, Professor Hallam,' Henri had grinned, cheekily.

'But dinnae worry lassie, ah'll be on hand tae help you wi' a' the research.' Maddie's faux Motherwell accent had earned her a dark look from Alice, before she realised they were teasing her—and then she'd laughed along with them.

The sound of Keir's boat engine drove the wisps of conversation from Henri's mind and she rushed over to the window where she watched him leap onto the jetty and enter the castle. Heart thumping, she stared blindly across the loch for several minutes steeling herself to receive bad news, wondering how she could put a positive spin on it. Turning, she walked over to the fire and added a few more logs, using the small hand bellows to breathe life into the dying embers. Next, she sprayed herself with perfume, ran her fingers through her sleep-knotted hair and climbed back into bed.

Keir entered the bedroom, closing the door quietly behind him, his expression neutral as he stood at the foot of the bed. 'You look beautiful . . .' he began. However, Henri swatted the compliment away, desperate to know what had happened at the Beach House.

'Well?' she prompted.

'*Very* well,' he replied. 'I apologised to Father for keeping him out of the loop and explained my reasons for doing so, all of which he accepted. He also admitted that I was probably the best person to handle any funds the treasure might bring, because—to use his words—he was *a complete idiot where money was concerned*.'

'So, good, then?' she ventured.

'Then he cried—'

'Oh no,' Henri put her hand over her mouth.

' . . . said that spending time in hospital, with little to do other than *think* about the past, made him realise what an appalling father he'd been.

He apologised for blaming me over what happened to Mother and young Malcolm. His change of heart is probably linked to Alice informing him that if he didn't do the right thing by me; us, the estate, she'd walk out of his life—for good.'

'Bless her . . .'

'Then we hugged, in proper manly fashion.' Keir tried to make light of it, but his voice was raw and he turned away, hiding his tears. 'And, we agreed that your arriving at Castle Tèarmannair was the best thing to have happened to the MacKenzies in a lo-ong, long time. At which point, Lachlan, said—'

'Lachlan was there the whole of the time?'

Keir nodded, seemingly more amused by Lachlan's boundary issues, than Henri.

'He said that if you left the castle, you'd take the good luck with you. So I'd better marry you and tie you down with a couple of weans, before some *Sassenach in a suit*, beats me to it.'

'Cheeky sod!' Henri breathed fire for a few moments, but then saw the funny side of Lachlan giving Keir relationship advice. 'However, he does have a point,' she dimpled.

'Does he now?' Vaulting over the end of the bed, Keir landed by her side and the half-tester creaked in protest at such rough handling. 'You'd prefer a *Sassenach in a suit* to the Master of Mountgarrie? Is that it, Dr Bruar?'

'I might,' Henri teased. 'Unless, said Master of Mountgarrie is wearing his kilt.'

'That could be arranged.' Looking over at the window, Keir murmured something like—*bang on cue*. Leading Henri out of the bed, he wrapped her in the ancient patchwork quilt with loving tenderness.

'My lady, if you please—' Pushing the bedroom window high enough for them to step over the sill and onto the battlements, he guided her over to the very edge of the castle. The freezing air took their breath away with its frosty kiss.

'What is this? More fireworks?' Gathering the quilt around her, Henri looked at Keir for enlightenment and then snuggled under his armpit for warmth.

'In a way; look—there in the north-east . . .'

What Henri had earlier taken to be her eyes adjusting to the darkness as she'd looked over the loch, now appeared as something quite different. The sky still had a greenish tinge, however other colours were merging with it—magenta, citrus green, yellow, great plumes of light which shifted and changed. Beneath the dancing colours, the night sky was clearly visible, the stars studding the shifting curtain of light like diamonds. The loch reflected the shimmering aurora and the village of MacKenzie appeared beneath the canopy, like a dream landscape.

'*Na Fir Chlis*—The Merry Dancers—the Aurora Borealis,' Keir announced as though he'd organised the light show especially for her.

'It's long been a dream of mine to see the Northern Lights.' She spoke in a whisper, as if her voice would chase the aurora away. 'How did you know?'

'I didn't. But I read, in the local paper as I waited for Alice and Maddie, that the aurora might appear tonight. And, bang on cue, here it is. You're shivering my love—' Noticing her bare feet, he removed his jacket and laid it down for her to stand on. Then, with the aurora as a backcloth, he stood before her, hand on heart. 'Henriette Bruar, you came into my life like a force of nature so it's fitting that I ask you this—as the *Na Fir Chlis* light up the sky over my castle, will you marry me? Share the responsibility for restoring this ancient castle to its rightful state? Have our children; love me for ever?'

'Of c-course I will.' After taking in a shuddering breath, she smiled. 'Who knew that, in running away from trouble at university, I was running into your arms?'

Keir turned her to face the aurora, pulling her back against him and enfolding her in his arms; his favourite position. 'Henri,' he whispered, 'the lights will have to stand in for the diamonds I hope, one day, to slip on your finger. However, I do have this.' Fumbling in his pocket, he brought out something warm and heavy which he placed in her hand, closing her fingers round it.

'Keir. It's the *Vigo* coin, your pirate gold.'

'Correction; *our* pirate gold. I kept it back because my mother gave it to me—and,' she heard the humour in his voice, 'as insurance. In case Himself reneges on his promise to spend MacKenzie's Gold restoring the estate.'

Henri laughed, pressing herself back against his chest. '*Can the leopard change his spots, or the tiger his skin*—that it?'

'Just about. Now, the lights are fading, mo chridhe. The show's over and you are freezing cold. We have no need of the aurora to bind us together.' Gathering her in his arms he carried her over the sill and laying her gently on the bed, whispered: '*Is tu an solas na mo bheatha*. You are the light of my life.' After closing the window, he returned to the bed and sat on the edge of it.

Her voice thick with emotion, Henri responded. 'I have a little saying Alice *learn't me*, as she puts it. Not in Gaelic, but in the broad Scots of her childhood. *I wisnae pushed, I didnae shove, I just met you and fell in love.*'

'The best of both worlds?'

'The best of all possible worlds. I don't mind which world I live in, Keir, as long as we are in it, together.'

There being nothing more to add, Keir switched off the lamp and lay down beside Henri on the too-short bed, the flames from the fire lighting one half of the room and the Na Fir Chlis growing fainter and fainter as they faded above the battlements of his castle.

THE END

A NOTE FROM THE AUTHOR

If you have a dream—go for it.
Life is not a rehearsal

When I was about seven years old I, along with two friends—Freda Wallace and Rosemary Smiley—went to Woolworths in Wishaw (Lanarkshire) and we each bought a notebook and pen. Rushing home, we sat on my back doorstep and started writing. I think my story was a version of *Greyfriars Bobby* which we'd seen the previous Saturday at the local cinema in Motherwell. I lost touch with Freda and Rosemary when my family moved to England, but I often wonder if they kept on writing, and how their lives turned out.

Fast forward to the present day and my novel **Girl in the Castle**. I have thoroughly enjoyed writing it and I hope you will enjoy reading it. In my head I'm still that optimistic seven-year-old sitting on a cold doorstep overlooking the Ravenscraig Steel Works, notebook in hand and scribbling away. I hope

I never lose that optimism or the compulsion to write and share my stories with others.

If you want to know more about me, my path to publication and progress with novel #5, go over to my website: www.lizzielamb.co.uk. Please click on the 'follow' button or sign up for my quarterly newsletter. I'd love to hear from you.

Lizzie x

TALL DARK AND KILTED—by Lizzie Lamb

A contemporary romance set in the Highlands of Scotland

Fliss Bagshawe longs for a passport out of Pimlico where she works as a holistic therapist. After attending a party in Notting Hill she loses her job and with it the dream of being her own boss. She's offered the chance to take over a failing therapy centre, but there's a catch. The centre lies five hundred miles north in Wester Ross, Scotland. Fliss's romantic view of the Highlands populated by Men in Kilts is shattered when she has an up-close and personal encounter with the Laird of Kinloch Mara, Ruairi Urquhart. He's determined to pull the plug on the business, bring his eccentric family to heel and eject undesirables from his estate—starting with Fliss. Facing the dole queue once more Fliss resolves to make sexy, infuriating Ruairi revise his unflattering opinion of her, turn the therapy centre around and sort out his dysfunctional family. Can Fliss tame the Monarch of the Glen and find the happiness she deserves?

Some reviews for Tall, Dark and Kilted

'This story is full of romantic Scottish themes; Kilts, bagpipes, scenery, Gaelic whisperings, Clan Urquhart tartans and Strathspey reels. Definitely an enjoyable read.'

'I really couldn't put it down. Makes me want to buy my hubby a kilt.'

'No complications, just a relaxing story that drags you in to the end. Quite sad to finish it'

'You won't be disappointed, ladies, and men, you could learn a thing or two.'

'I truly enjoyed this book. I stumbled across it on Twitter. I was looking for a light read. However, I had trouble putting this one down.'

BOOT CAMP BRIDE—by Lizzie Lamb
Romance and Intrigue on the Norfolk marshes

Take an up-for-anything rookie reporter. Add a world-weary photo-journalist. Put them together . . . light the blue touch paper and stand well back! Posing as a bride-to-be, Charlee Montague goes undercover at a boot camp for brides in Norfolk to photograph supermodel Anastasia Markova looking less than perfect. At Charlee's side and posing as her fiancé is Rafael Ffinch, award-winning photographer and survivor of a kidnap attempt in Colombia. He's in no mood to cut inexperienced Charlee any slack and has made it plain that once the investigation is over, their partnership—and fake engagement—will be terminated, too. Soon Charlee has more questions than answers. What's the real reason behind Ffinch's interest in the boot camp? How is it connected to his kidnap in Colombia? In setting out to uncover the truth, Charlee puts herself in danger ... As the investigation draws to a close, she wonders if she'll be able to hand back the engagement ring and walk away from Rafa without a backward glance.

Some reviews for Boot Camp Bride

'Another sparkling read, full of passion and laughter, but with a sinister undertone that keeps you turning the pages.'

'A definitely great read, as was Lizzie's Debut book, Tall Dark & Kilted... roll on book 3!'

'That good I read it twice!'

'The dialogue between the two main characters, rookie journalist Charlee Montague, and world-weary photographer, Rafael Ffinch is brilliant and full of repartee.'

Finalist—Festival of Romantic Fiction—romantic comedy

SCOTCH ON THE ROCKS—by Lizzie Lamb

Where the men wear kilts and the women are glad of it!

ISHABEL STUART is at the crossroads of her life.

Her wealthy industrialist father has died unexpectedly, leaving her a half-share in a ruined whisky distillery and the task of scattering his ashes on a Munro. After discovering her fiancé playing away from home, she cancels their lavish Christmas wedding at St Giles Cathedral, Edinburgh and heads for the only place she feels safe—Eilean na Sgairbh, a windswept island on Scotland's west coast where the cormorants outnumber the inhabitants, ten to one.

When she arrives at her family home, now a bed and breakfast managed by her left-wing, firebrand Aunt Esme, she finds a guest in situ —BRODIE. Issy longs for peace and the chance to lick her wounds, but gorgeous, sexy American Brodie, turns her world upside down.

In spite of her vow to steer clear of men, she grows to rely on Brodie. However, she suspects him of having an ulterior motive for staying at her aunt's B&B on remote Cormorant Island. Having been let down twice by the men in her life, will it be third time lucky for Issy? Is it wise to trust a man she knows nothing about—a man who presents her with more questions than answers?

As for Aunt Esme, she has secrets of her own.

Some reviews for Scotch on the Rocks

'A cracking book that stays with you long after you have finished'

'I like the way she weaves 'older characters' into the story; love isn't just for the young'

'lots of romance, humour, quirky secondary characters and a mad parrot. I was kept engaged, right up to the last page'

'A five star romance from a five star romantic novelist'

*FINALIST—THE EXETER NOVEL PRIZE

*Book Blogger Cathy Ryan's **TOP READS OF 2016**

Short listed for the contemporary fiction award (silver) by Rosie Amber's Review Team

ACKNOWLEDGMENTS

First of all, thank **YOU** for purchasing *Girl in the Castle*. It combines my love of history, the dream of living in a castle in the middle of a loch (complete with kilted hero), my love of Scotland—and my weakness for romance with a capital 'R'.

Writing can be a lonely occupation and I am grateful to my friends on Facebook and Twitter who encourage me to switch on the PC every morning and get down to it. I love finding out what they've got planned for the day, and sharing my news with them. It's even better when we meet at book signings and author events and I have the chance to meet them face to face.

♥♥♥♥♥♥♥♥♥♥♥

I should mention that Castle Tèarmannair exists only in my imagination. Two summers ago we were touring Argyll and Bute and stumbled across *Castle Stalker* sitting four square in the middle of Loch Laich, an inlet off Loch Linnhe. We discovered that the owner, Mr Ross Allward, conducted private tours of the castle and booked ourselves on one. The best bit? He fetches you from his boathouse on the shore and takes you across to the castle by dinghy—just like Lachlan did with Henriette. That visit was the inspiration for *Girl in the Castle*.

The Scots' dialect words in the novel, come courtesy of my family in Wishaw near Motherwell, and Whitburn; the 'Hoods' in Glasgow, especially Maggie, and my friend 'Maisie'. Readers tell me that they like the touch of authenticity these words bring to my writing and some of my Sassenach friends now litter their conversation with words like peely-wally/a drap o' the swally/palpatooral/scunner/ and dreich. Although, sadly, even after all these years my husband still can't pronounce 'po-liss', or order a 'fish supper', without getting into trouble in the chippy.

I've received valuable feedback and editorial advice from Miss Davies of Edge and the Diva from Dumbarton. Although, I suspect there still aren't enough murders in the novel for Miss Davies's tastes. Maybe I'll turn to the dark side one of these days and write *grit-lit*—but, don't hold your breath.

My novel, both paperback and kindle versions were formatted by *Sarah Houldcroft*—www.VAforAuthors.com. I must also mention my co-conspirators: Adrienne Vaughan, June Kearns and Mags Cullingford (**New Romantics Press**) who are never more than a phone call (or cup of coffee) away.

Once again, thanks to *Dr Nick Fiddes* at www.scotweb.co.uk who granted me permission to use one of his photographs for my front cover. I think it exactly catches the mood of the novel and the heroine, Henriette. I also got the idea for the *luckenbooth* which Henri wears at Samhain from his fabulous website (do check it out).

I have to say a great big *tapadh leibh* to Rachel McNeill of *Whisky for Girls (and Guys)* Islay, for help with Gaelic phrases and words. I'll make it over to Islay one of these days and share a wee dram with you, Rachel—*slainte mhath*. And, for the record, I'm not a bit jealous that you've met Sam Heughan (gorgeous Jamie from Outlander) and I haven't.

Many thanks to 'AL' in Human Resources, who helped with the background to disciplinary procedures in academic institutions. She prefers to remain anonymous, and who can blame her?

I wouldn't have progressed this far in my writing career without the support, expertise and knowledge of the **Romantic Novelists' Association.** In particular the talented writers in the **Leicester Chapter**, aka *The Belmont Belles*, organised by June Kearns and myself, which goes from strength to strength.

Big shout out also to *Mandy Greig* of Brisbane, Australia (formerly of Lenzie, Glasgow) in remembrance of the *'wee lassie* incident' in Falkland many years ago. It stuck in my mind and inspired the first meeting between Lachlan and Henriette.

And finally—thanks to *Bongo Man* for everything he does to ensure that I am left free to concentrate on my writing. It goes without saying that he is all of my heroes, rolled into one. When not looking after me and the parrot, he is busy erecting a reclaimed beach hut on an island in a secret location. I've been told there is *no way* it's becoming a writer's retreat.

My friends and I may have other ideas!

I'd love to hear from you so do get in touch

email: lizzielambwriter@gmail.com
website: www.lizzielamb.co.uk
twitter.com/@lizzie_lamb
www.facebook.com/LizzieLambwriter

Follow me on Pinterest and Instagram and subscribe to my newsletter

The New Romantics Press website: www.newromanticspress.com
twitter.com/@newromanticspress
www.facebook.com/NewRomanticsPress

Before you go . . .

Please Tweet/Share that you have finished *Girl in the Castle*

Rate this book ★★★★★

Novels published by New Romantics Press

Lizzie Lamb	Tall, Dark and Kilted
	Boot Camp Bride
	Scotch on the Rocks
	Girl in the Castle
Adrienne Vaughan	A Hollow Heart
	A Change of Heart
	Secrets of the Heart
	Fur Coat and No Knickers
June Kearns	An English Woman's Guide to the Cowboy
	Twenties Girl
Mags Cullingford	Last Bite of the Cherry
	Twins of a Gazelle
Collaboratively	Take a Chance on Us—a tapas of novels by NRP

If you've read and enjoyed our books, please leave a review on Amazon or Goodreads.

Look out for new books from The New Romantics Press autumn 2017/Spring 2018

Printed in Great Britain
by Amazon